Letters and Documents
of Heinrich Schütz
1656–1672
An Annotated Translation

Studies in Music, No. 106

George J. Buelow, Series Editor

Professor of Music
Indiana University

Other Titles in This Series

Letters and Documents of Heinrich Schütz 1656–1672
An Annotated Translation

by
Gina Spagnoli

With a Foreword by Werner Breig

UMI Research Press
Ann Arbor / London

Produced and distributed by
UMI Research Press
an imprint of
University Microfilms Inc.
Ann Arbor, Michigan 48106

Library of Congress Cataloging in Publication Data

Schütz, Heinrich, 1585-1672.
 Letters and documents of Heinrich Schütz, 1656-1672 ;
an annotated translation / by Gina Spagnoli.
  p. cm.—(Studies in music ; no. 106)
  Documents translated from the German.
  Includes bibliographical references.
  ISBN 0-8357-1902-2 (alk. paper)
  1. Schütz, Heinrich, 1585-1672—Correspondence. 2. Schütz,
Heinrich, 1585-1672—Archives. 3. Music—Germany—17th century—
History and criticism. I. Spagnoli, Gina. II. Title.
III. Series: Studies in music (Ann Arbor, Mich.) ; no. 106.
ML410.S35A4   1989
782.2'2'092—dc20   89-5204
                                                              CIP
                                                              MN

The paper used in this publication meets the minimum requirements of
American National Standard for Information Sciences—Permanence of
Paper for Printed Library Materials, ANSI Z39.48-1984. ⊚ ™

To Sarangan

Contents

Foreword

Whoever wishes to become familiar with the musical *oeuvre* of Heinrich Schütz can in the process rely on no fewer than three editions of his collected works. On the other hand, whoever wishes by means of the surviving documents to study Heinrich Schütz's biography—and that means the external circumstances of his creative work—must proceed on a difficult terrain. This is because a complete and reliable edition of the documents of his life, such as those we possess for J. S. Bach, Mozart, Schubert, or—to name a contemporary of Schütz—Monteverdi, does not exist for Schütz. Wolfram Steude, director of the Heinrich-Schütz-Archiv, which was opened in Dresden in 1988, considers producing such documentary work one of his most important missions. There can be no doubt, however, that the realization of this project will require preliminary studies for some time to come.

It is significant that Erich Hermann Müller's edition of the letters and documents of Heinrich Schütz, completed in manuscript in 1926 and printed in 1931, is still valued as "an indispensable collection"*—simply because it has not been superseded by one more up to date. Müller's edition was, for its time, certainly a pioneering achievement; today, however, a number of new documents have since come to light, and its contents are now no longer current. Moreover it cannot be denied that the usefulness of Müller's edition as a scholarly work was reduced from the beginning by the fact that the reproduction of the texts is frequently imprecise and that in many respects the commentary leaves the user in the lurch.

Thus the continuing work on the accessibility of the sources of Schütz's biography has been a pressing research desideratum for a long time. The work of Gina Spagnoli can for this reason be regarded as

---

*Allen Skei, *Heinrich Schütz: A Guide to Research* (New York and London: Garland Publishing, Inc., 1981), p. 57.

path-breaking. She concentrates on a relatively easily delimited time in the composer's life (the late period after the death of the Saxon elector Johann Georg I), examines anew within this domain the sources published by Müller, and supplements them with a thorough commentary and further documents which place the testimony from Schütz's pen in proper context.

The addition of an English translation to the original texts belongs to the fundamental conception of Gina Spagnoli's work. This is, first of all, an aid for those users who are not sufficiently familiar with the original language of the documents. In this sense her work serves a practical purpose, namely to make the documents of international research more easily accessible. This translation, however, is far more than an aid to overcoming language barriers. Anyone who has ever been involved with the translation of sources of this kind knows that "translation" comprises a tremendous effort toward fundamental understanding. Thus toward this end the German reader will also be grateful for the interpretation of the documents presented here.

Gina Spagnoli's work is the first publication since Müller's edition to be concerned with making the biographical Schütz documents accessible not merely sporadically but systematically. That such work was accomplished in America is a sign of the growing intensity with which a younger generation of American musicologists in recent years has devoted itself to the research of German music of the seventeenth century (one thinks, for example, of the Buxtehude studies of Kerala Snyder and Eva Linfield, the Biber research of Eric Chafe, or the theoretical-historical work of Paul Walker). With Gina Spagnoli's documentary work on Schütz, this line will be carried on and at the same time lay the foundation on which—it is to be hoped—further research in this area can be built.

Werner Breig

Preface

The modern view of Heinrich Schütz is based not only upon a substantial body of writings by the composer himself but also upon a wealth of archival material from the courts where he was active. The documents include the composer's own letters, letters from rulers and musicians at these courts, court ensemble lists, court diaries, receipts, musicians' contracts, court account books, music and instrument catalogs, and *Kantoreiordnungen,* the chapel orders in which guidelines for worship services throughout the year are set forth. All are of interest not only to musical scholars but to performers and general historians as well, for they provide a picture of the composer as a personality, details of his professional life, and abundant information about music and musicians in Schütz's milieu.

This is a study of Schütz's career based upon the important Schütz documents dating from 1656 to 1672, a period framed by the deaths of the elector Johann Georg I in 1656 and of Schütz himself in 1672. This period was chosen because Schütz's duties as Kapellmeister in Dresden changed drastically during this time as a result of the domination of Dresden's musical scene by Johann Georg II's Italian musicians. This period is further distinguished by Schütz's extensive involvement as musical advisor to other German courts. Some additional related documents outside this time frame are also included because they show the early stages of issues and relationships which developed during the reign of Johann Georg II.

The documents have been organized into four categories: Schütz's career at Dresden, where he served as Kapellmeister from ca. 1617 until his death in 1672; Schütz's relationship to the court at Wolfenbüttel, where he served as Kapellmeister *in absentia* from ca. 1644 to 1666; his efforts to establish a court ensemble in Zeitz; and the musical environment in which Schütz worked as defined by the duties of other musicians in Schütz's sphere. Each of the four chapters provides commentary upon various issues and trends raised in the documents and expands the view they provide through extensive quotation from other primary sources. The intent of the commentary is not to provide a comprehensive biography of Schütz or a cultural history of seventeenth-century Germany, but rather to clarify and interpret chosen documents from a delimited period. The primary focus of the Dresden chapter is the Italianate controversy and the change in musical taste at court after the death of Johann Georg I. The Wolfenbüttel chapter traces the development of a city devasted by war into one of Northern Germany's smaller artistic centers. The Zeitz material shows an interrelationship between music there and at Dresden, with Schütz as the linking figure. Finally, the chapter on the court musicians in Schütz's milieu outlines the responsibilities of the various members of the Dresden ensemble on both sacred and secular occasions. The reader is referred to the relevant documents at appropriate points in the text.

The search for primary source material on Schütz has been going on for well over a century. The first important study of Schütz documents was Moritz Fürstenau's article published in 1849 on music in Dresden in the seventeenth century.[1] More thorough treatment appears in Fürstenau's two-volume *Zur Geschichte der Musik und des Theaters am Hofe zu Dresden* published in 1861, covering music at the Dresden court from the Middle Ages through the late eighteenth century.[2] Fürstenau's remarkable collection of documents from the Dresden court remains of particular importance since it transmits many which have subsequently been either lost or destroyed.

In 1931 Erich H. Müller edited *Heinrich Schütz: Gesammelte Briefe und Schriften,* which is still the only collection of Schütz's letters.[3] Studies which preceded Müller's work and which are particularly pertinent in the present context include "Geschichte der Braunschweig-Wolfenbüttelschen Capelle und Oper vom sechzehnten bis zum achzehnten Jahrhunderts" by Friedrich Chrysander,[4] and *Städtische und fürstliche Musikpflege in Zeitz* by Arno Werner,[5] both of which presented documents from these courts for the first time. Hans Joachim Moser's monumental biography, *Heinrich Schütz: Sein Leben und Werk,* first published in 1936, revised in 1954, and translated into English in 1959, has been called "a work of exceptional scholarship and insight" which "merits inclusion among the greatest biographies in music history."[6] Moser's book makes extensive use of the work of earlier scholars such as Fürstenau, Müller, Chrysander, and Werner while adding new information, such as a previously unknown autograph letter from the year 1644.[7]

No student of seventeenth-century German music can ignore these ground-breaking studies; they are, however, not without problems. Neither Fürstenau nor Chrysander cited sources, which makes the relocation of the originals difficult if not impossible. Furthermore, Fürstenau's presentation of the documents is frequently misleading, for he summarized liberally and conflated multiple sources without comment. Müller's transcriptions are frequently unreliable; furthermore, his publication has been rendered somewhat out-of-date by the discovery of other letters in the fifty years since his collection first appeared, including some published as recently as 1988.[8]

After the publication of Moser's book, work on the Schütz documents ceased for a full twenty-five years. The first important study to appear after the war was Eberhard Schmidt's exhaustive theological dissertation on Dresden liturgical traditions of the sixteenth and seventeenth centuries,[9] which has been followed by significant documentary work by Wolfram Steude in the German Democratic Republic and Joshua Rifkin in the United States.[10]

The present study attempts to bring together all of Schütz's autographs from the years 1656 to 1672 in addition to a body of other relevant material (much of it previously unpublished) including musicians' contracts and letters, an undated chapel order from Johann Georg II's reign, a music catalog dated 1681, and various other documents which throw light on the role of the musician at the courts where Schütz was active. The difficulty of seventeenth-century German has rendered the documents inaccessible to all but German specialists. The sources, which are written in German script and contain countless abbreviations, present problems even for native speakers of German and are therefore presented here in German transcription. The translation of this material is intended to make them accessible to a broader range of scholars and performers. No attempt has been made to render the translations into modern English by improving awkwardness in language. Matters such as word repetition or complex, frequently perplexing syntax have been allowed to stand; bracketed material is occasionally inserted, however, where meaning is especially ambiguous.

Acknowledgments

This book could not have been completed without the assistance of various institutions that provided funds to support my work in the German Democratic Republic and the Federal Republic of Germany. I wish to thank Washington University for a Nussbaum Travel Grant for research in Wolfenbüttel during the summer of 1984; the Deutscher Akademischer Austausch Dienst for a Direktstipendium for language study at the University of Freiburg during the summer of 1984; and the International Research and Exchanges Board for a travel grant to the German Democratic Republic during fall and winter of 1984.

I am indebted to the personnel of the many libraries and archives where the research for this study was accomplished: Dr. Wolfgang Milde and Dr. Hans Haase of the Herzog-August-Bibliothek Wolfenbüttel; Dr. Wolfgang Reich and Herr Robert Schroller of the Sächsische Landesbibliothek Dresden; Herr Manfred Kobuch and Frau Dr. Agatha Kobuch of the Staatsarchiv Dresden; Herr Gunther Michel-Trilling of the Staatsarchiv Weimar; and the staffs of the Staatsarchiv Magdeburg, the Staats- und Universitätsbibliothek Hamburg, the Braunschweigische Landesmuseum, and the Pierpont Morgan Libary, who responded to my requests with microfilms, photographs, and xerox copies.

I also wish to thank the many individuals whose guidance and advice saw me through this project. Dr. Craig Monson of Washington University lent to this study that scholarly excellence which serves as a model for all of his students. I wish to express special thanks to Washington University faculty members Dr. William Matheson and Dr. Jeffrey Kurtzman for their particularly painstaking contributions and countless improvements both in matters of substance and style. The Reverend Vernon Nelson and Dr. Lothar Madeheim of the Moravian Archives, Bethlehem, Pennsylvania, gave me the expertise and confidence to read the documents on which this study is based in their excellent seminar in German script. I also wish to thank Dr. Wolfram Steude and Mr. Joshua Rifkin for their generosity in sharing ideas and resources. I especially wish to express my gratitude to Dr. Werner Breig of the University of Bochum for reviewing the manuscript, for sharing his invaluable suggestions and insights, and for his abiding support over the years.

Abbreviations

GBS	*Heinrich Schütz: Gesammelte Briefe und Schriften.* Müller, ed.
HAB	Herzog-August-Bibliothek
LAG	Landesarchiv Greiz
MGG	*Die Musik in Geschichte und Gegenwart*
NSA	Heinrich Schütz. *Neue Ausgabe sämtlicher Werke*
NSAW	Niedersächsisches Staatsarchiv Wolfenbüttel
OHMA	Oberhofmarschallamt
PML	Pierpont Morgan Library
SAD	Staatsarchiv Dresden
SAM	Staatsarchiv Magdeburg
SAW	Staatsarchiv Weimar
SGA	Heinrich Schütz. *Sämmtliche Werke*
SLB	Sächsische Landesbibliothek
SUBH	Staats- und Universitätsbibliothek Hamburg
SWV	*Schütz-Werke-Verzeichnis*

Part One

Commentary

1

Dresden

Documents show that Johann Georg I, ruler of the electorate of Saxony from 1611 until his death in 1656, was a pious ruler who attempted to enrich worship at his Lutheran court. He ordered a new organ built in the palace church in 1612, hired a senior court preacher in 1613, and (in 1616) examined the condition of the court ensemble. After a lengthy power struggle over Schütz with Duke Moritz in Kassel, the elector brought Schütz to Dresden as Kapellmeister.[1]

Johann Georg II, who succeeded his father in 1656, had already established his own court ensemble while still elector apparent. The earliest surviving documentary evidence for this ensemble is dated 14 September 1641 and lists four members: Matthias Weckmann, organist; Philipp Stolle, theorbo player and singer; Friedrich Werner, instrumentalist; and Augustus Tax, director of the instrumental music.[2] The young elector apparent, in his wish to engage Italian musicians, maintained an agent in Venice who sought out Italians there and in other European cities in hope of luring them to Dresden. Indeed, he was so assiduous that in 1652 the electress of Bavaria complained of the alienation of the affections of her Italian musicians by these attempts and demanded an explanation from Johann Georg I.[3] The elector apparent's ensemble grew until it rivaled the elector's own in size, as may be seen by the following lists.

[fol. 247r]

Musicians to His Electoral Highness of Saxony
Herr Heinrich Schütz, Kapellmeister

Singers

1. Johann Georg Hofkontz, tenor
2. Sebastian Hönschrödel, tenor
3. Jonas Kittel, bass
4. Georg Kaiser, bass

5. Christian Weber, alto and harpist
6. Christoph Bernhard, alto

Organists

7. Christoph Kittel
8. Johann Klemm

Instrumentalists

9. Zacharius Hertel
10. Friedrich Sulz
11. His two sons [Ludwig Sulz and
12. Jacob Sulz]
13. Johann Dixon
14. Clemens Thieme
15. Wolf Georg Ritter, timpanist
    Four choir boys
    An instrumental apprentice
    Samuel Pohle }
    David Pohle } both His Royal Grace Duke Christian's instrumentalists

[fol. 247v]

Musicians of the Elector Apparent

1. Senior Giovanni Andrea Bontempi, composer and discantist
2. Giovanni Severo, instrumentalist
3. Stefano Sauli, bass
4. Matthias Weckmann, organist
5. Philipp Stolle, tenor and theorbist
6. Friedrich Werner, cornettist and alto
7. Christian Kittel, bass and instrumentalist
8. Ferdinand Franke, tenor
9. Heinrich Groh, falsettist
10. Michael Schmidt, violinist [*Violiste*] and bass
11. Friedrich Westhoff, lutenist
12. Balthasar Sedenig, violinist and cornettist
13. Johann Friedrich Volprecht, lutenist and violinist

Choirboys

1. Gottfried Pasche, lutenist
2. Simon Leonhard, violinist and trumpeter
3. Daniel Philomethes, sackbut player and trumpeter
4. Andreas Winckler, instrumentalist
5. Georg Rumpf, instrumentalist.[4]

These lists are undated. But an examination of appointment records of members of the ensemble suggests that Fürstenau's date of 1651 is correct. Christian Weber was appointed in 1648,[5] Christoph Bernhard in 1649,[6] and Clemens Thieme in 1650.[7]

The elector apparent's ensemble includes the court ensemble's first castrato, Giovanni Andrea Bontempi, marking the beginnings of a golden age of Italian castrati in Dresden. Bontempi was born in Perugia ca. 1624 and studied singing in Rome with Virgilio Mazzocchi. Before coming to Dresden he was a singer at St. Mark's in Venice from 1643 to 1650. After serving as Kapellmeister in Dresden, he was appointed stage designer and master of the machines at the court theater.[8] His importance as an opera composer in Dresden will be discussed later in this chapter.

The presence of Italian musicians was nothing new in Dresden, of course. Schütz was himself a great admirer of the Italian style and traveled twice to Venice, first as Giovanni Gabrieli's student and again several years later during Monteverdi's tenure as *maestro di capella* at St. Mark's. As Kapellmeister Schütz brought Italian music, instruments, and musicians to Dresden. In a memorandum to the elector dated 28 September 1645 (which concerned rebuilding the court ensemble which had suffered from the depredations of the Thirty Years War), Schütz suggested dividing the musicians into three groups to be developed successively: the choirboys or discantists, the instrumentalists, and the singers. Schütz stated that the third group would be the most difficult to restore since he deemed hiring foreign singers quite necessary though the instrumentalists and choirboys could still be Germans.

> With the third company, however, namely that of the vocalists or singers, it would be somewhat more costly and more difficult to bring about [the improvement of the ensemble] because one would have to seek them abroad, perhaps even partially among the Italians.[9]

Indeed, the Thirty Years War had reached Saxony in 1631. The Dresden court ensemble, which had counted thirty-nine musicians among its members in 1632, had sunk to ten members by 1639. Schütz's efforts at reorganization were effective, for ensemble membership was up to twenty-one by 1647.[10]

In a memorandum dated 21 September 1647, Schütz proposed Agostino Fontana, then an alto at the Danish royal court, as successor to the recently departed vice-Kapellmeister Zacharius Hestius (doc. 1).[11] The court cantor Johann Georg Hofkontz challenged this appointment in a letter to the elector of 16 May 1649 in which he claimed the post was rightfully his and that Schütz had long delayed his advancement. He also criticized Schütz for attempting to hire a Catholic to fill such an important post at Dresden's Lutheran court. Hofkontz first petitioned the elector regarding the post on 20 March 1643. Apparently the Hausmarschall had promised Hofkontz the position when he had brought him to Dresden fifteen months earlier. Even though a contract had been drawn up for Hofkontz on 2 January 1642,[12] the Hausmarschall died shortly thereafter, leaving the post vacant. Hofkontz was forced to petition the elector repeatedly, arousing Schütz's ire. Fontana remained in Copenhagen as director of the royal ensemble. The position of vice-Kapellmeister was next offered to Christoph Werner of Danzig, but he died before he could assume the post. Hofkontz seems ultimately to have been successful in his challenge for he became vice-Kapellmeister in 1651.[13]

These early controversies centering around Schütz continued when, in 1653, an arrangement was made by which Schütz and Bontempi, whom Schütz himself had recommended as his assistant in 1651 (doc. 2),[14] were to alternate Sundays in conducting the music in church (doc. 3).[15] Schütz stated that the musical direction on ordinary Sundays had traditionally been the responsibility of the vice-Kapellmeister, and he therefore considered the new demand an affront. That year he was also forced to respond to accusations that he was responsible for the engagement of so many Italian musicians, a situation that must have aroused considerable resentment since the musicians were Catholics. In an appeal to the elector apparent on 23 August 1653 (doc. 4), Schütz persisted in his innocence and could only recall suggesting in a petition twenty years earlier that an Italian could have been a good instructor to the choir boys and the German singers.[16] Schütz is probably referring to his recommendation of 28 September 1645. The situation apparently worsened, for in a letter of 19 June 1654 Schütz described to an unnamed court official the growing resentment among the German musicians and begged for more equitable treatment for the Germans, probably with regard to salary (doc. 6).[17] Certainly by the time of the 1666 payment list, the Italians earned far greater salaries than the Germans.[18]

Johann Georg I's ensemble continued to decline in numbers during the last years of his rule. Johann Georg II mentions the lamentable state of the ensemble in a letter to his father in 1653 (doc. 5) in which he suggested improvements regarding personnel and pay.[19] In a letter addressed to the elector on 3 December 1654, the senior court preacher Jacob Weller, responding to a letter from Hofkontz and Christoph Kittel, bemoaned the fact that practically no one left in the electoral ensemble could sing a German "Our Father" (doc. 7), probably a reference to the presence of the Italians. In a letter to Weller dated 30 November 1654, Hofkontz and Kittel wrote of the "total ruin and decline of the royal ensemble" (doc. 7).[20] The unpublished list summarized below shows Johann Georg I's ensemble around this time. This list dates between 15 March 1654, the date of Constantin Christian Dedekind's appointment,[21] and Bernhard's appointment as vice-Kapellmeister on 1

August 1655 (doc. 10).

> Heinrich Schütz, Kapellmeister
> Johann Georg Hofkontz, vice-Kapellmeister
> Christoph Bernhard [and] Christian Weber, altos
> Constantin Christian Dedekind [and] Georg Kaiser, basses

Instrumentalists

> Christoph Kittel [and] Johann Klemm, organists
> Gabriel Mölich
> Friedrich Sulz
> Jonas Kittel
> Johann Dixon
> Clemens Thieme
> Ludwig Sulz
> Jacob Sulz
> Friedrich Werner, cornettist
> Gottfried Leschke, *Hofkirchner*
> Tobias Weller, organ builder
> Wolf Georg Ritter, timpanist
> Hans Huber, the old *Kalkant*
> Siegmund Recht, the new *Kalkant*[22]

The Death of Johann Georg I

Johann Georg I died on 8 October 1656. His funeral was an occasion both solemn and grandiose in which the court ensemble played an intricate role, as revealed by a rediscovered manuscript now in the Staatsarchiv Dresden. The details of the funeral services, held on 2–4 February 1657, are set forth in an elaborate record which enumerates every detail of the proceedings, including, for example, all of the hymns which were sung during each service and the processions.[23] The volume comprises 600 manuscript folios with a printed description of each of the services; a printed version of the text of the main funeral sermon is also bound at the front of the volume. Aside from occasional references by Fürstenau,[24] none of the material in this volume has been published.

According to Anton Weck in his 1680 history of Dresden, the body of the elector remained in the palace church hall from 9 October until 16 October, when it was moved to the palace church. There Jacob Weller delivered a funeral sermon.[25] While an elaborate funeral was prepared, the elector lay in state for more than three months. This period of time may seem extraordinary, but in fact embalming the dead had become quite sophisticated by the middle of the seventeenth century. For example, the body of Louis XIII was found in a nearly perfect state of preservation 150 years after his death in 1643, while the bodies of his predecessors were very badly decayed or mere skeletons.[26]

The obsequies for Johann Georg I began on Monday, 2 February, at 6:30 A.M., when all of the bells of the churches in and around Dresden rang. The first worship service took place at 7:00 A.M. in the palace church, with the first funeral sermon by M. Christoph Laurentius, the court preacher, on the text of the Canticum Simeonis, or the "Nunc dimittis," "Herr, nun lässest du deinen Diener im Frieden fahren" (Lord, now lettest thou thy servant depart in peace). The first page of the print bound in the front of the manuscript lists the order of service. The number of each item has been retained here.

Before the sermon:

1. "Ach wie elend ist unsre Zeit"
2. "Auf meinen lieben Gott"
3. The Collect and scripture readings
4. The Creed
5. The sermon

After the sermon:

6. "Was mein Gott will, das gescheh allzeit"
7. Collect and Benediction
8. "Mitten wir im Leben sind"

The service was over by 9:00 A.M. and the royal family assembled for a meal. At 11:00 A.M., members of the court formed a huge funeral procession which progressed through the city from the palace church to the Kreuzkirche. The procession was led by three groups of noblemen walking three by three, followed by the bass Jonas Kittel carrying a crucifix, which was a tradition according to the funeral description, then two hundred pupils and twenty-seven of the clergy. Next, walking in pairs led by six choirboys, came the entire court ensemble, all of whom had assembled before Schütz's house on the new marketplace. They were followed by three men of the court on horseback, one timpanist, twelve trumpeters, the Oberhofmarschall Baron von Rechenberg, a great many noblemen and officers from Dresden, Halle, Merseburg, Naumburg, Brandenburg, Anhalt, and other cities, and all of the elector's pages, servants, and lackeys, plus another timpanist and twelve trumpeters. Court noblemen were followed by twenty-two flags bearing the coats of arms of the various provinces of Saxony. The Hofmarschall

Heinrich Taube bore the electoral sword in its sheath while the great seal was carried by the privy chamberlain and chancellor Heinrich von Friesen the Elder. The senior Stallmeister Reinhard von Taube supported the electoral crown on a cushion. The mourning carriage itself was drawn by eight horses and was accompanied by twenty-four noblemen. Johann Georg II and his brothers August, Christian, and Moritz followed the mourning carriage. They were followed in turn by dignitaries from Bohemia, Hungary, Vienna, and Sweden. Other members of the royal family present included the elector apparent Johann Georg III, the elector's widow, the new electress, and other female members of the nobility, each accompanied by a prince, earl, general, baron, or colonel. According to Weck's description, every member of the Dresden court took part in the processions, from the new elector to the burghers and their wives, in addition to a large number of representatives from other courts both in Germany and abroad. Unfortunately it is impossible to estimate the total number of participants due to such general references as "all of the electoral Saxon chamberlains and noblemen."[27] Most assuredly, however, the processions were immense and were conducted with great pomp and ceremony. Organization must have been complicated as well as time-consuming: it is clear from the instructions given to various key members that the participants were required to stand in place for four to five hours before the processions began.[28]

The participants in the procession were instructed to sing a list of eight hymns until members of the royal family were in their seats and the procession had fully entered the Kreuzkirche, and, "if the hymns are insufficient [in length], others must be sung or the previous ones repeated."[29] These hymns were:

1. "Herzlich lieb hab ich dich o Herr"
2. "In dich hab ich gehoffet Herr"
3. "Herr Jesu Christ ich weiß"
4. "Herr Jesu Christ ich schrei zu dir"
5. "Ach lieben Christen seid getrost"
6. "Erbarm dich mein o Herre Gott"
8. "Ich weiß daß mein Erlöser lebt"

The procession was led into the church, where another service took place at 4:00 P.M. The morning and afternoon services were similar, with hymns and scripture readings framing a sermon, this time by Jacob Weller.

9.   "Wenn mein Stündlein vorhanden ist"
10. "Ein Würmlein bin ich arm und klein"

11. "Von Gott will ich nicht lassen"
12. The Collect and scripture reading
13. The Creed
14. Sermon by Jacob Weller

After the sermon:

15. "Herr Jesu Christ meins Lebens Licht"
16. "Ich weiß das mein Erlöser lebt"
17. Collect and Benediction
18. "Herr Jesu Christ wahr Mensch und Gott"

Following this service, hymns were sung until the procession emerged from the Kreuzkirche. All of the city bells rang while the procession was led back to the palace.

The following day, 3 February, a second procession took place from the Kreuzkirche to Freiberg, some twenty miles southwest of Dresden, for the burial in the royal vault in the Freiberg cathedral. In the Kreuzkirche the following hymns were sung:

1. "Mit Fried und Freud"
2. "In dich hab ich gehoffet Herr"
3. "Wenn mein Stündlein vorhanden ist"

While leaving the church:

1. "Ich ruf zu dir Herr Jesu Christ"
2. "Ach lieben Christen seid getrost"
3. "Si bona suscepimus"

The musicians were mercifully spared the greater part of the trip to Freiberg according to a memorandum to Schütz.

> A reminder to the Kapellmeister regarding the memorandum: The court musicians must be all together in the palace church shortly after 6:00 and carry out the singing. I find nothing that says that they [must] journey to Freiberg; but, because the three court preachers will provide a complete report, [the matter] shall not go undiscussed. The bass shall come with us, however, and carry the crucifix, which my lord the Hofmarschall has already commanded, as well as how it shall be borne on the way. [And written here in the margin] His Electoral Highness's aforementioned explanation: The assembled musicians shall walk with the procession as far as the little garden and then turn back.[30]

Another memorandum further elaborates on the responsibilities of the musicians for the three days of mourning.

The [duties which] the two Kapellmeisters [Schütz and Bontempi] and those for whom they are responsible are to perform at the electoral funeral procession.

1. On Monday, 2 February 1657, they shall all be in the palace church early in the morning just after 6:00 and sing before and after the sermon. Thereafter towards afternoon before 11:00 [they shall] assemble at the house of Kapellmeister Schütz, there arrange themselves in the order of the completed list, and when the pupils walk across the new marketplace toward the palace, [they shall] follow behind the clergymen into the palace court. As soon as the procession goes by, the bass shall follow the nine marshalls who lead the procession, and always carry the crucifix in the procession here and in Freiberg before them, and thereupon once again the two Kapellmeisters shall follow along with the musicians in their charge, as well as the choirboys walking before them, in correct order, two by two, in formation, into the Kreuzkirche, still [and] without singing, in suitable mourning, and they shall wait in their positions near the sacristy during the sermon and afterwards until the entire procession is out of the church, but then quietly make their way home.

2. On Tuesday, 3 February, they shall again arrange themselves all together early at 6:00 in the Kreuzkirche with the pupils and clergy, wait, and then follow at the onset of the procession as on the previous day as far as the Wilsdorfer Gate in the little garden, wherefrom they shall return to the city together with the clergymen and others and only the bass shall travel along to Freiberg.[31]

These instructions are corroborated by another memorandum to Schütz from Jacob Weller:

Directions from the electoral Saxon senior court preacher and father confessor Dr. Jacob Weller. That to which the Kapellmeister shall attend so that he establishes order.

a) On 2 February, the entire court ensemble shall be present in the palace church early precisely at 6:00.

b) When the bells stop ringing, sing the specified hymns before and after the sermon.

c) Be present at the palace again midday at 11:30 for the removal [of the body] in the Kreuzkirche.

d) On the day of 3 February, be present in the Kreuzkirche before 6:00 and accompany the electoral funeral procession as far as the electoral garden, when you may then again proceed home.[32]

The trumpeters and timpanists participating in the procession also had instructions which were enforced by trumpeter Hans Arnold:

The twenty-four trumpeters, timpanists, and those [men] who carry the two kettle-drums shall be present on Monday, 2 February, at midday about 11:00 in long mourning robes in the electoral stable and, according to the completed list, divide themselves into two troupes among the mounted grooms preassigned to them, and follow them as far as the green gate.[33]

During the service in the Kreuzkirche on 2 February, and prior to the trip to Freiberg on 3 February, the trumpeters, timpanists, mounted

grooms, and flagbearers were instructed to wait outside the church. They took their places as the procession emerged from the church. On 3 February, both troupes of trumpeters and timpanists traveled on horseback to Freiberg, the first troupe riding after the mounted grooms and before the three marshalls, and the second troupe before the court noblemen. Upon reaching the city, they dismounted and proceeded on foot to the furthermost courtyard of the palace.[34] On 4 February, the two troupes of trumpeters and timpanists were instructed to appear at 6:00 A.M., when the procession reassembled at the palace. At 11:00 A.M. all of the city bells rang and the procession, as in Dresden, advanced into the cathedral while singing hymns. Jacob Weller delivered the sermon. As mentioned earlier, a printed version of this sermon is bound in the front of the manuscript. The mourners left the cathedral in procession following the service, walking out behind the palace while singing hymns. The electoral sword was then carried unsheathed by Oberhofmarschall Baron von Rechenberg before Johann Georg II.[35]
In Freiberg these hymns were sung:

1. "Si bona suscepimus"
2. "Christus ist mein Leben und Sterben"
3. "Laßt uns folgen St. Pauli Lehr"
4. "Herzlich thut mich verlangen"
5. "Allein zu dir Herr Jesu Christ"
6. "Ich hab mein Sach Gott heim gestellt"
7. "Ach lieben Christen seid getrost"
8. "Was mein Gott will das gescheh allzeit"

The following hymns were sung on 4 February in Freiberg while the procession advanced into the cathedral:

1. "Ach lieben Christen seid getrost"
2. "Ich hab mein Sach Gott heimgestellt"
3. "Laßt uns folgen St. Pauli Lehr"
4. "Herr Jesu Christ ich schrei zu dir"
5. "Allein zu dir Herr Jesu Christ"
6. "Herzlich lieb hab ich dich o Herr"
7. "Herr Jesu Christ wahr Mensch und Gott"

Once inside the cathedral, the service proceeded as follows:

1. "In dich hab ich gehoffet Herr"
2. "Auf meinen lieben Gott"
3. "Von Gott will ich nicht lassen"
4. Collect and scripture reading

5. The Creed
6. Weller's sermon
7. "Mitten wir im Leben sind"
8. "Wenn mein Stündlein vorhanden ist"
9. "Was mein Gott will"
10. Collect and Benediction

While the mourners left the cathedral in procession, they walked out behind the palace while singing:

11. "Mit Fried und Freud ich fahr dahin"
12. "Nun laßt uns den Leib begraben"
13. "Ich hab mein Sach Gott heimgestellt"

Grandiose royal funerals such as the burial described here were symbols of the power of a dead ruler. According to Ralph Giesey, these ceremonies served a further purpose by

> situating the moment of transference of sovereignty neither at the death of the old king nor at the coronation of the new one but midway in between—that is, at the funeral and burial of the deceased.[36]

The European tradition for mourning a dead sovereign was set in medieval France, where the procedure for royal funeral processions became increasingly more elaborate over the centuries. By the fourteenth and fifteenth centuries, the order of the procession had been strictly laid down with those nearest the coffin representing the most important among the mourners.[37] It is this tradition that we see at Johann Georg I's funeral in 1657.

A list of the cost of 645 ells of number two cloth for mourning livery for the forty-seven members of the court ensemble appears in the expense records for the funeral. Each member of the ensemble is named with the cost of his robe.

Musicians

Heinrich Schütz, Kapellmeister
Giovanni Andrea Bontempi
Vincenzo Albrici
Christoph Bernhard
Gioseppe Peranda
Domenico Melani, soprano
Tobias Tille
Christian Weber

Matthias Erlemann
Georg Berthold [Giorgio Bertoldi]
Adam Merkel
Stefano Sauli
Christian Kittel
Constantin Christian Dedekind
Bartolomeo Albrici
Christoph Kittel
Georg Rumpf
Johann Klemm
Antoni [de Blasi?], Italian
Johann Bartholomäus Buhler
Vicoratorius, Italian
Jonas Kittel
Pietro Finati

Instrumentalists

Giovanni Severo
Friedrich Werner
Michael Schmidt
Balthasar Sedenig
Johann Friedrich Volprecht
Friedrich Westhoff
Wilhelm Burrowes
Friedrich Sulz
Jacob Sulz
Johann Friedrich Sulz
Clemens Thieme
Andreas Winckler
Johann Wilhelm Forchheim
Johann Dixon
Daniel Kreße
Tobias Weller, organ maker
Jeremias Seyffert
Christian Mildner, choirboy
Johann Thorian
Sebastian Ludwig Schulz

Choirboys

Gottfried Böhme
Georg Fritsche

Johann Gottfried Behr
Gottfried Janezky[38]

Fürstenau refers to this list but does not reproduce it.[39] This previously unpublished list is of particular significance since it supersedes Fürstenau's list dated 1662 as the earliest list of the court ensemble of Johann Georg II.[40]

Despite the number and multifaceted capabilities of the members of the court ensemble, their function at the 1657 funeral appears to have been to lead the hymn singing and, by their presence, to represent the enormity and significance of the elector's household and court. Beyond the lists of hymns, no reference is made to other music performed at Johann Georg I's funeral. Moser states that the two motets of Schütz's 1657 commemorative setting of the Canticum Simeonis (Luke 2:29–32), SWV 432–33, the only work in which he sets the same text twice with somewhat similar openings but otherwise quite differently, were intended to frame the funeral sermon.[41] Indeed the memorandum to Schütz regarding his responsibilities does instruct him to provide music both before and after the sermon, as mentioned earlier. Werner Breig points out in his edition of the Canticum Simeonis that Moser's suggestion is pure speculation, however.[42] The motets cannot have been performed in Freiberg since we now know that the musicians remained in Dresden. Given the details provided by the manuscript description of the funeral, including each and every hymn and the texts for the scripture readings and sermons, it does seem unlikely that a new work by the court Kapellmeister performed during the service would not have been mentioned by name as well.

Schütz's best-known funeral composition, the *Musicalische Exequien* (SWV 279–81), was in fact performed at the funeral of Heinrich Posthumus of Reuss-Gera. The printed order of service for this funeral describes the performance of a "Concerted motet . . . in the form of a German Missa," as well as a setting of "Herr, wenn ich nur dich habe," and a setting of the "Nunc dimittis," which we know to be the three parts of Schütz's *Musicalische Exequien,* for the title page of the work tells us that it was performed at the count's funeral on 4 February 1636. In contrast, the printed order of service for Johann Georg I's funeral contains no reference to the 1657 setting of the "Nunc dimittis" and the title page of the work states only that it commemorated the elector's death. The organizers of Johann Georg I's funeral apparently wished the music for the occasion to be somber, perhaps even plain. While many of the hymns celebrate the Christian belief in life after death, most are in minor modes, contributing further to the sober effect. The simplicity of the music for this ceremony is somewhat surprising, particularly in comparison to the music performed at Heinrich Posthumus' funeral.

The Italianate Controversy in Dresden

The death of Johann Georg I marks the beginning of a period of Italian domination of the Dresden musical scene although, as we have seen, the foreign presence had provoked discord much earlier. When the elector died, Schütz was allowed to go into semiretirement, his wish for many years, though a document from 1658 shows he was still expected to be at court three to four times each year (doc. 12).[43] The new ruler, Johann Georg II, was himself a composer, possibly having had music lessons from Schütz, who had dedicated the first part of the *Symphoniae sacrae* to the elector apparent in 1629.[44] The two Dresden ensembles were united under three Kapellmeisters (Schütz, Bontempi, and Vincenzo Albrici) and two vice-Kapellmeisters (Bernhard and Marco Gioseppe Peranda).

Vincenzo Albrici received his musical training at the German College in Rome, which he entered on 12 May 1641 as a *putto soprano*.[45] He had become a salaried musician of the college by 17 February 1646 as an *organista*, indicating that he played the instrument and kept it in repair as well.[46] In 1647, at the age of sixteen, he became *maestro di capella* at the Chiesa Nuova in Rome.[47] In 1652 he was one of sixteen Italian musicians, including his brother Bartolomeo and his father Domenico, who performed at the Swedish court in Stockholm, where they remained from December 1652 until June 1654.[48] When Queen Christina abdicated on 7 June 1654, Albrici, his brother Bartolomeo, and several of the other Italians joined the electoral ensemble in Dresden. A comparison of the list of the original sixteen Italians who visited the Swedish court and a list of Johann Georg II's musicians compiled in 1717 shows that the musicians coming from Stockholm to Dresden were Vincenzo Albrici, Bartolomeo Albrici, Domenico Melani, Vincenzo Cenni, Antonio Piermarini, Francesco Perotti, and Niccolai Milani.[49] Cenni, Piermarini, and Milani left Dresden in the same year while Pierotti remained until 1670, and Melani until his death in 1693.[50] Vincenzo Albrici's now-lost contract appointing him Kapellmeister is dated by Fürstenau as "probably 1656" (doc. 8).[51]

Vincenzo and Bartolomeo Albrici remained in the elector's service for many years (Bartolomeo until 1663 and Vincenzo until Johann Georg II's death in 1680) but they were frequently employed elsewhere as well. After their arrival in 1654, they stayed in Dresden but a short time, leaving to rejoin Queen Christina's entourage, probably in Rome. The exact date of their departure from Dresden is unclear but Vincenzo was definitely in Rome in Christina's service by the late summer of 1660.[52] They may have left Dresden as early as 31 August 1658, the date of written instructions to Domenico Melani,

> because His Electoral Highness's appointed Kapellmeister Vincenzo Albrici shall not be present for most humble service [in Dresden], but shall go elsewhere, the afore-mentioned Electoral Highness commands His privy chamberlain and chamber musician, Dominico Melani, to journey forth in all haste and to make inquiries as to where the aforementioned Albrici might be met.[53]

When Albrici returned to Dresden is uncertain as well, but he was present for the royal wedding festivities from 18 October to 13 November 1662 for he is listed with others in the court ensemble as having received ceremonial robes.[54] The Albrici brothers left Dresden in 1663 for London, where they served as composers in the Chapel Royal.[55] Bartolomeo remained in London, while Vincenzo left in 1668 for Dresden. He was in Cologne in 1671, but according to a previously unpublished travel pass, he had returned by 2 February of that year. The pass, issued by Johann Georg II, allowed Albrici to bring his wife and children and their belongings back from Cologne.[56] He was soon gone again, although we know that he returned to Dresden from France,[57] perhaps, as Richard Engländer suggests, after the sudden death of Marco Gioseppe Peranda in 1675.[58] Albrici seems to have been a special favorite of Johann Georg II, for the elector stood as godfather on 24 February 1662 to the Kapellmeister's son—who was named Johann Georg—in Albrici's Dresden home.[59] In 1680, upon the death of Johann Georg II, he and most of the other Italian musicians were relieved of their posts in Dresden. Albrici then went to the Thomaskirche in Leipzig as organist in 1681, where he converted to Protestantism. Within a year he converted back to Catholicism and from 1682 until his death in 1696 he was Kapellmeister at St. Augustin in Prague.

Marco Gioseppe Peranda was born in Rome or Mascera ca. 1625 and is believed to have been a pupil of Giacomo Carissimi in Rome. Johann Mattheson states that Peranda was brought to Dresden by Christoph Bernhard.[60] According to Fürstenau, Peranda is named as alto in the Dresden court ensemble in a list dating from 1656.[61] In 1661 he became vice-Kapellmeister and in 1663 he succeeded Albrici as Kapellmeister. After Schütz's death in 1672, Peranda became first court Kapellmeister in Dresden. Court journals reveal that he visited Italy in 1667. He died on 12 January 1675.[62]

Among Johann Georg II's Italian musicians, several attained higher positions at court. Both Donato de Amaducci and Gabriel Battistini were named privy chamberlains, in 1675 and 1667 respectively.[63] The castrati Domenico Melani and Bartolomeo Sorlisi were each named privy chamberlain while still retaining their duties as musicians.[64] The elector made them noblemen in 1666.[65] Sorlisi, in fact, married the daughter of a burgher of Dresden in 1666, causing considerable moral and religious indignation. Legal and theological authorities debated the issue for several decades thereafter.[66]

Sorlisi and Melani bought land together and built a summer house with a theater called the "Italian Garden." According to a court diary, Johann Georg II visited the garden on 31 July 1667. "The Italians Domenico Melani and Bartolomeo Sorlisi prepared a banquet in their newly built pleasure-garden on the outskirts of town. In between a German comedy or rather a festive spectacle was performed."[67] In 1668 Johann Georg II bought the garden, which was renamed the Royal Garden, as a gift for the electress.[68] In 1670, Sorlisi became an official of the town of Dippoldiswalde, just south of Dresden. Both Sorlisi and Melani are listed in 1671 as titled landowners.[69]

Preventing foreigners from practicing the Catholic faith in Lutheran Dresden became a concern of the elector who, on 27 March 1661, issued an order attempting to discourage the celebration of Mass in the homes of the Austrian and French envoys. When Sorlisi died on 3 March 1672 at the age of forty, the Kreuzministerium was apparently troubled by the fact that he received the last rites from a Catholic priest. On 27 February 1673 a newly printed electoral order was distributed, sharply forbidding the practice of the Catholic faith. Nevertheless 106 people were discovered on 6 April of that year at the home of the French envoy at a Catholic service. Among the worshippers were Albrici, Battistini, Melani, Carlo Pallavicino, and other Italian members of the court ensemble.[70]

Melani was sent frequently to Italy by Johann Georg II. Previously unknown letters dating from October 1660 to May 1661 between Johann Georg II and Wolf Caspar Klengel, the architect who built Dresden's first opera house (1667), show that Melani accompanied Klengel to Leipzig, Innsbruck, Florence, and Venice to purchase furnishings for the Dresden palace and costumes for the elector's lavish court spectacles.[71] A court diarist reported on 3 December 1669 that Melani had returned from Italy with the gift of a lion and a lioness from the archduke of Florence to the elector.[72] Melani became Sorlisi's successor in Dippoldiswalde.[73] He was one of the few Italians to remain in Dresden after the death of Johann Georg II, holding various court posts while continuing to be involved in organizing theatrical productions. In 1685

Melani endowed an *ospizio* in Florence for the purpose of providing food and lodging to pilgrims on their way to Rome. He specified in the constitution "that the musical oratorios already begun in the church of the hospital be continued, so that the members of [the congregation] might receive every delight and spiritual consolation, and for their greater inducement to frequent the said holy place." When Melani died in 1693, he left most of the fortune he had accumulated in Dresden to his *ospizio*.[74]

It is not known when Giovanni Novelli came to Dresden. He appears in the 1662 list as tenor and in the 1680 list he is named vice-Kapellmeister.

Sebastiano Cherici came to Dresden in September 1675, following Peranda's death on 12 January of that year. According to a court diary, he conducted in church for the first time on 12 September 1675.[75] He stayed in Dresden only until March 1676, when he returned to Ferrara.[76]

Carlo Pallavicino came to Dresden in 1667 as vice-Kapellmeister; in 1672 he was promoted to Kapellmeister.[77] He left in the following year to go to Padua as one of two principal organists at S. Antonio and in 1674 he became musical director of the Ospedale degli Incurabili in Venice. When Johann Georg III established Italian opera at his court, he appointed Pallavicino as director of chamber and theater music on 1 January 1687.[78] According to Fürstenau he wrote twenty operas for Dresden between 1666 and 1688.[79]

The inequity resulting from the preferential treatment given the Italians is well illustrated by the experiences of Schütz's pupil Christoph Bernhard. Exactly when Bernhard came to Dresden is unknown but his appointment as alto and singing instructor to the choirboys is dated 1 August 1649 (doc. 9).[80] Perhaps as a result of Hofkontz's appointment as vice-Kapellmeister, Bernhard petitioned Johann Georg I in a letter dated 17 November 1651, asking permission to leave his post.

> Your Royal Highness no doubt graciously knows that I have served humbly and diligently as a musician and alto in your court ensemble and chamber for more than two years. During this time, I put aside the studies which I was pursuing before so that I might practice music even better and satisfy Your Royal Highness. But because I notice that my current profession of music has not been helpful in securing me respectable advancement and also has not provided sufficient income for me to support myself [even] minimally, I therefore have decided to quit the profession of music from this time forward and in return to seek my support and advancement by taking up my previous studies again.[81]

The elector apparently responded by asking Bernhard to wait for Schütz's return to make a final decision, for Bernhard, who seems almost desperate to leave Dresden, wrote to the elector again on 19 November 1651.

> Although I hoped to obtain my dismissal from Your Royal Highness by my most humble petition delivered the day before yesterday, I am accordingly ready and willing to await in humility the Kapellmeister's arrival. But because the Kapellmeister's arrival will be delayed still longer and I would like to travel to Danzig to my friends before the very severe cold sets in, in order to confer with them concerning the place and means for study as well as other important matters, [I] therefore address my request to Your Royal Highness to grant me graciously a leave of absence of some months in order to carry out this trip.[82]

Although Bernhard petitioned the elector yet again on 24 January 1652 to be allowed to leave Dresden and return to his law studies,[83] he was not allowed to leave his post. He was, in fact, sent to Italy to recruit Italian singers for the court ensemble. Johann Mattheson describes Bernhard's two trips to Italy without dates in *Grundlage einer Ehrenpforte*.[84] Mattheson states that the purpose of Bernhard's first trip was to find two *castrati* in Rome. The date of Bernhard's second trip to Rome to find a Kapellmeister, a tenor, and an alto is established by a letter from Bernhard dated 13 September 1657, which appears in Constantin Christian Dedekind's *Aelbianische Musenlust* printed that year.[85] According to Mattheson, the alto whom Bernhard brought to Dresden was Peranda. Bernhard was appointed vice-Kapellmeister in 1655, after Hofkontz's death on 19 July (doc. 10).[86] When Albrici left Dresden for London in 1663, Bernhard probably expected to receive the position of Kapellmeister. When Peranda was chosen instead, Bernhard sought and obtained the position of cantor of the Johannisschule in Hamburg, recently vacated by the death of Thomas Selle. Johann Georg II allowed Bernhard to assume the post with the understanding that Bernhard was to return to Dresden on the elector's command.[87] Bernhard accepted the position in a letter to the Hamburg council dated 28 December 1663.[88] He returned to Dresden in 1674 as vice-Kapellmeister and as tutor to the princes Johann Georg IV and Friedrich August (later August II and subsequently the king of Poland). Bernhard's new appointment as vice-Kapellmeister of the Germans within the court ensemble is dated 31 March 1674.[89] Bernhard became privy chamberlain in 1679 and in 1681 was finally named Kapellmeister by Johann Georg III, a post he retained until his death in 1692.

The various registers of court musicians in Dresden indicate a predominance of Germans during the reign of Johann Georg I. However the 1651 list of the elector apparent Johann Georg II shows an ensemble with two Italian members, led by Bontempi. Of the forty-seven court musicians listed as participating in Johann Georg I's funeral, thirty-seven were German and ten Italian. The 1662 list shows a performing ensemble of thirteen Italians and twenty-seven Germans. Fürstenau produces a list dated 1666 in which the court ensemble numbers thirty-three Germans and seventeen Italians. In this list, the four Italian Kapellmeisters, Bontempi, Albrici, Peranda, and Pallavicino, are shown to have earned yearly salaries of 1200 Reichstalers while Schütz, by then semiretired, earned 800 Reichstalers. Vice-Kapellmeister Giovanni de Novelli earned 800 Reichstalers, while his German counterpart, vice-Kapellmeister Christoph Bernhard, had to be satisfied with a mere 500 Reichstalers.[90]

Music in Dresden during the Reign of Johann Georg II

The Italian domination produced a gradual shift in musical taste from the German to the Italianate style. An unpublished catalog compiled by Christian Kittel in 1681 for the new elector, Johann Georg III, lists prints and manuscripts used in both sacred and secular settings and contains almost exclusively Italian music (doc. 18), graphically illustrating the great extent of Italian domination.[91] The court diaries before ca. 1650 offer little musical information, but those recorded during Johann Georg I's final years and Johann Georg II's reign contain a large number of references to compositions by the Italian Kapellmeisters.[92] The diaries also present entire worship service orders during these years, showing a strong tendency toward Latin-texted church music. The diaries indicate that after 1660 the Masses and concerti of the Italian Kapellmeisters were performed in worship services in the palace church under the direction of the composers themselves. In fact, performances of over fifty Masses by Peranda, Albrici, and Pallavicino between 1650 and 1673 are mentioned.[93] In the diaries from 1662 until 1668, Peranda is mentioned as the principal director in worship services. In many descriptions the conductor's name is not given but after each work the composer is named. Therefore, if Peranda is named as composer, it is also likely that he conducted.[94]

In 1666 Albrici had left Dresden and only Schütz, Peranda, and Bontempi remained. Schütz was by this time quite old and in poor health and Peranda was frequently on journeys with the elector as director of the troupe of Italian musicians who traveled with him. Bontempi, who was by then concerned with theatrical events, seldom directed in church,[95] a duty which then fell to the court cantor, David Töpfer. To assure that musicians were always available, the court ensemble bass Constantin Christian Dedekind, in a letter to Johann Georg II dated 26 October 1666, proposed a formal division of the Italian and German musicians, suggesting that he, Dedekind, fill a newly created post of concert master rather than the position of secretary for which he had been recommended by Duke Wilhelm of Saxe-Altenburg:

> [S]o that in Your Highness's absence lovely music shall not be at all lacking, the appointment of a subject for the direction of a small German ensemble is almost necessary. [I] propose to Your Electoral Highness, may it please you, that the office of secretary suggested by the His aforementioned Royal Highness of Altenburg as friend and cousin, be transformed into a concert master's post and graciously allow me to be appointed to it.[96]

Fürstenau's 1666 list, cited above, shows that the court ensemble was divided into three groups: the first choir, or the Italian singers; the second choir, or the "kleine deutsche Musik" (the Little German Ensemble) consisting of the German singers; and the third choir of instrumentalists, a neutral group serving both groups of singers. While the Italians provided music for special celebrations and Sunday services, the "kleine deutsche Musik" under the direction of Dedekind was responsible for church music during the week or whenever the first choir was traveling. Dedekind's title of concert master indicated that he was to direct performances of concerti.[97]

After the death of Johann Georg II in 1680, the three factions of the ensemble were reunited and the Italians released from service. But when Pallavicino was reappointed as Kapellmeister in 1687, they returned, reawakening the old disputes and prompting Pallavicino to suggest to the elector in a letter dated 19 August 1687 that the ensemble be divided once more "for reasons of peace and unity between these wise nations, and it is necessary so that Your Electoral Highness shall be served properly."[98]

The performance of German music in church became more and more infrequent even during the last years of Johann Georg I's reign. A court diarist of 1656 reported that Schütz conducted the ensemble and further commented that "the music . . . was sung in German," as though it were unusual.[99] Schütz conducted the worship services in the electoral front chamber during the final weeks of Johann Georg I's rule and personally directed his *Historia der . . . Aufferstehung . . .* (SWV 50), probably for the last time.[100] Schütz conducted the music at Christmas of 1656,[101] and, as described earlier, he played an integral role in the

proceedings during the burial of the elector. It cannot be determ
whether Schütz ever directed the ensemble in church again.[102]

The music performed in church became codified ca. 1662, the date
of the completion of the renovation of the Renaissance church in the
Dresden palace. As Schmidt points out, Weck and the court diaries tell
us that worship services were held for three-fourths of the year 1662 in
the Sophienkirche and elsewhere during the renovation.[103] The chapel
was consecrated on 28 September 1662. After this date the court diary
descriptions of worship services reflect the format of Johann Georg II's
new chapel order, which is undated (doc. 13).[104] According to the description of the consecration service in the court diary, all of the music
was composed especially for the occasion by Albrici, who also conducted.
However a German setting of "Make a Joyful Noise unto the Lord, All
Ye Lands" (*Jauchzet dem Herren, alle Welt*) was sung as an introit, which
Wolfram Steude has shown to be Schütz's Psalm 100 (SWV 493).[105] The
work is mentioned again by a diarist on 15 October 1665, who positively
identifies it as a work by Schütz.[106]

Traditionally, after the middle of the seventeenth century, no instruments were played in the Dresden palace church during Passion Week
and Johann Georg II's new chapel order forbids even the use of the
organ during Lent. This restriction presented Schütz with the musical
challenge that provoked three of his most dramatic works, his Passion
settings. The new chapel order specifies that Passion settings should be
sung three times yearly: Judica, Palm Sunday, and Good Friday (doc.
13). Steude suggests that, with the new order, necessity dictated compositions of Luke and Mark Passions to complement the already existing
Matthew and John Passions by Rogier Michael. The diaries show that
this period included performances of Schütz's *Historia der . . . Geburth . . .
Jesu Christi* (SWV 435), traditionally performed on Christmas Day, his
three Passions for the weeks preceding Easter, and his *Historia der . . .
Aufferstehung . . .* (SWV 50) for Easter, as well as similar compositions by
Peranda, Johann Müller, Johann Wilhelm Forchheim, and Nicolaus
Adam Strungk. Indeed, Peranda's *Historia der . . . Geburth . . . Jesu Christi*
appears to have rivaled Schütz's composition of the same name after
1668, and completely supplanted it after Schütz's death.[107] In a fascinat-
ing survey of diary entries during Christmas, Lent, and Easter from
1656 to 1697, Steude has traced the history of Dresden performances
of these works.[108] Furthermore, in working with the manuscript copies
of Schütz's Matthew, Luke, and John Passions in the Musikbibliothek
der Stadt Leipzig, Steude has identified Peranda as the composer of the
St. Mark Passion, the attribution of which has puzzled scholars for over
a century.[109]

Peranda's *St. Mark Passion* was first performed on Good Friday 1668 in the Dresden palace church. Steude has further observed that stylistic similarities exist between the final chorus in Schütz's *St. Matthew Passion* and the choruses in Peranda's *St. Mark Passion*. Moser and other scholars had previously noted that the closing of the *Matthew Passion* is not typical of Schütz.[110] Steude has now raised the possibility that Schütz asked Peranda to complete the work, for Schütz in 1668 was probably occupied with his massive *opus ultimum* or *Schwanengesang, Königs und Propheten Davids hundert und neunzehender Psalm* (SWV 482–94), a complete setting of the 176 verses of Psalm 119 for two four-part choruses, a German Magnificat, and the Psalm 100 discussed earlier.[111]

Italian Influence in the Theater

The Italian domination extended beyond the church to Dresden's theatrical life as well, particularly after the opening in 1667 of the city's first opera house. Dresden's theatrical tradition, however, may be traced back to the late sixteenth century. Court festivities such as royal weddings, christenings, and other celebrations became highly organized and imaginative festivals in which fireworks, balls, banquets, masques, and theatrical presentations were organized around a common theme. These celebrations included a festive procession, or *Invention*, a word used not to connote "discovery" but "whimsy."[112] The *Inventionen* of Dresden were extraordinarily elaborate, with planets, mythological and sea creatures, and characters from exotic lands, and always included lavish use of musicians singing and playing in various groups as a decorative element. The great many illustrations of these processions include drawings and engravings of various sizes as long as several meters.[113] While the great *Inventionen* of the sixteenth century had been held outdoors, during the seventeenth century they were moved indoors, where they became connected with the development of the ballet. These court spectacles had various names. Older terms including *Aufzug, Tantz, Ritterspiel,* or *Mummerei,* later became *singend Ballett* or *Singballett.* Originally the court ballet had been nothing more than a part of a courtly celebration combining eating and drinking with dancing and music, in which the boundaries between theater and court ceremony were blurred.[114] Such ballets were performed during the seventeenth century at every German court and reached the height of their popularity in Germany between 1650 and 1680, by which time the popularity of French court ballets was declining.

Becker-Glauch places the first performance of a ballet at the Dresden court in 1615, at the christening of Johann Georg I's son Christian.[115]

Thereafter a great many ballets are mentioned in court documents. Since Fürstenau discusses all important theatrical events in chronological order, a list of all of these performances will not be repeated here.[116]

As Kapellmeister, Schütz composed a number of theatrical works for the Dresden court. As Werner Breig observes, however, most works composed for German court celebrations were never printed and therefore many have been lost.[117] Unfortunately Schütz's theatrical music is no exception. It is only through prints of texts and performance reports that we know of the existence of such works at all. Breig states that of the works composed for special occasions, only those usable beyond their original purpose were printed.[118]

Schütz's theatrical works for the Dresden court include a ballet composed for the Dresden visit of Emperor Matthias and his family on 15 July 1617; a musical tableau for the elector's birthday on 5 March 1621; the opera *Dafne,* a setting of a libretto adapted by Martin Opitz from Rinuccini, for the occasion of the wedding of Johann Georg I's daughter Sophia Eleonora to the Landgrave Georg II of Hessen-Darmstadt in Torgau in 1627; and a five-act opera-ballet on the Orpheus legend for the wedding of Johann Georg II and Magdalene Sibylla of Brandenburg in 1638. While we know from the court diaries that Schütz did compose music for the wedding of Johann Georg II's brothers, the dukes Christian and Moritz, to the princesses Christiana and Sophia Hedwig of Holstein-Glücksburg, his authorship of the ballet of *Paris und Helena* performed during the festivities lasting from 14 November to 11 December 1650 is uncertain.[119]

Giovanni Andrea Bontempi's five-act opera *Il Paride,* called "the decisive step toward the introduction of Italian opera in northern Germany,"[120] was performed during the celebrations for the wedding of Johann Georg II's daughter Erdmuth Sophia to Margrave Ernst Christian of Brandenburg-Bayreuth in 1662. The work consists of thirty-nine scenes. The four ballets, entitled Ballet of the Gods and Goddesses, Ballet of the Shepherds, Battle of the Trojans and Greeks, and Ballet of the Princes and Princesses, are not preserved in the printed score.[121] Another significant event in the development of opera in Dresden took place during the festivities celebrating the return of Johann Georg III from Copenhagen with his new bride, the princess Anna Sophia of Denmark, the eldest daughter of King Friedrich III. The occasion included the opening of the new opera house on 27 January 1667. The work performed was *Il Teseo* with G.A. Moniglia's libretto probably set by Moniglia or Bontempi.[122] In 1671 Bontempi and Peranda collaborated to produce *Apollo und Daphne,* which, as Engländer observes, is the first German opera to survive in both libretto and score and the first valid evidence of a full opera in German.[123] One year later Bontempi and Peranda collaborated again on *Jupiter und Jo*.[124]

The last major theatrical event held during the reign of Johann Georg II occurred in February 1678, when the elector was visited by his three brothers, Duke August of Saxe-Magdeburg, Duke Christian of Saxe-Merseburg, and Duke Moritz of Saxe-Zeitz. The performance of the *Opernballett von der Wirckung der sieben Planeten*, a work composed by Christoph Bernhard, as Gerhard Bittrich has shown, took place on 3 February.[125]

Schütz's Final Years

In 1663 or late 1662, Schütz apparently reminded the elector that his father Johann Georg I had assigned the composer 200 gulden yearly from taxes in Merseburg, for on 27 March 1663 Johann Georg II issued a command that the money should be paid (doc. 14).[126] In this order he refers to Schütz's "appended petition" which now seems to be lost. An account of the amount in arrears was produced on 24 October 1663 by court officials Tobias Berten and Georg Eysold:

> [According to the] contents of the prior most gracious order [from Johann Georg II], the following receipts for Kapellmeister Herr Heinrich Schütz's salary increase are thus to be put in order and paid immediately by the electoral Saxon chamber of revenues, namely

50 Reichstalers	Second Sunday in Lent	
50 Reichstalers	Trinity Sunday	1660
50 Reichstalers	September 14	
50 Reichstalers	December 13	
50 Reichstalers	Second Sunday in Lent	
50 Reichstalers	Trinity Sunday	1661
50 Reichstalers	September 14	
50 Reichstalers	December 13	
50 Reichstalers	Second Sunday in Lent	
50 Reichstalers	Trinity Sunday	1662
50 Reichstalers	September 14	
50 Reichstalers	December 13	
50 Reichstalers	Second Sunday in Lent	1663
50 Reichstalers	Trinity Sunday[127]	

In 1666 Schütz had to write to the elector twice more, for the privy president and councillor Haugwitz had neglected to resolve the matter (docs. 15 and 16).[128] In an undated letter to an unnamed court official, possibly during the same year, the exasperated Schütz seemed prepared to accept a compromise simply to bring the matter to a close (doc. 17).[129] Moser indicates that Schütz was granted his money, an erroneous conclusion apparently reached by misdating Johann Georg's letter of 27 March 1663 (doc. 14).[130] Evidence that Schütz was ever actually paid does not exist.

Schütz died on 6 November 1672, according to the court diaries, "at 4:00 . . . his age being 87 years, four weeks, and 19 and 3/4 hours. He was born 8 October 8:45 in the evening in the year 1585."[131] His funeral was held on 17 November in the Frauenkirche. The sermon was given by the senior court preacher Dr. Martin Geier, who used the occasion not only to eulogize Schütz but also to deliver a lengthy diatribe against Italians (Peranda in particular), the French style, and the secularization of the music performed in the palace church:

> Granted that many still join in the singing of a good song in church, how do things stand in your house? People may sing a good song with their mouths perhaps, but, good Sir, where is their heart? Many sing more for the melody's sake, perhaps because the song is new with a fine brisk way about it and a pleasant worldly ring, but who cares about the content? People like that remind me of a man who has a great fondness for the new styles in dress. When he sees a strange new bird finely and unusually dressed, he says, "Ah, that is nice! That suits me; that is the kind of man to get acquainted with; that is a man to welcome into your home." God defend us from the rascal that is hidden in such new clothes and from the misery and harm he afterwards causes for his host. . . . Here, there should be mentioned what so many old and new teachers of the church have complained of, that is, the unspiritual, dancelike, yes, even ridiculous, modes of song and music one often gets to hear in the churches. If a man were to be brought there blindfolded, he would be quite of the opinion that he was in a theatre where a ballet was to be danced or a comedy to be performed. . . . As a favor to the papists, we cite here the words of their man, Drexelius . . . [who shows] that this luxuriant church music is nothing, in fact but French comic opera. . . .
>
> Casalius . . . also inveighs mightily against such an unspiritual, dancerlike way of singing, particularly against those who for their voice's sake have been emasculated. . . . Oh, what great blessedness our gracious God has granted us in the bright light of the Gospel, beyond that of our ancestors and beyond that of those who are now still sitting in the darkness of the papacy![132]

Both before and after the sermon, the Germans of the court ensemble performed four compositions, the first of which was by Christoph Bernhard and the other three by Schütz himself, as recorded by a diarist. According to Mattheson, Schütz requested a work by Bernhard for his funeral, a setting of Psalm 119:54 in the style of Palestrina. Bernhard apparently submitted the work to Schütz for his approval, for Mattheson cites a letter from Schütz to Bernhard: "My son, you have done me a great favor by sending the motet which I requested. I would not know how to improve on a single note."[133] This work of Bernhard seems to be lost. As Schütz's body was carried from the church, another unnamed work by him was performed.

An incomplete last list of Johann Georg II's court ensemble, compiled in 1681 for his successor, Johann Georg III, has been published by Fürstenau.[134] In this list, the court ensemble at the time of Johann Georg II's death in 1680 is divided into three groups: first choir, second choir, and instrumentalists. The first choir was still primarily made up of Italians; all the members of the second choir were German; and the group of instrumentalists were all German except for Marziani. An unpublished list of Johann Georg II's musicians compiled in 1717 contains new information: the precise year in which the members received their last payment.[135]

The size of the court ensemble had grown during Johann Georg II's reign while the ratio of Italians to Germans had actually decreased. The combined lists of the ensemble in 1680 show a court ensemble of fifty-one members, eleven Italians and forty Germans, in which the Italians were paid much more handsomely than their German colleagues. An overview of the ensemble of Johann Georg II may be seen below.[136]

	Germans	Italians	Total
1657	37	10	47
1662	33	13	46
1666	33	17	50
1680	40	11	51

The large number of musicians in the Dresden ensemble during Johann Georg II's reign is quite in keeping with what we know about the repertoire performed at court during this period. Many of Schütz's works dating from Johann Georg II's reign, particulary after the consecration of the renovated Dresden chapel in 1662 (a date which Wolfram Steude believes designates the beginning of the composer's late style) show a return to the large polychoral forces of the *Psalms of David* (1619) and the *Symphoniae sacrae* III (1650).[137] The first of Schütz's late works is the Psalm 100 (SWV 493) performed at the 1662 consecration, a composition which a diarist describes as "composed anew."[138] The work was performed again in 1665 and the diarist again refers to Kapellmeister Schütz's Psalm 100 "composed anew." Steude suggests that the 1665 performance might have involved a revised version;[139] it seems more likely, however, that the diarist merely wished to differentiate this Psalm 100 from Schütz's earlier setting (SWV 36) from the 1619 *Psalms of David*. Other late works include the *Historia der ... Geburth ... Jesu Christi* (SWV 435), the three Passions, some of the last great Psalm settings, and a series of other works which are now lost.

As Joshua Rifkin points out, Schütz was plagued throughout his lifetime by economic conditions which prevented him from publishing many of his works.[140] As stated earlier, a great many of Schütz's lost compositions were unpublished, among them several works scored for large forces.

Performance Practice in Dresden

The lists of Johann Georg II's ensemble show numerous solo instrumentalists. Idiomatic instrumental writing in Schütz's works is first found in the *Symphoniae sacrae* I, a collection published in 1629 in Venice during Schütz's second visit to the city. The work contains settings of Latin texts in the concertato style in three to six solo parts with basso continuo. The solo instruments required are violins, recorders, cornetti or fiffari, sackbuts, bassoons or viole da gamba, and trumpets. The subsequent collection, *Symphoniae sacrae* II (1647), is scored for one, two, and three voices, two obbligato violins "or other like instruments," and continuo. *Symphoniae sacrae* III (1650), for three to six vocal parts, two violins, and continuo, has an optional four-part *complementum* for instruments or voices. The *Historia der ... Geburth ... Jesu Christi* (1664), which calls for a tenor evangelist, cantus, bass, three altos, three tenors, and four basses plus viole da gamba, violins, recorders, bassoon, sackbuts, clarini or cornetti, and basso continuo, is a score "requiring a diversity in instrumentation which had never before been employed in German church music."[141]

Although the lists of the ensemble consistently show forces large enough to sustain performances with several musicians on each part, the prefaces to Schütz's works reflect his wish that they be performed with smaller forces. In the preface to the *Psalms of David* (1619), he differentiates between an ensemble of solo voices, which he calls *cori favoriti*, and reinforcing groups, or *Capellen*. The *cori favoriti* parts are to be performed by four of the finest solo singers, except in the motets and sacred concerti which could be performed with one singer in each chorus and instruments playing the other parts. The *Capellen*, which are optional, may be performed by instruments alone or by a combination of instruments and voices. Schütz suggests in his preface that the parts of the small ensemble for certain Psalms in his collection may be reinforced in the tutti sections for the sake of balance.[142]

The *Psalms of David* was Schütz's first major publication after his return to Germany from Venice in 1613. The mode of performance described by Schütz is clearly related to Venetian musical practice at St. Mark's Basilica, as recently illuminated by the late James Moore.[143] Documents describing the salmi spezzati, works for two four-part ensembles and basso continuo, reveal that these works were not written for two equal choirs but for a first choir consisting of a group of four of the best singers and a second, a ripieno, consisting of the rest of the singers in the ensemble. Moore states that this practice reaches far back into the sixteenth century, perhaps as early as Willaert's salmi spezzati of 1550. There is, however, no clear evidence regarding instrumental doublings.[144]

Further evidence for limited forces in Schütz's polychoral works is provided by the composer in the form of a list of musicians who were to accompany Johann Georg I to Mühlhausen in Thuringia for the Electoral Diet between 4 October and 3 November 1627.[145] Besides himself, Schütz proposed eighteen additional musicians: six instrumentalists, four adult male singers, two organists, a cittern player, two discantists, and three *Instrumentistenknaben*. The work performed was the concerto for double chorus à 9 "Da pacem, Domine, in diebus nostris" (SWV 465). Schütz also provided a reduced list of four instrumentalists, three male adult singers, two organists, two discantists, and two *Instrumentistenknaben*. In the more expansive performance, Schütz may have intended some of the vocal lines to be doubled by instruments. The performance with reduced forces would have involved a combined vocal and instrumental realization as well, but with some parts played and not sung at all. It is interesting to note the importance of the two organists, undoubtedly one for each chorus. Schütz explains the necessity of two organists in any respectable court ensemble in a 1617 letter to Heinrich Posthumus, whom he advised on the reorganization of the music at the court at Gera.

> Your Grace, for such an extensive and excellent body of musicians at least two organists are absolutely necessary, if polychoral music is to be performed, for then the organists must provide the fundamental harmony [*das Fundament halten*], so that it is necessary to have an organist virtually with each choir. However, two organists can be placed opposite to each other, accompanying the adjacent choir on an organ or regal, so that the fundamental harmony can be heard at all times in the church. In my opinion this is the minimum number of organists necessary to perform Your Grace's music, and one or two organists can be a good adornment to the choirs which

are *minus principales*—or as I call them *Capellen* or *Choros adjunctos*. In my opinion, two such organists are necessary if one is to perform music in the latest fashion, with two trebles, alto, tenor and bass replying or adding [to what had gone before], producing fine echoes.[146]

The manuscript source of "Da pacem," destroyed in the bombing of Königsberg, contained an explanation of its origin and directions for performance:

[T]he first chorus of five parts may be played on viols, with one or two doubling voices singing *submisse;* the second chorus consists of four singers who must pronounce the words distinctly and sing strongly; this chorus may be placed apart from the first.[147]

The *Geistliche Chor-Music* (1648) is described on the title page as a work scored for "five, six, and seven voices, to be used both *vocaliter* and *instrumentaliter*."[148] In the preface, Schütz advises performers that the various compositions within the collection require different dispositions of voices and instruments so that some are best performed

by a full chorus of voices and instruments, whereas others are designed so that with best effect the parts are not doubled, tripled, or otherwise supported, but rather divided between vocal and instrumental performance and rendered by placing the choir at the organ or even antiphonally (if the work contains eight, twelve, or more parts). Examples of both kinds are to be found in this small work in which, for the time being, I have limited myself to the scoring of fewer voices—especially in the last few pieces, where with the mentioned style of execution in mind, I have not had the text placed under all the voice parts. The perceptive performer might apply the same principle to some of the earlier pieces in the volume and render them accordingly.[149]

Schütz personally inscribed the organ part to his *opus ultimum*, expressing his wishes for the performance of the work:

May my most humble request to you, most gracious and serene Lord Elector, be granted, that it please you most graciously, whensoever it may seem most favorable to your Highness, to allow this very modest little work to be tried and sung by eight good voices with two little organs in the two fine choir lofts that were constructed opposite each other on either side of the altar in your Highness's Court Chapel. The Author.[150]

According to Weck, the elector spared nothing in renovating the chapel. The two choir lofts rested on four red marble pillars and each contained a positif.[151] Other possibilities for the performance of the work seem to have existed, for the Dresden concert master, Constantin Christian

Dedekind, in the dedication of his own setting of Psalm 119 entitled *Königs Davids Göldnes Kleinod* (Dresden, 1674), writes:

> Herr Heinrich Schüzze [*sic*] / shortly before the end of his days / heroically, artistically, and diligently composed / [a setting of] the long 119th Psalm, until then never undertaken by a composer, / and entitled it the Swan-Song (doubtless / because he knew it would be his last work) / for eight voices divided into two choirs / and often reminded me to add instrumental parts to it *ad libitum*.[152]

The organ is the instrument which is mentioned most often in Schütz's prefaces, prints, and manuscripts. As already discussed, the polychoral works are best performed with two organs, a practice further supported by the manuscript copy to SWV 470 in which the organ part is divided between *Organo grande*, (which accompanies the *Capelle*) and *Organo picciolo* (a positif to accompany the solo singers and instrumental choruses).[153] In summarizing the use of the organ in Schütz's works, Gerhard Kirchner in his study *Der Generalbass bei Heinrich Schütz* states that works in which organ is the only basso continuo instrument mentioned can be performed without other supporting instruments while works in which other instruments are mentioned cannot be performed without organ.[154] Kirchner also emphasises that even in compositions in motet-style without continuo, the organist should double the vocal lines.[155] Schütz stresses this concept in the preface to the *Psalms of David:*

> The basso continuo part is intended only for the complete Psalm settings. Beginning with the Motet "Ist nicht Ephraim," and throughout the remainder of the volume, the interested organist might attempt to duplicate the part writing, and if more than one organ is used the different bass parts in the Psalms might again be doubled.[156]

Schütz refers often to the violone in his prefaces. Several of his printed works, such as *Symphoniae sacrae* II, the *Musicalische Exequien*, and the *Historia der . . . Geburth . . . Jesu Christi,* provide a separate violone part.[157] In the preface to the *Musicalische Exequien,* Schütz expresses his fondness for the violone as

> the most convenient, agreeable, and best instrument to go with the *concertato* voices (when the latter are sung to the sole accompaniment of a quiet organ), and is a particular ornament of concerted music when it is rightly employed—this is not only shown by its effect, but also confirmed by the example of the most famous musicians in Europe, who nowadays everywhere use this instrument in their arrangements of this sort.[158]

The only indication that other instruments were used in Schütz's compositions is a 1642 memorandum in which he refers to the violone, bass trombone, and bassoon as possible instruments to play the bass line.[159]

Several continuo parts in Schütz's works call for a choir of lutes. Kirchner quotes Praetorius in defining a lute choir as comprising other basso continuo instruments but not the organ,[160] including

> harpsichords or spinets, quilled instruments (commonly called *"Instrument"*), theorbos, lutes, pandoras, *Orphoreon*, citterns, a large bass lyra, or whatever and as many fundamental instruments of this kind as one is able to gather together.[161]

In support of this practice, Kirchner cites SWV 21, in which the basso continuo part calls for lutes and harpsichord to accompany the third choir. Generally, where the third chorus enters, the continuo part is marked "lute choir."[162] The preface to the *Historia der ... Aufferstehung ...* indicates that

> [t]he part of the Evangelist may be accompanied by organ, positif, or in addition a harpsichord, lutes, pandora, etc. . . . Whenever possible, it is better to omit the organ and other [instruments] and instead to use only four viole da gamba (for which [parts] are included here) to accompany the character of the Evangelist.[163]

Usually the lute choir accompanies a specific chorus. For example, in SWV 36 in the *Psalms of David*, the *coro di Liuti* accompanies Chorus II; in SWV 470 it accompanies a three-voice chorus of viols; and in SWV 274 in the *Symphoniae sacrae* I, the indication "Voce con la Tiorba" appears over the cantus and tenor solos of Chorus II.[164]

The 1681 catalog (doc. 18), which lists music and instruments borrowed from the Dresden instrument chamber during Johann Georg II's reign, gives information regarding the instrumentation used by Peranda in his sacred compositions. Of particular interest are the sacred concerti with scoring for various combinations of solo voices and instruments, most frequently violins, cornetti, bassoons, and trumpets. The Psalm composition by Johann Georg II (no. 1) and a Mass and Credo by Peranda (no. 6) have parts for six trumpets.

While Johann Georg I's court ensemble declined during the Thirty Years War and continued to suffer until his death in 1656, Johann Georg II as early as 1641 had established an ensemble of his own, which continued to expand until in 1651 it nearly surpassed the elector's own in size. When Johann Georg I died in 1656, the two Dresden court ensembles were united. A previously unpublished list of the Dresden musicians shows an increase from three Italian members in 1651 to ten in 1657, including the important figures Giovanni Andrea Bontempi,

Vincenzo Albrici, and Marco Gioseppe Peranda, all of whom were to exert great musical influence in Dresden during Johann Georg II's reign.

Schütz's semiretirement after Johann Georg I's death marks the beginning of a period of Italian domination of the Dresden musical scene. As the court diaries illustrate, sacred music, opera, and music at table were all composed primarily by the Italian Kapellmeisters and vice-Kapellmeisters. Even some of Schütz's own late works performed at court during this period were superseded by similar compositions by Peranda.

Controversy over the foreign presence had arisen as early as 1646, when Schütz proposed hiring Agostino Fontana as vice-Kapellmeister, an appointment successfully challenged by the court cantor, Johann Georg Hofkontz. Schütz found himself embroiled in further strife over his perceived role in the recruitment of Italian musicians in Dresden in the early 1650s. Strain between the Italian and German musicians may have prompted the formal division of the ensemble in 1666 into three groups, each with its specific duties as outlined above. After Johann Georg II's death in 1680, the Italian musicians were dismissed. They returned, however, when Johann Georg III established Italian opera at his court and thereby reawakened religious and nationalistic controversy at the Dresden court once again.

2

Wolfenbüttel

Schütz and the Guelf Courts

Schütz served as Kapellmeister *in absentia* to several courts in northern Germany. The first of these was Bückeburg, where Schütz acted as advisor to Count Ernst von Schaumburg-Lippe from 1615 until 1617.[1] Between the years 1638 and 1666, Schütz was involved in some capacity at various times with all three Guelf courts: Hanover-Calenburg, Celle-Lüneburg, and Wolfenbüttel-Brunswick. The earliest of these associations was the period in which Schütz was active at the court in Hanover. The ruler in Hanover, Duke Georg, met Schütz in Copenhagen in 1638, when the duke probably hired Schütz as advisor.[2] Little is known of Schütz's duties and influence, although the court account books contain several entries in his name for the years 1639–41. An entry for eight talers paid to a Curt Gruppe, a citizen of Hanover, for "that which Kapellmeister Schütz ... consumed in his home" indicates that Schütz was in Hanover on 24 December 1639.[3] In 1641–42 Schütz was paid for housing two choirboys whom he apparently had brought with him from Dresden to Hanover.[4] It was shortly after the duke's death on 12 April 1641 that Schütz's relationship with the Hanover court ended.[5]

Still less information has survived pertaining to Schütz's responsibilities at the court of Duke Georg's brother, Duke Friedrich of Celle-Lüneburg. The account books for the court in Celle show that Schütz was paid twenty talers sometime between 15 and 28 January 1648. As Jost Harro Schmidt suggests, the payment may have been for music; to show gratitude for the dedication of a composition; for professional advice; as a wedding gift for Schütz's daughter, Euphrosyne, who married on 25 January 1648; or as a payment for Schütz's services as Kapellmeister *in absentia,* even though a definite appointment has never been ascertained.[6]

Schütz's most intimate and long-lasting relationship with the courts of Lower Saxony was in Wolfenbüttel from ca. 1644 until 1666. Schütz, Duke August, and Duchess Sophie Elisabeth maintained a lively correspondence over a period of more than twenty years, and Schütz probably visited Wolfenbüttel on several occasions. Schütz was responsible for advising the duke and duchess and assisted them in refurbishing the Wolfenbüttel court ensemble, which had suffered from the depredations of the Thirty Years War. During Schütz's tenure as Kapellmeister *in absentia,* Wolfenbüttel became one of the most important musical centers of the smaller courts in Germany.

The Wolfenbüttel Court Ensemble before Schütz

The first period of musical prominence in Wolfenbüttel came during the reign of Duke Heinrich Julius (1589–1613) at a time when Protestant church music flourished in the cities and courts of Lower Saxony. A new palace church was built in Wolfenbüttel in 1570,[7] and by 1590 the court ensemble had seventeen members with an additional twelve trumpeters.[8] Michael Praetorius was named Kapellmeister in 1604, after having served since 1595 as organist. By this time, the court ensemble consisted of three basses, three tenors, three altos, eight choirboys, five instrumentalists, one instrumental apprentice, two organists, and two lutenists.[9]

On 9 January 1604, the citizens of Wolfenbüttel petitioned Duke Heinrich Julius for a new church which would serve both the city and the court. This church came to be known as the Beatae Mariae Virginis, Marienkirche, or Hauptkirche, and replaced the palace church as the central place of worship in Wolfenbüttel.[10] We know of the interior of the church from two engravings completed by Sebastian Furck from originals by Albert Freise in 1650.[11] The two engravings show views of the church looking east, toward the high altar, the ducal crypt, and the ducal gallery, and looking west, where the organ and the court ensemble are depicted. The view to the west shows the musicians and the organ sharing one gallery (fig. 1). To the right of the organ are the instrumentalists, including two stringed instruments and four winds (cornetto, recorder, sackbut, and curtal). To the left of the organ are two groups of singers consisting of three and four men.[12]

The successor to Duke Heinrich Julius was his son, Duke Friedrich Ulrich (1613–34). In a letter dated 1614 Praetorius encouraged the new duke to reorganize the ensemble, suggesting the addition of another five or six instrumentalists to the current six singers and six instrumentalists.[13] The new duke, however, was not musical like his father, and the number of performers in the ensemble fell still further.[14] Praetorius remained Kapellmeister but was often away, sometimes in Dresden serving elector Johann Georg I. In 1616, however, Praetorius arranged for Gottfried Fritzsche to come to Wolfenbüttel. Fritzsche was royal organ builder to the elector in Dresden and had close connections to important organists and composers of his time, including Schütz. Fritzsche's first great organ, which Hans Leo Haßler designed shortly before he died in 1612, was built in the Dresden palace church in 1612.[15]

Fritzsche and Praetorius also planned the building of a new organ in the Marienkirche, culminating in a contract with Fritzsche dated 15 February 1620.[16] The organ was inspected in 1679 by Friedrich Besser, whose notes show that the construction of the organ followed Praetorius's original plan.[17] Praetorius died 15 February 1621, before the organ was completed, and he was, in fact, buried beneath it. Fritzsche completed the instrument, which was his first three-manual organ, in 1623. His pupil Jonas Weigel remained in Wolfenbüttel and performed several repairs on the organ.[18] While Fritzsche was in Wolfenbüttel he also built a new organ in the palace church, although little is known about it.[19] After the completion of the organ in the Marienkirche, some of the best-known organists of the North German organ school were employed there, including Sweelinck's pupil Melchoir Schildt and his brother Ludolph Schildt, as well as Schütz's personal friend, Delphin Strungk.[20]

The New Duke and Duchess

When Duke Friedrich Ulrich died childless on 11 August 1634, August of the Lüneburg-Dannenberg line became duke. The chronicler Philipp Jakob Rehtmeier described August as a ruler gifted in body and mind.[21] He was the seventh child of Duke Heinrich of Brunswick, who provided him with an exceptionally good education. August studied in Rostock and Tübingen. At fifteen, he was rector of the University of Rostock and could converse fluently in Latin. He visited Italy, Sicily, Malta, France, and England while maintaining a residence in Hitzacker. During his younger years, he wrote books about his life and travels; his correspondence from this period fills thirty volumes.

Duke August's wife, Sophie Elisabeth, was the first member of the most prestigious seventeenth-century German literary society, the Fruit-Bearing Society (*Fruchtbringende Gesellschaft*) and was known both as an author and composer. She was born in 1613 in Güstrow to Duke Johann Albrecht of Mecklenburg-Güstrow. After the death of Sophie Elisabeth's mother in 1618, the duke married Elisabeth von Hesse, a daughter of Moritz the Learned. Duchess Elisabeth saw that Sophie Elisabeth received a fine musical education, for she employed the English lutenist John Stanley as lute instructor for the princesses when Sophie Elisabeth was twelve. Sophie Elisabeth was also surrounded by other excellent English musicians at her father's court, such as William Brade, appointed court Kapellmeister in 1618, and the English gambist Walter Rowe and his sons, who visited the Güstrow court in 1626.[22]

It is said frequently that Sophie Elisabeth was at the court of Moritz the Learned in Kassel (where Schütz spent his early years before going to Dresden) when her father, Duke Johann Albrecht, suffered the imperial ban for high treason. He was banished in 1629 because of his sympathies for Christian of Denmark.[23] While the duke was in exile, some of his children were housed at other courts. Sievers cites a contemporary report which states that at the age of sixteen, Sophie Elisabeth fled with her sister to Kassel. He further suggests that it was there that Sophie Elisabeth first became acquainted with Schütz's music.[24] In 1632 the house of Mecklenburg was restored by Gustav Adolf of Sweden and Duke Johann Albrecht was reconciled with Emperor Ferdinand II in the Peace of Prague in 1635.

When Sophie Elisabeth married Duke August, she was not quite twenty-two years old, and he was fifty-seven with four small children. She and August had three more children, although one died shortly after birth. Her greatest achievement at court was in the realm of music. She saw that all of the children received musical instruction. These musical pursuits are commemorated in an anonymous painting in which the children are depicted playing six gambas with either Sophie Elisabeth or August's oldest daughter at the harpsichord, while August and other family members play at a board game (fig. 2).[25]

Herzog-August-Bibliothek possesses six volumes of Sophie Elisabeth's poems, dating from 1650 until her death in 1676. She maintained close connections with the poets Georg Philipp Harsdörffer (1607–58) and Sigmund von Birken (1626–81) of Nuremberg and she brought Justus Georg Schottelius (1612–76) to Wolfenbüttel in 1638, where he remained until 1646 as tutor to August's children.[26] Birken was also in Wolfenbüttel as tutor to the duke's gifted son, Anton Ulrich.

Rebuilding the Court Ensemble

In 1635 August moved with his children and Sophie Elisabeth to Brunswick, where they lived for eight years until the emperor's troops withdrew from Wolfenbüttel after the signing of the Treaty of Goslar on 16 January 1642. Before moving his court from Brunswick to Wolfenbüttel, August had begun to reassemble the court ensemble and had appointed Sylvester Hancke as organist for the Marienkirche. In a previously unpublished contract signed in Wolfenbüttel on Easter 1637, Hancke agreed

> always to serve diligently at worship services on Sundays and feast days or, when necessity demands, at burials or weddings and on occasion willingly to provide *choraliter* pieces as well as *figuraliter* pieces which are agreeable and appropriate to the time of year. . . .[27]

Hancke's salary was 100 talers per year; an increase to 120 talers on 27 March 1638 is indicated at the bottom of the page.[28]

In 1638 August engaged Stephan Körner, who had been a court musician when Praetorius was Kapellmeister, to rebuild the court ensemble.[29] In an undated letter to August, Körner provides some suggestions regarding personnel,[30] and in a second undated memorandum, Körner further suggests that the musicians should be provided one meal at court, "especially since this [policy] was always maintained by the previous prince and lord of blessed memory and without this their wages in the current difficult times are insufficient."[31] To fulfill the wishes of the duke, Körner states that he will

> betake myself personally to Hamburg and Lübeck and without any doubt shall find good, well-trained musicians. The singers, however, [are another matter] because there is a great difference [in their training] and they are simply not so qualified that they can offer both [singing and playing instruments] well.[32]

Finally, he asks for the full authority to engage musicians for the ensemble. In a document dated 12 June 1638 August empowers Körner

> to organize an excellent, good ensemble for the purpose of the worship service in church as well as service at our royal table in our chamber to the special praise and honor of God the Almighty, and furthermore for the enjoyment of us and ours, and for this purpose to seek in our name, near and far, carefully chosen, excellent musicians who have an understanding not only of all sorts of musical instruments but also know how to play them beautifully.[33]

August then empowers Körner to make final agreements with musicians regarding salary. August also includes a specific list of the types of musicians Körner is to find, summarizing Körner's suggestions with his own wishes added, clear evidence that musicians were expected to be extremely versatile.

> An alto who is also an instrumentalist, 120 talers; a tenor who also plays the pandora and is also an instrumentalist; a bass who along with [singing] bass can also play a

bass instrument and hold a singer's post [at the same time] and could teach the boys singing [and who can] play the violin or something else, 100 talers; a good violone player and [who is] perhaps a good lutenist in addition, 140 talers; a cornettist and violinist, 120 talers; a curtal player and bassoonist, 120 talers.[34]

He adds to the list two choirboys and a *Kalkant* to care for the instruments, copy music, and perform various other duties. As Kapellmeister, Körner was to maintain a household in Wolfenbüttel and was to be responsible for the daily tutoring of the two choirboys in music. Körner's contract was settled shortly thereafter and is dated 24 June 1638.[35]

Körner's contract served some seventeen years later as rough copy for the contract of his successor Johann Jacob Löwe von Eisenach, dated 24 June 1655. Körner's name is simply crossed out and Löwe's inserted throughout. Fair copy for Löwe's contract appears as document 24. When Löwe left Wolfenbüttel to become Kapellmeister in Zeitz in 1663, his contract apparently served in turn as rough copy for the contract of his successor, Martin Colerus, for the contracts for Körner, Löwe, and Colerus differ in no significant detail.[36]

On 5 December 1638 August appointed Martin Dröge as watchman of the tower, a post which carried both civic and musical duties.[37] A later agreement dated Brunswick, 29 September 1643, states that Dröge

shall always keep watch from our palace and the tower built upon it along with four companions who are skilled in music. . . . And occasionally, if need be, [he shall] assist our ensemble in the palace or at other times in the court chapel with his musical instrument along with his companions. . . . He shall also play at weddings, christenings, and other banquets . . . in Wolfenbüttel as well as the entire district of Wolfenbüttel in the country with his and other musical instruments alone and with his companions. . . . However, when he is employed at these weddings and feasts, he shall always have at least one of his companions on the palace tower. . . .[38]

For this service, Dröge was paid a small salary and a *deputat* (an allowance paid in goods such as rye, barley, peas, wood, and livestock).

Following his appointment, Körner began to concern himself with the instrument and music collections. Letters between Philipp Hainhofer and Duke August in the years 1639 and 1640 show that Hainhofer was purchasing music for Körner, probably for use by the Wolfenbüttel court ensemble. Hainhofer mentions sending

sacred and secular vocal concerti in Latin and German for four and more voices for instrumental and vocal performances by all kinds of distinguished Italian and German composers from Rome, Florence, Venice, Vienna, and Munich (besides that of Schütz, Scheidt, and Schein already sent) for Your Royal Grace's Kapellmeister. . . .[39]

Hainhofer also writes of obtaining a number of instruments, including six Venetian violins, four glass flutes, cross flutes, cornetti, sackbuts, a small Spanish pandora, crumhorns, bagpipes, and shawms.[40] Körner himself was purchasing instruments, for a previously unpublished receipt signed by Körner and dated 19 November 1641 shows that he bought three instruments for twenty-eight talers: a new English viola da gamba, an English cittern (chitarina), and a tenor viola da braccio.[41] A second receipt, also dated 19 November 1641 and cosigned by Jorg Beflandt von Eisleben, pipemaker, shows that Körner had several instruments made or repaired: the repair of a great bombard, which had not been used for many years, and a curtal; butts, reeds, and mouthpieces made for the shawms and sordunes; and two new discant shawms and a new discant crumhorn.[42]

News of Duke August's new court ensemble must have spread, for together with a letter dated Halle, 19 June 1642, Samuel Scheidt apparently sent the duke a set of over one hundred sacred madrigals for five voices and a set of instrumental sinfonias for use as preludes to vocal music, which he dedicated to August's ensemble.[43] In 1644 the duke was again seeking musicians and a Kapellmeister, apparently due to Körner's departure, according to a letter dated 27 November 1644 from a Johann Martin Rubert, an organist in Hamburg. Rubert writes:

> I have it on good authority in Brunswick that His Royal Grace in Wolfenbüttel, due to the recent resignations of his Kapellmeister and other musicians, seeks to engage again some very good people by this coming summer (please God!).[44]

Körner must have left sometime in 1644, for a document shows that the court owed him money for service from 24 June 1638 to 24 June 1643,[45] and he is listed in the court account books as having received a payment in 1644.[46]

Rebuilding Wolfenbüttel

Before establishing his court in Wolfenbüttel, August had to rebuild the city. It had first been occupied in 1626 by Danish troops, followed a year later by Emperor Ferdinand II's troops, which continued to hold Wolfenbüttel in spite of several Danish attacks that destroyed much of the city.[47] By the end of the occupation in 1642, scarcely 150 of Wolfenbüttel's 1200 residents remained. Of 890 houses, 330 had been destroyed and many of the remaining 560 houses stood empty.[48] When August began to rebuild the city, records show that the costs for the palace alone amounted to just over 12,526 talers from Michaelmas 1643 to Michaelmas 1644.[49]

After the rebuilding was under way, August moved his residence from Brunswick to Wolfenbüttel. The church records of the Marien-kirche read, "On 26 February 1644, our gracious prince and lord, Lord August, duke of Brunswick and Lüneburg, has moved with his household from Brunswick to us and established his residence here."[50] Thereafter August and Sophie Elisabeth rebuilt Wolfenbüttel until it became an important cultural center of seventeenth-century Germany. August, an avid book collector, founded the Bibliotheca Augusta to house his treasures. By 1649, with the help of agents such as Philipp Hainhofer, he had assembled 60,000 works in 16,950 volumes, including 764 manu-scripts. By 1661, the collection had grown to 116,350 works in 28,415 volumes with 2003 manuscripts.[51]

Schütz's Earliest Contacts with Wolfenbüttel

The earliest surviving correspondence between Schütz and the Wolfenbüttel court is a letter from Schütz to Sophie Elisabeth dated 22 October 1644 (doc. 19).[52] He hints at a musical collaboration between himself and the duchess and mentions plans to meet her in Wolfenbüttel on his way to Hildesheim on business. Schütz is probably referring to the *Theatralische neue Vorstellung von der Maria Magdalena*. In 1647 Justus Georg Schottelius published a collection of his poetry under the title *Fruchtbringender Lustgarte voller Geistlicher und Weltlicher Neuen erfin-dungen zu Ergetzlichen Nutz zubereitet*. Schottelius claims that two of the poems were set by Schütz: "The widely renowned Herr Schütz pre-sented this New Theatrical Presentation of Mary Magdalen in Wolfenbüttel to great praise."[53] Schottelius later reused both poems in *Ausführliche Arbeit Von der Teutschen HaubtSprache*, published in Bruns-wick in 1663, reaffirming that Schütz had set the poems. Unfortunately, the music is lost.

The probable year of the performance of the Mary Magdalen Sing-spiel has been extensively studied by Jörg Jochen Berns.[54] The third and seventh lines of the first poem refer to the celebration of the New Year, suggesting that the performance may have taken place in the hall of the Wolfenbüttel palace at that time. To follow Berns's reasoning, Wolfenbüttel had been occupied by the emperor's troops until 14 Sep-tember 1643. After their departure the city was in such desolate condi-tion that the court could not move there until 26 February 1644. The

Lustgarte was dedicated 5 February 1647. These facts suggest that the performance must have taken place at New Year's 1644/45 or 1645/46, the earliest possible dates that Schütz could have been in Wolfenbüttel. The earliest evidence of Schütz's presence in Brunswick is 23 February 1645, when he stood as godfather to his friend Delphin Strungk's third child.[55] It is unlikely that Schütz was in Wolfenbüttel at New Year's 1645/46, however, since just before Michaelmas 1645 he asked Johann Georg I for permission to remain in Weissenfels until Easter 1646.[56] Considering the travel conditions of the time, it is unlikely that Schütz traveled to Dresden from Brunswick in November 1645 only to return at the end of the year to present the Mary Magdalen drama himself. It therefore seems probable that Schütz's first visit to Wolfenbüttel took place at New Year's 1644/45.

Schütz's earliest association with Wolfenbüttel remains a mystery. The published sermon delivered at Schütz's funeral follows the seventeenth-century German custom of appending a biography of the deceased, which still remains our primary source of biographical information about the composer. According to the biography, Schütz first visited Brunswick in 1638, a date accepted by many historians down to the present day.[57] Sievers suggests that Schütz visited the duke and duchess in 1638 in Brunswick on the return trip from Copenhagen. Rifkin, however, states that while Schütz had petitioned the elector on 1 February 1637 for permission to return to Denmark, the journey never materialized.[58] Chrysander had suggested, on the other hand, that Sophie Elisabeth only became acquainted with Schütz through the publication of the *Becker Psalter* by her uncle Adolph Friedrich in 1640 in Güstrow.[59] Hans Haase considers this unlikely, however, because Sophie Elisabeth had already married August and had been living in Brunswick since 1635. Haase raises the possibility that Delphin Strungk had initiated the relationship since, as mentioned earlier, Schütz stood as godfather to Strungk's third child in 1645 in Brunswick and Strungk is named as distributor in the *Symphoniae sacrae* II (1647) and the *Geistliche Chor-Musik* (1648).[60]

Schütz was clearly serving in an advisory capacity in Wolfenbüttel by 1645, for in a letter written in Brunswick on 17 March 1645 to the duchess, he reports that a musician whom he had recommended for the court ensemble had left the area (doc. 20). In an undated memorandum, which Chrysander suggests originated at approximately the same time as the 17 March 1645 letter,[61] Schütz enumerates several points on which he has been asked to give advice (doc. 21).[62] These include the ensemble personnel as well as appropriate occasions and locations for various types of repertoire.

Growth of the Ensemble

Schütz's early years as Kapellmeister *in absentia* in Wolfenbüttel were a period of expansion for the court ensemble in which the musical staff grew substantially. Benedict Höfer, who is listed in a court account book as an "instrumentalist and tenor,"[63] was appointed 17 October 1643 "to serve willingly and humbly in the court ensemble with his voice or other musical instruments [such as] organ positif and the like."[64] Höfer had been employed by Duke Wilhelm IV in Weimar according to a contract dated 24 June 1639.[65] Höfer did not stay long in Wolfenbüttel, however; August provided him with a letter dated 6 July 1646 to recommend him to his next post: "Benedict Höfer has served faithfully and diligently in our royal chapel as a musician and court organist now for nearly three years."[66] Höfer is still listed as a court musician in 1647–48. He must have left Wolfenbüttel in 1648. His successor, Andreas Körner, is not mentioned at all by Chrysander. Körner purchased two clavichords for one of the princesses, for which he submitted a receipt dated 22 March 1643. Payment of a sum of nine talers for the clavichords was made to "Andreas Körner, choirboy" (*Capelknabe*).[67] In a letter to Sophie Elisabeth dated 23 November 1648, Körner asks the duchess to intercede on his behalf with August, whom he has served for ten years, seven of which almost gratis.[68] Körner writes that he seeks to improve his salary of sixty talers yearly, for he is aware that his predecessor was paid one hundred talers yearly and even with that amount did not make ends meet. (Benedict Höfer's contract, dated 17 October 1643, shows that he was indeed paid one hundred talers.)[69] Körner writes, "I shall not be able to hold out much longer either, if I am not otherwise to become a beggar altogether."[70] He also indicates that he is the music instructor for the youngest princess. At the end of the letter, instructions are written in the duke's hand that Andreas Körner's salary is to be raised to one hundred talers. The duke's instruction are postdated effective 29 September 1648. A new contract was drawn up, also postdated 29 September 1648, replacing his original contract of 1646 and appointing him court organist and musician.[71] Payment lists show that he continued as court organist in Wolfenbüttel for one hundred talers yearly until his death in 1685.[72]

The court account books for the year from Trinity 1647, the eighth Sunday after Easter, to Trinity 1648, list the following members in the court ensemble:

Court Trumpeters

    Wentzel Humpoletzky
    Johann Busse
    Johann Heinen, court trumpeter no longer employed

Court Musicians

    Philipp Roth, chamber musician
    Wolf Teubener, harpist[73]
    Peter Groskopf, violinist
    Andreas Körner, organist
    Benedict Höfer, instrumentalist and tenor
    Sylvester Hancke, organist[74]

Another musician, Theodor Krummtinger, was hired at Christmas 1648 as a musician and instrumentalist.[75] By the end of the year, the court ensemble consisted of two trumpeters and seven ensemble members in addition to the two choirboys. Although the choirboys do not appear in the list, we know of their existence from a receipt submitted by Peter Groskopf dated 2 April 1650 for payment of their expenses amounting to forty talers for the years 1648–50.[76]

Court Spectacles

The growth of the court ensemble coincided with a new interest at Wolfenbüttel in court spectacles involving music, theater, and dance. Sophie Elisabeth not only acted as the organizer of these events, but she contributed as a composer as well. Her first known composition in this genre, the *Neuerfundenes FreudenSpiel genandt Friedens = Sieg*, was performed at least five times, first in February 1642 in the hall of Burg Dankwarderode in Brunswick on the occasion of the Treaty of Goslar, according to the title page of the 1648 print.[77] The copper engravings by Conrad Buno which illustrate the 1648 print show how the event was staged (figs. 3–11). The guests assembled in the great hall and were seated along the outer edges of the hall (figs. 3–5). No stage was present and the action took place in the center of the hall (figs. 6–9). An entryway, decorated to give the illusion of clouds, was used for entrances and exits by the numerous performers (figs. 3, 4, 10, and 11). Situated to the right of the entryway are an organ and the court ensemble in which approximately twelve singers and instrumentalists are visible (figs. 3 and 4). The instrumentalists are positioned to the far right of the entryway with a harpist and gambist in front of them. The singers are standing to the immediate right of the entryway. To the rear of the hall, behind the musicians, is an organ.[78]

The birthdays of rulers in seventeenth-century Germany were also occasions for celebrations. Since 1639 August's birthday had been celebrated with poems, Singspiele, and ballets. The poems for these occasions were issued in various single prints until 1648. Thereafter, until August's death in 1666, collections of poems were printed in the duke's honor. One such collection, Martin Gosky's *Arbustum vel Arboretum Augusteum,* printed in Wolfenbüttel in 1650, contains a poem by Schütz (doc. 22). Sophie Elisabeth was also a poet, and in 1648 she wrote her first birthday poem to Duke August in honor of his seventieth birthday.[79]

Beginning in 1652, Sophie Elisabeth arranged special court celebrations in honor of the duke's birthday. The first of these, the *Glückwünschende Freuden-Darstellung,*[80] was representative of court theater in seventeenth-century Germany. Royalty, noble relatives, and other members of court mimed, sang, and danced before those related to the court either by blood or service.[81] The texts were seldom printed and often little of them survives beyond reports and other accounts. The repertory consisted of pastorals, Singspiele, short Italian operas, masques, and ballets.

Three masques by Sophie Elisabeth were performed in Wolfenbüttel in the years 1654, 1655, and 1656 for the celebrations of Duke August's birthday. In the earliest, *Der Natur Ballet,*[82] Sophie Elisabeth played the role of Nature, while other members of the nobility played the roles of the four temperaments and the seven planets.[83] Each of the planets was accompanied by instruments appropriate to its character: the sun by lutes, the moon by hunting horns, Mars by trumpets and timpani, Mercury by flutes, Jupiter by sackbuts and cornetti, Venus by violins, and Saturn by shawms.[84] The ninety to one hundred performers who took part in the masque walked together in procession into the ballroom before dinner. After supper the company proceeded to the theater for a performance of *Seelewig,* sometimes called "the first surviving German opera,"[85] with a libretto by Georg Philipp Harsdörffer set by Sigmund Theophil Staden.[86]

The duke's son, Anton Ulrich (1633–1714), who is chiefly remembered for his novels, also wrote the texts for several Singspiele performed at August's birthday celebrations. Unfortunately none of the music for his Singspiele survives. The music for these works is generally attributed to Johann Jacob Löwe von Eisenach, Kapellmeister from 1655 until 1663. However, according to Frederick Lehmeyer in his study of Anton Ulrich's Singspiele, the only libretto in which he is actually named as composer is *Orpheus* (1659); the other libretti acknowledge no composer at all.[87] *Orpheus* is one of the few Singspiele by Anton Ulrich not dedicated to August, but to Sophie Elisabeth. Both the acknowledgment of Löwe as composer and the dedication to Sophie Elisabeth set *Orpheus* apart from Anton Ulrich's other Singspiele. Lehmeyer therefore suggests that those of Anton Ulrich's Singspiele dedicated to August were composed by Sophie Elisabeth herself.[88]

The ballets, masques, and comedies produced at Wolfenbüttel evidently required the expertise of a dancing master, for Ulrich Roboam de la Marche was appointed to that post on 21 September 1658. He was also to instruct members of the court and the princesses daily in dancing.[89] The dancing master was an integral part of court life. The young princes and princesses began to learn court ceremony at a young age, receiving two to three hours of instruction daily in what was necessary for court functions: proper bearing, curtsies and bows, the language of the fan, the carrying of swords, cloaks, and gloves, not to mention the court dances themselves with their turns and leaps, complicated step combinations, spatial plans, and dramatic execution.[90]

As pointed out by Werner Breig, there is little evidence that Schütz participated directly in court events at Wolfenbüttel. His activities were probably limited to the instruction given to Sophie Elisabeth, his setting of Schottelius's Singspiel, and his responsibilities as advisor in the reorganization of the court ensemble.[91]

Schütz's Later Contacts with Wolfenbüttel

In 1655 Schütz continued to concern himself with providing suitable musicians for the court ensemble. Although his letter of 12 June 1655 is lost, Sophie Elisabeth's answer (doc. 23) refers to a falsettist, a new Kapellmeister, choirboys, and a bass from Kassel.[92] The name of the bass is not revealed. He can probably be identified as Gerhard Wilcke, who was appointed on 7 August 1655 as instrumentalist and bass for sixty talers yearly, with the stipulation that he

> serve at all feast days and Sundays in the performance of the worship service as well as at and before our royal table in the presence of foreign princes or their emissaries and otherwise to serve among others of his colleagues and always at our command to perform on all sorts of musical instruments that they have with them and on which he is skilled, as well as in the vocal music. . . .[93]

In a letter dated 24 July 1655, Schütz informs the duchess of the departure from Dresden of her new Kapellmeister, Johann Jacob Löwe von Eisenach, with two choirboys. In a postscript, Schütz reminds Sophie Elisabeth that his appointment as Kapellmeister *in absentia* is only verbal and he would like a written agreement. He also mentions that his payment is in arrears. On the last page of this letter, Sophie Elisabeth penned a sketch of her answer (doc. 25).[94] Schütz soon received his contract dated 23 August 1655 (doc. 26).[95] Löwe von Eisenach's contract is dated 24 June 1655 (doc. 24).[96]

Schütz apparently was forced to mention his wages again in another lost letter of 30 October 1655, for Sophie Elisabeth's response on 10 November suggests a means of paying Schütz and arrangements for the delivery of "things" (*Sachen*), which must mean Schütz's compositions (doc. 27).[97] She also approves of both the new Kapellmeister and a theorbo player and painter whom Schütz had recommended. On 27 November 1655 (doc. 28), Schütz responds to Sophie Elisabeth's letter, which he says was not sent until 20 November.[98] His response refers again to "the falsettist or artist," who must also be the theorbo player mentioned by Sophie Elisabeth in her letter of 10 November. Schütz recommends a salary of 150 to 200 talers and adds that the person is also a poet who performs his own settings, accompanying himself on his theorbo. Schütz also makes clear in this letter that the matter of the payment of his own salary and the conveyance of his compositions to Wolfenbüttel had still not been resolved. Sophie Elisabeth in her response of 2 January 1656 (doc. 29) agrees that the falsettist should be paid 200 talers.[99] This man of such diverse talents is probably Heinrich Gödke, who was appointed on 3 August 1657 as a singer and instrumentalist for 200 talers.[100]

A summary drawn up by Jobst Barthold Krankenfeld on 18 December 1657 (doc. 33) dates Schütz's first payment as Kapellmeister *in absentia* on 5 October 1655. However, this payment had not reached Schütz at the time of his letter to Sophie Elisabeth dated 27 November 1655 (doc. 28).[101] By 29 September 1656 the money had arrived, for Schütz responded with a receipt (doc. 33)[102] listed in item 3 of document 33.[103] Schütz's receipt mentioned in item 4 of document 16 is lost. There seems to have been considerable confusion regarding the payment of Schütz's salary, for in a letter from Krankenfeld to August dated 18 December 1657, the writer indicates that at the duke's request he has taken over Schütz's account from Freudenhammer, another court official. Krankenfeld informs the duke that Schütz had actually been overpaid seventy-five talers and that his pay should be cut at Easter. He goes on to say that this information had already been passed to Gieseken, a local merchant.[104] In a previously unknown autograph receipt, Schütz acknowledges receiving payment from Heinrich Günther, a merchant of Wolfenbüttel, at the end of September 1658 (doc. 31). The reverse side of the receipt is a continuation of the previous summary in which Schütz's salary is noted as 225 talers in arrears, information duplicated in documents 33 and 34. Document 34, however, contains a reference to fifty talers for travel costs paid 6 June 1660. Schütz was clearly in Wolfenbüttel at this time. Moser states without supporting evidence that Schütz arrived in Wolfenbüttel at Easter 1660.[105] Rifkin suggests that Schütz's visit may have coincided with Duke August's birthday on 10 April, stating further that Schütz was definitely in Wolfenbüttel at the writing of a letter from Löwe von Eisenach addressed to Schütz on 5 May (doc. 32).[106] Since the letter, now in NSAW, is a fair copy, Schütz must have received the letter in Wolfenbüttel.[107] Schütz also refers to a recent visit in his letter dated 10 April 1661 (doc. 35).[108]

The payment made by Günther is verified by the court account books with this entry: "The senior Kapellmeister *in absentia,* Heinrich Schütz in Dresden, is due at Michaelmas 1658 one-half year's [payment] and was paid at that time by Heinrich Günther in Leipzig."[109]

Schütz was still supplying musicians at that time, as is evident from a court account book entry which reads: "30 August 1658. To the electoral Saxon Kapellmeister H. Schütz's servant Georg Schell, who brought two choirboys from Dresden. 14 talers."[110] By the fiscal year 1658–59, the Wolfenbüttel ensemble consisted of the following members:

Johann Jacob Löwe von Eisenach, Kapellmeister
Julius Johann Weilandt, vice-Kapellmeister
Andreas Körner, court organist
Johann Selner, harpist
Kilian Fabritius, musician
Johann Philipp Roth, chamber musician[111]
Heinrich Gödke, singer and instrumentalist
Friederich Jobst, cornettist
Gerhard Wilcke, bass
Martin Dröge, watchman and wind player
Wenzel Humpoletzky, court trumpeter
Gottfried Janusch, court trumpeter
Hans Hassel, court trumpeter
Georg Gruntzenbach, court trumpeter
Hans Schuster, timpanist
Johann Busse, court trumpeter *in absentia*[112]

According to a preface to one of his own compositions, the new vice-Kapellmeister, Julius Johann Weilandt, had been educated at the court in Brunswick and had probably served as a choirboy in the interim ensemble maintained by August in Brunswick before the court moved to Wolfenbüttel.[113] After serving a short time in Petershagen, he was appointed to the Wolfenbüttel court ensemble on 5 March 1655.[114] In a payment list dated 13 May 1661, he signs himself as vice-Kapellmeister.[115]

Schütz's letter to Duke August dated 10 April 1661 (doc. 35) accompanied a birthday gift of two copies of the *Becker Psalter* of 1661. The copy now in HAB bears the inscription, "My own copy. Heinrich Schütz. In his own hand," indicating that Schütz had sent his own personal copy, or *Handexemplar*.[116] The second copy is now in the Houghton Library of Harvard University. Duke August's initials are on the binding.[117] Schütz's letter of 10 January 1664 (doc. 38)[118] also accompanied a birthday gift of Schütz's own compositions, which he listed in a catalog (doc. 39). The catalog was found recently by Horst Walter, who places its origin at the end of December 1663 or early January 1664. Walter states that the paper is the same as that of Schütz's letter of 10 January 1664.[119] The catalog itself was written by a scribe with the commentary and the title on the cover written by Schütz. According to Haase, the scribe who wrote the catalog was undoubtedly the same one who inscribed the titles on the bindings of the volumes, proving that the shortened titles of Schütz's works were written on the volumes under his supervision before they were conveyed to Wolfenbüttel by Stephan Daniel.[120] All of the works designated by an asterisk in the catalog are currently in HAB.[121] Schütz later sent the manuscript of the *St. John Passion*, the so-called early version (SWV 481a) dated "Weissenfels, 10 April 1665" in the composer's hand, as a birthday gift to August.

The court account books for the fiscal year 1665–66 show a court ensemble with the following members:

Martin Colerus, Kapellmeister
Andreas Körner, organist
Christoph Hartwig, musician[122]
Johann Philipp Roth, chamber musician
Kilian Fabritius, musician
Johann Selner, Hofmeister
Johann Paul Roth, musician
Christoph Jäger, musician[123]
Georg Schell, musician and cornettist[124]
Alexander Heinrich Schmidt, musician[125]
Hieronijmo Hagen, bass
Simon Hassel, court cantor
Andreas Ernst Dröge, watchman

Ulrich Roboam de la Marche, dancing master
Gottfried Janusch, trumpeter
Johann Hassel, trumpeter
Georg Gruntzenbach, trumpeter
Johann Busch, trumpeter
Johann Koch, trumpeter[126]

The last court records attesting to Schütz's employment at Wolfenbüttel are dated Easter 1665 (doc. 40). Duke August died at the age of eighty-eight on 17 September 1666 and Sophie Elisabeth retired to Lüchow, where she remained until her death on 12 July 1676. Although there is no evidence that Schütz continued his relationship with the Wolfenbüttel court as Kapellmeister *in absentia,* he did maintain contact with the court in Lüchow where Sophie Elisabeth resided. The only surviving copy of the first print of Schütz's *Historia der . . . Geburth . . . Jesu Christi* (SWV 435), now in the Staatsbibliothek Preussischer Kulturbesitz, Berlin, has written on the title page the letters "RAHZBUL" and, below, "Luchaw [Lüchow] 1671." Spitta interpreted the letters as "Rudolph August Herzog zu Braunschweig und Lüneburg," a dedication to Duke August's son who, with his brother Anton Ulrich, became coregent in Wolfenbüttel after August's death. Spitta further observed that Rudolph August would have received the print before June 1671, since he left Lüchow that month for Celle, and that Schütz may have sent him the work.[127] Eva Linfield points out that, because the copies of Schütz's music now in HAB are Schütz's own *Handexemplare,* sent by the composer himself to the duke, it is likely that SWV 435 is also Schütz's own copy. Linfield further suggests that Schütz had continued contact with the Wolfenbüttel-Brunswick court because of his relationship to the duchess and that he sent his copy of the 1664 print not to Wolfenbüttel but to Lüchow.[128]

As shown by correspondence and other documents spanning twenty years, Schütz played a major role in Duke August's efforts to establish his court as an important musical and literary center of seventeenth-century Germany. Schütz's influence at Wolfenbüttel appears largely to have consisted of his advice to the duke and duchess as they built their court ensemble. Schütz recruited musicians on their behalf, and during his tenure as Kapellmeister *in absentia,* the ensemble expanded from nine musicians and two trumpeters in 1648 to thirteen musicians, one dancing master, and five trumpeters in 1666. Although there is no evidence that Schütz composed any music for Wolfenbüttel aside from one lost Singspiel, he did send August a large number of his personal copies of prints of his works, as well as one early manuscript version of the *St. John Passion* for his personal library, where they have remained to this day.

3

Zeitz

In 1653 Johann Georg I divided the electorate of Saxony among his four sons. His death in 1656 marked the beginning of the collateral lines of Merseburg, Weissenfels, and Zeitz. Moritz, the youngest son of Johann Georg I and the administrator of the Naumburg-Zeitz bishopric, chose to move his official residence from Naumburg to Zeitz in 1663. As duke of Zeitz he began by rebuilding the palace and church and hired Schütz as senior Kapellmeister *in absentia* to advise him in the establishment of the Zeitz court ensemble.

The earliest correspondence between Schütz and Moritz is dated 14 July 1663 (doc. 41).[1] Newly discovered evidence in SAW and SAD suggests, however, that Moritz and Schütz may have begun devising their plans for the Zeitz court ensemble as early as 1658.

Johann Georg II traveled to Frankfurt in March 1658 to attend the Electoral Diet, an assembly held to elect a new emperor to succeed Ferdinand III, who had died 2 April 1657. On 2 June 1658, Duke Wilhelm IV of Saxe-Weimar sent an invitation to Johann Georg II to visit Weimar on the latter's return to Dresden from Frankfurt.[2] Johann Georg II responded with an acceptance on 6 July 1658.[3] On 18 July 1658 the assembly elected Ferdinand's son Leopold as the new emperor. According to Wilhelm's journal, Johann Georg II arrived in Weimar on 16 August 1658.[4] Wilhelm's journal also reveals new information on Schütz: the composer had also arrived in Weimar on 11 August.[5] Moritz, whose wife at this time was Dorothea Maria, a daughter of Duke Wilhelm,[6] arrived in Weimar on 14 August. According to a recent article by Hans Rudolf Jung, it was during this visit on 18 August that Johann Georg II became a member of the Fruit-Bearing Society.[7] Moritz left Weimar on 18 August and Johann Georg II departed on 19 August, both for Naumburg. The date of Schütz's departure from Weimar is not mentioned in the journal.

According to Wilhelm's journal, Schütz and Moritz were again in

Weimar in July 1659. The journal entry reads, "On Saturday, 29 July, Kapellmeister Schütz arrived here from Weissenfels."[8] Moritz arrived some four days later on 2 August.[9] Although there is no existing evidence, Jung speculates that Schütz had specific musical duties in Weimar in both 1658 and 1659 and that the music performed at the festivities was composed by him. A more reasonable explanation might be that these previously unnoticed visits to Weimar would have provided Schütz and Duke Moritz with opportunities to discuss the duke's musical establishment five years before their earliest surviving correspondence.[10]

Schütz's first duties involved seeking out singers and instrumentalists for the court ensemble, providing music, and stocking the instrument collection. Schütz accomplished this task partly by shifting personnel from Dresden and Wolfenbüttel, other courts where he served as Kapellmeister. He recommended Johann Jacob Löwe von Eisenach as Kapellmeister, who came from Wolfenbüttel in 1663 to assume the post.[11] Clemens Thieme, whom Schütz had recommended as a member of the the Dresden court ensemble in 1650,[12] was engaged as concertmaster. Gottfried Kühnel, on the other hand, had met Moritz in Naumburg, where he was city cantor. In 1663 the duke brought him to Zeitz as court cantor. A document dating from ca. 1664–65 lists a court ensemble of fourteen members.

> Heinrich Schütz, Kapellmeister *in absentia*. Johann Jacob Löwe, Kapellmeister. Clemens Thieme, director of the little ensemble. Gottfried Kühnel, singer at all events. Christoph Dörffel, bass. August Kühnel, violist da gamba. Ludwig Sulz, instrumentalist. Johannes Bohl. The organist, four discantists, one alto.[13]

Of these musicians, Ludwig Sulz had previously been listed as an instrumentalist in Dresden, and was probably recommended by Schütz in addition to Löwe and Thieme.[14]

In a letter dated 14 July 1663 (doc. 41) from Dresden, Schütz wrote to Moritz about a matter he considered of great importance: the training of the choirboys for the new court ensemble. Schütz preferred that two choirboys who had been apprenticed in Merseburg to Gottfried Kühnel be sent to Dresden for two months to join two other boys and an alto already in Dresden for training. In the same letter, Schütz mentioned the reconstruction of the organ in the palace church at Zeitz, which also had fallen under his supervision. He stated that he had sent the builder the plans and description for a new positif which could be carried in two pieces. The organ builder, however, had delivered an already existing organ, and Schütz had to be satisfied with that instrument and postpone

the building of the new one. Schütz had also arranged for various instruments to be constructed. Duke Moritz overruled Schütz in an undated letter (doc. 42), in which he informed Schütz that the two choirboys would be trained locally and that any action on the new positif
would be postponed indefinitely.[15]

Schütz's suggestions had also been ignored once again in connection
with the reconstruction of the palace church, a matter on which the
composer's advice had been solicited. Schütz had recommended that the
lofts should be positioned opposite one another next to the church pillars. The architect obviously ignored his advice concerning the placement of the choir lofts, which were rebuilt in such a fashion that they
were behind the pillars. Schütz voiced his displeasure in a letter dated
29 September 1663 (doc. 43), pointing out that the musicians would
have to stand behind pillars.[16] He advised, because of the unfavorable
acoustical results, that the lofts be moved forward.

Among his most important duties as Kapellmeister *in absentia,* Schütz
was expected to provide compositions for church and table, as is indicated in an undated letter from Schütz to the superintendent in Zeitz
(doc. 44).[17] Yet here, too, he had reason to complain of the results.
Schütz had sent quite a few of his own compositions through his servant
and was vexed that the manuscripts had not been properly cared for.
He then proposed a register for organizing his works, which he appended to the letter.[18]

The same letter also makes clear that Moritz had decided to introduce
the *Becker Psalter* in the palace church. Schütz sent three copies and
suggested that the cantor come to pick up the part books for his choir.
He also arranged for copies of the text alone to be printed in Lüneburg
for the congregation so that they might begin to learn the psalms. The
Dresden court diaries make frequent reference to the use of settings
from the *Becker Psalter* in worship services in the court chapel after the
revised edition appeared in 1661. Johann Georg II had a fourth edition
published through Christoph Bernhard in 1676. In a previously unpublished letter to his brother, Duke Moritz, dated 28 July 1676, the elector
wrote:

> Because I have reissued the hymns in Dr. Cornelius Becker's Psalms, customary in
> our true religion of the Augsburg Confession [of 1530], with their melodies beneath
> the discant and bass, together with the usual church prayers and other ingenious
> songs as they are traditionally sung here in my court chapel, and had it published in
> this readable print and form, I wish to send Your Love a pair of copies with best
> wishes.[19]

The *Becker Psalter* continued to be used in the palace church in Zeitz for some seventy-five years until it was replaced with the *Schemelli Gesangbuch* in 1736.[20]

On 1 May 1664 the completely renovated palace church was consecrated in a celebratory worship service. The order of service, while specifying that concerti on Psalm 122, Psalm 100, and a third concerto with an unidentified text were performed, names no composer.[21] Werner writes, "Without doubt Schütz wrote the music,"[22] an opinion supported by Moser.[23] Rifkin believes that the music performed was more likely to have been written by Löwe, since composing music for court functions was normally the responsibility of the Kapellmeister.[24] Wolfram Steude writes, however, that the Psalm 100 performed for the consecration in Zeitz is definitely the same work composed for the consecration of the renovated Dresden palace church on 28 September 1662 (SWV 493). Steude states (without supporting evidence, however) that Schütz conducted the service in Zeitz, which would also make it likely that he composed the music.[25] Schütz was in fact in Zeitz by 6 May 1664 according to a letter to Duke Moritz by Clemens Thieme, who refers to being in Schütz's presence on that day.[26]

At the time of the consecration of the palace church, the musicians of the Zeitz court ensemble still had no signed agreements regarding their appointments. Furthermore, the exact delineation of duties and rights had yet to be established, causing conflict and strife among the court ensemble members and its leaders. A bitter quarrel had arisen between Löwe and Thieme concerning the direction of the Sunday services. In an attempt to bring an end to this disagreement, Schütz and the court preacher wrote a set of guidelines for the court musicians dated 7 May 1664, a *Discourse on Some Points in Dispute*.[27] This document is an early draft of the undated *Royal Saxon Chapel Order for the Moritzburg on the Elster*, which enumerates the duties of the court musicians and identifies in general terms the music to be performed on each day of the church year.[28] The opening nine sections of the Zeitz order, which outline the structure of worship services on feast days, regular Sundays, the elector's birthday, services during the week, Vespers, and prayer meetings, reveal once again the strength of the Dresden influence at Zeitz. These portions show a direct relationship to the corresponding portions of Johann Georg II's undated order for Dresden (doc. 13).[29] Since both orders are undated, the sequence of their origin is unknown. A comparison of both reveals only slight variations in the directives regarding the worship services, such as the two extra concerti performed in Dresden for Vespers on apostles' days. Portions of the Zeitz Sunday services were divided between the *Stadtkantorei* and the court ensemble, with a distinction made between *choraliter* Sundays and *figuraliter* Sundays.[30] Prayer meetings in Dresden were held Mondays, Tuesdays, Thursdays, and Fridays, while in Zeitz they were held only on Wednesdays and Fridays. The only work attributed to Schütz in the Zeitz order is the *Becker Psalter;* but the performances of "The Resurrection of Our Lord and Savior Jesus Christ *figuraliter*" for Easter Vespers and "The Birth of Our Lord and Savior Jesus Christ *figuraliter*" for Christmas Day Vespers called for in the order probably indicate Schütz's settings.

The Zeitz order concludes with fifteen points elaborating the various duties of the court musicians. As in Dresden, performance in church services was the most important duty of the court musician. Overseeing the sacred music was the responsibility of the Kapellmeister, who was to keep the court preacher informed of matters regarding the texts to be sung and the number of musicians performing. Compositions of both the Kapellmeister and the concertmaster were performed in church. The concertmaster conducted the sacred music every other Sunday; however, he was still subordinate to the Kapellmeister. The direction of the Tafelmusik was divided between the Kapellmeister and the concertmaster and performed by the court ensemble.[31] On *choraliter* Sundays, which occurred every other week, the *Stadtkantorei* performed the *choraliter* music while the court ensemble performed the concerti before and after the sermon. On feast days and *figuraliter* Sundays, the court ensemble also performed the Kyrie and Mass. Regarding the choirboys, the order specifies that they were to sing only in the palace church and in the royal residence, lest they miss their regular duties with the other members of the ensemble or suffer harm to their voices. Finally, the musicians were instructed to behave circumspectly in church and to refrain from walking about, since the two lofts in the palace church were in full view of the worshippers. The musicians were also instructed to close the doors to the lofts to prevent others who were not members of the court ensemble or the *Stadtkantorei* from entering.

In spite of the new order, the dispute between Löwe and Thieme continued. Peace was only restored with Löwe's departure. Duke Moritz recommended him for a musical post to the elector of Brandenburg on 20 March 1665 and to the council of the city of Frankfurt on 24 May 1665.[32] Both applications were unsuccessful, however, and the unemployed Löwe went to Jena. He died in extreme poverty in Lüneburg in 1703. Thieme continued as Kapellmeister in Zeitz until his death in 1668.[33] He was succeeded by Gottfried Kühnel, who managed the ensemble until it was finally dissolved in 1682 after Duke Moritz's death.

The nature of Schütz's influence at Zeitz as Kapellmeister *in absentia* is most strikingly apparent in the close interrelationship of music at Duke Moritz's court and that at Dresden. Of the fourteen musicians of the Zeitz court ensemble listed ca. 1664–65, Löwe had been Schütz's pupil at Dresden and both Thieme and Sulz had been members of the court ensemble there. Schütz also trained two discantists and an alto in Dresden before sending them to Zeitz. Furthermore, the Zeitz chapel order and Johann Georg II's undated order contain numerous verbatim sections. Finally, several compositions of Schütz performed at Dresden during this period, including the Psalm 100 setting of the *opus ultimum*, the *Becker Psalter*, and probably the *Historia der . . . Aufferstehung . . .* and the *Historia der . . . Geburth . . . Jesu Christi* (both of which are listed in the Zeitz order without composer) also became part of the repertory at Zeitz.

4

Duties of the Court Musician
in Schütz's Sphere

The central position of worship in court life in Dresden is clearly evident in the *Kantoreiordnungen* and court diaries of the sixteenth and seventeenth centuries. The *Kantoreiordnungen,* which enumerate the duties of the members of the Dresden court ensemble, make clear that providing music for worship services was their most important task throughout this period. The various revisions of these orders by succeeding monarchs help to clarify both the size of the ensemble and the changing responsibilities of its members. The charter *Kantoreiordnung* was prepared in 1548 during the reign of the elector Moritz who, after assuming power in 1541, began the construction of a new palace church. The second edition of the order, completed in 1555 during the reign of the elector August, reveals the predominance of the sacred over the secular when it states in its preamble that the principal motive for the founding and maintenance of a court ensemble is the glorification of God.[1]

In 1637 Johann Georg I assembled another new order which also emphasized the importance of worship at court and the pervasive intermingling of secular and sacred in all facets of court life.[2] In his thorough study of the structure of the Dresden worship services, Schmidt observes that the numerous descriptions of worship services during Johann Georg II's reign are not preserved in the consistorial records or in the correspondence of the senior court preacher but among the documents of daily court life. Schmidt further raises the possibility that Johann Georg II may have dictated these descriptions himself and had them written by scribes into fair copy.[3]

The size of the court ensemble had varied as much in the sixteenth century as during Schütz's tenure as Kapellmeister. The charter group of 1548 consisted only of singers: eleven adult basses, altos, and tenors, and nine boys as discantists. By 1555 the ensemble had grown to thirty-eight members, including fourteen boys and ten instrumentalists. By

1590 the ensemble numbered forty-three musicians, among them three organists, sixteen instrumentalists, and eight discant voices. Just before Schütz came to Dresden, the ensemble had twenty-seven members: four altos, four tenors, three basses, five discantists, and eleven instrumentalists.[4]

During Johann Georg II's reign, the various liturgical duties for the musicians were borne by various factions within the ensemble. The vice-Kapellmeister, for example, generally conducted the music in church on regular Sundays. The Little German Ensemble under the direction of the concertmaster Dedekind performed the worship services when the larger part of the ensemble and the Italian Kapellmeisters were on trips with the elector.[5] According to Johann Georg II's undated order, during the week the singers (*die Choralisten*), together with the court cantor and one organist, performed in church for the services on Wednesdays, Fridays, and Saturdays, and for the prayer meetings on Mondays, Tuesdays, Thursdays, and Fridays. They were also responsible for the services on the feast days of St. John the Baptist and St. Mary Magdalen.[6] Apparently the Kapellmeister, with the large ensemble including the Italian singers and instrumentalists, performed on feast days, holy eves, and some Sundays, for the order specifies the performance of motets and concerti on these days, whereas the weekday services call for German Psalms sung *choraliter*.

The musicians seem traditionally to have performed in the middle of the nave in the palace church. According to Johann Georg I's 1637 order, the organ gallery and side galleries cannot have been used to accommodate the ensemble, for they were occupied by the congregation.[7] Schmidt reports that the *Kantoreiordnung* of 1592 states that the musicians were to remain before the music lectern (*vor dem Pult*) during the service and none of them was "to sneak off to a corner" (*in den Winckell verkriechen*).[8] *Vor dem Pult* seems to signify in the middle of the church as illustrated by David Conrad's well-known engraving which depicts Schütz and the court ensemble assembled around a three-sided music lectern placed in the middle of the nave in such a manner that all the performers could see and sing in the direction of the altar.[9] Schmidt indicates that although Conrad's engraving is an allegorical representation, Johann Georg II's order confirms that the place for the singers during the *choraliter* Psalm singing at Vespers, on feast days, and holy eves was "*vor dem Pult*" (doc. 13).[10] Schmidt further points out that Conrad's positioning of the choir on the floor before a lectern had also been discussed by Praetorius, former Kapellmeister *in absentia* at Dresden.[11] The importance of this location for the ensemble is clear from the constant admonition in the *Kantoreiordnungen* that the ensemble should take seriously its duty to lead the hymn singing and not disappear from the view of the congregation after the polyphonic music.[12] The practice of singing *vor dem Pult* seems to have been abolished in the course of the seventeenth century. When the palace church was renovated in 1662, the organ gallery was enlarged by means of a wooden gallery resting upon four marble pillars built in front of it. The congregation stood or sat above and beneath galleries encircling the interior of the church. The large space in the nave had no seats in the seventeenth century and Schmidt suggests that celebrants also stood in this area during worship.[13] The altar was enclosed by the musicians' galleries overtopped by the organ to the east. The two choir lofts built over the altar in 1662 were surely intended to accommodate the spatial demands of polychoral music. Conrad's engraving shows instrumentalists in the far corner of the side galleries: a choir of wind instruments in the southern gallery, and a choir of strings in the northern gallery.[14] Furthermore, Schütz's dedication for the *opus ultimum* specifies positioning eight singers in the two lofts.[15]

The Kapellmeister

In determining the duties of the Dresden Kapellmeisters, Schmidt cites the appointment records of Antonius Scandellus (Kapellmeister from 1568–80), Georg Förster (1586–87), and Rogier Michael (1587–1613).[16] Besides leading the ensemble in church and at table, these Kapellmeisters trained the boys in singing and composed for the ensemble. The court Kapellmeister was also expected to contribute to the greater glory of the ruler, as is evident from the occasion of the emperor's visit to Dresden in 1617. Johann Georg I set forth specific duties for the musicians in an order containing nine points for Kapellmeister Schütz alone, meant to assure "that His Electoral Grace's ensemble ... acquit itself with honor and glory before the visitors."[17]

Although Schütz's original appointment contract has never been found, a letter to Johann Georg I from his privy counselor Christoph von Loss dated 11 December 1616 makes clear some of Schütz's duties.

> [I]f the music at the church and at the table is to be conducted as before, a person who is practiced in composition, conversant with instruments, and familiar with the repertoire of church music cannot be dispensed with. In my humble opinion, I know of no one to be preferred to Schütz in these matters.

Loss further states that without Schütz or Praetorius, the latter serving only as Kapellmeister *in absentia,* the performance of concerted music would be impossible, rehearsals would cease altogether, and the ensemble itself would suffer great harm.[18] Direction of the music in church for the weekday and regular Sunday services ultimately became the responsiblity of the vice-Kapellmeister. Schütz objected to requests that he direct the music in church both on Sundays and during the week. In his memorandum dated 30 July 1646 he summarized his duties:

> [T]he principal and best performance of my office consists not so much in my perpetual presence and attendance but rather in the composition and arrangement of all sorts of good musical works, as well as in the supervision of the entire operation.[19]

Schütz's bitter response to the demand that he and Bontempi direct in church on alternate Sundays has already been discussed in chapter 1 (doc. 3). In his memorandum of 14 January 1651 (doc. 2), Schütz refers to the specific occasions of his service to the elector

> at many past diverse festivities which occurred during this time, at imperial, royal, electoral, and princely gatherings, in this country and abroad, but particularly at each and every one of your own royal children's weddings, not less, too, at the receiving of their sacred christenings. . . .

Schmidt observes that Schütz's leaves from Dresden always fell during periods when no festivites were planned.[20]

Hofkontz, seeking the post of vice-Kapellmeister, describes his expectations of Schütz as Kapellmeister in his letter to Johann Georg I dated 16 May 1649:

> Although, most gracious elector and lord, it would be quite honorable and fitting that Kapellmeister Schütz, as the principal member and leader of the ensemble, remain steadfast by the ensemble entrusted to him, provide it with musical compositions, attend it with various sorts of advice and assistance, and fulfill the duties of that office; but it is known to Your Serene Highness and nearly everyone else that he, otherwise charged as shepherd, has for many years attended little to his flock, but has abandoned it, traveling from one province to the next, [not caring whether] Your Serene Highness's ensemble was provided for or remained abandoned. In this regard, Your Serene Highness might graciously bear in mind that not only during the three years that Herr Schütz resided in Denmark, Brunswick, and Weissenfels, I have served your electoral ensemble with the utmost diligence to the best of my ability, serving at princely christenings, noble weddings, and other duties at table, but I have also . . . during the present four years, served on feast days, Sundays, and holidays with requisite music as well as the weekday services and daily prayer meetings with respectable singing, and thus at the same time have had to earn for Kapellmeister Schütz his appointment and his bread.[21]

Schütz's duties as Kapellmeister, therefore, may be seen to consist of composing music primarily for church but also theatrical and festival music for court occasions;[22] directing the ensemble on high feast days, particularly, as he wrote in his memorandum of 21 May 1645, "in the presence of foreign rulers or emissaries;"[23] and making artistic judgments regarding the entire ensemble.

After Albrici's appointment as Kapellmeister, Schütz was still expected to provide "musical service" at the elector's command (doc. 8). Albrici, on the other hand, was to conduct in church, at table, and for theatrical works, using his own compositions or those of others. He was free to arrange for the vice-Kapellmeister to conduct in church in his place as often as he wished (doc. 8). Schmidt, however, has deduced from the court diaries that the Italian Kapellmeisters did not have their vice-Kapellmeisters substitute for them, at least on feast days.[24] Finally, Albrici was also specifically responsible for settling quarrels among the court musicians, perhaps yet another indication of the ever present strife between the Germans and the Italians.

The Vice-Kapellmeister

The vice-Kapellmeister freed the Kapellmeister of daily liturgical duties. Hofkontz's 1646 contract shows that he was responsible for the daily Vespers and other services during the week and on Sunday, teaching the choirboys, and singing tenor when needed. Musical composition is not mentioned among his duties.[25] The post changed during Bernhard's tenure as vice-Kapellmeister. The vice-Kapellmeister served as a replacement for the Kapellmeister in directing the figural music, as discussed above. Bernhard, however, was no longer responsible for placing music on the lectern, a duty mentioned in Zacharias Hestius's contract.[26] This and other duties passed to the court cantor during Bernhard's tenure as vice-Kapellmeister (see below). Bernhard's contract instructed him to teach the choirboys, a duty later entrusted to Christoph Kittel and the court cantor.

The Court Cantor

The position of court cantor, as described by Fürstenau from the appointment contract of an unnamed musician, involved the direction of the music in the weekday and prayer services, as recorded in Johann Georg II's order, and in the Sunday services, when he led the singing of hymns. The court cantor was also charged with the instruction of the choirboys in religion, Latin, and occasionally, in Greek. He was also expected to sing in church and at table, and, in the absence of the Kapellmeister and vice-Kapellmeister, to conduct the polyphonic music. During the sixteenth century, the Kapellmeister served as the *cantor choralis*. The singers were reminded in the *Kantoreiordnungen* to take the tempo set by the Kapellmeister in figural and hymn singing. Although leading the hymn singing is among the duties named in the contracts of Hestius and Hofkontz, when Bernhard assumed the post, it was not the vice-Kapellmeister who was responsible for these daily duties but the court cantor.[27]

The Organists

The *Kantoreiordnung* of 1555 lists three organists; the lists of the court ensemble throughout the reigns of Johann Georg I and Johann Georg II show two to three organists at any given time.[28] The organists in the palace church were expected to: 1) improvise preludes or play some other work given to them in advance; 2) play continuo; 3) play before and after the sermon; and 4) to be responsible on occasion for the direction of the singers in worship. They were often responsible for composing music for the ensemble.[29] Organists also played at table.

The *Kalkant*

Stephan Körner, in a memorandum to Duke August of Wolfenbüttel, summarized his expectations of the *Kalkant:* "A *Kalkant* . . . one can take as an apprentice for service at the organ and moreover for removing [instruments, etc.], copying, and other matters such as robes and wages."[30] The *Kalkant* was at the disposal of the Kapellmeister to arrange rehearsals and performances and to bring the instruments to and from the instrument chamber.[31] According to Philipp Hainhofer, an acquaintance of Schütz and a patrician from Augsburg who visited Dresden in both 1617 and 1629, the instruments at the court in Dresden were kept in a great chamber

> within which is the painting of the Last Judgement from which one can go into the court church to the great organ, and for major holidays trumpeters and kettle drummers have to play instrumental music in this chamber and make echoes.[32]

The Court Trumpeters

The court trumpeters formed one of the largest groups of musicians in Dresden and were used in both musical and military settings. Court trumpeters in Germany belonged to a *Kameradschaft* (fellowship). Beginning in the seventeenth century, all German court and military trumpeters were subject to the statutes of the Dresden *Oberkameradschaft* ratified by the 1623 Regensburg *Reichstag*. These statutes were renewed in 1630; in 1653 the constitution of the *Oberkameradschaft* was increased from eleven to twenty-two articles.[33] According to Don L. Smithers,

> these *Vorrechte* or *Privilegi* made various demands on the court trumpeters, but they also guaranteed various rights. They restricted the performance of trumpet music to the privileged players; they gave members of the *Kameradschaft* free access to all kingdoms and territories that came under the aegis of the emperor's mandate; and they allowed privileged trumpeters right of appeal to royal authority in cases of dispute or legal actions.[34]

Johann Georg II declared himself Reicherzmarschall, making him the most powerful representative of the *Kameradschaft* in the empire.[35]

Frequent disputes arose between the privileged court trumpeters and the *Stadtpfeifer*, or the municipal musicians, who provided music at various city proceedings. Johann Georg II issued a mandate in March 1661 forbidding the *Stadtpfeifer* to play trumpets at most town functions. The *Stadtpfeifer*, however, not willing to make financial sacrifices,

> strained the rules and regulations by playing on waldhorns, trumpets with tuning crooks (*Inventionstrompeten mit Setzstücken*) and curiously wound instruments made so as not to resemble trumpets but sounding none the less just the same.[36]

In 1658 Johann Georg II had thirty-one trumpeters and one timpanist in his employ.[37] The 1680 list shows nineteen "court and field trumpeters" and five "musical trumpeters."[38] Music at Johann Georg II's court frequently employed trumpets as obbligato instruments as may be seen in the 1681 catalog compiled for Johann Georg III (doc. 18). The musical trumpeters must have been required to play the more complicated parts while the court and field trumpeters played signals, cavalry calls and flourishes, and sounded the call to table.

Tafelmusik

During the seventeenth century, the responsibilities of ensemble members came increasingly to include more secular performances in the theater and at table as well. Indeed, among the many responsibilities of seventeenth-century court musicians, one of the most frequent was to provide Tafelmusik. Music historians, however, often leave us with a somewhat bland impression of music performed at table. For example,

Werner Braun, in his book *Die Music des 17. Jahrhunderts,* suggests that "in the chamber (at mealtime) great importance was attached to beautiful, soft, and diverse sounds more or less attentively listened to."[39] A clearer picture of the much more varied character of Tafelmusik can be gained from the Dresden court diaries, musicians' contracts, catalogs of the period, and Schütz's letters.[40]

Tafelmusik is mentioned in the original Dresden *Kantoreiordnung* of 1548, in which the elector Moritz orders the members of his court ensemble to serve "in church and at our table."[41] A hundred years later the court appointment books in Dresden still show musicians dividing their time between church and table. For example, in his appointment as instrumentalist and musician dated 22 February 1651, Friedrich Sulz

> is ordered, commanded and bid regarding service in our court ensemble, at table, and elsewhere. . . . [I]n addition he shall have charge and management of all of our wind and reed instruments, violins, and other instruments, as well as the room in our palace organized for that purpose, and to give diligent attention that none of them is damaged or lost, failing which, however, he is responsible for restoring the damage or loss. [He is ordered] to keep ready at all times those instruments needed for church, at table, or other circumstances, and to have them brought by the *Kalkant* or by the boys to the place where they are to be used.[42]

When Christoph Bernhard was promoted from alto to vice-Kapellmeister in 1655, Tafelmusik was listed in his contract as one of his most important duties (doc. 10). In a letter accompanying Bernhard's contract, Heinrich Taube, Hofmarschall to Johann Georg I, writes of Bernhard that "in the absence of [either] the electoral Kapellmeister Heinrich Schütz or the elector apparent's Kapellmeister, or else at their command, he [will] direct and organize the music both in church and at the electoral and princely table" (doc. 10). This note confirms that Schütz conducted Tafelmusik as a regular part of his duties, otherwise known only from a document from 1655 in which he requests to be released from the demands of his position due to advanced age and weakened health "in church as well as at table."[43]

Aside from documents relating directly to the running of the court ensemble, contemporary descriptions considerably expand the view of music at court. Philipp Hainhofer provides especially vivid details of his second visit to Dresden, including descriptions of Tafelmusik.[44] Describing one meal in the upper hall of the royal garden house which contained a great many lifesized portraits, he writes,

> Behind every picture it is hollow and set up in such a way that behind one can perform a certain kind of music. When one dines in this upper hall, the musicians

are positioned in the lower hall as well, the doors are closed, and so the resonance ascends delightfully through the ventilators. Above, under the ceiling, there is also an arrangement for hidden music, so that one can hear such music from thirty-two different locations, each separated.[45]

He describes yet another meal at which the elector Johann Georg I was present. Meals at court must have been somewhat boisterous, or as Hainhofer states,

namely, too many guests make much too much commotion and noise. Everything, however, at this royal meal progressed very quietly, solemnly, and respectfully, and no one at table spoke but the elector and whoever responded to him.[46]

This excerpt is followed by a description of Tafelmusik during which several soloists alternate, including John Price the Englishman, who played the viola da gamba and, at the same time, a little English pipe held in his right hand.[47] This kind of variety is borne out by the description of another meal, at the home of Georg Reichbrodt, lord chamberlain of the exchequer.

Then a pretty feast was set up, with vocal music outside before the room, [and] a room with instrumental music (being an instrumentalist and a lutenist who waited especially on the electress and alternated with one another).[48]

One of the most important witnesses to court life in Dresden, the court diaries often go no further than to point out that "the court musicians were in attendance at table." The diaries do, however, provide detailed descriptions of special celebrations, indicating that Tafelmusik was provided not only for important royal gatherings but at regular meals as well. An entry on 6 January 1658 provides details of one royal meal at which music served not only as entertainment but also as a ceremonial manifestation of royal power.

Your Serene Highness's entire trumpet choir sounded in the New Year which was conducted in the following manner:

Finally in the afternoon you took your places in the Great Hall near the window, and when Your Serene Highness went to the table as soon as the Oberhofmarschall entered the Great Hall, the trumpets played "Nun Last uns Gott den Herren," which they continued until Your Serene Highness and all of your high officers and servants were in the dining room. Afterwards, when Her Serene Highness and the princess came to the table, the aforementioned song was played again until they were in the dining room. However, when the emissaries, barons of the king of Hungary and the archduke of Austria, were led to the table, only a trumpet flourish was played.

But as the royal company [came] to the table, the trumpeters arranged themselves on one side of the giant chamber in the antechamber near the middle entrance and there played "Joseph, lieber Joseph mein," after which the drummers and pipers also did their part in the entrance between the Great Chamber and Great Hall, and thus it ended.[49]

Meals frequently included theatrical performances as entertainment along with Tafelmusik. An entry from 6 March 1650 reads:

Your Serene Highness celebrated with God's grace your sixty-sixth birthday . . . and during the celebrations at table, the elector apparent, Duke Johann Georg [II], had a singing ballet presented by the musicians at 9:00 in the evening.[50]

On 8 May 1671,

at 5:00 the call to table was sounded with trumpets and drums . . . there on the stage the comedy of Orlando Furioso was performed, and the Mountain Singers, the Little Turkish Drum and Shawm Players were in attendance during the meal.[51]

Wedding banquets were often concluded by a ball such as the festivities held in a great tapestried hall in the palace on Sunday 19 November 1665. The emperor himself was in attendance, but seems to have spent the evening playing cards.

Most of the *Dames* and *Cavaliers* began to dance a bransle for which the royal prince's eight violins, sent by the king of France, were in attendance. After the bransle, courantes were danced, passing a couple of hours. . . . After the meal the dancing continued with courantes, bransles, and German dances, between which food and wine was carried around, and the ball ended with an English dance.[52]

A diary entry from 2 March 1680, describing the wedding festivities in Merseburg of Duke Johann Ernst of Saxe-Gotha with Princess Sophia Hedwig of Saxe-Merseburg, contains the banquet seating arrangement, or *Tafelsitz*, commonly incorporated into diary accounts of feasts (fig. 12). However this seating arrangement includes not only the names and locations of the guests at the table but lists the musicians and shows their placement as well. The guests are shown seated to the right of the table while the musicians are placed directly in the center before them. The performers included the French Violinists, the Chamber Cymbalist, Royal and Military Shawm Players, Mountain Singers, Wallachian Bag-pipers, and the *Stadtpfeifer*.[53]

The ensembles specifically indicated on the *Tafelsitz* represent the extreme diversity in the resident ensembles of Dresden, confirmed else-where by numerous other references throughout the court diaries. One of the most active groups was the Court and Field Trumpeters and Timpanist (*Hof- und Feldtrompeter und Heerpaucker*). The court trumpeters served as couriers, accompanied royalty on trips, performed at all festivities, and sounded the call to meals. According to Fürstenau, the Shawm Players (die *Schallmeypfeiffer*) consisted of a quartet of two trebles, one alto, and one bass shawm with pipes and timpani.[54] Among the most intriguing are the various more exotic ensembles, such as the Little Turkish Drum with the Little Shawms (*das türkische Päuklein mit den kleinen Schallmeyen*); bagpipers known as the Six Wallachians or Haiduks with bagpipes (*die sechs Wallachen oder Heyducken mit dem Bocke* or simply *Bockpfeifer*); and the Dulcimer Players (*die Hackbretirer*). The French Violinists (*die französische Geiger*), not mentioned in the court diaries until the last quarter of the century, were probably an imitation of the *petits violons* of Louis XIV and Lully. According to Fürstenau, the Mountain Singers (*die Bergsänger*) performed national songs in traditional costumes with and without instrumental accompaniment in ensembles consisting of two singers, two shawms, two violins, one *Spitzharfe,* and one lute.[55] These ensembles occasionally played at court meals, dances, and at pageants.

Aside from these more unusual ensembles, instrumentalists and singers from the court ensemble were also regularly expected to perform at table. Schütz, in his search for musicians to restock Duke August's court ensemble in Wolfenbüttel, suggests

> a reasonably good poet who is capable of especially good inventions which he composes himself and afterwards sings to his theorbo, which is then very well-suited to a royal table and provides a good variety to other compositions. (doc. 28)

The court diaries include entries such as "the Italian and German musicians were in attendance at table with your ensemble,"[56] or "Kapellmeister Vincenzo [Albrici] was in attendance with the entire electoral ensemble."[57] Smaller combinations were also available as is illustrated by references to "evening meals in the dining hall at which the chamber musician Balthasar Sedenig was in attendance with the viola da gamba,"[58] or "at table two guest musicians from Brandenburg performed, one on the lute and the other on the viola da gamba."[59]

Central to the performance of Tafelmusik were the boys of the court ensemble, who were also referred to as *Tafelknaben* or *Tischknaben.* Schütz mentions them frequently and stresses their importance in a 1617 letter to Heinrich Posthumus of Reuss-Gera.

Concerning the two table boys who are to be kept there, most gracious lord, it is my opinion that Your Grace could build the entire foundation of your ensemble on them. . . . These same boys must be (be they many or few) trained in expression in singing and, of Your Grace's court instruments, definitely all on the violin, but on such other instruments as zinks, sackbuts, according to the desire and interest of the boys.[60]

In a letter to Johann Georg I dated 7 March 1641, Schütz suggests the addition of eight boys to the court ensemble, four as singers and four as instrumentalists, to remedy its current state, which Schütz compares to a patient at the point of death.

This is, most gracious elector, in my humble opinion the one and most suitable way in which Your Serene Highness could not only in some respects maintain a small ensemble for your royal table, but also in [these] eventful, [but,] God help us, soon better times (with the engagement of a genuinely good Italian or other instrumentalist, and a singer just as good), make the Collegium musicum, according to Your Highness's desire, always complete and whole.[61]

Schütz apparently made certain that the boys practiced their table duties, for in an earlier letter dated 17 December 1625, he had requested: "If Your Serene Highness can permit me sometime this week when there is otherwise no service to have all the boys, big and little, serve perhaps one time at table."[62] This scene was no doubt training for more important occasions such as the royal banquet described in a court diary of 1668:

Your Highness the elector apparent dined in the evening with your princess. . . . Your Serene Highness sent for the choir boys who performed at table to honor the newly engaged couple. After that there was dancing into the night.[63]

In *Syntagma musicum* III (1619), Michael Praetorius addresses the variety expected of musicians performing at table, suggesting the alternation of various instruments and voices.

Thus and in this manner can one arrange to have good music for the table of great lords or for other happy events so that, if one has two or more boys or in addition other alto, tenor, and bass voices (which I call concerted voices) singing with harpsichord, regal, or a similar basso continuo instrument, and then begin to play the lute, pandora, violins, zinks, sackbuts, and similar instruments somewhat differently alone and without singing voices, and then again with voices, and thus alternating singing and instruments one after the other. Likewise, after a concerto or else a splendid motet, one could then bring forth a jolly canzona, galliard, courant, or something similarly frivolous, which then an organist or lutenist can also play alone, taking care that if he plays a motet or madrigal very slowly and solemnly at a banquet, soon afterwards to begin a happy allemande, intrada, bransle, or galliard. After that he could take up perhaps another motet, madrigal, pavan, or artistic fugue.[64]

Since few seventeenth-century collections are actually designated for use at table, we must draw conclusions regarding repertoire from other sources. Schütz himself offers clues about Tafelmusik in his letters. During his second trip to Venice on 3 November 1628, he notes new Italian musical tastes.

> I detect that since the time before when I came to these parts for the first time, this entire style has quite changed, and that music used at the royal table for comedies, ballets, and similar productions has noticeably improved and advanced.[65]

In his letter to the superintendent in Zeitz (doc. 44), Schütz includes a list of new compositions which he will provide for the royal ensemble, including

> large Psalms, large sacred concerti, *Te Deum laudamus,* and similarly full-voiced compositions with vocal and instrumental parts to be used at any time at one's own discretion. . . . Small Psalms and concerti or those only intended for few voices, some of which can be occasionally used at the beginning of a royal banquet. . . . Secular and moralistic songs for royal Tafelmusik.

As Kapellmeister *in absentia* at the court in Wolfenbüttel, Schütz suggests to Duke August both sacred and secular music for use at table (doc. 21).

In a letter to Philipp Hainhofer in 1632, Schütz asks his friend's assistance in obtaining a list of madrigals, canzonettas, frottolas, motets, and sacred works by several Italian composers, including Gesualdo (doc. 45). It is easy to imagine that Schütz was interested in these compositions for use at table, particularly in view of the catalog compiled by Christian Kittel in 1681 for the new elector, Johann Georg III (doc. 18). This catalog, which lists prints and manuscripts used in both sacred and secular settings, is mentioned by Eberhard Schmidt, for it lists Latin masses by Peranda and Albrici.[66] It also contains an inventory of Tafelmusik in use during the reign of Johann Georg II. Recorded are madrigals by Peranda for various vocal combinations, frequently with instruments. Most of the madrigals are for five voices and when instruments are specified they are two trumpets with or without timpani. Other vocal combinations include two tenors; two treble voices and tenor; and treble, tenor, and bass. Other compositions by Peranda intended for Tafelmusik listed here include three symphonias, one for six instruments (two trumpets and drums, two violins, and bassoon); another for nine instruments (four trumpets, four violins, and bassoon); and a third for five instruments (two trumpets, two violins, and bassoon). The consistent use of trumpets should dispel any notion that all Tafelmusik was soft enough so that those at table could carry on a conversation. Listed as well is an introit by Christoph Bernhard, designated *Festo Trinitas,* for four voices with instruments, followed by a list of printed music borrowed by privy chamberlain Gabriel Angelo de Battistini, listed in the 1680 court ensemble registers as a soprano and one of the ensemble's highest paid members.[67] This collection includes canzonas by Antonio Mortaro and madrigals by Orazio Brognonico, Luca Marenzio, Domenico Obizzi, Giovanni Rovetta, Steffano Bernardi (or Etienne Bernard), and Claudio Monteverdi. The madrigals are nearly all for five voices except the Obizzi collection for two, three, four and five voices, and the Rovetta, a volume of concerted madrigals for two, three, four, five, six, and eight parts with violins. The most interesting repertoire is, of course, the inclusion of Marenzio's Books Three, Four, and Seven for five voices and Monteverdi's Books Four, Five, Six, and Seven. These and Schütz's request to Philipp Hainhofer for Gesualdo's Book Eight for six voices, a posthumous collection which survives incomplete,[68] show an abiding interest in the late Italian virtuoso madrigal. Battistini borrowed six volumes each of the madrigals by Monteverdi and Obizzi and Rovetta, and five volumes of the canzonas by Mortaro, suggesting that a performance did in fact take place.

We know of at least one work that Schütz composed specifically for performance at table. "Wie wenn der Adler sich aus seiner Klippe schwingt" (SWV 434), a lovely solo song for treble voice and basso continuo, was composed for the 1651 betrothal of Johann Georg I's daughter Magdalene Sibylle to Friedrich Wilhelm of Saxe-Altenburg. The text is a six-verse ode by David Schirmer, which he published in 1663 under the heading, "Ode most humbly set to music and sung before the elector's table in the aforementioned illustrious occasion of the Altenburg betrothal."[69] Schirmer published the music and first verse with the heading, "The following melody, composed by Heinrich Schütz, the highly respected Kapellmeister to the electoral Saxon court, belongs to the ode on the illustrious Altenburg betrothal on page 125."[70]

Judging by the numerous references in court documents, Tafelmusik in Dresden was an integral aspect of court life and was considerably more diverse than one might have imagined. The music performed at table was both sacred and secular, using small and large ensembles of instrumentalists and singers in innumerable combinations. It contained elements of the exotic and fantastic so characteristic of the ceremonial processions of the period with musicians parading in ethnic costumes and playing unusual instruments. Theatrical presentations and dancing were frequently part of an evening's revelry. The repertoire ranged from the simple, uncomplicated, and intimate to the complex late madrigals of Gesualdo, Marenzio, and Monteverdi and the festiveness of trumpets, offering a cross section of the musical tastes of the time.

5

Conclusion

The aim of this study has been to analyze and interpret an important collection of documents which expands our knowledge of Heinrich Schütz and the environment in which he worked. It also makes more accessible materials that provide us with a clearer view of the Schütz milieu. Although scholars may have been aware of the existence of some of these documents, many are previously unpublished, and a significant number are newly discovered.

The specific dates and concrete details relevant to Schütz's biography and creative output that can be gleaned from these documents are relatively few:

21 September 1657	Schütz's letter in Constantin Christian Dedekind's *Aelbianische Musenlust* places him in Weissenfels.
8 April 1658	The date of an order from Johann Georg II for Schütz to travel from Weissenfels to Dresden three to four times each year.
11 August 1658	The journal of Duke Wilhelm IV of Saxe-Weimar records Schütz's presence in Weimar.
29 July 1659	Duke Wilhelm's journal reveals Schütz's arrival in Weimar from Weissenfels.
5 May 1660	The date of a letter from Löwe indicating Schütz's presence in Wolfenbüttel at this time. Duke August's account books show Schütz was paid travel money on

	6 June 1660, probably for his departure.
25 December 1660	A court diarist recorded a performance of "the birth of Christ in recitative style," unquestionably a reference to Schütz's *Historia der ... Geburth ... Jesu Christi* (SWV 435).
10 April 1661	In his letter to Duke August, Schütz wrote of his plan to return to Weissenfels after spending more than eight months in Dresden.
30 March 1662	A court diarist recorded a performance of Schütz's *Historia der Aufferstehung ...* (SWV 50).
15 June 1662	A court diarist recorded the performance of Schütz's *Aquae tuae, Domine,* a work which does not survive.
28 September 1662	A court diarist recorded the performance of Schütz's setting of Psalm 100 (SWV 493) for the consecration of the palace church.
7 October 1662	An epigram by Schütz for the *Geistliche Arien, Dialogen und Concerten* of Werner Fabricius places him in Leipzig.
18 October to 13 November 1662	Festivities for the wedding of the elector's daughter Erdmuth Sophia to Margrave Ernst Christian of Brandenburg-Bayreuth. Schütz's presence is recorded in a payment list for ceremonial robes for the musicians.
23 November 1662	A court diarist recorded a second performance of *Aquae tuae, Domine.*
21 May 1663	The date of a receipt in Schütz's hand for 300 talers signed in Teplitz.
14 July 1663	The date of a letter from Schütz to Duke Moritz of Zeitz from Dresden.

29 September 1663	The date of a letter from Schütz to Duke Moritz of Zeitz from Dresden.
10 January 1664	The date of a letter from Schütz to Duke August of Wolfenbüttel from Leipzig.
1 May 1664	The consecration ceremony of the palace church in Zeitz with the performance of Schütz's Psalm 100 (SWV 493). Schütz's presence in Zeitz around this time is recorded in a letter from Clemens Thieme and in the statutes for the Zeitz musicians.
24 March 1665	A court diarist recorded the first performance of Schütz's *St. John Passion* (SWV 481).
26 March 1665	A court diarist recorded a performance of Schütz's *Historia der ... Aufferstehung ...* (SWV 50).
10 April 1665	Schütz's signature on the early version of the *St. John Passion* (SWV 481a) sent to Duke August places Schütz in Weissenfels.
10 July 1665	Schütz in Halle for the baptism of a friend's son.
15 October 1665	A court diarist recorded a performance of Schütz's Psalm 100 (SWV 493) for the birthday of the electress.
16 December 1665	A court diarist recorded the performance of *Renunciate Johannis quae audistis,* a lost work.
25 December 1665	A court diarist recorded a performance of Schütz's *Historia der ... Geburth ... Jesu Christi* (SWV 435).
1 April 1666	A court diarist recorded the first performance of Schütz's *St. Matthew Passion* (SWV 479).

8 April 1666	A court diarist recorded the first performance of Schütz's *St. Luke Passion* (SWV 480).
13 April 1666	A court diarist recorded a performance of Schütz's *St. John Passion* (SWV 481).
15 April 1666	A court diarist recorded a performance of Schütz's *Historia der . . . Aufferstehung . . .* (SWV 50).
1 and 3 May 1666	Schütz's letters to Johann Georg II place him in Dresden.
1 January 1667	A court diarist recorded a performance of Psalm 150 as "Kapellmeister Schütz's new composition with trumpets and timpani," now lost.
5 April 1667	A court diarist recorded a performance of Schütz's *St. Luke Passion* (SWV 480).
7 April 1667	A court diarist recorded a performance of Schütz's *Historia der . . . Aufferstehung . . .* (SWV 50).
22 July 1668	A court diarist recorded another performance of Psalm 150.
1669	Schütz honored with a gilded cup from Johann Georg II.
4 April 1669	A court diarist recorded a performance of Schütz's *St. Luke Passion* (SWV 480).
14 January 1672	The date of a Weissenfels testamentary contract disposing of Schütz's family property.
6 November 1672	Schütz's death in Dresden.
17 November 1672	Schütz's funeral in Dresden's Frauenkirche.

The documents make clear that Schütz, as the semiretired court Kapellmeister, retained certain musical responsibilities at Dresden, although during much of Johann Georg II's reign he resided in Weissenfels: the payment schedules document that he received a salary during this period; several court diary references to new works by Schütz show that he continued to compose for the Dresden court; and Johann Georg II required him to travel to Dresden three to four times a year, perhaps to serve in an advisory capacity. The biographical information contained in the sources, however, is surprisingly limited, so that any new discoveries that help to fill in the details of Schütz's biography take on considerable importance. For example, the Wolfenbüttel material includes a new receipt in Schütz's hand dated Michaelmas 1658 (doc. 31) which was cataloged at NSAW but was previously unknown to Schütz scholars. Of much greater significance is the information the documents transmit about Schütz's environment, his role as Kapellmeister in Dresden, and his involvement at other courts outside Dresden as Kapellmeister *in absentia*.

Although Schütz had served as Kapellmeister *von Haus aus* at other courts earlier in his lifetime, his influence had never been as extensive as at Wolfenbüttel and Zeitz. His respective roles at Wolfenbüttel and Zeitz, however, appear to have been quite different from one another. As we have seen, the nature of Schütz's duties at Wolfenbüttel was outlined by the composer himself in a memorandum of ca. 1645. In this he listed the areas in which he was to advise the duke and duchess: the makeup of the ensemble, the language for the vocal music, the uses of sacred and secular music, and the purchase of instruments (doc. 21). The contract signed by Duke August and Schütz in 1655 tells us further that Schütz was to supply musicians for the court ensemble, advise Kapellmeister Löwe, and attend to musical matters in person on occasion, all for 150 talers per year.

The large body of correspondence and documents related to the Wolfenbüttel court ensemble show Schütz's influence there to have been primarily in recruiting musicians for the duke and duchess. New lists of the court ensemble in Wolfenbüttel chart its growth from eight members in 1647–48 to sixteen members in 1658–59, to its peak of eighteen members in 1665–66, precisely the years during which Schütz served as Kapellmeister *in absentia*. He also supplied choirboys, for whom he showed particular concern. In his letter of 24 July 1655 (doc. 25), Schütz informed Sophie Elisabeth that Löwe was leaving Dresden with "both discantists," asking her to watch over them, especially since he feared that Kapellmeister Löwe tended to work them "perhaps a little too hard and they then complain about him." The Wolfenbüttel court account book shows that Schütz sent two more choirboys to Wolfenbüttel in 1658.

The extent to which Schütz was to provide the Wolfenbüttel court ensemble with music is still unclear. There is no indication that Schütz ever composed anything especially for Wolfenbüttel aside from one Singspiel, now lost; the composer in fact wrote in a letter of 27 November 1655 (doc. 28) that he wished Löwe's compositions to be performed at August's court. He did mention his intention to send his own compositions to Wolfenbüttel, however, and, indeed, his letter of 10 April 1661 (doc. 35) accompanied two copies of the *Becker Psalter* for the duke and the duchess, and "just as many continuo parts for the organists," a clear indication that the Psalms were for use in August's church. He also stated that he had "been reminded of my incumbent responsibilities" and that he planned to go to Weissenfels soon to assemble from his private collection the music "of the most distinguished composers" to send to Wolfenbüttel. On 10 January 1664 (doc. 38) he wrote to the duke that he was sending his "published musical works which you graciously desired," indicating his gratitude that the duke was willing to "show my modest work the honor and high favor graciously to grant it a little space in your royal library, famous throughout Europe." It seems likely that, except for the *Becker Psalter,* the music sent to Duke August was probably not for use by his ensemble but intended as a gift to remain on the shelves of the Biblioteca Augusta, particularly since many of the works, notably all three parts of the *Symphoniae sacrae*, call for forces larger than the Wolfenbüttel ensemble.

On the other hand, music at Zeitz during Schütz's tenure as Kapellmeister *in absentia* was clearly influenced by the Dresden court. Just as Schütz presented two copies of the revised *Becker Psalter* to August for his eighty-second birthday in 1661, he also sent two copies to Zeitz, again for the duke and duchess. Not only were settings from the *Becker Psalter* performed at Zeitz but also the Psalm 100 of Schütz's *opus ultimum.* This Psalm was performed at the consecration ceremonies for both the renovated palace churches, in Dresden in 1662 and in Zeitz in 1664. The strongest evidence for the close interrelationship between Dresden and Zeitz, however, is the discovery that the Zeitz chapel order and Johann Georg II's undated order for Dresden are in most respects identical.

Schütz appears to have been much less effective at Zeitz than at Wolfenbüttel, perhaps because Zeitz lacked the strong musical presence of someone like Duchess Sophie Elisabeth, who did much to shape music at her court in Wolfenbüttel and who seems to have been receptive to Schütz's recommendations. At Zeitz, on the other hand, Schütz's advice in musical matters was repeatedly ignored. For example, he would have preferred to train all the choirboys for Zeitz at Dresden, as he did the Wolfenbüttel choirboys. But here, as in other matters, such as the renovation of the interior of the palace church, the building of a new organ, and the proper care of the music he sent, he encountered little cooperation from the authorities at Zeitz. While Schütz did recruit musicians for both Wolfenbüttel and Zeitz, it is perhaps significant that he did not send Italian musicians to either court, perhaps because of the controversy over their presence in Dresden. No Italian musicians were in the employ of either Duke August or Duke Moritz.

Finally, the documents presented here greatly expand our knowledge of the role of court musicians in seventeenth-century Germany, from the most exalted, such as Schütz himself, to the more modest who worked under him. Newly discovered *Hofkapelle* lists from Dresden and Wolfenbüttel further our understanding of the size and makeup of these court ensembles. Previously unpublished contracts of court musicians, which specifically enumerate many of their duties, in addition to the Dresden court diaries and Johann Georg II's undated chapel order, clarify court musicians' responsibilities in a variety of settings.

During the reign of Johann Georg I, there were wide discrepancies in pay among the musicians at Dresden and Wolfenbüttel. For example, Wolfenbüttel's Kapellmeister Stephan Körner in 1638 proposed salaries from 100 to 140 talers for musicians. The musicians' contracts from ca. 1655 to 1666 show salaries from 50 to 230 talers, information corroborated by autograph receipts in NSAW. It is possible that higher pay was allotted to the musicians of greater skill. For example, a falsettist who set his own poems and accompanied himself on the theorbo, and was the subject of correspondence between Sophie Elisabeth and Schütz in 1655 (docs. 23, 27, and 28), received a salary of 200 talers. In Dresden, Clemens Thieme earned 150 talers as an instrumentalist in 1650.[1] Constantin Christian Dedekind earned 150 gulden in 1654.[2] As vice-Kapellmeister in Wolfenbüttel, Weilandt received 150 talers, as revealed in an autograph receipt dated 24 December 1662.[3] In Dresden, Christoph Bernhard earned 200 gulden in 1649 as alto (doc. 9); as vice-Kapellmeister he earned 350 gulden in 1655 (doc. 10).[4]

Körner's 1638 contract allots him 400 talers as Wolfenbüttel's Kapellmeister;[5] Chrysander states, however, that he actually received only about 100 talers.[6] Both Löwe's and Colerus's contracts indicate that they were to be paid 300 talers as Kapellmeister, showing a certain stability in the salary for that post. Schütz is listed as to having earned 400 talers in both the 1680 and 1717 lists (see appendix). In comparison, Wolfenbüttel's court artist (*Hofmahler*) Albert Freise, who created the originals from which the engravings of the interior of Wolfenbüttel's Hauptkirche were made (see fig. 1), earned a yearly salary of 100 talers in 1644, and the brazier (*Rothgiesser*) Michael Apper earned 200 talers yearly in 1642.[7]

The amounts paid to some musicians increased in Dresden during the

reign of Johann Georg II. As may be seen in the payment lists reproduced in the appendix, the Italians generally earned salaries which were
much larger than those of the Germans. In 1680, the members of the
first choir, who were nearly all Italians, earned as much as ten times the
salaries of their German colleagues in the second choir, a situation which
surely contributed to German animosity regarding the foreign presence
in Dresden.

The three ensembles at Dresden, Wolfenbüttel, and Zeitz differed
widely in size. Dresden, as an electoral court, maintained a larger ensemble than the lesser courts of Wolfenbüttel and Zeitz. In 1651 the
combined ensembles of the elector and the elector apparent numbered
forty musicians, while in Wolfenbüttel in 1648 (not long after Schütz
had begun his tenure as Kapellmeister *in absentia*) the ensemble com-
prised only nine musicians and two trumpeters. By the year 1658–59,
Wolfenbüttel's ensemble had grown to ten musicians, four trumpeters,
and one timpanist, while in Dresden the new elector Johann Georg II
had in his employ in 1657 forty-seven musicians. A 1658 list shows that
he employed an additional thirty-one trumpeters and one timpanist.
By the end of Schütz's tenure in Wolfenbüttel in 1666, the court ensemble included thirteen musicians, one dancing master, and five trumpeters, while in Dresden in the same year there were fifty musicians. In
Zeitz the ensemble included fourteen members in 1664–65. By 1680 the
Dresden ensemble contained fifty-one musicians, sixteen trumpeters,
and four timpanists.

The eventual increase in the size of these court ensembles may be
seen as a reflection of the gradual easing of the pressures resulting from
the Thirty Years War. Furthermore, Dresden's ensemble remained
fairly stable throughout Johann Georg II's reign, probably as a result
of his commitment to maintaining a fine musical establishment. The
importance which he attached to music at court and his compassion for
the court musicians is clearly apparent in his 1653 letter to his father
(doc. 5), in which he sought both to improve his father's waning ensemble and to relieve the economic hardships of the electoral musicians.

It appears that approximately equal numbers of singers and instrumentalists were retained in the ensembles at these courts. Stephan
Körner, in his 1638 list, proposed an ensemble for Wolfenbüttel of ten
members: six musicians, two choirboys, a *Kalkant*, and a Kapellmeister.
The three adult singers, an alto, a tenor, and a bass, were also to play
instruments; the three instrumentalists were expected to play more than
one instrument. Johann Georg II's 1653 letter (doc. 5) proposes an
ensemble of twenty singers (two tenors, two altos, two basses, and four
choirboys) and some twenty instrumentalists, including two cornettists,

six sackbut players, one bassoon and bombard player, violinists (probably two), two organists, seven general instrumentalists, and one timpanist.

The newly discovered 1657 list of the electoral ensemble shows not only an equal distribution of singers and instrumentalists but also reveals the expectation that seventeenth-century German musicians be extremely versatile. The singers listed include two castrati, three male altos, two tenors, four basses, and six choirboys, bringing the total number of singers to nineteen, including vice-Kapellmeister Bernhard, who was also an alto, and cantor Erlemann, a bass. The remainder of the ensemble consisted of four organists and seventeen instrumentalists. Christian Weber, listed here among the singers, also played the harp, lute, theorbo, and other instruments, according a memorandum from Schütz dated 31 March 1648.[8] The bass Jonas Kittel apparently played theorbo as well, as Schütz wrote in a memorandum dated 31 September 1631.[9] Furthermore, Johann Georg II indicated that Kittel also played the bass viol (doc. 5). Johann Wilhelm Forchheim, appointed as an instrumentalist on 20 December 1655, is designated a violinist, *Oberinstrumentist,* and organist in Fürstenau's 1666 list.[10] Schütz also wrote in a memorandum dated 14 September 1641 that Friedrich Werner played "all sorts of wind as well as string instruments as fitting for an instrumentalist."[11] This definition is supported by Praetorius, who describes *Instrumentisten* as "those who play various melody instruments such as cornetti, sackbuts, recorders, bassoons, violins, viols, and the like."[12] It is clear from the lists of Johann Georg II's musicians, however, that many performers were specialized virtuosi, particularly the castrati.

Various sources provide information about the repertory performed by the court ensemble in Dresden during the reign of Johann Georg II. During this period, the court diaries contain numerous worship service orders showing that primarily Masses and concerti by the Italian Kapellmeisters were performed in church. The diaries also reveal that secular music in the theater and at table was also Italianate, a fact corroborated by the 1681 catalog of prints and manuscripts intended for use in sacred and secular settings (doc. 18). The list includes works by the Italian Kapellmeisters as well as late Italian virtuoso madrigals by such composers as Marenzio and Monteverdi, showing continued interest in these works many decades after they were published.

Unfortunately, similarly detailed information for Zeitz and Wolfenbüttel has yet to come to light. Several of Schütz's late works were performed at both Dresden and Zeitz; it is not known at this time, however, whether Zeitz also imitated Dresden's preference for Italian music. The Wolfenbüttel sources reveal a strong commitment to the

Singspiel, but little is known of the sacred music performed by August's court ensemble.

The study of Schütz's letters and documents is an area replete with possibilities for further research. At the time of this study, for example, materials in the Staatsarchiv Magdeburg which could provide us with more information about Schütz's activities in Zeitz were largely unavailable. Many unanswered questions remain regarding the Zeitz chapel and organ, growth of the court ensemble there during Schütz's tenure as Kapellmeister *in absentia,* and other links between Dresden and Zeitz, particularly other works by Schütz which may have been performed at Moritz's court. Furthermore, this study presents only the late documents related to Schütz's long and productive life. A worthy future project would be an international edition of all of Schütz's letters and prefaces in their original language, in English, and in facsimile. An available and readable presentation of Schütz's letters and documents, great in number and rich in information about the composer and his times, would be a valuable asset to musical scholarship.

Appendix

Dresden Court Ensemble Lists
from 1662, 1680, and 1717

Court Ensemble, 1662

[SAD OHMA B no. 13/b. *Beylager Marggrafens zu Brandenburg, Herrn Christian Ernsts mit Churfürstens zu Sachßen Herrn Johann Georgens des andern Fräulein Tochter Fräul. Erdmuth Sophien in Dresden 1662.* Vol. II, fols. 750v–752r.]

List of the most graciously allotted ceremonial robes [*Verzeichnüß der gnädigst verwilligten Ehrenkleidung*]
[fol. 750v]

Persons Belonging to the Electoral Court Ensemble

		[Reichstalers and gulden]
Heinrico Sagittari	⎫	109,9
Vincenzo Albrici	⎬ Kapellmeisters	109,9
Giovanni Andrea Bontempi	⎭	109,9
Gioseppe Peranda	⎱ vice-Kapellmeisters	87,12
Christoph Bernhard	⎰	87,12
Dominico Melani	⎫	87,12
Bartolomeo Sorlisi	⎬ soprani	87,12
Francesco Perotti		87,12
Antonio de Blasi	⎭	87,12
Francesco Santi, alto		87,12
[fol. 751r]		
Giovanni Novelli	⎱ tenors	87,12
Giorgio Bertoldi	⎰	87,12
Stefano Sauli	⎱ basses	87,12
Christian Kittel	⎰	87,12
Giovanni Severo, violinist		87,12
Bartolomeo Albrici, organist		87,12

Friedrich Werner	87,12
Adam Kriegner, organist	65,15
Michael Schmidt	65,15
Friedrich Westhoff	65,15
Balthasar Sedenig	65,15
Johann Friedrich Volprecht	65,15
Sebastian Andreas Volprecht	65,15
Johann Wilhelm Forchheim	65,15
Simon Leonhard ⎫ musical trumpeters	65,15
Daniel Philomethes ⎭	65,15
Sebastian Ludwig Schulz	65,15
[fol. 751v]	
Clemens Thieme	65,15
Johann Dixon	65,15
Andreas Winckler	65,15
Johann Jäger	65,15
Jacob Sulz	65,15
Tobias Weller ⎫ organ and instrument makers	65,15
Jeremias Seyffert ⎭	65,15
Johann Georg Feistel, copyist	65,15
Gottfried Leschke, *Hofkirchner*	52,12
Johann Kaschwicz ⎫ *Kalkanten*	21,21
Johann Christoph Schricker ⎭	21,21

Choristers

Christoph Kittel, organist	65,15
Matthias Erlemann, court cantor ⎫ basses	65,15
Constantin Christian Dedekind ⎭	65,15
Adam Merkel ⎫ tenors	65,15
Johann Gottfried Behr ⎭	43,18
[fol. 752r]	
Christian Weber ⎫ altos	65,15
Gottfried Janezkÿ ⎭	43,18
Ephraim Büchner, whose voice	43,18
has changed [*so mutiert*]	

Court Ensemble, 1680

[SAD Loc. 8687. *Kantoreiordnung*, fols. 355r–359r.]

[fol. 355r]
[Talers]
Yearly:

1000	Giovanni Andrea Bontempi
100	Carlo Pallavicino
400	Sebastian Andreas Volprecht
400	Heinrich Schütz
500	Friedrich Werner
400	Johann Gottfried Ursinus
350	Johann Arnold
300	Daniel Philomethes
300	Jacob Michael

Pensioners [*Erben*]

3750 talers

[fol. 356v]
Yearly:

300	Johann Jacob Studer
250	Gottfried Janezky
175	Samuel Jägersdörfer the elder
175	Christian Mohr
175	Christian Weber
50	Johann Georg Koch
35	Johann Kaschwicz
35	Johann Christoph Schricker

Pensioners

1195 talers

Total: 4945 talers

[fol. 356r]

List of all of the electoral Saxon ensemble members in the year 1680 [*Verzeichnüß Derer Churfl. Sächs. Capellbedienten Anno 1680*]

Choir 1

Yearly:

1000	Vincenzo Albrici, maestro di capella
700	Giuseppe Novelli, vice maestro di capella
800	Gabriel Angelo de Battistini, soprano
700	Antonio Fidi ⎫ contraltos
600	Paolo Sieppi ⎭
700	Donato de Amaducci ⎫ tenors
700	Galeazzo Pesenti ⎭
700	Antonio Cottini ⎫ basses
700	Johann Jäger ⎭
400	Johann Heinrich Kittel, organist
500	Pietro Paolo Morelli, copyist
1000	Domenico Melani

700   Christian Kittel
――――
9200 talers
[fol. 356v]

Choir 2

Yearly:
700   Christoph Bernhard, Vice-Kapellmeister
500   Johann Wilhelm Forchheim, concert master
300   David Töpfer, court cantor
150   Johann Müller
100   Gottfried Siegmund Engert   } altos
200   Johann Füssel, d. 25 October 1680
200   Johann Georg Krause   } tenors
350   Ephraim Limner, bass
120   Johann Christian Böhme, organist
150   Johann Jacob Lindner, copyist
400   Johann Friedrich Volprecht
100   Tobias Beutel, *Kunstkämmerer*
600   Georg Bentle, toward salary in arrears
――――
3870 talers

[fol. 357r]

Instrumentalists

Yearly:
700   Johann Jacob Walther
700   Ludovico Marziani   } violinists
150   Johann Paul Westhoff
250   Simon Leonhard
250   Christoph Richter
250   Johann Heinrich Lizsche   } musical trumpeters
300   Friedrich Sulz
300   Christian Krausche
250   Johann David Janezky, musical timpanist
200   Salomon Kriegner
200   Johann Merkel   } cornettists
200   Paul Kaiser, bassoonist
200   Andreas Winckler
200   Friedrich Westhoff   } sackbut/musical timpanists
200   Georg Taschenberg

50	Caspar Koch	
50	Heinrich Koch	musical shawm players
50	Gottfried Hering	
50	Christian Elste	

4550 talers

[fol. 357v]
Yearly:

200	Jeremias Seyffert	organ makers
60	Andreas Tamitius	
130	Johann Gräbe, *Hofkirchner*	
50	Rudolf Beit, *Haußmann*	
40	Johann Wilhelm Billich	*Kalkanten*
40	Wenzel Klemzschkÿ	

520 talers
Total 18140 talers

[fol. 358r]
List of all of the electoral Saxon court and field trumpeters and timpanists in the year 1680 [*Verzeichnüs Derer Churfl. Sächs. sämbtl. Hof- und Feldtrompeter auch Herrpäucker*]

Court and Field Trumpeters and Timpanists

Yearly:
350	Christian Haßert
199,12	Wolfgang Voigt
199,12	Christian Rockstroh
225	Johann Christoph Hartmann
225	Johann Christoph Lindenberg
175	Johann Georg Loch
175	Christian Kläre
175	Georg Zacharowicz
175	Sebastian Nicolaus Knaud
175	Augustus Müller
175	Johann Jacob Nesiczkÿ
175	David Zapf
175	Christian Percolÿ
175	Friedrich Teichmann
175	Andreas Mehlich
175	Samuel Jägersdörffer, d. 23 August 1680
175	Nicolaus Sperber, d. 8 November 1679

175	Gottfried Herrnhoff ⎫	with His Grace Duke Christian of
175	Martin Böhmisch ⎭	Saxe-Halle
50	Joachim Friedrich Lindenberg, d. 29 July 1679	

3609 talers

Timpanists

Yearly:

131,6	Johann Georg Mohr ⎫	
131,6	Johann Georg Eschenderling ⎬	Timpanists
262,12	Emanuel Allmoÿ the Moor ⎭	
50	Johann Michael Koch, trumpetmaker	
131,6	Christoph Beiz, timpanist, d. 7 September 1680	

706,6

Total 4405 talers, 6 gulden

[fol. 359r]
Total in all: 22,545 talers, 6 gulden

Court Ensemble, 1717

[SAD Loc. 32751. *Kammerkollegium.* Rep. LII. Gen. no. 849, fols. 145r–148v.]

[fol. 145r]
List of the Italian and German musicians, the singers as well as the instrumentalists, who were in service to His Serene Highness Johann Georg the Second of illustrious memory [*Verzeichnüs Der Italienischen und Teutzschen Musicorum so wohl die Vocalisten als Instrumentisten so beÿ Ihro Churfürstl. Durchl. Johann George des Andern, Glorwürdigsten andenckens in Diensten gestanden*]

Reichstalers

Yearly salary		until
	Kapellmeisters	
400	Heinrich Schütz, the older Kapellmeister	1672
1200	Marco Gioseppe Peranda	1675
1200	Sebastiano Cherici	1676
1200	Vincenzo Albrici	1679
1500	Giovanni Andrea Bontempi	1680
1200	Carlo Pallavicino	1680

Vice-Kapellmeisters

744	Giovanni Novelli	1680
744	Christoph Bernhard	1680

Concert Masters

1000	Balthasar Manganoni	1654
500	Johann Wilhelm Forchheim	1680
175	Constantin Christian Dedekind	1676

[fol. 145v]

Yearly salary		until
	Soprani	
744	Gioseppe Maria Donati	1654
600	Antonio Piermarini	1654
744	Antonio Protogagi	1656
744	Angelo Maria Marchesini	1667
900	Francesco Perotti	1670
1000	Giovanni Antonio Pivido	1672
1000	Bartolomeo Sorlisi	1672
1000	Antonio de Blasi	1678
1000	Domenico Melani	1680
1000	Gabriel Angelo de Battistini	1680
	Altos	
480	Niccolai Milani	1654
300	Heinrich Groh, Falcettist	1654
744	Sefarino Jacobuti	1660
175	Tobias Tille	1660
744	Francesco Santi	1670
744	Giovanni Battista Ruggieri	1673
400	Johann Gottfried Ursinus	1674
744	Antonio Fidi	1680
600	Paolo Sieppi	1680
150	Johann Müller	1680
100	Gottfried Siegmund Engert	1680

[fol. 146r]

Yearly salary		until
	Tenors	
500	Francisco Ferdinand Franke	1653
840	Stefano Boni	1654
300	Philipp Stolle	1654

175	Peter Wenig	1659
744	Giorgio Bertoldi	1666
200	Wilhelm Alexander Mibes	1666
150	Christoph Krause	1669
400	Georg Cleÿer	1676
400	Adam Merkel	1678
700	Galeazzo Pesenti	1680
744	Donato de Amaducci	1680
250	Johann Georg Krause	1680
200	Johann Füssel	1680

Basses

600	Vincenzo Cenni	1654
480	Angelo Maria Donati	1654
175	Jonas Kittel	1659
175	Georg Kaiser	1659
744	Stefano Sauli	1663
744	Pietro Paolo Scandalibeni	1674
500	Michael Schmidt	1675
100	Donat Rößler	1677

[fol. 146v]

Yearly salary		until
744	Antonio Cottini	1680
700	Johann Jäger	1680
350	Ephraim Limner	1680

Chamber and Court Organists

300	Matthias Weckmann	1655
200	Georg Rumpf	1659
157	Johann Klemm	1659
744	Bartolomeo Albrici	1663
744	Carlo Capelli	1665
600	Adam Krieger	1666
350	Christoph Kittel	1677
400	Johann Heinrich Kittel	1680
120	Johann Christoph Böhme	1680

Bass Violists [*Violonisten*]

400	Sebastian Andreas Volprecht	1678
500	Pietro Paolo Morelli	1680
300	Christoph Richter, senior instrumentalist	1680

	[*Oberinstrumentist*]	
500	Georg Werner	1667

[fol. 147r]

Yearly salary		until
	Violinists [*Violinisten*]	
148	Andreas Künzgen	1648
300	Samuel Skahn	1654
300	Sebastian Ludwig Schulz	1663
744	Giovanni Battista Bascucci	1669
800	Giovanni Severo	1670
500	Michael Schmidt	1675
600	Johann Balthasar Sedenig	1677
944	Johann Jacob Walther	1680
744	Ludovico Marziani	1680
200	Johann Paul Westhoff	1680
	Violists [*Bracisten*]	
400	Johann Friedrich Volprecht	1680
300	Christian Krausche	1680
	Bassoonists	
300	Clemens Thieme	1666
200	Paul Kaiser	1680
	Cornettists	
250	Gottfried Janezky	1676

[fol. 147v]

Yearly salary		until
200	Johann Merkel	1680
250	Salomon Kriegner	1680
	Sackbut Players	
500	Christoph Magnus Naumann	1653
500	Christoph Magnus Helwig	1661
200	Johann Friedrich Sulz	1662
300	Jacob Sulz	1663
131	Johann Dixon	1666
262	Andreas Winckler	1666
300	Johann Friedrich Westhoff	1680
218	Georg Taschenberg	1680

Trumpeters

300	Daniel Philomethes	1675
300	Simon Leonhard	1680
300	Johann Heinrich Lizsche	1680
300	Friedrich Sulz	1680

Musical Timpanists

| 300 | Thomas Eschenderling | 1667 |
| 250 | Johann David Janezky | 1685 |

[fol. 148r]
Yearly salary   until

Violist da Gamba [*Viol di Gambiste*]

| 400 | Wilhelm Burrowes | 1656 |

Lutenist

| 100 | Gottfried Rasch | 1654 |

Poet

| 175 | Johann Georg Richter | 1672 |

General Instrumentalists [*Instrumentl: in genere*]

100	Friedrich Sulz	1656
80	Christian Hoffmann	1666
150	Balthasar Sedenig Junior	1679

Copyists

| 200 | Johann Georg Feistel | 1667 |
| 200 | Johann Jakob Lindner | 1680 |

Court Cantors

| 306 | Matthias Erlemann | 1665 |

[fol. 148v]
Yearly salary   until
| 175 | Christian Weber | 1679 |
| 300 | David Töpfer | 1680 |

Court Organ Makers

43	Tobias Weller	1664
200	Andreas Janictius	1680

Kalkanten

35	Johann Christoph Schricker	1677
35	Johann Kaschwicz	1678
40	Johann Wilhelm Billich	1680
40	Wenzel Klemzschkÿ	1680

The Musical Shawm Players

50	Johann Georg Koch	1678
50	Kaspar Koch	1680
50	Heinrich Koch	1680
50	Gottfried Hering	1680
50	Christian Elste	1680

Total:
53,676 talers
Signed Dresden
10 March 1717
Georg Gottfried Barkstroh

Figure 1.   The Interior of the Marienkirche in Wolfenbüttel,
            Looking West
            Engraving from Martin Gosky's *Arbustrum seu Arboretum*
            (1650) by Sebastian Furck from an original by Albert
            Friese.
            (NSAW)

Figure 2. Anonymous Portrait of Duke August and His Family
(*Braunschweigisches Landesmuseum*)

Figure 3. Staging of Sophie Elisabeth's *Neuerfundenes FreudenSpiel genandt Friedens = Sieg* in the Great Hall of Burg Dankwarderode Engraving by Conrad Buno, 1648. (*HAB Sign. 166.1 Eth. [1]; Lo 6992*).

Figure 4. Staging of Sophie Elisabeth's *Neuerfundenes FreudenSpiel genandt Friedens = Sieg*
in the Great Hall of Burg Dankwarderode
Intrumentalists positioned next to an entry decorated
to give the illusion of clouds. Engraving by Conrad Buno, 1648.
(HAB Sign. 166.1 Eth. [1]; Lo 6992)

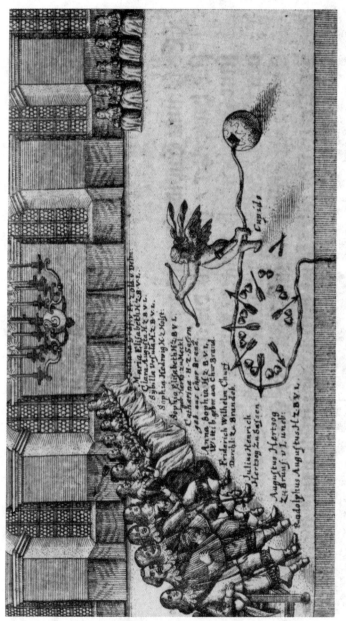

Figure 5. Staging of Sophie Elisabeth's *Neuerfundenes FreudenSpiel genandt Friedens = Sieg* in the Great Hall of Burg Dankwarderode. Guests seated along the outer edges of the Great Hall. Engraving by Conrad Buno, 1648.
(*HAB Sign. 166.1 Eth. [1]; Lo 6992*)

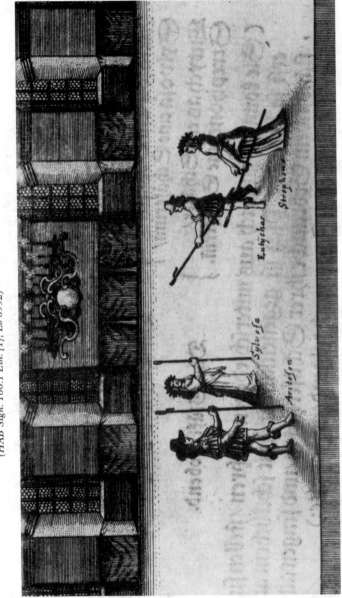

Figure 6. Staging of Sophie Elisabeth's *Neuerfundenes FreudenSpiel genandt Friedens = Sieg*
in the Great Hall of Burg Dankwarderode
Costumed performers. Engraving by Conrad Buno, 1648.
(HAB Sign. 166.1 Eth. [1]; Lo 6992)

Figure 7. Staging of Sophie Elisabeth's *Neuerfundenes FreudenSpiel genandt Friedens = Sieg* in the Great Hall of Burg Dankwarderode
Costumed performers in the center of the hall.
Engraving by Conrad Buno, 1648.
(HAB Sign. 166.1 Eth. [1]; Lo 6992)

Figure 8.   Staging of Sophie Elisabeth's *Neuerfundenes FreudenSpiel genandt Friedens = Sieg*
in the Great Hall of Burg Dankwarderode
Costumed performers in the center of the hall.
Engraving by Conrad Buno, 1648.
(HAB Sign. 166.1 Eth. [1]; Lo 6992)

Figure 9.   Staging of Sophie Elisabeth's *Neuerfundenes FreudenSpiel genandt Friedens = Sieg*
in the Great Hall of Burg Dankwarderode
Costumed performers in the center of the hall.
Engraving by Conrad Buno, 1648.
(HAB Sign. 166.1 Eth. [1]; Lo 6992)

Figure 10. Staging of Sophie Elisabeth's *Neuerfundenes FreudenSpiel genandt Friedens = Sieg*
in the Great Hall of Burg Dankwarderode
Closer view of the performers' entryway. Engraving by Conrad Buno, 1648.
(HAB Sign. 166.1 Eth. [1]; Lo 6992)

Figure 11.   Staging of Sophie Elisabeth's *Neuerfundenes FreudenSpiel genandt Friedens = Sieg*
in the Great Hall of Burg Dankwarderode
Closer view of the performers' entryway. Engraving by Conrad Buno, 1648.
(HAB Sign. 166.1 Eth. [1]; Lo 6992)

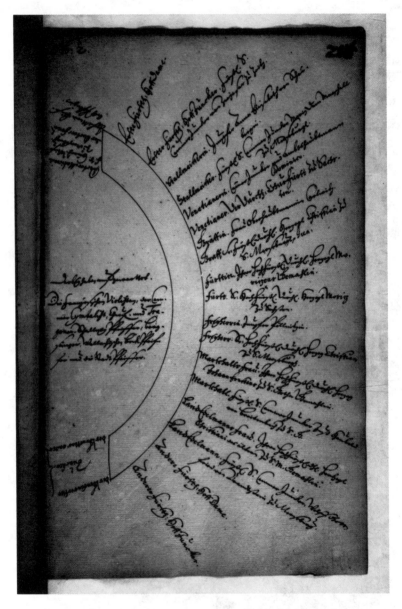

Figure 12.   The *Tafelsitz*, or Banquet Seating Arrangement, from
a Dresden Court Diary
Entry dated 2 March 1680.
(SAD Loc. 8682. nr. 13. Hof Diaria 1679-80, fol. 286r)

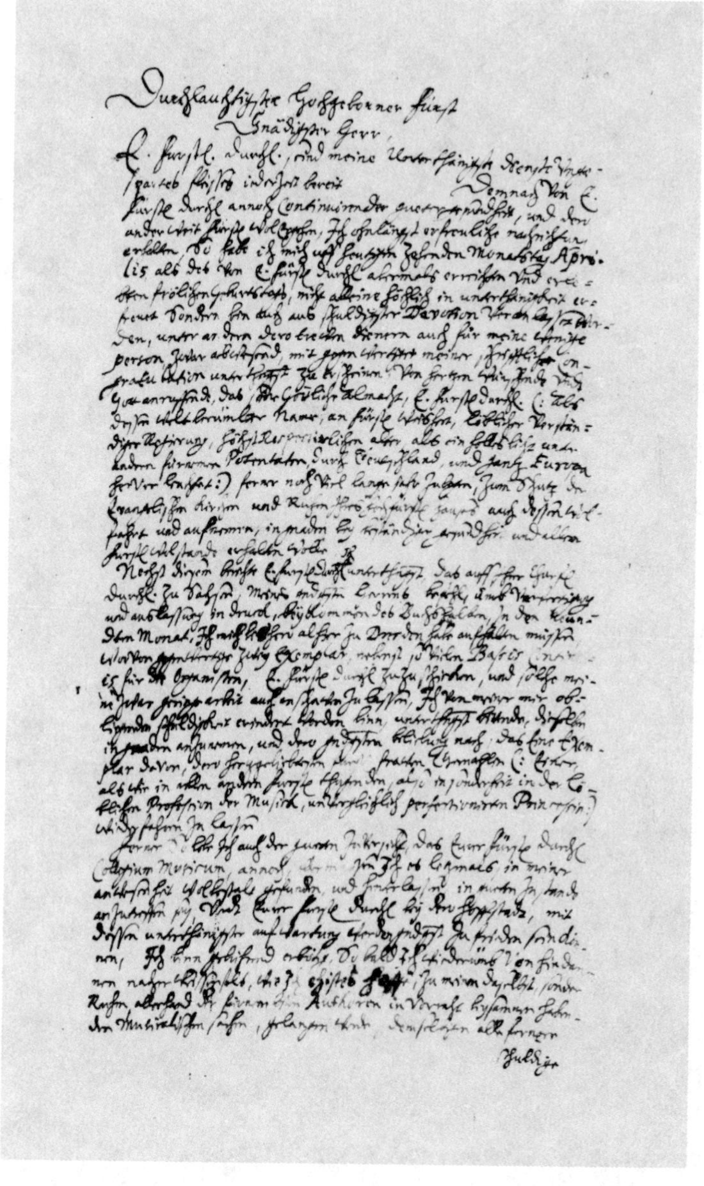

Figure 13.   Schütz's Autograph Letter to Duke August of
Wolfenbüttel, 10 April 1661
(HAB Cod. Guelf 376 Nov., fol. 320)

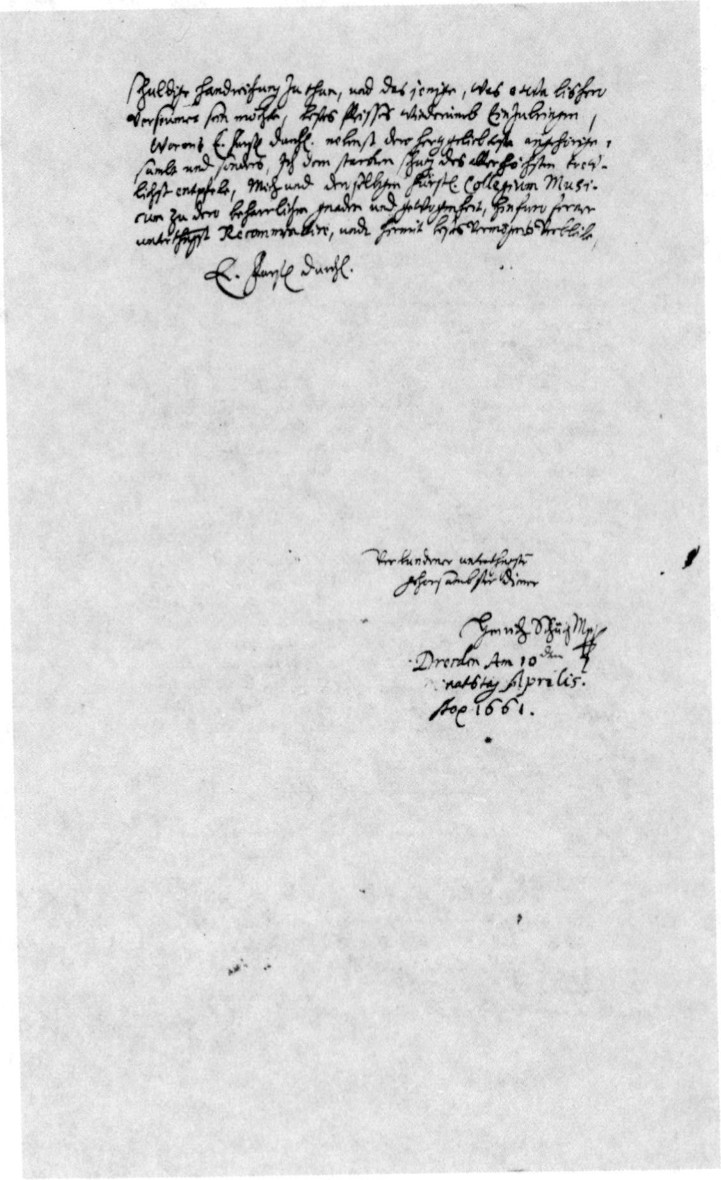

Figure 13 (cont.)

Part Two

Documents

Commonly Used Seventeenth-Century German Abbreviations

Ao	Anno
D	Doktor
E. f. Gn.	Euer fürstliche Gnaden
f., fl.	Gulden
gndgst	gnädigst
H	Herr
Lbd.	Liebden
m.p., m.p.p.	manu propria
rtlr	Reichsthaler
s. f. Durchl.	seine fürstliche Durchlaucht
thlr	Thaler
unterthgst	unterthänigst
Xbr	December
7bris	Septembris
9bris	Novembris

1

Schütz to Christian Reichbrodt.
Dresden, 21 September 1647

[SAD Loc. 8687. *Kantoreiordnung*, fols. 244–45]

[fol. 244r]
Dreßden am 21 Monatstag September. 1647.
Unterthänigst Memorial
Was etwa beÿ vnserm gndgstn Churfürsten vndt Herren [flourish] Wegen des Italianischen Musici Augustin Fontana zu erindern die Notturfft scheinen thut:

1.

Ihrer churfl. durchl. unterthenigste nachrichtung zu geben, das obgedachter Italianer, (:ohngeacht er itzo bey dem König zu dennenmark 500 Rther jährliche gewisse besoldung hatt, bey dem hertzog zu Gottorp ihme auch nebenst dem Capellmeisterambt derogleichen jährliche unterhaltung, hirüber auch die erbawung Einer newen wohnung, angeboten worden ist:) annoch gantz begierig ist in dero dienste undt bestallung sich unterthenigst einzulassen, seinem zuschreiben nach, auch sein übriges gantzes leben, bey diesem churfurstl. hause sollen das zuzubringen [flourish]

2.

Wegen seiner jährlichen besoldung, hatt er für seinem abreisen, vndt nach meiner mit Ihm gehaltenen vnterredung, sich dahin erkleret, mit 400 Thlrn zufrieden zu sein, welche dann (:iedoch sonder eintzige masgebung:) von vnsern gndgstn herrn, ihme derogestalt gndgst bewilliget, undt seine schrifftliche bestallung auff solche weise eingerichtet werden könte, das 300 Thlr als ein Vicecapelmeister (:NB nach welchem Officio Er insonderheit strebet:) vndt hirüber noch 100 thlr wegen unterrichtung und exercirung nicht alleine der Discantisten, Sondern auch das andern collegii aller Sänger oder Vocalisten, Er jährlichen zu entpfahen, vndt also Qvartaliter 100 Thlr zu erheben haben solte.

3.

Hirüber So hatt er mich auch beydes in seinem anwesen alhier, mündlich vndt itzo schrifftlich [*gebeten* crossed out] fleissig gebeten, beÿ vnserm gndgsten churfursten v. herrn Ihn dahin unterthenigst zu re-commendiren (:weil doch von solcher seiner Ordinar bestallung er wenig würde erübrigen oder prosperiren können:) das von hochgedachter Ihrer churfl. durchl. Ihme gndgste promission wegen einer begnedigung zu erkeuffung eines hausses [flourish] wiederfahren möchte.   Wie nun das nottürfftige accomodent dieses frembdlings, solches wol erfordern wirdt, also verhoffe Ich auch, Ihrer churf durchl. an mitteln es nicht ermangeln, [*werde* crossed out] vndt dahero auch dieses puncts halben, Ihme von mir gndgste vndt zarte vertröstung überschreiben lassen werden.

4.

Er begerte zwar auch als er hier war, das seine besoldung alhier also baldt angehen möchte, wann seine bestallung in dennenmarck ausgehen würde, da es aber Ihrer churfl durchl. belieben [*würde* crossed out] thete, wolte Ich Ihm derogestalt zu schreiben das zu seiner anherokunfft [*Er* crossed out] am stadt der Reisekosten vndt ohne abgang seiner besoldung, Er 100 Thlr haben, vndt alsdann seine bestal-lung anfahen solte [flourish] Alles aber zu Ihrer churfl. durch. gdste bereiffung v. erklerung anheimb gegeben.

Henrich Schütz Mpp

[fol. 245v]
[Flourish] Churfl. durchl. zu Sachsen wolverordneten geheimbden Herrn Cammersecretario H. Christian Reichbrohdt zu grosgönstigen handen [closing flourish]

1: Translation

Schütz to Christian Reichbrodt.
Dresden, 21 September 1647

[SAD Loc. 8687. *Kantoreiordnung*, fols. 244–45]

[fol. 244r]
Dresden on the twenty-first day of the month of September, 1647.
Most humble memorandum
That which seems to be somewhat necessary to remind our most gracious elector and lord regarding the Italian musician Augusto Fontana:

1.

To give His Electoral Highness a most humble report, the aforementioned Italian (even though he now has a dependable salary of 500 Reichstalers from the king of Denmark, and has also been offered by the duke of Gottorp, along with the position of Kapellmeister, the same yearly salary and the building of a new house as well) is still most eager to enter most humbly into your service and employ, according to his written agreement, and he shall spend the rest of his entire life in this electoral household.

2.

Regarding his yearly salary, before his departure and after the conversation I had with him, he declared himself to be satisfied with 400 talers, which then (indeed subject to correction) was granted to him most graciously by our most gracious lord, and his written contract could be arranged in such a manner that he shall receive yearly 300 talers as a vice-Kapellmeister (*nota bene* toward which office he especially strives) and beyond this another 100 talers for teaching and rehearsing not only the discantists but the other group of all of the singers or vocalists and [this amount] should be raised 100 talers.

3.

Furthermore he has asked me diligently both verbally while he was here and now in writing to recommend humbly to our most gracious elector and lord (because from such a regular salary as his he could save little or [scarcely] prosper) that he would like to receive the aforementioned His Electoral Highness's most gracious pledge regarding an extra sum for the purchase of a house.

Since this is what is absolutely necessary for the accommodation of this foreigner, I thus hope that His Electoral Highness does not lack the means and shall therefore permit me to convey to him most gracious and tender consolation on this small point as well.

4.

When he was here, he did in fact request in addition that his salary here might begin as soon as his salary in Denmark ceases. If His Electoral Highness prefers, I shall write to him that upon his arrival, instead of the travel costs and without deduction from his salary, he shall be given 100 talers and then his salary shall begin. All however submitted for His Electoral Highness's most gracious inspection and clarification.

Heinrich Schütz
In his own hand

[fol. 245v]
To the benevolent hands of Lord Christian Reichbrodt, most illustrious Lord and Privy Chamber Secretary to His Electoral Highness of Saxony.

2

Schütz to Johann Georg I.
Dresden, 14 January 1651

[SAD Loc. 8687. *Kantoreiordnung*, fols. 291–94]

[fol. 291r]
Durchlauchtigster Hochgeborner Churfürst
    Gnädigster Herr,
Mit gegenwertiger vnterthänigster überreichung, meines vnter E.
churfl. durchl. hohen Namen, Itzo an den tag kommenden Werckleins
werde ich zugleich veranlasset, meinen von Jugend auff bishero
geführten fast mühseeligen lebenslauff, in etwas mit zu berüren, In
tieffer Devotion bittende, E. churfl. durchl. mir solches zu gnaden halten, von und zu dero beliebigen gelegenheit, zu vernemen Ihr nicht
entgegen wolle sein lassen, Nemblichen: Wie das (:nachdem Ich Ao etc.
1585. am tage Burckhardi auff diese Weld gebohren worden binn:)
nicht gar lange hernacher, Sondern so bald im dreyzehenden Jahre
meines alters, aus meiner Seeligen Eltern hause zu Weissenfels Ich
gekommen binn, auch von selbiger Zeit an, mich allezeit in der frembde
auffgehalten, vnd anfenglich zwar in Herrn landgraff Moritzens etc.
Hoffcapell zu Cassel etliche jahr für einen Capellknaben mit auffgewartet habe, nebenst der Music aber zur Schulen, und erlernung der
Lateinischen undt anderer sprachen zugleich gehalten undt erzogen
worden binn,   Vndt dieweil meiner Seeligen Eltern wille niemahls
war, das heute oder morgen, Ich gar Profession von der Music machen
solte, habe auff dero gutachten (:in gesellschafft eines meines andern
Bruders, der hernacher ein Doctor Juris worden, und vor wenig Jahren
zu Leibzigk im Oberhoffgerichte, und in E. churfl. durchl. bestallung
verstorben ist:) Ich mich, nach dem Ich meine Discantstimme verlohren,
auff die Universitet Marpurgk begeben, In willens meine, ausser der
Music, anderweit zimlicher massen angefangene Studia daselbst fortzu-
stellen, Eine gewisse Profession mir zu erwehlen, und dermahl eins

einen Ehrlichen Gradum darinnen zu erlangen, Es wurde aber solcher
mein fürsatz (:sonder zweiffel aus schickung Gottes:) mir baldt
verrücket, In dem, nemblich, Herr landgraff Moritz einsten nacher
Marpurgk kam, (:welcher die zeit über, als an Seinem hoffe Ich für
einen Capellknaben mich gebrauchen lassen, vieleicht vermercket haben mochte, ob zu der Music Ich von Natur in etwas geschickt were:)
vnd nachfolgenden vorschlag mir thun lies: weil dero zeit in Italia, zwar
ein hochberümbter, aber doch zimlich alter Musicus undt Componist
noch am leben were, So solte Ich nicht verabseumen, denselbigen auch
zu hören, vndt etwas von ihm zu ergreiffen, vndt liessen hochgedachte
Ihr ft. Gnaden, zu volle streckung solcher Reise, mir zugleich Ein Sti-
pendium von 200 thlrn Jährlichen anpraesentiren, welchen vorschlag
dann (:als ein Junger, und die Weld zu durchsehen auch begieriger
mensch:) Ich zu unterthänigen danck, gantz willigst annam, vnd darauff
Ao etc. 1609. gleichsamb wieder meiner Eltern Willen, nacher Venedig
fortzoge, ob nun zwar zu meiner anhinkunfft (:nach dem bey meinem
lehrherrn Ich mich in etwas weniges aufgehalten:) Ich die wichtigkeit
vndt Schwere des mir fürgenommenen Studii der Composition, und das
hierinnen ich noch einen vngegründeten schlechten anfang hette, bald
vermerket, vndt dahero mich fast sehr gerewet gehabt, das von denen
auff den Teutschen Universi [fol. 291v] teten gebreuchlichen, und von
mir albereit zimlich weit gebrachten Studiis Ich mich abgewendet, Habe
ich mich doch nichts desto minder zur gedult, bequemen, und demjenigen, worumb Ich dahin gekommen war, obliegen müssen, derowegen
auch von solcher zeit an, alle meine vorigen Studia ausser handen ge-
legt, und das Studium Musices alleine mit allem möglichsten grösten
fleis zu tractiren, und zu versuchen wie solches mir von statten gehen
wollen, angefangen, da ichs dann mit gottlicher hülffe, sonder ruhm so
weit gebracht habe, das nach dreyen Jahren (:undt ein jahr zuvohr ehe
Ich aus Italia wieder zurücke gereiset:) Ich mein Erstes musicalisches
wercklein, in Italianischer sprache, mit sonderbahren lobe, der damahls
fürnembsten Musicorum zu Venedig, daselbste [*habe* crossed out]
drücken lassen, vnd von daraus herrn landgraff Moritzen (:deme Ichs
auch zu unterthäniger dancksagung Dedicirt) zugeschickt habe, Nach
welcher publicirung Itzo gedachtes meines Ersten werckleins, Ich nicht
alleine von meinem Praeceptor, dem Johann Gabriel, Sondern auch von
dem Capellmeister vndt andern fürnembsten Musicis daselbst ver-
mahnet und angefrischet worden binn, das bey dem Studio Musices Ich
verharren, und alles glücklichen successes hierinnen mich zu getrösten
haben solte,   Vnd als Ich nach diesem mich noch Ein jahr (:wiewol
auff meiner Eltern unkosten:) auffhielte, noch etwas mehres in solchem
Studio zu erfahren, Begab sichs eben, das oberwehnter mein Praecep-

tor, zu Venedig verstarbe, dem Ich auch das gleite zu seinem Ruhbette gegeben, Er mir auch auff seinem thodbette, aus sonderbahrer affection, einen aus seinen hinterbliebenen Ringen zu seinem gueten andencken verordnet gehabt, welcher mir von seinem Beichtvater Einem Augustiner Mönch, (:aus dem kloster da D. Luther sich für diesen auch einsten auffgehalten:) nach seinem erfolgten thodesfall, auch praesentirt und zugestalt worden ist, das also vorhergedachte, H. landtgraff Moritzens, zu Marpurgk gehabte beysorge, war worden, [*vndt* crossed out] das wer von diesem gewislich sehr hochbegabten Manne Etwas hette lernen wollen, nicht lenger als Ich ausbleiben dürffen,

Als Ich nun Ao etc. 1613. das Erste mahl aus Italia wieder zu rücke nach Teutschlandt gelangete, beschlos Ich zwar bey mir, mit meinen in der Music numehr gelegten gueten fundamenten, noch etliche jahr zu rücke, und mit denenselbigen mich gleichsamb verborgen zu halten, bis Ich dieselbigen noch etwas weiter Excolieret haben, vndt hierauff mit auslassung einer würdigen arbeit, mich würde herfür than können,   Vndt ermangelte damahls auch an meiner Eltern vndt anverwandten Raht und antrieb noch nicht, welcher meinung kurtz ümb war, das durch anderweit meine zwar geringe Qvaliteten, Ich mich bedient zu machen und förderung zu erlangen trachten, [*soll* crossed out] die Music aber als eine nebensache tractiren solte, von derer wiederholten unnachläslichen Vermahnung dann folge zuleisten, Ich entlichen überredet wurde, vndt meine vorhin ausser handen gelegte Bücher wieder hervor zu suchen, gleich begriffen war,   Es schickte es aber Gott der almechtige [fol. 292r] (:der mich sonder zweiffell zu der Profession der Music von Mutterleibe an abgesondert gehabt:) auch also, das Ao etc. 1614 (:weis nicht ob vieleicht durch herrn Christoff von Loos, damals geheimbden Rahts, oder des Cammerrahts Wolffersdorffs, auch Heubtmans zu Weissenfels angeben,:) Ich anhero nacher Dresden zur auffwartung, bey deme damals bevorstehenden fürstl. kindteuffen, Herrn Hertzogen Augusti, Itzigen Administratoris des Ertzstiffts Magdeburgk, beschrieben, und nach meiner erfolgten anhero kunfft, undt abgelegten Prob, In E. churfl. durchl. namen das Directorium über dero Music, mir alsbaldt gnedigst angeboten wurde, woraus dann meine Eltern undt anverwandten nebenst mir, den unwandelbahren Willen Gottes mit meiner Person, augenscheinlich verspüret, und hierdurch meinen umbschweiffenden gedancken, ein ziel gestecket, und Ich veranlasset worden binn, die mir angetragene Ehrliche condition nicht abzuschlagen, sondern mit unterthänigsten dancksagung anzunemen, undt demselbigen nach meinem besten fleis vorzustehen, anzugeloben,

Was nun de Ao etc. 1615 an (:im welchem jahr in hiesische Bestallung

Ich persönlich angetreten binn, und als lange Es Gott und E. churfl.
durchl. gefallen wirdt mich ferner darinnen enthalten werde:) vndt also
uber 35 Jahr lang, bishero, meine zwar geringschätzige, doch nicht sonder mühe abgelegte verrichtungen gewesen sindt, werden E. churfl.
durchl. verhoffentlich, sich noch etlicher massen erindern können,
     Vndt mag Ich die (:solche lange Zeit über:) von Gott mir ver-
liehene wolthat und gnade, so weit wol rühmen, das nebenst meinem
Studio Privato, undt auslassung unterschiedlicher Musicalischer
Wercke, E. churfl. durchl. bey inzwischen fürgegangenen allerhandt
vielen Solenniteten, Als kayserlichen, königl. Chur- und fürstlichen
zusammenkunfften, inn und ausser landes, Insonderheit aber auch
deroselbigen churfurstl. geliebten kindern ausstattungen sambt und
sonders, nichts minder auch bey entpfahung Ihre christlichen Tauffe
(:keines ausgenommen, als die Itzige fraw landgräffin zu darmstadt,
vndt herrn hertzogen Johann Georgen Churprintzen,:) Ich aller unterthänigst auffgewartet, vom anfange meines Directorii E. churfl. durchl.
hoff Capell [fol. 292v] auch, fur andern in Teutschlandt berümbt zu
machen mich allezeit bester massen beflissen, dero lob und ruhm verhoffentlich auch bis auff diese stunde, zimlicher massen habe erhalten
helffen,   Nun möchte ich zwar hertzlich gerne wunschen, das auff
bishero von mir gepflogene weise Eurer churfl. durchl. hoffCapell, hinfuro auch von mir vorgestanden werden könte, demnach aber nicht
alleine wegen meines, sonder ruhm von jugendt auff obgelegen Stetigen
Studirens, Reisens, [*undt* crossed out] schreibens, und anderer
continuirlicher arbeit, (:deren meine Schwere Profession undt Ambt,
ohnümbgänglich benötiget gewesen ist, von dero difficultet und
Schwere, dann, meines erachtens, die wenigsten, ja auch unsere geler-
then zum gueten theill selbst, nicht eigentlich möchten vrtheilen
können, alldieweil auff unsern Teutschen Universiteten solch Studium
nicht getrieben wirdt:) Sondern auch wegen meines numehr herange-
kommenen hohen alters, abgenommen gesichts, undt aller lebens
Kräffte, dieselbige geburlich mehr zu bedienen, auch den in meinen
Jungen jahren etlicher massen erlangeten gueten namen, bey Itzigen
meinem alter zu behaubten, Ich mir keines weges getrauen, noch mich
unterfangen kann, Im fall ich auch meine gesundheit ehistes nicht in
gefahr stellen, und gar zu boden stürtzen will, [*mich* crossed out] des
Stetigen Studierens, schreibens und nachsinnens, der Medicorum Raht
nach, mich numehr so viel mir möglich, enthalten und entbrechen mus,
So werde dahero, E. churfl. durchl. zu dero gndsten behertzigung solches hirbey mit geburlichen bescheidenheit zu hinterbringen, vndt
daneben in vnterthanigster Devotion anzulangen Ich ohnümbgäntzlich
genotiget, Sie geruhen Gnädigst, (:nicht alleine umb Itzo von mir

angezogener ursachen willen, Sondern auch im betrachtung, des Eurer churfl. durchl. liebste churfurstliche kinder, numehr ingesambt ausgestattet seint:) mich hinfuro auch in einen etwas geruhigeren zustandt zu versetzen, vndt (:damit Ich meine anderweit in meiner Jugendt angefangene Musicalische Wercke colligiren, [*und* crossed out] Completieren, undt zu meinem andencken auch in den druck geben könne:) von der ordentlichen auffwartung mich zu befreyen, vnd auff eine Eurer churfl. durchl. selbst beliebende masse, gleichsamb fur einen Provisioner halten undt erkleren zu lassen, Auff welchen fall Ich es auch geschehen lassen müste [fol. 293r] wann E. churfl. durchl. meine Itzige besoldung vieleicht in etwas zu moderiren, Ihr gndgst belieben lassen würde,   Jedoch binn ich so erbötig als schuldig, (:wo fern E. churfl. durchl. von dero Capell mich nicht gerne abkommen lassen, auch noch zur zeit keinen andern Capellmeister annemen, Sondern mit meiner geringen auffwartung, welche Ich, bey meinem teglich mehr abnemenden Kräfften [*gnädigsten zufrieden* crossed out] werde darstellen können, weiter zufrieden sein wollen:) ferner dabey zu verharren, alle mögliche handreichung zu thun, und mich zu befleissigen, den Tittels Eines (:E. churfl. durchl. und dero hohen hausses:) weiter zu verdienen, vndt mit mir verhoffentlich entlich in mein grab mit zu nemen, wann hinfuro nur (:demnach zumahl auch alle diejenigen alten Musicanten, mit welchen Ich für 35 Jahren mein Directorium erstlich angefangen habe, numehr alle verstorben, die übrigen sehr wenigen aber, leibesbeschwerung und alters halben, zu weiterer auffwartung, nicht sonderlich mehr geschickt seint:) Eine andere, zu erleichterung meiner arbeit qvalificirte Person mir zugeordnet werden möchte, welche, mit denen in der churfürstl. Capell Itzo auffkommenden Jungen leuten, teglich umbgienge, das nohtwendige Exercitium fortstellete, mehrmahls auch die Music anorden und vnter Ihnen den Tact geben thete,   Sintemahl bey meinem hirnechst noch weiter abnemenden Kräfften, (:wann mich Gott noch lenger leben lassen solte:) es vieleicht geschehen undt mir auch ergehen möchte (:E. churfl. durchl. verzeyhen mir gndgst das Ich dieses mit anführe:) wie einem, an einem Namhafften ort wohnenden mir wol bekandten, nicht übel qvalificirten Alten Cantor, welcher für etlicher zeit an mich geschrieben vnd mir höchlich geklagt hatt, das seine junge Rathsherren, mit seiner alten Manier der Music, sehr übell zufrieden, und dahero seiner sehr gerne loos weren, Ihme dahero ausdrücklich auff dem Rahthausse ins angesicht gesagt hetten, Ein dreÿsig jähriger Schneider, vnd drÿsig jähriger Cantor dieneten nicht mehr in die welt, wie es denn auch nicht ohne ist, das die Junge weldt der alten sitten und Manier bald pfleget [*zu* crossed out] überdrüssig zu werden und zu endern, vndt ob ich wol deren keines, von E. churfl. durchl. Herrn Söhnen, (:als meinen in allen gnaden mir wolzugethanen gnädigen herren:) vermutens binn, So könte mir doch derogleichen von andern, auch wol von etlichen new ankommenden Jungen Musicanten selbst wiederfahren, welche mit hindansetzung der alten, gemeiniglich [*die* crossed out] Ihre newe Manier wie wol mit schlechten grunde pflegen hirvor zu ziehen, [fol. 293v] Vndt demnach Herrn Hertzogen Johan Georgens churprintzens Italianische Eunuchus, Andrea Buontempi, Sich vielmals verlauten hatt lassen, das insonderheit auch von jugendt auff Er der Composition, noch mehr als des Singens beflissen gewesen were, Sich auch aus eigener bewegung gegen mich erbothen, das auff mein begeren Er iedesmahl gerne fur mich auffwarten vnd die Music dirigiren wolte, Als habe zum beschlus dieses meines schreibens E. churfl. durchl. solches auch entdecken, vndt hiruber Ihre Gnadigste meinung [*auch* crossed out] einholen wollen, Ob nemblich mit dero gndgsten Consens, Ich gedachtes Andrea Buontempi, anerbieten, annemen, und denselbigen an meiner stelle die Music mehrmahls Dirigiren lassen [*kö* crossed out] möge? Welches dann meinem geringen verstande nach, E. churfl. durchl. (:doch ohne einige maasgebung:) desto ehe geschehen lassen, und gleichsamb zur probe Eine zeitlang mit ansehen und anhören könten, Aldieweil für solche seine auffwartung Einige erhöhung seiner Besoldung oder verenderung seines Tittels nicht begeret, Sondern mit seines gndgsten Herrens des churprintzens Ihme angeordneten verpflegung, einen wegk wie dem andern content zu sein, erbötig Ist So ist dieser junge mensch auch, zu solcher verrichtung fast wol qvalificirt, habe auch von venedig [strikeout] (:alda Er sich in die 8 Jahr lang auffgehalten hatt:) genungsame nachrichtung erlanget, das bey etlichen celebrirten festagen daselbst, Er mehrmahls an Capellmeisters stadt die Music in ihren kirchen öffentlich Dirigiret hatt, das dahero an seinen Qvaliteten desto minder zu zweiffell, wie er dann sonst auch in seinen andern proceduren, Ein discreter höfflicher, undt verträglicher feiner junge mensch bishero scheinet. Was nun E. churfl. durchl. gndgster wille in dieser sache sein werde, Bitte Ich umb eine gndgste nachrichtung, Sintemahl ohne E. Churfl. durchl. vorwissen, mir nicht geburen will, solcher Person dienstes, mich continuirlich zu gebrauchen,   Entpfele hirauff dieselbige, dem Starken schutz des aller höchsten, zu langwüriger, volständiger gueter leibes gesundheit, langen leben, [*und* crossed out] glückseeliger Regierung vndt aller anderer am Seel und leibe selbst gewünschten wolergehen [fol. 294r] trewlich, mich aber zu beharlichen churfl. Gnaden unterthänigst undt gehorsamblich. Datum Dresden am 14 Monatstag Januarii. Anno Christi vnsers Einigen Erlösers und Seeligmachers, 1651.

E. Churfl. durchl
vnterthänigster pflichtschuldigster
alter diener
Henrich Schütz
Capellmeister Mpp

[fol. 294v]
Unterthanigst Memorial An den durchleuchtigsten etc. Churfürsten zu
Sachsen, Burggraffen zu Magdeburgk etc. Meinem gndgsten Herren,

2: Translation

Schütz to Johann Georg I.
Dresden, 14 January 1651

[SAD Loc. 8687. *Kantoreiordnung*, fols. 291–94]

[fol. 291r]
Most Illustrious, Noble Elector,
    Most Gracious Lord,
    With the present most humble offering of my little work which has just appeared under Your Electoral Highness's exalted name, I am at the same time moved to touch somewhat briefly on the course of my rather troubled life from youth to the present, begging in deep devotion that Your Electoral Highness receive it graciously and, if you are not opposed, to examine it at your leisure. Namely: that (after I was born into this world on St. Burkhard's Day, 1585) not very long thereafter but as early as my thirteenth year of age, I left my late parents' house in Weissenfels, and from that time on always lived abroad, and at first in fact I served as a choirboy for several years in the court ensemble of my lord the Landgrave Moritz in Cassel, but I both lived and was educated in school, and learned Latin and other languages in addition to music.
    And as it was never my late parents' wish that I should now or ever make a profession of music, after I lost my soprano voice, on their advice I betook myself to the University of Marburg (in the company of my second brother, who thereafter became a Doctor of Law and who died a few years ago in Leipzig as a member of the Supreme Court of the Judicature and in Your Electoral Highness's employ). There I intended to pursue the studies I had extensively undertaken elsewhere outside of music to choose a reliable profession and therein attain an honorable station. However, my plan was soon altered for me (undoubtedly by the will of God), namely in that my lord the Landgrave Moritz came to Marburg one day (who may perhaps have observed at the time

when I was allowed to serve as a choirboy at his court that in some respects I was musically gifted by nature) and made me the following proposal: Because at that time a truly celebrated but quite old musician and composer was still living in Italy, I should not miss the opportunity to hear him and to learn something from him, and the aforementioned His noble Grace generously offered me at the time a stipend of 200 talers yearly to carry out such a journey, which proposal I thereupon accepted most willingly with humble thanks (as a youth eager to see the world), and in 1609 departed for Venice, contrary, however, to my parents' wishes. Upon my arrival (after I had spent a little time with my master), I soon realized the importance and difficulty of the study of composition which I had undertaken and what an unfounded and poor beginning I had made in it so far, and therefore I regretted very much having turned away from those studies which were customary at German universities [fol. 291v] and in which I had already become rather advanced. I nonetheless patiently submitted and had to apply myself to that which had brought me there. So from that time on, all my previous studies laid aside, I began to deal only with the study of music with the greatest of all possible diligence to see how I would succeed. Then, with divine help, I progressed so far, without boasting, that after three years (and one year before I returned from Italy) I had published there my first little musical work in the Italian language, with superior praise from the most distinguished musicians then in Venice, whence I sent it to my lord the Landgrave Moritz (to whom I dedicated it with humble acknowledgment). After the publication of my first little work, mentioned above, I was urged and encouraged not only by my teacher, Giovanni Gabrieli, but also by the Kapellmeister and other distinguished musicians there that I should persist in the study of music and that I should anticipate every auspicious success therein.

And after I remained there another year (although at the expense of my parents) to learn yet something further from my studies, it happened that my aforementioned teacher died in Venice, whom I also accompanied to his final resting place. On his deathbed, he also bequeathed to me out of special affection, in his blessed memory, one of his rings he left behind which was presented and delivered after his death by his father confessor, an Augustinian monk (from the cloister where Dr. Luther once stayed). Thus the aforesaid premonition of my lord the Landgrave Moritz in Marburg proved true, that whoever wished to learn something from this certainly very highly talented man need remain absent no longer than I.

When I then returned to Germany from Italy for the first time in 1613, I indeed resolved to keep to myself my musical foundations, by now well established for some years, and to keep them hidden until I had developed them somewhat further and thereupon could distinguish myself with the publication of a worthy piece of work. And also at that time, I was not lacking advice and incentive from my parents and relatives, whose opinion was, in short, that I should make use of my other truly modest abilities and strive for advancement, and should treat music, however, as an avocation. As a result of their repeated unremitting admonition, I was finally persuaded and was about to seek out my books which I had previously laid aside when God Almighty [fol. 292r] (who no doubt had singled me out in the womb for the profession of music) ordained that in 1614 I be called to service in Dresden for the then impending royal christening of my lord the Duke August, now administrator of the archbishopric of Magdeburg (I do not know whether perhaps through the advice of Christoph von Loss, then privy councillor, or of Chamber Counselor Wolffersdorff, also designated commander of Weissenfels). After my arrival and passing an audition, the directorship of your music was soon thereafter graciously offered to me in Your Electoral Highness's name, from which then my parents and relatives as well as I obviously perceived the immutable will of God regarding my person, and hereby a goal was set for my vacillating plans, and I was persuaded not to refuse the honored position offered me, but to accept with humble thanks and to vow to fulfill it with my best efforts.

I hope Your Electoral Highness will to some extent remember my truly insignificant duties, indeed performed not without difficulty since the year 1615 (the year in which I personally assumed this post, and, as long as it pleases God and Your Electoral Highness, I shall hold in the future) until now, and thus over thirty-five years.

And if I may go so far as to praise the charity and favor granted to me by God (over such a long time), along with my private studies and the publication of various works, I have most humbly served Your Electoral Highness at many past diverse festivities which occured during this time, at imperial, royal, electoral, and princely gatherings, in this country and abroad, but particularly at each and every one of your own royal children's weddings, not less, too, at the receiving of their sacred christenings (except for my lady, now the Landgravine of Darmstadt, and my lord the Duke Johann Georg, the elector apparent). From the beginning of my directorship of Your Electoral Highness's court ensemble, [fol. 292v] I have also always endeavored to spread its fame above all others in Germany to the best of my ability, and, I hope, have always devoted myself to help uphold its praise and fame in some measure even up to the present.

Now I would indeed gladly and sincerely hope that the course of

Your Electoral Highness's court ensemble which I have tended up until now could be directed by me in the future; however, not only due to my ceaseless study, travel, writing, and other constant work, which has been, without boasting, continuous since my youth (which my arduous profession and position unavoidably require, the smallest difficulties and hardships of which, then, in my opinion, even our own scholars themselves are in fact unable to judge, because at our German universities such studies are not pursued) but also due to my now advancing old age, diminishing eyesight, and spent vitality, I am now unable to serve it suitably any longer, nor uphold my good name, which I gained to some extent in my youth. I in no way dare continue, nor can I attempt, unless I want to endanger my health and collapse ere long, the constant studying, writing, and contemplation, [from which,] according to the physician's advice, I must henceforth refrain and forbear as much as possible. Therefore, Your Electoral Highness, I hereby submit this for your gracious consideration with due humility, and moreover in most humble devotion I respectfully entreat you, may it please Your Grace (not only because of the reasons I have already cited, but also in consideration of the fact that Your Electoral Highness's most beloved royal children are now all married) to remove me in future to a somewhat calmer situation, and (in order that I might again collect and complete my musical works, begun in my youth, and have them published in my memory) to free me from steady service, and to the extent that pleases Your Electoral Highness, to have me recognized and declared, as it were, a pensioner, in which case I must perhaps accept the situation [fol. 293r] if Your Electoral Highness were to modify somewhat my present wages, if it please Your Grace.

Nevertheless, I am as willing as I am indebted (in that Your Electoral Highness is unwilling to spare me from your chapel and to employ another Kapellmeister at this time, but will continue to be satisfied with the poor service which I will be able to offer in my daily waning strength), yet to persevere in being of all possible aid and to devote myself further to serving the title of [Kapellmeister] (of Your Electoral Highness's honored house) and I would hope finally to take [that title] with me to my grave, only if in future (especially since all those old musicians with whom I first began my directorship thirty-five years ago are now all dead and the very few remaining, owing to physical infirmity and old age, are not particularly suited to further service) another qualified person may be allied with me to relieve me in my work, who could daily manage the young people now thriving in the electoral ensemble, continuing the necessary rehearsals, frequently organize the music, and conduct.

Whereas with the imminent waning of my strength yet further (if God should allow me to live still longer) it is perhaps possible that I will experience (if Your Electoral Highness will graciously pardon me for bringing this up) what has happened to one not poorly qualified old cantor, who lives in a noteworthy place and whom I know well, who for some time has written to me and complained bitterly that his young town councillors are quite dissatisfied with his old-fashioned music and therefore would like very much to be rid of him, saying intentionally to his face in the town hall that a tailor of thirty years and a cantor of thirty years are of no use to anyone. And although I am certain that the fact that the young world soon becomes weary of the old customs and ways and changes them is not without its advantages, and though to be sure I anticipate none of this from my lords the sons of Your Electoral Highness (as my gracious lords have treated me kindly), I could encounter it from some other newly arrived young musicians who, with the rejection of the old, usually give preference to all of their new ways, although for poor reasons.

[fol. 293v] And since my lord the Duke Johann Georg the elector apparent's Italian eunuch, [Giovanni] Andrea Bontempi, has many times made it known that especially since his youth he has been more devoted to composition than to singing and he has volunteered out of his own free will that at my request he would always willingly serve in my place and direct the ensemble, I therefore wish at the conclusion of this writing of mine to Your Electoral Highness to discover and moreover to learn your most gracious opinion in this matter: Namely, whether I may, with your most gracious consent, offer and employ the aforementioned Andrea Bontempi and allow him frequently to direct the ensemble in my place? This, in my modest judgment, Your Electoral Highness (indeed subject to correction) should allow immediately, and could observe and listen awhile for a trial period, so to speak, since he does not seek a salary increase or a change of title for his service, but is willing to be as content one way as the other with the support ordered by his most gracious lord the elector apparent. This young man is thus willing and very well qualified for such work. He has also acquired satisfactory recommendations in Venice (he remained there for eight years) where for several holiday celebrations he often took the Kapellmeister's place in publicly directing the music in their churches. Therefore there is little to doubt regarding his qualifications; besides, he seems then to be, in his other transactions, a discrete, polite, goodnatured, fine young man. Regarding Your Electoral Highness's most gracious will in this matter, I request a most gracious report, since without Your Electoral Highness's prior knowledge, it would not be proper for me to make constant use of the services of such a person.

Commending you hereupon to the powerful protection of the Almighty for prolonged [and] complete bodily health, long life, blissful reign, and your every other hope for the well-being of body and soul, [fol. 294r] while [commending] myself to the constant electoral grace most humbly and obediently. Dated Dresden on the fourteenth day of January. In the year of Christ our only Redeemer and Savior, 1651.

> Your Electoral Highness's most
> humble duty-bound old servant
> Heinrich Schütz
> Kapellmeister
> In his own hand

[fol. 294v]

Most humble memorial to the most illustrious Elector of Saxony, Burgrave of Magdeburg, etc. my most gracious Lord.

3

Schütz to Heinrich Taube, Jacob Weller, and Christian Reichbrodt.
Dresden, 21 August 1653

[SAD Loc. 8687. *Kantoreiordnung,* fol. 327]

[fol. 327r]

Hochgeehrte Patronen

Was bey herrn Hertzogen Johann Georgen, Unser Gndgn Churprintzen zu nothwendiger Rettung einer mir Unverdienter Weise
[strikeout] beÿ gemessen Beschuldigung, ich unterthnst eingeben
müssen, geruhen dieselbigen zu dero gelegenheit, aus dieser bey kommenen abschrifft ohnbeschwert grosgönstig zu vernemen. Undt
demnach ich die beÿsorge haben mus, das derogleichen ungegründete
Zeitung von mir entlich wol gar zu unsers Gndgsten Churfursten vnd
Herrn ohren gelangen möchten, Als ist an meine hochgeehrte Herrn
mein gantz unterdinstliches bitten, das auf begebenden solchen fall, Sie
in dieser gerechten sache mir so weit nur beÿstehen und beÿ unserm
gndgsten Herrn es dahinn unterthngst vermitteln helffen wollen, das
ich zu mündlicher oder schrifftlicher meiner Verandtwortung ferner
auch zu gelassen werden möge.

Belangende sonst die von hochgedachten churprintzen gemachte
anordnung ümb Sontägliche abwexlung der Music in der Schloskirchen,
So kann meinen hochgeehrten herren deswegen Ich auch nicht bergen,
was massen es mir, als gleichwol einen alten undt verhoffentlich nicht
unverdienten mann, fast verkleinerlich und schmertzlich furfallen will,
an solchen Sontagen (:an welchen hiebevor zu H. D. Hoen Zeiten, nicht
mir sonder dem Vice capelmeister das Directorium obgelegen ist:) ich
mit des Herrn Churprintzens Directore als einen 3 mahl jüngern [*menschen* crossed out] als ich, undt hirüber Castrirten menschen, ordentlich
und stetig ümbwexeln [*soll* crossed out] und unter, ungleichen undt zum

gueten theil unverständigen zuhörer und Richter urtheil mit ihm gleichsamb pro loco disputiren soll. Dahero ich dann verhoffentlich auch nicht ohnbillig ümb ein gndgsts Privilegium mich zu bewerben habe, das dem vice capelmeister auf selbige zeit, das Directorium von mir auf getragen werden möge, vndt zwar so würde wol der music halben in der churfl. Schloskirchen kein sonderlicher mangel iemals zu verspüren sein, wann nur die Musicanten, und bevorab die churfürstl. (:deren companey ohne des gar gering, und deren etliche, wegen ermangelnden Verpflegung alhier, sich fast stets anderswo aufhalten:) mit bezahlung ihrer besoldungen zur stetigen aufwartung verbunden werden möchten, In Verbleibung welcher dann Ich für meine Person selbst auch hirmit protestiret haben will, das nachdem Ich numehr alles, bis auf das bluth aus dem adern gleichsamb theils zugesetzt, theils unter etliche nohtleidende Musicanten verstreket habe, mir lenger alhier in Dresden zu dauern gantz vnmöglich fallen wirdt, wor von in specie dieses orts Ich itzo nichts melden, Sondern dieses nur bezeuget haben will, das lieber den thodt als lenger so thanen bedrengten zustandt beyzuwohnen, Ich mir wunschen wolte.

Meiner hochgeehrten Patronen
dinstschuldiger
Henrich Schütz Mpp

Signatum Dresden am 21 Augusti Ao etc. 1653
[fol. 327v]
Churfl. durchl. zu Sachsen wol verordneten herrn Oberhoffmarschalle etc. Herrn Henrich von Taube. Wie auch dero selbigen wolbestalten herrn Beichtvatern, kirchen Raht vndt Oberhoffpredigern Herrn Doctor Jacobi Weller. Dan auch Herrn Christian Reichbrohdt Hochgedachter Churfl. Durchl. fürnemen Raht, und Geheimbden Secretario Meinem grosgönstigen hochgeehrter Patronen in Dresden.

3: Translation

Schütz to Heinrich Taube, Jacob Weller, and Christian Reichbrodt. Dresden, 21 August 1653

[SAD Loc. 8687. *Kantoreiordnung*, fol. 327]

[fol. 327r]
Most Venerable Patrons,
    May it please you to look most favorably upon the enclosed copy unencumbered at your leisure. I must present the unjust manner in which formal duty has been imposed on me by my lord the Duke Johann Georg, our gracious elector apparent, from which I require deliverance. And because I fear that this unfounded news about me quite surely will ultimately reach the ears of our most gracious elector and lord, it is my most humble request to my honorable lords that in such a case they would only stand beside me in this rightful matter so far and help intercede humbly in this with our most gracious lord so that later I might also be allowed a verbal or written response.
    As for the command made by the aforementioned elector apparent regarding the alternation of the music in the palace church on Sundays, I can not disguise from my most honorable lords to what extent it would be demeaning and painful to me as an old as well as, I hope, not undeserving man, on those Sundays (on which previously, in Dr. Hoe's day, the direction was not my responsibility but that of the vice-Kapellmeister) to alternate regularly and continuously with my lord the elector apparent's director [Giovanni Andrea Bontempi], a man three times younger than I and castrated to boot, and to compete with him for favor, pro loco, as it were, before biased and for the most part injudicious audiences and judges. Therefore I hope to obtain, I hope not unreasonably, a most gracious privilege in which the directorship shall be conferred by me upon the vice-Kapellmeister at that time, and indeed no

particular deficiency would ever be perceptible in the music of the palace church if only the musicians were to receive the payment of their salaries for continuous service, and above all those of the elector (of whose company some scarcely sustain themselves, and others, because of the lack of provisioning here, almost constantly live elsewhere). In conclusion, I wish to protest in my own person, now that everything I have unto the very blood in my veins has in part been sacrificed and in part spread among a few suffering musicians, it will be altogether impossible for me to continue in Dresden any longer. I wish now to report nothing in particular about this place but only to certify that I prefer death to living any longer in such oppressive conditions.

My most venerable patrons'
everwilling
Heinrich Schütz

Signed Dresden 21 August 1653
[fol. 327v]
His Electoral Highness of Saxony's highly ordained Oberhofmarschall, my lord Heinrich von Taube, as well as the same highly appointed lord and spiritual leader, member of the consistory, and senior court preacher, my lord Dr. Jacob Weller, and also my lord Christian Reichbrodt, nobly born advisor and privy secretary to the aforementioned His Serene Highness. My most favorable venerable patrons in Dresden.

4

Schütz to Johann Georg II.
23 August 1653

[SAD Loc. 8687. *Kantoreiordnung,* fols. 328–29]

[fol. 328r. Not in Schütz's hand]
Durchlauchtigster Hochgeborner ChurPrintz,
  Gnadigster Herr,
Eur Churprintzl. Durchl. kan ich keinen vmbgang haben mit gegenwertigen meinem Vnterthstn Memorial Klagendte zu berichten, was maßen ich täglich ie mehr vndt mehr in erfahrung komme, wie das (:wegen E. Durchl. aus Italia anhero beschriebenen, vndt in die Churfl. HoffCapell eingeführten Musicanten:) von allerhandt Geistlichen vndt weltlichen Persohnen, nicht alleine vnterschiedliche wiederwertige Vrtheil gefallen, Sondern ich darneben innsonderheit mit meiner grösten befrembdung, vernemen mus, das für des Vhrheber vndt Rathgeber zu dieser Neüerung ich gehalten vndt beredet werden will, wordurch ich mich dann, leider albereit in vieler fürnemer Leüte (:denen solche frembde Nationen vieleicht dergestalt nicht beliebig:) bößen concept vndt heimblichen Haß vermercket habe. Weill dann E. Hochfürstl. Durchl. meine vnschuldt, vndt das ümb beschreibung einiger Persohn, aus denen ietzo allhier vorhandenen Italianern, Ich die geringste wißenschaft niemahls bekommen noch erlanget habe, genugsamb bekandt ist, die Vhrheber solcher sache auch, welche mit E. Durchl. hieraus vertraulich communiciret, vndt hernacher gedachte Musicanten aus Italia abgeholet haben, Vnuerborgen seint, So gelanget hierbeÿ an dieselbige mein vnterthnigstes [fol. 328v] hochflehentliches bitten, Sie geruhen Gndst (:zuuor vndt ehe ich vielleicht beÿ dero gnstn Herrn Vatern deswegen von iemands follends auch in Vnuerdienten Verdacht gestellet werden möge:) dieses argwohn gst von mir abzuwenden, vndt beuorab, beÿ dem Ehrwürdigen Ministerio der Churfl. HoffCapell, beÿ welchen ich mich deßwegen auch im wiedriegen Credit befinde) deßen mich gst entnemen

zulaßen, Vndt demnach mir auch von etlichen furgeworffen worden ist, alß ob zum beweise meiner beschuldigung, Eine schrifft (:worinnen Eur Churfl. durchl. zu solchen Italianern ich gerathen:) vnter meiner eigener Handt vorhanden sein solte, Ich mich aber doch dergleichen nichts sondern nur dieses zu errindern weiß, das numehr vor 20 Jahren oder mehr auf dero gsts begehren, Ich eine nachrichtung aufsetzen müßen, auf was weiße etwa eine Capella anzurichten, vndt was für Musicanten zu dero Complirung gehörig waren, da ich denn vnter denen Vocalisten, etwa eines Italianers, von welchen die Capellknaben vndt Teütschen Sänger eine gute manier begreiffen könten, So wohl auch vnter denen Instrumentisten, dergleichen qualificirten Italianern, mit erwehnet haben mag. Welchem meinen vor viell langen Jahren numehr gethanenen Vorschlag, dann, verhoffentlich noch niemandt zu taddeln, vndt auf die [fol. 329r] ietzo allhier anwesende Italianer zu ziehen haben wirdt, Wenn von E. Durchl. erwehnte meine schrifft, verständigen sich darinnen zuersehen, vntergeben werden möchte, maßen an meinem orte, vmb communication einer Copeÿ daßelbigen zu meiner nachrichtung ich auch vnterthänigst zu bitten.

Im übrigen so betheüere Ich mit Gott, das mir an meinem orte, solch von E. Hochfürstl. Durchl. neu angerichtetes Italianische Directorium Musicum, (:ob es gleich mir vndt andern Teütschen allhier, mehr zur verkleinerung alß erhöhung vnserer qualiteten gereichet:) niemahls zu wieder gewesen ist, daßelbe ich auch, vndt alles das ienige was E. durchl. mit Ihrem Corpore Musico hinfüro weiter disponiren möchten, mir albereit auch gefellig, vndt von mir vngetaldelt vndt vnuerachtet bleiben soll, Nun aber so mus ich dieses schmertzlich beklagen, das gegen das Ende meines Lebens, vndt nach meinen so lange Zeitt an diesem Churfl. Hoffe abgelegten vnterthstn mühsamen vndt wohlgemeinten diensten, ietzo erst alle planeten vndt Element, gleichsamb Sich wieder mich auflehnen vndt mich bekriegen wollen In dem es nemblich nicht genug gewesen ist (:das ich mich bißhero in hindangesetzten vndt armsehligen zustande, mehr alß mir von iugendt auf nicht wiederfahren, vndt ein anderer auch noch wol von wenigern qualiteten alß ich, vieleicht nicht übertragen haben werde:) in vnterthgstr großer gedult hinbracht, dabeÿ auch gutt vndt muth zugesetzet, [fol. 329v] vndt eine beßerung gehoffet habe, Sondern mir hirüber auch ietzo diese wiederwertikeit zustehet, das ich die schuldt habe, als ob E. durchl. ich zu Vnuerantwordlichen händeln, vndt großen spesen veranleite, so vieler fürnemer Leüte vngunst auf mich laden, vndt an stadt meines verdientes danks dauon tragen soll [closing flourish] Welchs ich aber entlich Gott vndt der Zeitt befehlen muß, welche meiner vnschuldt verhoffentlich einmahl Zeügnüß geben werden.

Eüre ChurPrintzliche durchl. aber bitte ich allerunterthgst Sie mir diese abgenötigte Klage, in vngnaden nicht vermercken, zu dero hohen protection dann, in dieser meiner gerechten sache, wie auch zu bißhero gepflogenen ferneren beharrlichen Gnaden, hiermitt in aller vnterthänigkeit, ich mich nochmahls treuestes fleißes, vnterthngst recommendiret vndt empfolen haben will [closing flourish]

> E. Churprintzl. Durchl.
> Vnterthgstr Gehorsambster alter diener
> Henrich Schütz [closing flourish]

Dreßden am 23. Augusti
Anno 1653.

Dem Durchlauchtigsten Hochgebornen fürsten vndt herrn, herrn Johann Georgen Hertzogen vndt ChurPrintzen zu Sachßen [closing flourish] Meinem Gndstn Herrn [flourish]

4: Translation

Schütz to Johann Georg II.
23 August 1653

[SAD Loc. 8687. *Kantoreiordnung,* fols. 328–29]

[fol. 328r. Not in Schütz's hand]
Most Serene Illustrious Elector Apparent,
   Most Gracious Lord,
I can gain no access to Your Royal Highness with my current most
humble memorandum plaintively to report the extent to which I am
given to understand how more and more each day that (regarding Your
Highness's musicians from Italy described here and those installed in
the electoral court ensemble) not only repeatedly unpleasant judgment
is passed on me by various ecclesiastical and secular persons but in
addition, to my particularly great surprise, I have become aware that I
am considered to be, and slandered as, the cause and instigator of this
change. Because of this I have unfortunately already observed miscon-
ception and secret hatred in many people of rank (who perhaps hold
such foreign nations dear in no way whatever). Because my innocence
is sufficiently known to Your Serene Highness and that I have never
received or obtained the slightest knowledge [regarding the hiring] of
any person among the Italians now present here, [and] the perpetrators
of this matter, who communicate with Your Highness confidentially
from here and who subsequently have fetched the aforementioned musicians from Italy do so openly, I then direct this my most humble [fol.
328v] fervent request, may it most graciously please you (before and ere
I am perhaps placed for this reason by someone else under the undeserved suspicion of my most gracious lord, your father) graciously to
avert this mistrust from me and especially graciously to relieve me of
that [mistrust] of your honorable minister of the electoral court ensemble, with whom for that reason I also find myself held in low esteem.
And accordingly I have also been reproached by some, as though in

proof of the charge brought against me, for a writing in my own hand (in which I recommended some Italians to His Serene Highness) is supposed to exist. Indeed I know nothing of the sort but remember only this: That now twenty years ago or more, at His [Highness's] most gracious command, I was to draw up a report in what manner an ensemble might be assembled and what musicians were necessary to complete it. At that time I had suggested for the vocalists the possibility of an Italian from whom the choir boys and German singers could learn good style, and a similarly qualified Italian for the instrumentalists as well. It is to be hoped then that no one criticizes my suggestion, made now many years ago, and the [fol. 329r] Italians now present here will be drawn upon [for such appointments]. If Your Highness agrees, my writing could be submitted to judge what is contained in it, because for my part I also most humbly request the communication of a copy of it for my own information.

Moreover I swear to God that I for my part do not oppose Your Serene Highness's newly installed Italian director of music [Giovanni Andrea Bontempi] (even though for me and other Germans here it serves more to the detriment of our abilities than the advancement of them). I am content in this and in everything which Your Highness might in future decide for your body of musicians, who shall remain unblamed and undespised by me. Now however I must complain bitterly that toward the end of my life and, after my many years of most humble persevering and well-intentioned service at this electoral court now behind me, it is now as if all of the planets and elements rise up against me and wage war upon me. If that namely were not enough (that until now I have not experienced a more continuous and wretched state even in my youth, which another possessed of still less ability than I perhaps could not have endured), [I am] brought hither in most humble great forbearance, to which good cheer and a hope for improvement are also added, [fol. 329v] but now in addition this unpleasantness is my due, as if I were guilty of misleading Your Highness into irresponsible behavior and great expense. Thus many people of rank heap disfavor upon me and I bear this instead of the thanks I deserve. I must finally trust in God and time, it is to be hoped, to give witness to my innocence once and for all. I beg Your Royal Highness most humbly not to receive with disfavor this complaint that has been wrung from me. I commend and entrust myself once again with most faithful diligence herewith in all humility to your noble patronage in this my rightful cause as well as to your steadfast grace which I have cherished to the present and shall forevermore.

Your Serene Highness, the Elector
Apparent's
Most humble obedient old servant
Heinrich Schütz

Dresden 23 August 1653

To the serene noble Prince and Lord, Lord Johann Georg, Duke and Elector Apparent of Saxony, My most gracious Lord.

5

Johann Georg II to Johann Georg I.
30 September 1653

[SAD Loc. 8687. *Kantoreiordnung*, fols. 337–38]

[fol. 337r]
Durchlauchstigster Hochgeborner Churfürst, aller gndigster Herr vnd Vatter [flourish]
E. Gn. Habe Ich vmb vorgebung zu bitten, das Ich dieselbige beÿ Ihren hohen gescheften hirmitt belestige, hoffende aber es werden E. Gn. solches in gnaden Vormercke, deroselben meine wenige doch wohl gemeinte gedancken nicht übel auffnemen, Und betrieft solches E. Gn. eugene Musica welche sie iederzeitt rümlichen Vor anderen Potentaten gehalten, Die weill aber an itzo es mitt selbiger gentzlichen auff die neuge kommen, das sie vollendt gätzlich zergöhet, als habe Ich meinen wenigen gedancken nach, zu Dero gndigsten gefallen stellende, wie selbige an itzo mitt wenigen zu erhalten vnd wieder auff zu bringen wehre, Darmitt von E. Gn. so viel darauff gewandte kosten nicht gentzlich vorgebens, als könde darmitt die kirchen auch E. Gn. Taffel dienst ordenglich mitt rumh vorsehen wirde, vnd E. Gn. itzo ballt wieder zu einer volkömmenglichen Compani vnd Corpo gelangen, volgendes gemacht werden. Der Herr Cappellmeister bliebe wie ieder Zeit vnd ob er gleich seines hohen alters halber nicht allezeitt auff warden könte, er selbiges schon wirdt einen auff zu tragen wissen, dar mitt an E. Gn. dienst nichts hirrin vorseimet würde, vnd bekemen also E. Gn. 20 Vocalisten vnd 8 Instrumentalisten nebenst zweÿ organisten, welche zwar alle schon in Euer Gnaden [fol. 337v] Diensten sindt, als der Vice Cappellmeister Hoffkuntze, so ein Tenorist, Vnd weill Ich ohne das mitt bewußten vorsehen als wolle Ich E. Gn. Philip Stollen vor ein Tenoristen so auch die Teorba pfleget vberlassen, wehren also 2 Tenoristen, die 2 Altisten wehren so an itzo auch in bestallung Christopf Bernhardi, und weber so auch ein Harffeniste, die 2 Bassisten der Keÿser worbey Ich

zuerinneren, das Ja E. Gn. selbigen nicht weck lassen wollen, dan gewiß
dergleichen nicht zu bekommen, vnd Jonas Kittel, so den fiolon auch
brauchet, nebenst 4 Cappellknaben, die Instrumentisten, so wehre Friederich sultze vnd seine 3 Söhne der von der eine noch ein Junge, Clemens, der Engelander, der herbaucker, vnd der Junge so aussen Cornet
lernet, hetten also E. Gn. 2 gutte Zincken bleser vnd 6 posaunen, so
wehren die geigen vnd fagott und Pommert hirmitt auch bestellet,
nebenst den zweÿ organisten Kitteln und hans Klemmen, und könten
also E. Gn. mitt meinen ieder Zeit abwexselung haben, beÿdes in der
kirchen und beÿ der Taffell, vnd wirden gewiß von allen Potentaten E.
Gn. eine perfecta musica haben. Dan mitt mein allein dieselbe zu bestellen es nicht möglich zu mahl die kirchen musica, vnd die weill diese
leute ohne vnter halt oder gelt nicht zu leben, das quanto auch nicht gar
hoch, ob E. Gn. sich gndigst gefallen lassen [fol. 338r] wolten darmitt sie
an itzo ein Quartal bekommen, auch ins künftige von merckten zu
merkten bezahlet werden möchten. Bitt hirnebenst E. Gn. wollen solches in keinen vngnaden vormercken, sondern diesen Vorschlack so zu
E. Gn. reputation vnd zu Gottes ehren gemeinet gndigst an vnd auffnemen, vnd wie bis anhero ieder zeit mein allergndigster Herr und Vatter
sein vnd vorbleiben, vorbleibe E. Gn.

                   Vnttertenigster gehorsammer Sohn

Dreßden
den 30 Septembris
1653
               J G Sachßen

5: Translation

Johann Georg II to Johann Georg I.
30 September 1653

[SAD Loc. 8687. *Kantoreiordnung*, fols. 337–38]

[fol. 337r]
Most Serene Noble Elector, Most Gracious Lord and Father,
   I must beg Your Grace's forgiveness for troubling you herewith as
one concerned with high duties, but hoping that Your Grace shall look
upon it graciously, not take offense at my trivial, yet well-intentioned
thoughts. It concerns your own ensemble which you have always held
more glorious than other potentates. Because it is now down to the
heeltap and has dwindled to nothing, I therefore present my humble
opinion to your most gracious favor as to how it could now be maintained and restored with little [expense]. Lest Your Grace's considerable
costs related to this be borne entirely in vain, the following could be
done so that the service in church and at Your Grace's table could be
properly conducted with glory, and Your Grace's [ensemble] could soon
be raised again to a complete company and body. The Kapellmeister
[Heinrich Schütz] should continue as always, and though he cannot
serve at all times due to his advanced age, he can select another in his
stead so that nothing is neglected in Your Grace's service. And were
Your Grace to have [in your employ] twenty vocalists and eight instrumentalists as well as two organists, who are in fact already in Your
Grace's service, [fol. 337v] as well as the vice-Kapellmeister Hofkontz,
who is a tenor, and, moreover, because I have made arrangements with
him, I shall give up to Your Grace Philipp Stolle as a tenor, who plays
the theorbo as well: thus, two tenors; the two altos, Christoph Bernhard,
now in your employ, and Weber, who is also a harpist; the two basses
[including Georg] Kaiser, who, in fact, Your Grace personally reminded
me was not to be let go, for certainly another like him cannot be had,
and Jonas Kittel, who also plays the violone; in addition to four choir-

boys; the instrumentalists Friedrich Sulz and his three sons, one of whom is still a boy; Clemens [Thieme?]; the Englishman; the timpanist; and the boy who is learning to play the hunting horn; [and] if Your Grace had two good zink players and six sackbut players, and if the violin[ists] and bassoon[ist] and bombard [player] were also appointed, in addition to the two organists Kittel and Johann Klemm, and thus Your Grace's musicians could alternate with mine both in church and at table, then certainly Your Grace would have a perfect ensemble in the eyes of all potentates. Because it is not possible to hire them with my own [resources] alone, especially the church musicians, and because these people cannot live without livelihood or money and the amount is not at all high, if Your Grace graciously consents [fol. 338r] they might now receive one fourth of their pay and shall be paid henceforth from one fair to the next. I ask Your Grace not look upon this with disfavor but graciously accept and receive these suggestions as they are intended for Your Grace's reputation and the glory of God, and now as always you are and remain my most gracious lord and father, I remain Your Grace's

Most humble obedient son

Dresden
30 September
1653

Johann Georg [II of] Saxony

6

Schütz to the Chamberlain.
Dresden, 19 June 1654

[SAD Loc. 7287. *Einzelne Schriften, Kammersachen.* 1492–1677, fol. 210]

[fol. 210r]

Hochgeehrter Herr Cammermeister [flourish]
Denselbigen bitte ich dinstlich ümb Verzeyhung, das seinem an mich
gethanen begehren zur folge, Ich keinen absonderlichen auszugk oder
specification, der Vffwartenden, oder Müssigen Musicanten, aufsetzen
kann, Vndt kann der Herr Cammermeister bey sich selbst wol ermessen,
was ohngelegenheit ich mir hirdurch zuziehen, auch was für trennung
undt misverstendt unter der Companey hirdurch entstehen würde,
dahero dann an den H. Cammermeister mein dienstliches bitten ist, Er
es dahin Vermitteln helffen wolle das eine gleichheit gehalten [*werden*
crossed out], oder aber im Wiedrigen fall Von Vnserm Gndstn
Churfurst v. herrn selbst zu dero gndstn befindung disponiret werden
moge, Gott mit uns in Gnaden
des herrn Cammermeisters dienstwilligster
Henrich Schütz Mpp
Dresd. am 19 Junii
Ao etc. 1654

6: Translation

Schütz to the Chamberlain.
Dresden, 19 June 1654

[SAD Loc. 7287. *Einzelne Schriften, Kammersachen,* 1492–1677, fol. 210]

[fol. 210r]
My Honorable Lord Chamberlain,
From whom I dutifully beg forgiveness that I cannot comply with his request to draw up a separate summary or detailed account of the servants or idle musicians, and my Lord Chamberlain can well imagine himself what trouble I have been involved in here and what divisiveness and misunderstanding has arisen here within the company. Therefore it is my dutiful request of my Lord Chamberlain that he, or, failing that, our most gracious elector and lord himself, might help to mediate so that equity be maintained, determined by your most gracious discretion. The divine grace of God be with us.
> My Lord Chamberlain's most dutiful
> Heinrich Schütz
> In his own hand
Dresden
19 June 1654

7

Johann Georg Hofkontz and Christoph Kittel to Jacob Weller. Dresden, 30 November 1654.

Jacob Weller to Johann Georg I. Dresden, 3 December 1654

[SAD Loc. 8560. *Schreiben von und an Oberhofprediger Jacob Weller, 1646–1651*, fols. 28–29]

Hofkontz and Kittel to Weller

[fol. 29r]
Hochwürdiger, Großachbahrer Vnd hochgelahrter herr Oberhoffprediger, hochgeehrter herr Vnd Großer beföderer;
E. hochw. ist Vnser iüngstes suppliciren guter maßen bewust, wir können aber, Vngeachtet wir Vns sehr darumb bemühet, keine Gnädigste erklärung erlangen: Sondern Vernehmen aus etlichen Vmständen, daß wir, wie sonst allezeit, also auch vor dißmahl Von besoldung nichts zu hoffen haben: Immittelst, weil Vnsere Mitconsorten, wie E. hochw. selbsten täglich Vnd Sonntäglich sehen, sich aller dienste Vnd aufwartungen entbrechen, vnd der gäntzliche ruin Vnd Vntergang der Churf. Capelle nur auf Vns 4. oder 5. Personen, die wir noch alleine täglich trewe Vnd fleißige dienste in dem Gotteshause leisten, beruhet; haben wir noch diß letzere mittel Versuchen wollen, Vnd gelanget an E. hochw. als Vnser hochverordneten Inspectorem Vnser Vnterdienstliches flehentliches bitten, weil wir mit Vnserm Vielfaltigen suppliciren nichts ausrichten können, Sie geruhe, Vor obgedachter endlicher ruin, morgen oder Vbermorgens an Churf. Durchl. intercendendo Vor Vns zu [fol. 29v] Suppliciren, das, wo sie ia nicht allen dero Capellbedienten etwas durch die banck wolten geben laßen, Sie doch nur <u>denen 4. oder</u>

5. Personen, durch welche der höchstnothwendige Gottesdienst mit gesang v. klang noch erhalten Vnd Verrichtet wird, ein eintziges Quartal besoldung zu erhaltung ihres elenden Lebens nur möchte angeordnet Vnd gegeben werden: Welches denn gar ein schlechtes austräget, Vnd uns, wann gleich sonsten gantz kein entziges mittel Vorhanden wehre, Von dem Geheimbten Cammerdiener H. Martin Ratken, oder aus dem Accisen Ambte gar leichte so viel könte gezahlt werden. Dafern wir aber wieder alles Verhoffen abermahl Vnd noch ferner Von aller hülffe solten Verlaßen bleiben, Vnd wir übrigen aus noth V. armuth gezwungen wurden, theils in Vnserm Vaterlande, theils anderer orten die h. Advent, Vnd Weinachtzeit über, Vnser brod zusuchen, daß Vnser Weib und kinder nicht noth leiden dürffen; wollen wir an dem Vor augenschwebenden Vntergange endschuldiget sein. Welches E. hochw. wir im Nahmen Vnser Vnd der noch übrigen mitgehülffen gebührend beÿbringen sollen: höchlich bittende, Sich eüserste zu bemühen, ob etwa das Churfürstliche Herz gegen vns arme diener noch möchte zu erweichen sein? Deroselben glückliche Verrichtung wünschende. Dreßden den 30 Novemb. A 1654.

E. hochw.

> Vntergebene und dienstschuldige
> Johann Georg Hofkontz
> V. C. mpp
> Christoph Kittel Hoforganist
> mpp

Weller to Johann Georg I

[fol. 28r. Not in Weller's hand]
Durchlauchtigster Churfürst Gnädigster Herr
Die Eü. Churfürstl. Durchlaucht [*ich* crossed out] nicht allein zu Hauß mit den lieben meinigen, sondern auch öffentlich in der Gemeine Gottes beÿ abweichnus des Alten und antrettung des Neüen kirchen Jahres ich von grund meiner Seelen durch Jesum Christum alle zu Seel und leib hochersprießliche Wohlfarth, den himmlischen Segen und die unaussprechliche Barmherzigkeit Gottes, langes leben, bestendige gesundtheit, undt daß mit dem eintritt das Neüen KirchenJahres, die gnade Unsers Heilandes Jesu Christi reichlich eintrete, gewünschet: Alß wiederhole ich solches mit herzlichen seüfzen undt bitte: O Herr Jesu Hilff! O Herr Jesu laß alles wohl gelingen, übersende auch E. Churfürstl. Dhl. unterthenigst, der Musicanten in der Schloskirchen an mich abgelaßenes schreiben, mit unterthenigster bitte, Sie geruhen gnädigst den elenden Zustandt der guten Leüthe zuerwegen, und daß wenn sie

nicht mit gnädigen augen solten angesehen werden, diese Fünffe, so bis
anhero fast einig und allein den Gottes dienst bestellet, weichen und
also fast nie [fol. 28v] mand sein würde der nur den Corall und ein
deütsches Vater Unser in der Kirchen würde sing können, dieweil aber
E. Churfürstl Durchl. Christ Fürstliches gemüth, damit Sie denen, so
den dienst Jesu Christi bestellen höchstrühmlichst zugethann, und daß
Sie mich bishero keine feilbitte, deßen ich mich in Gott zuerfreüen, thun
laßen, mir bekandt: Alß habe als über sie gesezter Inspector hiermit aus
unterthenigsten vortrauen für sie bitten und flehen wollen: Gewis E.
Churfürstl. Durchl. werden deßen für Gott dermahl eins und auch hier
zeitlich ruhm und ehr haben, und meine Herzens seüfzer, ia augen
thränen, damit deroselben besten für Gott ich ohne unziemblichen
Ruhm täglich suche, werden denn für freüden fließen, wenn E. Churf.
Durchl. dero Seelsorgern hierinnen abermahl in gnaden werden angesehen haben, Befehle Sie in die theüern Wunden Christi Jesu, und
verbleibe
Eü. Churfürstl. Durchl.
Datum Dreßden
den 3. Decemb. Ao 1654

[In Weller's hand] Unterthenigster treuer diener
und teglicher andachtiger Fürbitter
bey Gott so lang ich lebe,
   Jacoby Weller D.

7: Translation

Johann Georg Hofkontz and Christoph Kittel to Jacob Weller. Dresden, 30 November 1654.

Jacob Weller to Johann Georg I. Dresden, 3 December 1654

[SAD Loc. 8560. *Schreiben von und an Oberhofprediger Jacob Weller, 1646–1651*, fols. 28–29]

Hofkontz and Kittel to Weller

[fol. 29r]
Our Reverend, Respected, and Most Learned Senior Court Preacher, Our Highly Esteemed Lord and Great Advisor,

Your Reverence is to a great extent aware of our most recent plea. We could, however, obtain no gracious explanation despite our great trouble about it but have learned from certain circumstances that we, just as at all other times previous, have no hope of payment of our wages. Meanwhile, because our colleagues, as Your Reverence sees every day and every Sunday yourself, avoid all service and attendance, and the total ruin and decline of the royal ensemble, [whose duties] we fulfill faithfully and diligently every day in God's house, rests only upon us four or five persons. We wish to attempt yet this last means, and address our most servile, fervent plea to Your Reverence as our highly ordained inspector because we have been able to accomplish nothing with our repeated petitioning. May it please you, before the aforementioned final ruination, interceding in our behalf, to petition His Serene Highness tomorrow or the day after tomorrow, [fol. 29v] in which all of your ensemble members should not be presented all together, but only those four or five persons through whom the most necessary worship service is still maintained and carried out with singing and playing, to grant and give a single quarter of their salary only to maintain their miserable lives. This amounts to very little, and if no single other means were at hand, so much could quite easily be paid out to us by the privy chamberlain Herr Martin Ratke or from the excise officer.

Should we, however, remain deprived once again of all hope and furthermore of all help, and if, moreover, we are forced out of need and poverty to seek our bread partly in our Fatherland, partly in other places, over the holy Advent and Christmas season so that our wives and children shall not suffer need, we wish to be exonerated from the decline which is waving before our eyes. We beg Your Reverence mightily to strive to the utmost on our behalf and on [the behalf of] those remaining to bring about the assistance we deserve. Might perhaps the royal heart yet be softened toward us, your poor servants? Wishing you every success therein. Dresden 30 November 1654.

> Your Reverence's
> Subordinate and dutybound
> Johann Georg Hofkontz
> Vice-Kapellmeister
> In his own hand
> Christoph Kittel
> Court organist
> In his own hand

Weller to Johann Georg I

[fol. 28r. Not in Weller's hand]
Most Serene Elector, My Most Gracious Lord,
I wish Your Serene Highness from the depth of my soul, through Jesus Christ, all the most prosperous welfare of body and soul, the divine blessing and the inexpressible mercy of God, long life, enduring good health, and the grace of our Savior Jesus Christ, and that, with the arrival of the new church year, the grace of our Savior Jesus Christ will enter in abundance not only at home with your beloved family but also openly in God's community at the passing of the old and the approach of the new church year. I also transmit this with heartfelt sighs and supplication: O Lord Jesus, help! O Lord Jesus, lend success in all things and transmit graciously to Your Serene Highness the writing that has been forwarded to me by the musicians in the palace church. May it please you graciously to consider the miserable condition of the good people and [to be mindful] that if they are not looked upon with gracious eyes, these five will leave, who until now have been carrying out

the worship service virtually alone and by themselves, and so there would be almost [fol. 28v] no one who could simply sing hymns and a German "Our Father" in church. Since, however, I know of Your Serene Highness's royal Christian disposition which you most honorably show those who carry out the service of Jesus Christ, and because you have as yet denied me no request, for which I rejoice in God, I therefore in most humble faith beg and implore you in their behalf as their duty-bound inspector. Surely Your Serene Highness will then have peace and honor before God in the hereafter and here on earth as well, and the sighs of my heart, indeed the tears of my eyes, opened wide, with which I seek daily an undeserved peace with God, shall then flow for joy if Your Serene Highness will look with grace anew upon your spiritual advisor. I commend you to the precious wounds of Jesus Christ and remain

Your Serene Highness's

Dated Dresden 3 December 1654

    [In Weller's hand] Most humble faithful servant

    and intecessor who is more devout daily,

    with God as long as I live,

        Dr. Jacob Weller

8

Vincenzo Albrici's Contract as Kapellmeister.
Undated

[Moritz Fürstenau, *Zur Geschichte der Musik und des Theaters am Hofe zu Dresden* (1861–62; rpt. Leipzig: Peters, 1979), pp. 160–62]

Von GOTTES gnaden Wir Johann Georg der Ander, Herzog zu Sachßen, Jülich, Cleve und Berg, des heil. Röm. Reichs Erz = Marschall und Churfürst, Landgrafe in Thüringen, Marg = Grafe zu Meißen auch Ober = und Nieder = Lausiz, Burggrafe zu Magdeburg, Grafe zu der Marck und Ravensberg, Herr zu Ravenstein etc. Thun hiermit kund und bekennen; Daß Wir Unsern lieben getreuen Vincentium Albrici zu Unserm würcklichen Capelmeister bestellet und angenommen haben; Thun auch solches hiermit und in Krafft dieses dergestalt und also, daß Uns er getreü, hold, dienstgewärttig und schuldig seyn soll, Unsern Nuzen, Ehre, Wohlfarth und frommen nach seinem besten Vermögen Zuschaffen und Zubefördern, dargegen allen Schimpff, Schaden und nachtheil so viel an ihme zu hindern und fürzukommen, insonderheit aber soll er schuldig seyn die ordentlichen Musicalischen Aufwarttungen (außer wann Wir solches Unsern Alten verdienten Capellmeister Heinrich Schüzen, oder auch Unsern Capelmeister Johanni Andreae Bontempi absonderlich anbefehlen würden) sowohl in der Kirchen alß für der Taffel, ingleichen zu Theatrischen Compositionen, wie und wo Wir es verordnen werden, fleißigst zu verrichten, wobey ihm freistehen soll, entweder seine eigene Compositiones oder auch andere nach seinen eigenen guhtbefinden Zugebrauchen, doch, daß diejenigen Texte, so er in der Kirchen musiciren will, fürhero dem Oberhoffprediger gecommuniciret und von selbigen geapprobiret seyn; Ingleichen soll ihme freystehen, Unserm Vice = Capelmeister die Kirchen = Aufwarttung so offt es ihme beliebet, anzubefehlen; Maßen denn so wohl derselbige alß auch alle andere Unsere Capel = Bedieneten Crafft dieses und nach inhalt ihrer Bestallung an ihn hiermit vollkömlich gewiesen seyn sollen; Und da sich über verhoffen zwischen denen Musicis ein Mißverstand oder Zanck ereügnen solte, hat er solches nach seinem besten vermögen beyzulegen, oder aber, da es nicht verfangen wolte, Unserm Oberhoff = Marschall solches fürzubringen und seiner decision zu untergeben; Da aber die entstandene Streitigkeiten dadurch noch nicht möchten hingeleget werden, Uns sodann die Sache zu endlicher resolution gehorsamst fürzutragen; Auch soll er denen Musicis keinesweges zugeben, ohne Unsere erlaubnüs bey Banqueten, Hochzeiten oder Kind = Tauffen aufzuwartten, vielweniger ohne sein Vorwissen und genugsame erhebliche Uhrsachen und Ehehafften [*Gesetzliche Entschuldigung* added by Fürstenau] Zuverreysen, oder durch außenbleiben die Kirchen = und Taffeldienste und fürhabendes probiren Zuverseümen. Damit auch Unsere Musica recht versehen werde, soll er schuldig seyn, Uns mit dergleichen tauglichen subjectis seinen besten befinden nach, Zuversehen, welche in der Kunst perfect, auch von denen Wir Ehre und gute dienste haben mögen, iedoch soll er ohne Unsern willen und wißen keinen annehmen noch abschaffen, und hingegen Kürzlich alles dasjenige thun, und leisten, was einen getreüen Capelmeister und diener gegen seinen Chürfürsten und Herrn eignet und gebühret; Welches er dann also zuhalten durch einen Handschlag an Eydesstadt angelobet und seinen schrifftlichen revers darüber außgehändiget. Dargegen wollen Wir ihme etc.

8: Translation

Vincenzo Albrici's Contract as Kapellmeister. Undated

[Moritz Fürstenau, *Zur Geschichte der Musik und des Theaters am Hofe zu Dresden* (1861–62; rpt. Leipzig: Peters, 1979), pp. 160–62]

By the grace of GOD, We, Johann Georg the Second, Duke of Saxony, Jülich, Cleve, and Berg, Erzmarschall and Elector of the Holy Roman Empire, Landgrave in Thuringia, Margrave of Meissen and Upper and Lower Lausitz, Burgrave of Magdeburg, Earl of Marburg and Ravensberg, Lord of Ravenstein etc. attest and acknowledge herewith that we have appointed and accepted our beloved faithful [servant], Vincenzo Albrici, as our true Kapellmeister, done herewith by the power of this [document] so that he shall be faithful, loyal, prepared to serve us, and dutiful; to see to and protect our interests, honor, well-being, and concerns to the best of his ability; [and] to hinder and prevent dishonor, injury, and wrong to his person. He shall especially, however, be responsible for musical service (except when we particularly command this of our old Kapellmeister of merit, Heinrich Schütz, or our Kapellmeister Giovanni Andrea Bontempi) in church as well as at table, likewise to perform [his duty] in theatrical compositions most diligently, however and wherever we decree. For this he is free to use either his own compositions or others according to his own discretion; those texts, however, which he wishes to perform in church shall be communicated to the senior court preacher and approved by him beforehand. Likewise he shall be free to command our vice-Kapellmeister to serve in church as often as he wishes. Inasmuch as he [the vice-Kapellmeister] as well as all of our other ensemble members are completely [responsible] to him [Albrici] by power of this [deed] and according to the contents of their contracts. And if contrary to our expectations, a misunderstanding or quarrel should arise between those musicians, he shall settle it to the best of his ability, or, if that is not effective, [he shall] bring it before our

Oberhofmarschall and submit to his decision. If, however, the disputes which have arisen are still not resolved therefrom, then the matter shall be obediently brought before us for final resolution. And he shall in no way allow the musicians to serve at banquets, weddings, or christenings without our permission, much less to travel without his prior knowledge and sufficent reasonable cause and excuse ["legitimate excuse" added by Fürstenau] or through absence to miss service in church and at table and scheduled rehearsals. So that our ensemble is properly managed, he shall be responsible for serving us with those same fit subjects as best he can, whom we wish to be perfect in art and from whom we desire honor and good service. At the same time he shall neither appoint nor discharge anyone without our will and knowledge and again in short do and be all that is due and worthy of his elector and lord as a true Kapellmeister and servant. This he then pledges to keep by a ceremonial handshake and has given his written agreement thereon. We on the other hand shall etc.

9

Christoph Bernhard's Contract as Alto.
Dresden, 1 August 1649

[SAD Loc. 33345. 1953. *Registratur über das 11te Bestallungs Buch*, fol. 367]

[fol. 367r]
Von Gottes gnaden Wir Johann Georg, Hertzogk zu Sachssen, Jülich, Cleve vnd Berg, das Heiligenn Römischen Reichs Erzmarschall vnnd Churfürst, Landtgraff in Düringenn, Marggraff zu Meißen, auch Ober: vnd NiederLausiz, Burggraff zu Magdeburgk, Graff zu der Marck vnnd Ravensperg, Herr zu Ravenstein etc. Vrkundenn hiemit vnd bekennenn, Daß wir vnsern liebenn getreuenn, Christoffen Bernhardi, zu vnserm Musico vnd Singer bestellet vnd auffgenommen habenn, Thue das auch hiemit vnd in Kraft dieses briefes, dergestalt vnd also, daß er Vns getrew, holdt, vnd dienstgewerttig sein, Vnser Ehre, Nuz vnnd wohlfarth befördern, Schimpf, schadenn vnd nachtheil aber warnen, Wennden vnd vorkommenn, Insonderheit aber, alle dem, was die Cantoreÿ Ordenung vermag, vnd dabeÿ von Vnß, oder Vnsertwegen, durch Vnserm HofMarschall, Inspectorn vnd Capellmeister, wegenn der Aufwartung in Vnser HoffCapell oder vor der Taffel, weiter geschafft, verordnet vnd befohlenn wirdt, gehorsambst nachleben, Danebenn auch die Capellknabenn täglichenn zu gewißen stundenn im Singenn Vnterweisenn vnd vfs beste [fol. 367v] abrichtenn, Auch sonstenn alles andere, was Vnß zu Ehrenn, nuz vnnd wolfarth gereichet, mitt allem getreuen fleiß, seines höchsten vnnd besten vermögens befördern, Vnnd in summa in solchem seinem dienste sich allenthalben also, wie einem getreuen vnd fleißigenn diener Kegenn seinem herrn eignet vnd gebuhret, iederzeit bezeigenn soll, Welches er denn auch alß vnterthenigst versprochenn vnd mit einem Cörperlichenn Eide angelobet, danebenn in einem schrieftlichenn Reverße sich verpflichtet hat, Da kegenn wollenn wir ihme von dato an Jährlichenn Zweÿ hundert

gülden, fur Soldt, Kost, Kleidung vnd alles andere, aus vnser Renth-Cammer reichenn vnd folgenn laßenn,

Zu Vrkundt habenn Wir diesenn brieff mit eigenen handenn Vnterschriebenn, vnd mit vnserm RentCammer secret wißentlich bedrucken laßenn, Beschehen vnd gebenn zu Dreßden am Ersten Augusti Nach Christi vnsers Erlösers vnd Seeligmachers geburt, Des Sechzehenhundert vnd Neun vnd Vierzigsten Jahres

[Johann Georg I's hand] Johann George Churfürst,

9: Translation

Christoph Bernhard's Contract as Alto.
Dresden, 1 August 1649

[SAD Loc. 33345. 1953. *Registratur über das 11te Bestallungs Buch,* fol. 367]

[fol. 367r]
By the grace of God, we, Johann Georg, Duke of Saxony, Jülich, Cleve and Berg, Erzmarschall and Elector of the Holy Roman Empire, Landgrave in Thuringia, Margrave of Meissen and Upper and Lower Lausitz, Burgrave of Magdeburg, Earl of Margberg and Ravensberg, Lord of Ravenstein etc. attest and acknowledge herewith that we have appointed and accepted our beloved faithful [servant], Christoph Bernhard, as our musician and singer, done herewith and by the power of this letter so that he shall be faithful, loyal, and prepared to serve us; to protect our honor, interests, and well-being; but to ward off, avert, and prevent dishonor, injury, and wrong; but in particular to comply most obediently with everything that the *Kantoreiordnung* signifies; and in addition is further ordered, charged, and commanded to carry out [commands] on behalf of us or ours through our Hofmarschall, inspector, and Kapellmeister concerning service in our court chapel or at table; and moreover to instruct the choirboys in singing every day at the appointed times and to do his best [fol. 367v] to teach them; and in addition to promote to the utmost and best of his ability otherwise all else which pertains to our honor, interests, and well-being with all true diligence; and in summation shall show himself in service in all things at all times to be a true and diligent servant dutiful towards his lord. He has promised most humbly and has sworn by a bodily vow and in addition has made a pledge in a written agreement. We on the other hand shall have given and presented to him 200 gulden from our chamber of the exchequer for wages, board, clothing, and all else from this date forward.

In verification we have undersigned this letter in our own hand and knowingly have had it imprinted with our official seal. Signed and sealed in Dresden on the first of August of the sixteen hundred and forty-ninth year after the birth of Christ our Redeemer and Savior,

[Johann Georg I's hand] Johann Georg, Elector.

10

Christoph Bernhard's Contract as Vice-Kapellmeister. Heinrich Taube to Johann Georg I. Dresden, 1 August 1655

[SAD Loc. 33345. 1953. *Registratur über das 11te Bestallungs Buch,* fols. 366–69]

Christoph Bernhard's Contract as Vice-Kapellmeister

[fol. 366r]
Bestallung
Vor den Vice Capellmeister Christoff Bernhardi. JEP. 1 August Ao 1655.
Von GOTTES gnaden WIR Johann George, Herzog zu Sachßen, Jülich, Cleve, vnd Berg etc. Churfürst etc.
Thun hiermit kund und bekennen, daß Wir Unsern lieben getrewen, Christoph Bernharden, gewesenen Altisten beÿ Unser HoffCapelle, von newen, zu Unserm Diener und vice Capellmeister angenommen, und thun solches krafft dieses, daß Unser getrew, holdt und dienstgewärttig, auch schuldig seÿn soll, in abwesenheit Unsers, alß auch des durchleüchtigen Hochgebornen Fürstens, Unsers freündlichen lieben Sohns und Gevatters, Herrn Johann Georgens, Herzogens zu Sachßens Ld. iziger oder künfftiger Capellmeistere, oder sonsten auff derer Anordnung die Music beydes in der Kirchen, so wohle auch beÿ denen Chur: und fürstlichen Taffeln zu dirigiren und zu bestellen, Insonderheit aber, soll er (:er dirigire selbsten oder aber ein Capellmeister:) den Tact vorm Pulde beÿ der Coral-Music iedes mahl geben, auch allzeit Unserm Ober:Hoff:Predi [fol 366v] ger (:dehme Wir die Inspection über unsere HoffCapelle anbefohlen:) oder wer sonsten das Predigen verrichtet, die Texte der Musicalischen Stücken zuvorhero communiciren, wie nichts weniger, da ein Capellmeister dirigiret, und seiner

Stimme bedürfftig seÿn würde, soll er auff daßelben anordnung (:an dehm Wir ihn dann Ordinarie und allerdings verwiesen haben wollen:) sich keines weges deßen verweigeren, sondern iederzeit bereit und willig erzeigen, auch darneben, wann ihme Capellknaben Untergeben würden, dieselben in Musicis unterrichten, Im übrigen auch in solchem seinen dienste sich allenthalben, alß einem getrewen und fleißigen diener kegen seinen herren eignet und gebühret, ieder Zeit bezeigen, und keine klage über sich nicht einkommen laßen, Welches er dann auch also unterthänigst zu halten, beÿ seiner vorhin geleisteten [fol. 369r] Pflicht versprochen, und in einem schrifftlichen Revers sich verpflichtet hatt,

Hinwegen, und damit er solches Unsers dienstes desto beßer und fleissiger abwartten könne, wollen wir ihme zu seiner besoldung Jährlichen Dreÿhundert und funffzig Gülden, aus unserer Rent Cammer reichen und geben laßen, Sonder gefehrde,

Zu Urkund haben wir Unß mit eigenen handen unterschrieben undt unser Cammer Secret hierauff drücken laßen, Geschehen und geben zu Dreßden, den 1. Augusti, Nach Christi 1655.

Heinrich Taube to Johann Georg I

[fol. 368r]
Demnach der Durchlauchtigste Churfürst zu Sachssen, unndt Burggraff zu Magdeburgk etc. mein gnädigster Herr, den zeithero gewesenen Altisten Christoph Bernhardten, zu dero Vice Capellmeistern angenommen, daß Er nemblich beÿ der abwesenheit des Churf. Capellmeisters Heinrich Schüzens, so wohl Sr ChurPrinzl. Durchl. ieziger undt kunfftiger Capellmeisterr, oder sonst auff deroselben anordtnunge die Music beÿdes in der Kirchen, undt beÿ denen Chur. und Furstl. Tafeln dirigiren, undt bestellen, Insonderheit aber schuldig sein solle, (er dirigire selbsten, oder ein Capellmeister;) iedesmahl den Tact vorm Pulte beÿ der Coral Music zugeben, auch allezeit dem Herrn Oberhoff Prediger, oder wer sonsten das Predigen verrichtet, die Texte derer Musicalischen Stücken zu vorher zu communiciren, wie nichts weniger, Da ein Capellmeister dirigiret undt seiner Stimme bedurfftig seÿn wurde, sich willig gebrauchen zu laßen, auch darneben, wenn ihme Capellknaben untergeben wurden, solche in Musicis zu unterrichten.

Alß wirdt denen Churf. S. Wohlverordneten herren Cammerräthen solches dienstlich vermeldet und werden dieselbe nach erfolgenden handtschlagk Ihme seine bestallung auff obige Puncta, undt der besoldung halben nach derer Vorigen ViceCapellmeisters Bestallungen ausfertigen und aushändigen laßen, doch daß dargegen seine Altisten besoldung von dato an wegfalle, und nebenst den freÿen tisch, so der vorige Vice-Capellmeister gehabt, dem künfftigen hoff-Cantori zu seiner ergezlichkeit verbleibe Signatum Dreßden am 1. Augusti Ao etc. 1655.

Churfn Durchl. zu Sachssen etc. bestaldter Oberhoffmarschall, Ober-Cammer vor und habtmannerer Ambter Torgau und Eilenburgk etc.

Heinrich Taube Mp

10: Translation

Christoph Bernhard's Contract as Vice-Kapellmeister. Heinrich Taube to Johann Georg I. Dresden, 1 August 1655

[SAD Loc. 33345. 1953. *Registratur über das 11te Bestallungs Buch,* fols. 366–69]

Christoph Bernhard's Contract as Vice-Kapellmeister

[fol. 366r]
Appointment
Of the vice-Kapellmeister Christoph Bernhard. JEP. 1 August 1655.

By the grace of GOD, WE, Johann Georg, Duke of Saxony, Jülich, Kleve, and Berg, etc., Elector etc. declare and acknowledge herewith that we newly appoint our beloved and faithful servant, Christoph Bernhard, alto, who has been serving in our court ensemble, as our servant and vice-Kapellmeister, and do this by power of this [document, in order] that he shall be faithful, loyal, and prepared to serve and be dutiful to Us now or in future in the absence of our Kapellmeister or that of the serene noble prince, our benevolent beloved son and kinsman, Lord Johann Georg [II], My Lord the Duke of Saxony, His Dilection, or at other times, at their command, to direct and organize the music both in church as well as at the electoral and princely table. In particular, however, (whether he himself or a Kapellmeister conducts) he always shall beat time from the lectern for the *choraliter* singing, and always communicate the texts of the musical pieces beforehand to our senior court preacher [fol. 366v] (whom we charge with the inspection of our court ensemble) or to whoever delivers the sermon. Furthermore, when a Kapellmeister conducts and needs his voice, he shall in no way refuse this command [of the Kapellmeister] (whom we wish to have consulted in general and in all matters) but show himself to be ready and willing at all times. And in addition, should choir boys be entrusted to him, he shall instruct them in music. Furthermore, in all aspects of his service, at all times, he shall also present himself as is fitting and suitable for a faithful and diligent servant to his lord, and cause no complaint to be lodged against himself. He has recently promised to uphold his sworn [fol. 369v] duty most humbly and has made a pledge in a written agreement.

For that reason and so that he therewith might serve us even better and more diligently, we shall have presented and given to him 350 gulden from our chamber of the exchequer for his yearly salary, without penalty.

In verification we have undersigned in our own hand and have had our official seal imprinted hereupon.

Signed and sealed in Dresden, 1 August 1655 after Christ

Heinrich Taube to Johann Georg I

[fol. 368r]

The most serene elector of Saxony and burgrave of Magdeburg, etc. my most gracious lord, accordingly appointed the former alto Christoph Bernhard as your vice-Kapellmeister, and ordered that now or in future, in the absence of [either] the electoral Kapellmeister Heinrich Schütz or the elector apparent's Kapellmeister, or else at their command, he direct and organize the music both in church and at the electoral and princely table. In particular, however (whether he himself or a Kapellmeister conducts), he shall always beat time from the lectern for the *choraliter* singing, and always communicate the texts of the musical pieces beforehand to the senior court preacher or to whoever delivers the sermon. Furthermore, when a Kapellmeister conducts and needs his voice, he shall serve willingly; and, in addition, should choir boys be entrusted to him, he shall instruct them in music.

This will be officially announced to the elector's rightfully designated lords of the exchequer, and these will have his appointment, after the ceremonial handshake has taken place on the above points, and his salary drawn and handed out to him according to the appointment of the previous vice-Kapellmeister. Indeed, his salary as alto shall cease from this date forward and will be, in addition to the open table, which had been given to the previous vice-Kapellmeister, granted to the future Hofkantor for his pleasure.

Signed Dresden. 1 August 1655.

His Serene Highness of Saxony's appointed Hofmarschall, Lord High Chamberlain and Chief Government Official for Torgau and Eilenburg etc.
Heinrich Taube
In his own hand

11

Schütz's Prefatory Letter to Constantin Christian Dedekind's *Aelbianische Musenlust.* Weissenfels, 21 September 1657

[Müller no. 100, reprinted from Constantin Christian Dedekind, *Aelbianische Musenlust*]

An
Herrn Constantin Christian
Dedekinden
Keiserl. gekröhnten Poeten/
Kuhrfl.-Sächs. fürnehmen Hof-Musicum.
Insonders vielgünstiger Herr und wehrter Freund!

DAß derselbe aus guhtem Zutrauen in meine Persohn/eine Ansuchung getahn und gebehten/mein Guhtachten über die AElbianische MusenLust/wie er das unter Händen habende Werk obgeschrieben und vohrgetitult/zu eröffnen/habe ich aus seinem Zuschreiben mit mehrerm vernommen. Nuhn ich dänn das/was die Musik betrifft/wohl überleget und befunden/daß die Melodeien nicht alleine nach den Regulis und modis Musicis Kunstmässig/sondern auch hierüber dero modulationes anmuhtig übersäzzet und geführet seind/dahero gänzlich dahrfür halte/ der Herr solte nicht unterlassen dieses Werklein in Druk zugeben und also der Wält mit zu teilen:

Alß erinnere ich ihn hiermit freundlich/er wolle das dargeliehene und von GOtt her empfangene Pfund nicht vergraben/sondern diese seine aufgesäzte Arien neben der Poesie, in Gottes Nahmen den Kunst- und Liebhabern zum bästen heraus geben. Wovon er dann anders nichts/als Ehr und Loob erlangen wird. Dahrzu ich Ihme alles Glück wünsche und Göttlicher Obacht ergebe/im übrigen aber verbleibe
des Herrn allezeit

Dienstwilliger.
Weissenfels/den 21. Septemb 1657.
Heinrich Schütz/
Kuhrfl. Sächs. Kapell-Meister

11: Translation

Schütz's Prefatory Letter to Constantin Christian Dedekind's *Aelbianische Musenlust*. Weissenfels, 21 September 1657

[Müller no. 100, reprinted from Constantin Christian Dedekind, *Aelbianische Musenlust*.

To
Herr Constantin Christian
Dedekind
Imperial Crowned Poet
Foremost Electoral Saxon Court Musician
Most noble gentleman and valued friend!

I have learned from his [Dedekind's] letter among other things that, out of good confidence in my person, he has asked me to give my opinion on the *Aelbianische Musenlust*, as he has superscribed and entitled the work at hand. Now that I have given careful consideration to that which concerns the music and found that the melodies are rendered and carried out artistically not only according to the rules and church modes but moreover delightful in their modulation, I therefore think without qualification that the gentleman should not neglect to publish this little work and thus share it with the world.

Therefore I remind him herewith as a friend that he should not conceal the talent bestowed and received from God but publish the arias he has composed along with the poetry for professionals and amateurs, for which he can receive nothing but honor and praise. I wish him the best of luck and hope for divine observance, but remain moreover
the gentleman's obedient [servant] always
Weissenfels, 21 September 1657
Heinrich Schütz
Royal Saxon Kapellmeister

12

Schütz's Travel Pass from Johann Georg II.
Frankfurt am Main, 8 April 1658

[SAD Loc. 8297. *Päße von reisende Personen 1634–93*, fol. 25]

[fol. 25r]
Ordinanz
An die beambten zu Leipzig Wurzen Oschaz und Meißen dem Capell-
meister Heinrich Schüzen, Jährlichen dreÿ biß vier mahl mit zweÿen
Pferden vorspannung zuschaffen.
JGC. franckfurt am Main den 8. Aprilis 1658.
Johann George der Ander Churfürst und Reichs vicarius./.
Demnach Wir Unsern Capellmeister und lieben getreüen Heinrich
Schüzen zu Unserer dienstwartung Jährlichen 3. biß 4. mahl von
Weißenfelß zu erfordern gemeinet seÿn, und ihn mit einer Vorspan-
nung mit zweÿ Pferden von Ambte zu Ambte iedes mahl wollen ver-
sehen wissen, Als ist hiermit Unser befehl, daß Unsere beambten zu
Leipzig, Wurzen, Oschaz und Meissen sich darnach gebührende achten
und ermelten Unsern Capellmeister benennete vorspannung verschaf-
fen sollen, An dehme beschiehet Unser wille und meinung, Geben zu
franckfuhrt am Main den 8. Aprilis Anno 1658.

12: Translation

Schütz's Travel Pass from Johann Georg II. Frankfurt am Main, 8 April 1658

[SAD Loc. 8297. *Päße von reisende Personen 1634–93*, fol. 25]

[fol. 25r]
Ordinance
To the officials of Leipzig, Wurzen, Oschatz, and Meissen to provide the Kapellmeister Heinrich Schütz three to four times yearly with two fresh horses.
JGC [Johann Georg Churfürst]
Frankfurt am Main on 8 April 1658.
Johann Georg the Second, Elector and Vice Regent.
Because we are disposed to call our Kapellmeister and beloved loyal servant Heinrich Schütz from Weissenfels to our service three to four times yearly, and wish him furnished with two fresh horses each time from exchange point to exchange point, it is therefore our command that our servants in Leipzig, Wurzen, Oschatz, and Meissen shall heed what is required and provide the designated fresh horses to our aforementioned Kapellmeister. By this our will and intention will be carried out. Administered in Frankfurt am Main on 8 April 1658.

13

Johann Georg II's Chapel Order.
Undated

[SLB Msc. K. 89, fols. 1–23]

[fol. 1r]
Ordnung
Wie der Durchlauchtigste Hochgebohrne Fürst und Herr, Herr Johann
Georg, der Ander, Hertzog zu Sachßen, Jülich, Cleve, und Bergk, des
Heiligen Römischen Reichs ErtzMarschall, und Churfürst, Landgraff
in Thüringen, Marggraff zu Meißen, auch Ober= und Nieder Lausitz,
Burggraff zu Magdeburg, Graff zu der Margk und Ravensberg, Herr
zu Ravenstein etc. es in Dero Hoff=Cappella, mit der Musica, an denen
Fest= und Sontagen, auch in der Wochen, hinführo wolle gehalten
haben.
[fol. 2r]

Erstlichen.

Das die Teützschen Lieder anlanget, Soll jedes mahl dem Herrn
Ober=HoffPrediger freÿstehen, Ob er beÿ nachverzeichneten verbleiben, oder seiner beliebung nach, es ändern, auch die andern Texte,
in denen concerten, und Motetten zu componiren geben will, So wohl
die lateinischen und Teützschen, welche jedesmahl ihme von dem Cappellmeister gezeiget werden sollen. Ingleichen soll auch Ihme freÿ
gelaßen seÿn, ein oder mehr Lieder anzuordnen und auch zumindern.
Wobeÿ auch dieses zuerinnern, daß wann die Herrschafft nicht in Dero
Residentz sich befindet, die Musica zu des Herrn Ober Hoff Predigers
fernern Ordnung stehen soll.

Zum Andern.

Vor allen Hohen Fest Tagen wie solche nachverzeichnet (:außer die
dreÿ Haupt Feste:) alß Ersten Advent SonTag, Neü Jahr, Ephiphaniae,

Pürificationis, Annünciationis Mariae, SonTag Qvasimodogeniti, Himmelfahrt, Trinitatis, Johannis Baptistae, Visitationis Mariae, Mariae Magdalenae, und Michaëlis,
Ingleichen alle SonnAbende, Sonntäge, und MittWochen,
[fol. 2v]
So wohl den FestTag [*Ephiphaniae* crossed out] Johannis Baptistae, Undt Mariae Magdalenae, Soll wie bißhero und vor diesen bräuchlich gewesen, eine lateinische Vesper, nebenst mit untergemengeten Teützschen Liedern gehalten werden.
Diese Vesperen, Wie auch die Wochen Predigten und Beht Stunden, bestellet der Hoff = Cantor, mit den Choralisten, und darzugehörigen Organist.

Zum Dritten.

Werden die Vesperen und Beht Stunden folgender gestalt gehalten:

Vesper.

1. Wird von dem Priester vor dem Altar intonirt:
   Deus in adjutorium, Worauff der Chor antworttet.
2. Die Fest Tage und Heilige Abende, wird ein Teützscher Psalm choraliter vor dem Bulde, wie ihn der Herr Ober Hoff Prediger ordnen wird, gesungen; Des SonnTags, [fol. 3r] Mittwochs, und SonnAbends ingleichen ein Teützscher Psalm, wie sie nacheinander folgen.
3. Alle Hohe Feste, Heilige Abende, und Sonntäge, wirdt ein lateinisch oder Teüzsch Concert, oder Motetto, musicirt.
4. Ein Teüzsch Lied.
5. Wird von dem Priester vor dem Altar ein Psalm, oder ander Text, und darauff das gewöhnliche Gebeht, und Vater Unser abgelesen.
   Die Heilige Abende, vor den Fest Tagen (:außer die Dreÿ Hohen Fest:) aber, lieset ein Knabe, die Epistel vom Chor ab.
6. Die Hohen Feste, Heilige Abende, und SonnTage, wirdt das Magnificat lateinisch figuraliter musicirt. Des MittWochs und SonnAbends aber choraliter, lateinisch oder Teüzsch, wechßelsweise.
7. Ein Teüzsch Liedt.
8. Collecta und Segen.
   [fol. 3v]

Beht Stünden.

So des Monntags, Dienstags, Donnerstags, undt Freÿtags gehalten werden,

1. Deus in adjutorium.
2. Ein Psalm, nach der Ordnung, aus dem Becker.
3. Ein Teüzsch Lied.
4. Wird vor dem Altar, vom Priester ein Psalm oder ander Text, neben dem gewöhnlichen Gebeht und Vater Unser abgelesen.
5. Ein Teüzsch Lied.
6. Collecta und Segen.

Nota.

In der Fasten, vom Montag nach Laetare ahn biß auff den Char Freÿtag, außer den Feste Annunciationis [fol. 4r] Mariae, und Abend zuvor, wird keine lateinische Vesper, Sondern nur Beht Stunde gehalten.

Zum Vierden.

Wird den Ersten Advent Sonntag alß Kirchen Neü Jahr, nach dem zum drittenmahl geläutet alß umb 1/2 Acht Uhr, es folgends gehalten:
1. Zum Introitu: Rorate Coeli de super. Auff die andern Sonntage aber, durchs ganze Jahr, Ein Teüzsch Lied, anstatt des Introitus.
2. Kÿrie, Christe, Kÿrie. ⎫
3. Völlige Missa.   ⎬ musicaliter

Nota.

Wann aber die Herrschafft communiciret, es seÿ auff [fol. 4v] welche Zeit es wolle, werden zwischen dem Kÿrie, dreÿ Teützsche Lieder, oder Psalmen gesungen, welche der Ober Hoff Prediger zuordnen hat, darauff intonirt der Priester vor dem Altar, das Gloria, Worauff die Missa, und alßdenn:
4. Allein Gott in der Höh seÿ Ehr.
5. Collect und die Epistel.
6. Nun komm der Heÿden Heÿland.
   So aber Communion, die Litania teüzsch, figuraliter, oder choral, Wann das leztere gebraucht wird, singen die Knaben kniend vor dem Altar, Wann selbige aber an den zweÿen Haupt Festen, den Christ= und Oster Tagk gehalten wird, wird ein Teützschen Fest Lied, anstatt der Litaniae gebraucht.
7. Evangelium.

Nota.

Wann Communion, intonirt der Priester das Credo.
8. Das Credo figural, die andern Sontäge Ein kurz Concert oder Motetto.

9. Der Teützsche Glaube.
   [fol. 5r]
10. Predigt, und vor derselben, Ein kurz Lied oder Versicul, einer
    oder mehr, welches aber nur den Ersten Advent Sonntagk, oder
    wann Communion gehalten wird, gebraucht werden soll.
11. Nach der Predigt, ein Concert oder Motetto.
12. Darauff ein Teüzsch Lied.

Nota.

Wann Communion, Wird das Concert oder Motetto außen gelaßen und
anstatt deßen gesungen:
Allein zu dir Herr Jesu Christ.
13. Consecration und Austheilung des Heiligen Abendmahls, wobeÿ
    die gewöhnlichen Teützschen Lieder gesungen werden.
14. Collecta und der Segen.
15. Ein kurz Teüzsch Lied, oder Versicul zum Beschluß.
    Den Ersten Advent Sontag, wird auch, nach dem umb 2. Uhr, zum
    drittenmahl geläutet, Vesper, nebenst einer Predigt gehalten, Wie
    denn auch sonsten jedesmahl, so die Herrschafft communicirt,
    Vesper und Predigt zuhalten.
    [fol. 5v]

Zum Fünfften.

Den Andern, dritten, vnd Vierden Sontag im Advent, den Sonntag nach
dem Heiligen Christag, Sontag nach dem Neüen Jahrs Tag, und die 4.
Sonntage in der Fasten, alß Invocavit, Reminiscere, Oculi und Laetare,
Ingleichen Rogationum, und den 10. Sontag Trinitatis wird à Cappella
musicirt, Ingleichen, wenn ein Sonntag an einem heiligen Abend
gefällig ist.
Auff den Sonntag Judica, Palmarum und CharFreÿtag, wird die Passion
gesungen.

Heilig Christ = Fest.

Am Heiligen Abend, wird umb halbweg zweÿ, zum Ersten und umb [fol.
6r] dreÿ Viertel zum andernmahl geläutet.

Vesper.

1. Deus in adjutorium.
2. Ein lateinischer Psalm, musicaliter.
3. Ein Concert oder Motetto.
4. Ein Teüzsch Lied.

5. Lieset der Priester vor dem Altar einen Psalm, oder andern Text abe.
6. Magnificat.
7. Ein Concert, oder Motetto.
8. Ein Teüzsch Lied.
9. Collecta.
10. Benedicamus.

Am Heiligen Christ Tage.

Erstlich

Werden umb 4. Uhr, vom Creüz Thurm, Dreÿ Stücken, [fol. 6v] gelöst, Worauff alsobald auffm Schloß, Inn= und außerhalb der Stadt, so wohl auch zu Alten Dreßden, mit allen Glocken, das Fest biß halbweg 5. Uhr, eingeläutet wird, Welcher Gebrauch jedesmahl zuhalten, es seÿ die Herrschafft in der Residentz oder nicht.

Zum Andern.

Nachdem zum Erstenmahl halbweg 7. Uhr geläutet, ziehen alle Guardien auff, und wird aus dreÿ halben Carthaunen, dreÿmahl Feüer, Wie auch von denen Guardien dreÿmahl salve gegeben.

Zum Dritten.

Umb halbweg 7. Uhr, wird zum Ersten, umb 7. Uhr zum Andern, und halbweg Acht Uhr, zum drittenmahl geläutet, wie es denn auch alle andere Fest= und Sonntage, also damit zuhalten.

Zum Vierden.

Wird der Gottesdienst, in der Kirchen folgender Ordnung verrichtet: [fol. 7r]
1. Introitus: Puer natus est nobis.
2. Kÿrie, Christe, Kÿrie.
3. Intonirt der Priester vor dem Altar das Gloria, Hierauff:
4. Missa.
5. Allein Gott in der Höh seÿ Ehr.
6. Collecta und die Epistel.
7. Gelobet seÿst du Jesu Christ.
8. Evangelium.
9. Intonirt der Priester das Credo.
10. Das Credo musicaliter.
11. Der Glaube.
12. Predigt, und vor derselben: Ein Kindelein so löbelich.

13. Ein groß Concert.
14. Collecta und der Segen
15. Zum Beschluß: Ach mein herzliebes Jesulein.

Zum Fünfften.

Vesper.

Zu welcher umb 1. Uhr zum Ersten, halbweg 2. Uhr [fol. 7v] zum Andern, und umb 2. Uhr zum drittenmahl geläutet wird.

1. Intonirt der Priester vor dem Altar: Deus in adjutorium vorauff der Chor antworttet.
2. Ein lateinischer Psalm musicaliter.
3. Die Gebuhrt unsers Herrn und Heilandes Jesu Christi, figuraliter.
4. Predigt, Und für dem Vater Unser: Ein Kindelein so löbelich.
5. Magnificat, Wozwischen die gewöhnlichen Teützschen Lieder, alß:
    1. Lobt Gott ihr Christen all.
    2. Wir Christen Leüth, und
    3. In dulci jubilo.
6. Collecta.
7. Benedicamus Domino.

[fol. 8r]

Den Andern Feÿer = oder St: Stephans Tag.

Wird es nachfolgender gestalt gehalten:

1. Zum Introitu: Grates nunc omnes, mit dem Teützschen, choraliter.
2. Missa, musicaliter.
3. Allein Gott in der Höh seÿ Ehr.
4. Collecta und die Epistel.
5. Vom Himmel hoch da komm ich her.
6. Evangelium.
7. Ein Concert.
8. Der Glaube.
9. Predigt, und für dem Vater Unser: Ein Kindelein so löbelich.
10. Ein Concert oder Motetto.

[fol. 8v]

11. Ein Teüzsch Lied.
12. Collecta und der Segen.
13. Ein kurz Lied oder Versicul zum Beschluß.

Vesper.

1. Deus in adjutorium.
2. Ein lateinischer Psalm, musicaliter.

3. Ein kurz Concert oder Motetto.
4. Lieset der Priester vorm Altar, einen Text, oder Psalmen abe.
5. Ein Teüzsch Lied.
6. Predigt, und für derselben, Ein Kindelein so löbelich.
7. Magnificat.
8. Ein Concert oder Motetto.
9. Ein Teüzsch Lied.
10. Collecta.
11. Benedicamus.
[fol. 9r]

Den Dritten Feÿer = oder St. Johannis Tag.

1. Zum Introitu: Christum Wir sollen loben schon.
2. Missa musicaliter.
3. Allein Gott in der Höh seÿ Ehr.
4. Collecta und die Epistel.
5. Vom Himmel kam der Engel Schaar.
6. Evangelium.
7. Concert oder Motetto.
8. Der Glaube.
9. Predigt, welche der hiesige Superintendens, Wie auch den Oster = und Pfingst dienstag verrichtet, und für derselben: Ein Kindelein so löbelich.
10. Ein Concert oder Motetto.
[fol. 9v]
11. Ein Teüzsch Lied.
12. Collecta und der Segen.
13. Ein kurz Lied, oder Versicul zum Beschluß.

Vesper.

1. Deus in adjutorium.
2. Ein lateinischer Psalm musicaliter.
3. Ein Concert oder Motetto.
4. Ein Teüzsch Lied.
5. Lieset der Priester, vor dem Altar einen Psalm, oder andern Text abe.
6. Magnificat.
7. Ein Concert oder Motetto.
8. Ein Teüzsch Lied.
9. Collecta.
10. Benedicamus.
[fol. 10r]

Am Heiligen Neüen Jahrs Tage.

Ziehen wiederumb alle Guardien auff, wird aber nicht geschoßen, Und wird der Gottes Dienst, folgender Ordnung nach verrichtet:
1. Zum Introitu: Helfft mir Gottes Güte preisen.
2. Missa, musicaliter.
3. Allein Gott in der Höh seÿ Ehr.
4. Collect und die Epistel.
5. Jesu nun seÿ gepreiset.
6. Evangelium.
7. Ein Teüzsch Concert, das alte Jahr vergangen ist, oder ein lateinisches.
8. Der Glaube.
9. Predigt, und für dem Vater Unser: Nun lasst uns Gott dem HERREN.
   [fol. 10v]
10. Concert.
11. Ein Teüzsch Lied.
12. Collecta und der Segen.
13. Ein kurz Lied zum Beschluß.

Mit der Vesper Predigt, wird es, wie am andern Feÿer Tage gehalten.

Am Fest Epiphaniae.

1. Introitus: Ecce advenit Dominator Dominus.
2. Missa.
3. Allein Gott in der Höh seÿ Ehr.
4. Collecta und die Epistel.
5. Puer natus in Bethlehem.

[fol. 11r]
6. Evangelium
7. Credo.
8. Der Glaube.
9. Predigt, und für dem Vater Unser: Ein Kindelein so löbelich.
10. Concert.
11. Was fürchtst du Feÿnd Herodes sehr.
12. Collecta und der Segen.
13. Zum Beschluß: Dancksagen Wir alle Gott.

Mit der Vesper wird es, wie am dritten Christ Feÿer Tage gehalten.

Am Fest Purificationis Mariae.

1. Introitus: Suscepimus Deus Misericordiam tuam.
2. Missa.

3. Allein Gott in der Höh seÿ Ehr.
[fol. 11v]
4. Collecta und die Epistel.
5. Gelobet seÿst du Jesu Christ.
6. Evangelium
7. Credo.
8. Der Glaube.
9. Predigt, und für dem Vater Unser Ein Kindelein so löbelich.

Nota.

Hierbeÿ zuerinnern, daß vom Christ Tage, biß auff dieses Fest, vor allen Sonntags Predigten, iztermeldtes Lied zu singen.
10. Lob Gesang Simeonis Teüzsch, oder lateinisch, musicaliter.
11. Mit Fried und Freüd fahr ich dahin.
12. Collecta, und der Segen.
13. Zum Beschluß: So fahr ich hin zu Jesu Christ.
Oder: Ach mein Herzliebes Jesulein.
Mit der Vesper wird es, wie am dritten Christ Feÿer Tage gehalten.
[fol. 12r]

Am Fest Annunciationis Mariae.

1. Introitus: Vultum tuum deprecabuntur omnes divites plebis.
2. Missa.
3. Allein Gott in der Höh seÿ Ehr.
4. Collecta und die Epistel.
5. Alß der gütige Gott vollenden wolt.
6. Evangelium.
7. Credo.
8. Der Glaube.
9. Predigt, und für dem Vater Unser: Ein kurzer Versicul, so sich auf das Fest schickt.
10. Concert.
11. Ein Teüzsch Lied.
12. Collecta und der Segen.
13. Ein kurz Lied zum Beschluß.
Auff dieses Fest, wird eine Vesper [fol. 12v] Predigt gehalten, wie bräuchlichen.

Nota.

Hierbeÿ zumercken: Wenn dieses Fest in der Char Wochen, oder am Heiligen Oster Tag gefällig, es jedesmahl auf den Palmen Sonntag zu celebriren.

In der Char Wochen.

Wird Montag, Dienstag, MittWoch, Grün Donnerstag, und Char Freÿtag gepredigt.
Wann die Herrschafft am Grünen Donnerstage communiciret, wird es wie gebräuchlichen, mit der Music gehalten und eine Vesper Predigt, beÿ welcher keine Music, und Orgel gebraucht wirdt.

Am Heiligen Oster Abend.

Wird es wie am Heiligen Christ Abend, mit der Vesper gehalten.
[fol. 13r]

Am Heiligen Oster = Tage.

Wird mit dem Schießen, Läuten, und auffziehen, gleich wie am Heiligen Christ Tage gehalten:

1. Introitus: Salve festa dies, Wozwischen zu dreÿen mahlen: Also heilig ist der Tag. 3. halbe Cartaunen gelöset werden.
2. Kÿrie, Christe, Kÿrie.
3. Intonirt der Priester vor dem Altar das Gloria.

Hierauff:

4. Missa.
5. Allein Gott in der Höh seÿ Ehr.
6. Collecta und die Epistel.
7. Christ lag in Todesbanden.
8. Evangelium.
9. Intonirt der Priester das Credo.
[fol. 13v]
10. Das Credo musicaliter.
11. Der Teützsche Glaube.
12. Predigt, und für derselben: Christ ist erstanden.
13. Ein Groß Concert.
14. Collecta und der Segen.
15. Zum Beschluß: Jesus Christus unser Heÿland.

Vesper.

1. Deus in adjutorium.
2. Der 114. Psalm, da Israel aus Egÿpten zog, Teüzsch, choraliter vor dem Bulde.
3. Die Aufferstehung unser Herrn und Heÿlandes Jesu Christi, figuraliter.
4. Predigt, und für dem Vater Unser: Also heilig ist der Tag.

 5. Magnificat.
 6. Ein Concert oder Motetto.
 7. Erschienen ist der herrliche Tag.
 8. Collecta.
 9. Benedicamus.
[fol. 14r]

Am Oster Montage.

 1. Zum Introitu: Surrexit Christus hodie.
 2. Missa.
 3. Allein Gott in der Höh seÿ Ehr.
 4. Collecta und die Epistel.
 5. Erschienen ist der herrlich Tag.
 6. Evangelium.
 7. Ein Concert.
 8. Der Glaube.
 9. Predigt, und für dem Vater Unser: Christ ist erstanden.
10. Ein Concert.
11. Ein Teüzsch Lied.
12. Collecta und der Segen.
13. Ein kurz Lied, oder Versicul zum Beschluß.
Mit der Vesper Predigt, wird es gleich dem Andern Christ Tag gehalten.
[fol. 14v]

Am Oster Dienstage.

 1. Zum Introitu: Erstanden ist der Heilige Christ.
 2. Missa musicaliter.
 3. Allein Gott in der Höh seÿ Ehr.
 4. Collecta und die Epistel.
 5. Christ lag in Todesbanden.
 6. Evangelium.
 7. Ein Concert.
 8. Der Glaube.
 9. Predigt, und für derselben, Christ ist erstanden, So auch die fol-
    gende Sonntage, biß auff Himmelfahrt gesung wird.
10. Ein Concert.
11. Ein Teüzsch Lied.
12. Collecta und der Segen.
[fol. 15r]
13. Ein kurz Lied, oder Versicul zum Beschluß.

Mit der Vesper wird es gleich wie am dritten Christ Tage gehalten.

Am Sonntage Qvasimodogeniti.

Ziehen die Guardien, wie am Neüen Jahrs Tage auff, und wird zweÿmahl geprediget, wie am andern feÿer Tage.

Am Himmelfahrts Tage.

1. Introitus: Viri Galilaei quid admiramini aspicientes in coelum.
[fol. 15v]
2. Missa musicaliter.
3. Allein Gott in der Höh seÿ Ehr.
4. Collecta und die Epistel.
5. Nun freüt eüch lieben Christen gemein.
6. Evangelium.
7. Credo.
8. Der Glaube.
9. Predigt, und für derselben: Christ fuhr gen Himmel, so den folgenden Sonntag.
10. Concert.
11. Ein Teüzsch Lied.
12. Collecta und der Segen.
13. Ein kurz Teüzsch Lied zum Beschluß.
Wird auch diesen Tag eine Vesper Predigt gehalten.

Am Heiligen Pfingst Abend.

Wird es wie am Heiligen Christ = und Oster Abend mit der Vesper gehalten.
[fol. 16r]

Am Heiligen Pfingst = Tage.

Wird es mit dem Schießen, Läuten, auffziehen, gleich wie an Weihnachten, und Ostern gehalten.
1. Introitus: Spiritus Domini replevit orbem Terrarum.
2. Kÿrie, Christe, Kÿrie.
3. Intonirt vor dem Altar, der Priester das Gloria.

Hierauff.

4. Missa.
5. Allein Gott in der Höh seÿ Ehr.
6. Collecta und die Epistel.
7. Nun bitten Wir den Heiligen Geist.
8. Evangelium.

9. Intonirt der Priester das Credo.
10. Das Credo musicaliter.
[fol. 16v]
11. Der Teützsche Glaube.
12. Predigt, und vor derselben: Komm Heiliger Geist Herre etc.
13. Ein Groß Concert.
14. Collecta und der Segen.
15. Ein kurz Teüzsch Lied, oder Versicul zum Beschluß.

Vesper.

1. Deus in adjutorium.
2. Ein lateinisher Psalm musicaliter.
3. Veni Sancte Spiritus.
4. Lieset der Priester vor dem Altar, einen Psalm, oder andern Text abe.
5. Komm Gott Schöpffer Heiliger Geist.
6. Predigt, und für derselben: Nun bitten Wir den Heiligen Geist.
7. Magnificat.
8. Ein Concert oder Motetto.
9. Komm Heiliger Geist Herre Gott.
[fol. 17r]
10. Collecta.
11. Benedicamus.

Den Pfingst Montag, und Dienstag.

Wird es, wie am Oster Montage, und Dienstage gehalten.

Am Fest der Heiligen Dreÿfaltigkeit.

Ziehen die Guardien, wie am Neüen Jahrs Tage, und [fol. 17v] Qvasimodogeniti auff, und wird der Gottesdienst folgender Ordnung nach verrichtet:

1. Introitus: Benedicta sit Sancta Trinitas.
2. Missa.
3. Collecta und die Epistel.
4. Gott der Vater Wohn uns beÿ.
5. Evangelium.
6. Credo.
7. Der Teützsche Glaube.
8. Predigt, und für dem Vater Unser: Allein Gott in der Höh seÿ Ehr.
9. Das Te Deum laudamus, lateinisch, musicaliter.
10. Collecta und der Segen.
11. Der du bist dreÿ in Einigkeit.

Wird auch diesen Tag, eine Vesper Predigt gehalten.
[fol. 18r]

Am S. Johannis Tage.

Nachdem zum Erstenmahl, halbweg Sieben Uhr geläutet, ziehen alle Guardien auff, und wird von denenselben, unter dem Te Deum laudamus, Wie auch aus denen Stücken Salve gegeben.

1. Introitus: De Ventre matris meae, vocavit me Dominus.
2. Missa.
3. Allein Gott in der Höh seÿ Ehr.
4. Collecta und die Epistel.
[fol. 18v]
5. Gelobet seÿ der HERR, der Gott Israel.
6. Evangelium.
7. Credo.
8. Der Glaube.
9. Predigt, und für derselben: Ein kurz Lied.
10. Das Te Deum laudamus teüzsch.
    Worzu die Trompeten und Heer Paucken gebraucht, und 3. Salven gegeben werden, alß:
    Die Erste unter den Wortten: Heilig, Heilig, Heilig, die andere: Täglich HERR Gott etc.
11. Collecta und der Segen.
    Worauff die Dritte Salve.
12. Ein kurz Lied zum Beschluß.
Die Vesper wird wie am Heiligen Abend gehalten.
[fol. 19r]

Am Fest Visitationis Mariae.

1. Introitus: Gaudeamus in Domino omnes.
2. Missa.
3. Allein Gott in der Höh seÿ Ehr.
4. Collecta und die Epistel.
5. Meine Seele erhebt den HERREN.
6. Evangelium.
7. Credo.
8. Der Glaube.
9. Predigt, und für derselben: Ein kurz Lied oder Versicul.
10. Concert.
11. Collecta und der Segen.
12. Ein kurz Lied zum Beschluß.

Die Vesper, wie am dritten Pfingsttage bräuchlichen ist.
[fol. 19v]

Am Tage Mariae Magdalenae.

1. Zum Introitu: Erbarm dich mein o Herre Gott.
2. Missa musicaliter.
3. Allein Gott in der Höh seÿ Ehr.
4. Collecta und die Epistel.
5. Ach Gott und Herr, wie groß etc.
6. Evangelium.
7. Litania Teüzsch, musicaliter.
8. Der Glaube.
9. Predigt, und für derselben: Ein kurz Liedt, oder Versicul.
10. Herr Gott dich loben Wir.
11. Ein Concert, oder Motetto.
12. Collecta und der Segen.
[fol. 20r]
13. Ein kurz Lied zum Beschluß.
Wird Vesper wie am Heiligen Abend.

Am Fest St: Michäelis.

1. Introitus: Benedicite Domino omnes Angelicjus.
2. Missa.
3. Allein Gott in der Höh seÿ Ehr.
4. Collecta und die Epistel.
5. Nun lob meine Seele den HERREN.
6. Evangelium.
7. Credo.
8. Der Glaube.
[fol. 20v]
9. Predigt, und für derselben: Ein kurz Lied, oder Versicul.
10. Ein Concert.
11. Ein Teüzsch Lied.
12. Collecta und der Segen.
13. Gott seÿ uns gnädig und barmherzig.
Und wird diesen Tag eine Vesper Predigt gehalten.

Nota.

Wann ein Gebuhrts Tag einfällt, alß den 31. Maÿ, steht jedesmahl sich zu vergleichen, wie es damit zuhalten.
[fol. 21r]

Ordnung.

Der Wochen Predigten, Mittwochs, und Freÿtags.

Erstlichen.

Von Ostern biß Michäelis, und frühe Dreÿ Vierteil auff Sieben Uhr, der Gottes Dienst angefangen, und von Michäelis biß wiederumb Ostern umb Sieben Uhr.

Zum Andern.

Würd es MittWochs, und Freÿtags also gehalten:
[fol. 21v]
Daß die Orgel jedesmahl, außer in der Fasten, Von Laetare ahn gebraucht würde.

1. Und Erstlich, zum Anfange, nach der Ordnung durch, ein Psalm D. Cornelii Beckers, nach den Melodien, des Cappellmeisters, Heinrich Schüzens, Wann es aber ein langer, wird solcher auff zweÿmahl, auch wohl dreÿmahl, und der 119. Psalm offter getheilt.
2. Ein Teüzsch Lied.
3. Collect, und ein Capittel aus dem Neüen Testament (:wo selbiges auch zu lang, wird es ebenfalls getheilt:) In der Fasten aber, wird ein Stück aus der Passion gelesen.
4. Teützscher Glaube.
5. Predigt.
6. Wiederumb ein Teüzsch Lied, des Freÿtags aber die Litaneÿ.
7. Collect und der Segen.

Drittens.

Wann ein Apostel Tag gefällig, Alß:
[fol. 22r]

1.	Den 30. Novembris	St. Andreas.
2.	Den 21. Decembris	Thomas.
3.	Den 25. Januarÿ	Pauli Bekehrung.
4.	Den 24. im Schalt Jahr 25 Februarÿ	Matthias.
5.	Den 1. Maÿ	Philippi Iacobi.
6.	Den 29. Junÿ	Petri Pauli.
7.	Den 25. Julÿ	Iacobi.
8.	Den 24. Augusti	Bartholomaei.
9.	Den 21. Septembris	Matthaei, und
10.	Den 28. Octobris	Simon Iudae.

So dieser Tag einer auff den Sonntag gefiele, blieb er selbiges Jahr außen.

Gefällt solcher aber auff den Montag, dienstag, oder Mittwoch, Würde er MittWochs gehalten.

Gefällt derselbe auff den Donnerstag, Freÿtag, oder SonnAbend, würde er Freÿtags in folgender Ordnung gehalten:

1. Zum Introitu: Ein Psalm D. Cornelii Beckers, [fol. 22v] nach des Cappellmeisters, Heinrich Schüzens Melodien, wie selbiger in der Ordnung gefällig.
2. Kÿrie, Gott Vater in Ewigkeit.
3. All Ehr und Lob soll Gottes seÿn.
4. Collecta und gewöhnliche Epistel.
5. Ein Teüzsch Lied.
6. Das Evangelium.
7. Ein Concert.
8. Teützscher Glaube.
9. Die Predigt.
10. Ein Concert.
11. Wiederumb ein Teüzsch Lied.
12. Collecta und der Segen.

Zum Vierden.

Der 31. Octobris, er falle, auff was vor einen Tag er wolle, Würde zum Gedächtnüs, Weill diesen Tag, das Heilige Evan= [fol. 23r] gelium durch herrn Lutherum wiederumb aus Liecht bracht, folgender gestalt gehalten und celebrirt:

Gefällt er aber auff einen Sontag, wird die Musica mitgebraucht wie an ander Sontägen bräuchlich.

Die Missa und das Credo.

1. Zum Introitu: Ein Veste Burg ist unser Gott.
2. Kÿrie Gott Vater in Ewigkeit.
3. Allein Gott in der Höh seÿ Ehr.
4. Collect, und ein Text, anstatt der Epistel welchen der Herr Ober Hoff Prediger ordenen wirdt.
5. O Herre Gott, dein Göttlich Wortt.
6. Ein Text anstatt des Evangelii, so ebenfalls der Herr Ober Hoff Prediger zuordnen.
7. Nun lob meine Seele den HERRN.
8. Wir gläuben all an einen Gott.
9. Predigt.
10. Erhalt uns Herr beÿ deinem Wortt.

[fol. 23v]

11.   Collect und der Segen.

12.   Ach bleib beÿ uns Herr Jesu Christ.

Der St. Martini Tag, wird dem herrn Luthero zum Gedächtnüs, gleich wie ein Apostel Tag, begangen, den 10. oder 11. Novembris.

Wann aber selbiger auffn Sonntag gefällig, wird er ingleichen mitbegangen

13: Translation

Johann Georg II's Chapel Order.
Undated

[SLB Msc. K. 89, fols. 1–23]

[fol. 1r]

Order

How the most serene nobly born Prince and Lord, Lord Johann Georg II, Duke of Saxony, Jülich, Cleve, and Berg, Erzmarschall and Elector of the Holy Roman Empire, Landgrave in Thuringia, Margrave of Meissen and Upper and Lower Lausitz, Burgrave of Magdeburg, Earl of Marburg and Ravensberg, Lord of Ravenstein, etc. shall henceforth celebrate feast days, Sundays, and weekdays in your palace chapel with your court ensemble.

[fol. 2r]

First.

Concerning the German hymns, the senior court preacher shall always be at liberty to keep [the] main prescribed [order] or, at his discretion, to change it, including the other texts, those in Latin as well as in German, provided for the composition of the concerti and motets which shall always be shown to him by the Kapellmeister. He shall be likewise free to reorder or subtract one or more hymns.

Whereby this is also to be remembered: When the sovereign is not in his residence, the court ensemble shall stand at the further command of the senior court preacher.

Second.

For all feast days, as they are prescribed (except the three main feast days), namely the first Sunday in Advent, New Years, Epiphany, Feast of the Purification, Feast of the Annunciation, Quasimogeniti Sunday, Ascension, Trinity, St. John's Day, Feast of the Visitation, Feast of Mary

Magdalen, and Michaelmas as well as all Saturdays, Sundays, and Wednesdays.

[fol. 2v]

It shall now be customary to celebrate a Latin Vesper interspersed with German hymns on both the feast days of St. John the Baptist and St. Mary Magdalen.

These Vespers, as well as the weekday services and prayer meetings, shall be carried out by the court cantor, the choristers, and the organist assigned [to play for these services].

Third.

The Vespers and prayer meetings shall be celebrated in the following manner:

Vespers.

1. The priest shall intone from the altar:
   Deus in adjutorium, whereupon the choir answers.
2. On feast days and holy eves, a German Psalm shall be sung *choraliter* from the lectern, as ordered by the senior court preacher. Sundays, [fol. 3r] Wednesdays, and Saturdays, a German Psalm likewise [shall be sung] in order of succession.
3. On all high feast days, holy eves, and Sundays, a Latin or German concerto or motet shall be performed.
4. A German hymn.
5. The priest shall read a Psalm or another text from the altar, and thereafter the customary prayer and Our Father [shall be read].
   The holy eves before the feast days (except the three high feast days), however, a boy shall read the Epistle from the gallery.
6. On high feast days, holy eves, and Sundays, the Magnificat shall be performed in Latin but on Wednesdays and Saturdays *choraliter,* in Latin or German alternately.
7. A German hymn.
8. Collect and Benediction.

[fol. 3v]

Prayer Meetings.

Mondays, Tuesdays, Thursdays, and Fridays shall be celebrated:
1. *Deus in adjutorium.*
2. A Psalm, according to the order, from the Becker [Psalter].
3. A German hymn.
4. From the altar, the priest shall read a Psalm or another text along with the customary prayer and Our Father.

5. A German hymn.
6. Collect and Benediction.

Note.

During Lent from Monday after Laetare Sunday until Good Friday, except for the Feast of the Annunciation [fol. 4r] and the previous evening a prayer meeting and not a Latin Vesper shall be celebrated.

Fourth.

After the bells are rung a third time, the first Sunday of Advent as the beginning of the church year shall be celebrated as follows:
1. Introit: *Rorate Coeli de super.* On the other Sundays, however, throughout the entire year, a German hymn [shall be sung] instead of the introit.
2. Kyrie, Christe, Kyrie ⎫ *musicaliter*
3. The complete Mass ⎭

Note.

When, however, the sovereign receives communion, at that [fol. 4v] time three German hymns or Psalms chosen by the senior court preacher shall be sung between the [sections of the] Kyrie. Thereafter the priest shall intone the Gloria from the altar, followed by the Mass, and then:
4. "Allein Gott in der Höh sei Ehr."
5. Collect and the Epistle.
6. "Nun komm der Heiden Heiland."
If [there is] communion, however, the Litany [shall be sung] in German, *figuraliter* or *choraliter*. If the latter is used, the boys shall sing kneeling before the altar. When [communion] is celebrated on the two main feast days, Christmas and Easter, a German feast day hymn shall be used instead of the Litany.
7. Gospel.

Note.

If [there is] communion, the priest shall intone the Credo.
8. The Credo *figuraliter* [but] a short concerto or motet on other Sundays.
9. The Creed in German.
[fol. 5r]
10. The sermon, and before it, a short hymn or versicle, one or more, which shall be used only on the first Sunday in Advent or when communion is received.

11. After the sermon, a concerto or motet.
12. Thereupon a German hymn.

Note.

When communion [is taken], the concerto or motet shall be omitted and [there shall be] sung instead "Allein zu dir Herr Jesu Christ."
13. Consecration and administering of the holy sacrament, during which the customary German hymns shall be sung.
14. Collect and Benediction.
15. In conclusion, a short German hymn or versicle.

On the first Sunday in Advent, after the bells have been rung a third time at 2:00, Vespers accompanied by a sermon shall be celebrated, for Vespers and a sermon is otherwise always celebrated if the sovereign receives communion.
[fol. 5v]

Fifth.

[The music on] the second, third, and fourth Sundays in Advent, the Sunday after Christmas, the Sunday after New Years Day, and the four Sundays in Lent, namely Invocavit, Reminiscere, Oculi, and Laetare, likewise the Feast of Rogations and the tenth Sunday after Trinity shall be performed a capella, likewise if Christmas Eve falls on a Sunday.

On Judica Sunday, Palm Sunday, and Good Friday, the Passion shall be sung.

Holy Christmas.

On Christmas Eve, the bells shall be rung at 1:30 the first time and at [fol. 16r] 1:45 a second time.

Vespers.

1. *Deus in adjutorium.*
2. A Latin Psalm, *musicaliter.*
3. A concerto or motet.
4. A German hymn.
5. The priest shall read a Psalm or another text from the altar.
6. Magnificat.
7. A concerto, or motet.
8. A German hymn.
9. Collect.
10. *Benedicamus.*

On Holy Christmas Day.

First.

At 4:00 three shots shall be fired from the Kreuzturm [fol. 6v] whereupon immediately in the palace, in and outside the city, and in old Dresden, the feast day shall be announced with the ringing of all the bells until 4:30. This custom shall always be observed whether the sovereign is in his residence or not.

Second.

After the bells are rung for a second time at 6:30, the guards shall come on duty and three shots fired from three demi-cannon and the guards shall fire three salutes.

Third.

The bells shall be rung at 6:30 a first time, at 7:00 a second time, and at 7:30 a third time as all other feast days and Sundays are observed.

Fourth.

The worship service in church shall be celebrated in the following order: [fol. 7r]

1. Introit: *Puer natus est nobis.*
2. Kyrie, Christe, Kyrie.
3. The priest shall intone the Gloria from the altar, hereupon:
4. Mass.
5. "Allein Gott in der Höh sei Ehr."
6. Collect and the Epistle.
7. "Gelobet seist du Jesu Christ."
8. Gospel.
9. The priest shall intone the Credo from the altar.
10. The Credo *musicaliter.*
11. The Creed.
12. Sermon, and before it: "Ein Kindelein so löbelich."
13. A great concerto.
14. Collect and Benediction.
15. In conclusion: "Ach mein herzliebes Jesulein."

Fifth.

Vespers.

At which the bells shall be rung at 1:00 a first time, at 1:30 [fol. 7v] a second time, and at 2:00 a third time.

1. The priest shall intone from the altar: *Deus in adjutorium,* whereupon the choir answers.
2. A Latin Psalm *musicaliter.*
3. *Die Geburt unsers Herrn und Heilandes Jesu Christi, figuraliter.*
4. Sermon and before the Our Father: "Ein Kindelein so löbelich."
5. Magnificat, in-between the customary German hymns, namely:
    1. "Lobt Gott ihr Christen all."
    2. "Wir Christenleut," and
    3. "In dulci jubilo."
6. Collect.
7. *Benedicamus Domino.*

[fol. 8r]

The Second Holiday or St. Stephen's Day.

Shall be celebrated in the following manner:
1. Introit: *Grates nunc omnes,* in German, *choraliter.*
2. Mass, *musicaliter.*
3. "Allein Gott in der Höh sei Ehr."
4. Collect and Epistle.
5. "Vom Himmel hoch da komm ich her."
6. Gospel.
7. A concerto.
8. The Creed.
9. Sermon, and before the Our Father: "Ein Kindelein so löbelich."
10. A concerto or motet.

[fol. 8v]

11. A German hymn.
12. Collect and Benediction.
13. In conclusion, a short hymn or versicle.

Vespers.

1. *Deus in adjutorium.*
2. A Latin Psalm, *musicaliter.*
3. A short concerto or motet.
4. The priest shall read a text or Psalm at the altar.
5. A German hymn.
6. Sermon, and before it: "Ein Kindelein so löbelich."
7. Magnificat.
8. A concerto or motet.
9. A German hymn.
10. Collect.

11. *Benedicamus.*
[fol. 9r]

The Third Holiday or St. John's Day.

1. Introit: "Christum wir sollen loben schon."
2. Mass *musicaliter.*
3. "Allein Gott in der Höh sei Ehr."
4. Collect and Epistle.
5. "Vom Himmel kam der Engel Schaar."
6. Gospel.
7. Concerto or motet.
8. The Creed.
9. A sermon preached by the current superintendent as well as on Easter and Whittuesday, and before it: "Ein Kindelein so löbelich."
10. A concerto or motet.
[fol. 9v]
11. A German hymn.
12. Collect and Benediction.
13. In conclusion, a short hymn or versicle.

Vespers.

1. *Deus in adjutorium.*
2. A Latin Psalm *musicaliter.*
3. A concerto or motet.
4. A German hymn.
5. The priest shall read a Psalm or another text at the altar.
6. Magnificat.
7. A concerto or motet.
8. A German hymn.
9. Collect.
10. *Benedicamus.*
[fol. 10r]

On Holy New Years Day.

All the guards shall again come on duty, but no shots fired, and the worship services celebrated in the following order:
1. Introit: "Helft mir Gottes Güte preisen."
2. Mass, *musicaliter.*
3. "Allein Gott in der Höh sei Ehr."
4. Collect and Epistle.
5. "Jesu nun sei gepreiset."
6. Gospel.

7. A German or Latin concerto [celebrating] the end of the year.
8. The Creed.
9. Sermon, and before the Our Father: "Nun lasst uns Gott dem HERREN."

[fol. 10v]

10. Concerto.
11. A German hymn.
12. Collect and Benediction.
13. In conclusion, a short hymn.

Vespers with a sermon shall be celebrated as on other holidays.

On the Feast of Epiphany.

1. Introit: *Ecce advenit Dominator Dominus.*
2. Mass.
3. "Allein Gott in der Höh sei Ehr."
4. Collect and Epistle.
5. *Puer natus in Bethlehem.*

[fol. 11r]

6. Gospel.
7. Credo.
8. The Creed.
9. Sermon, and before the Our Father: "Ein Kindelein so löbelich."
10. Concerto.
11. "Was fürchtst du Feind Herodes sehr."
12. Collect and Benediction.
13. In conclusion: "Danksagen wir alle Gott."

Vespers shall be celebrated as on the third day of Christmas.

On the Feast of the Purification.

1. Introit: *Suscepimus Deus Misericordiam tuam."*
2. Mass.
3. "Allein Gott in der Höh sei Ehr."

[fol. 11v]

4. Collect and Epistle.
5. "Gelobet seist du Jesu Christ."
6. Gospel.
7. Credo.
8. The Creed.
9. Sermon, and before the Our Father: "Ein Kindelein so löbelich."

Note.

As a reminder, the now-mentioned hymn shall be sung before all Sunday sermons from Christmas until this feast day.

10. Canticle of Simon in German or Latin, *musicaliter.*
11. "Mit Fried und Freud fahr ich dahin."
12. Collect, and Benediction.
13. In conclusion: "So fahr ich hin zu Jesu Christ."
     Or: "Ach mein herzliebes Jesulein."
Vespers shall be celebrated as on the third day of Christmas.
[fol. 12r]

On the Feast of the Annunciation.

1. Introit: *Vultum tuum deprecabuntur omnes dirites plebis.*
2. Mass.
3. "Allein Gott in der Höh sei Ehr."
4. Collect and Epistle.
5. "Als der gütige Gott vollenden wolt."
6. Gospel.
7. Credo.
8. The Creed.
9. Sermon, and before the Our Father: a short versicle appropriate to the feast day.
10. Concerto.
11. A German hymn.
12. Collect and Benediction.
13. In conclusion, a short hymn.
On this feast day, Vespers [fol. 12v] with a sermon shall be celebrated, as is customary.

Note.

It is to be noted herewith: If this feast day falls during Passion or on holy Easter, it shall always be celebrated on Palm Sunday.

During Passion Week.

Services shall be held Monday, Tuesday, Wednesday, Maundy Thursday, and Good Friday.

When the sovereign receives communion on Maundy Thursday, which shall be celebrated with the court ensemble, as is customary, and Vespers with a sermon [shall be celebrated] at which the ensemble and organ shall not be used.

On Holy Easter Eve.

Shall be celebrated as on Christmas Eve with Vespers.
[fol. 13r]

On Holy Easter Sunday.

Shall be celebrated with shooting, bell ringing, and [guards] parading exactly as on Holy Christmas:
1. Introit: *Salve festa dies.* Three times in-between "Also heilig ist der Tag," three demi-cannon shall be fired.
2. Kyrie, Christe, Kyrie.
3. The priest shall intone the Gloria from the altar.

Whereupon.

4. Mass.
5. "Allein Gott in der Höh sei Ehr."
6. Collect and Epistle.
7. "Christ lag in Todesbanden."
8. Gospel.
9. The priest shall intone the Credo.
[fol. 13v]
10. The Credo *musicaliter.*
11. The German Creed.
12. Sermon, and before it: "Christ ist erstanden."
13. A great concerto.
14. Collect and Benediction.
15. In conclusion: "Jesus Christus unser Heiland."

Vespers.

1. *Deus in adjutorium.*
2. Psalm 114, "Da Israel aus Egypten zog," in German, *choraliter* at the lectern.
3. *Die Auferstehung unser Herrn und Heilandes Jesu Christi, figuraliter.*
4. Sermon, and before the Our Father: "Also heilig ist der Tag."
5. Magnificat.
6. A concerto or motet.
7. "Erschienen ist der herrliche Tag."
8. Collect.
9. *Benedicamus.*
[fol. 14r]

On Easter Monday.

1. Introit: *Surrexit Christus hodie.*
2. Mass.
3. "Allein Gott in der Höh sei Ehr."
4. Collect and Epistle.
5. "Erschienen ist der herrlich Tag."
6. Gospel.
7. A concerto.
8. The Creed.
9. Sermon, and before the Our Father: "Christ ist erstanden."
10. A concerto.
11. A German hymn.
12. Collect and Benediction.
13. In conclusion, a short hymn or versicle.

Vespers with a sermon shall be celebrated exactly as on the second day of Christmas.
[fol. 14v]

On Easter Tuesday.

1. Introit: "Erstanden ist der heilige Christ."
2. Mass *musicaliter.*
3. "Allein Gott in der Höh sei Ehr."
4. Collect and Epistle.
5. "Christ lag in Todesbanden."
6. Gospel.
7. A concerto.
8. The Creed.
9. Sermon, and before it, "Christ ist erstanden," which shall be sung as well on the following Sunday until Ascension.
10. A concerto.
11. A German hymn.
12. Collect and Benediction.
[fol. 15r]
13. In conclusion, a short hymn or versicle.

Vespers shall be celebrated exactly as on the third day of Christmas.

On Quasimodogeniti Sunday.

The guard shall come on duty, as on New Year's Day, and two services shall take place, as on other holidays.

On Ascension.

1. Introit: *Viri Galilaei grid admiramini aspicientes in coelum.*
[fol. 15v]
2. Mass *musicaliter.*
3. "Allein Gott in der Höh sei Ehr."
4. Collect and Epistle.
5. "Nun freut euch lieben Christen gemein."
6. Gospel.
7. Credo.
8. The Creed.
9. Sermon, and before it: "Christ fuhr gen Himmel," as on the following Sunday.
10. Concerto.
11. A German hymn.
12. Collect and Benediction.
13. In conclusion, a short hymn.
Vespers with a sermon shall also be celebrated on this day.

On Holy Eve of Whitsunday.

Shall be celebrated with Vespers as on Christmas Eve and Easter Eve.
[fol. 16r]

On Holy Whitsunday.

It shall be celebrated with shooting, bell ringing, and [guards] parading exactly as on Christmas and Easter.
1. Introit: *Spiritus Domini replevit orbem Terrarum.*
2. Kyrie, Christe, Kyrie.
3. The priest shall intone the Gloria from the altar.

Hereupon.

4. Mass.
5. "Allein Gott in der Höh sei Ehr."
6. Collect and Epistle.
7. "Nun bitten wir den heiligen Geist."
8. Gospel.
9. The priest shall intone the Credo.
10. The Credo *musicaliter.*
[fol. 16v]
11. The German Creed.
12. Sermon, and before it: "Komm heiliger Geist Herre [Gott]"
13. A great concerto.

14. Collect and Benediction.
15. In conclusion, a short German hymn or versicle.

Vespers.

1. *Deus in adjutorium.*
2. A Latin Psalm *musicaliter.*
3. *Veni Sancte Spiritus.*
4. The priest shall read a Psalm or another text from the altar.
5. "Komm Gott Schöpfer heiliger Geist."
6. Sermon, and before it: "Nun bitten wir den heiligen Geist."
7. Magnificat.
8. A concerto or motet.
9. "Komm heiliger Geist Herre Gott."
[fol. 17r]
10. Collect.
11. *Benedicamus.*

Whitmonday and Whittuesday.

They shall be celebrated as on Easter Monday and Tuesday.

On the Feast of the Holy Trinity.

The guards shall come on duty as on New Year's Day and [fol. 17v] Quasimodogeniti and the worship service shall be celebrated according to the following order:
1. Introit: *Benedicta sit Sancta Trinitas.*
2. Mass.
3. Collect and Epistle.
4. "Gott der Vater wohn uns bei."
5. Gospel.
6. Credo.
7. The German Creed.
8. Sermon, and before the Our Father: "Allein Gott in der Höh sei Ehr."
9. The *Te Deum laudamus,* in Latin, *musicaliter.*
10. Collect and Benediction.
11. "Der du bist drei in Einigkeit."
Vespers with a sermon shall also be celebrated on this day.
[fol. 18r]

On St. John's Day.

After the bells are rung for a first time at 6:30, the guards shall come on duty and during the *Te Deum laudamus* fire three salutes from their guns.

1. Introit: *De ventre matris meae, vocavit me Dominus.*
2. Mass.
3. "Allein Gott in der Höh sei Ehr."
4. Collect and Epistle.

[fol. 18v]

5. "Gelobet sei der HERR, der Gott Israel."
6. Gospel.
7. Credo.
8. The Creed.
9. Sermon, and before it: a short hymn.
10. The *Te Deum laudamus* in German for which the trumpets and timpani are used and three salutes sounded, namely:
    The first during the words: "Heilig, Heilig, Heilig," the second: "Täglich HERR Gott, etc."
11. Collect and Benediction.
    Whereupon the third salute [shall be fired].
12. In conclusion, a short hymn.

Vespers shall be celebrated as on Christmas Eve.

[fol. 19r]

On the Feast of the Visitation.

1. Introit: *Gaudeamus in Domino omnes.*
2. Mass.
3. "Allein Gott in der Höh sei Ehr."
4. Collect and Epistle.
5. "Meine Seele erhebt den HERREN."
6. Gospel.
7. Credo.
8. The Creed.
9. Sermon, and before it: A short hymn or versicle.
10. Concerto.
11. Collect and Benediction.
12. In conclusion, a short hymn.

Vespers [shall be celebrated] as is customary on the third day of Whitsuntide.

[fol. 19v]

On the Feast of Mary Magdalen.

1. Introit: "Erbarm dich mein o Herre Gott."
2. Mass *musicaliter*.
3. "Allein Gott in der Höh sei Ehr."
4. Collect and Epistle.
5. "Ach Gott und Herr, wie groß [und schwer]"
6. Gospel.
7. Litany in German, *musicaliter*.
8. The Creed.
9. Sermon, and before it: A short hymn or versicle.
10. "Herr Gott dich loben wir."
11. A concerto or motet.
12. Collect and Benediction.
[fol. 20r]
13. In conclusion, a short hymn.

Vespers [shall be celebrated] as on Christmas Eve.

On the Feast of St. Michael.

1. Introit: *Benedicite Domino omnes Angelicus*.
2. Mass.
3. "Allein Gott in der Höh sei Ehr."
4. Collect and Epistle.
5. "Nun lob meine Seele den HERREN."
6. Gospel.
7. Credo.
8. The Creed.
[fol. 20v]
9. Sermon, and before it: A short hymn or versicle.
10. A concerto.
11. A German hymn.
12. Collect and Benediction.
13. "Gott sei uns gnädig und barmherzig."

On this day, Vespers with a sermon shall be held.

Note.

When a birthday falls [on this holiday], such as 31 May [Johann Georg II's birthday], they shall always be celebrated equally.
[fol. 21r]

Order.

Of the weekday services [on] Wednesdays and Fridays.

First.

From Easter to Michaelmas, the worship service shall begin early at 6:45, and from Michaelmas until Easter again at 7:00.

Second.

Wednesdays and Fridays shall be celebrated:
[fol. 21v]
The organ shall be used at all times from Laetare except in Lent.

1. And first, the beginning [of the service], according to the order throughout, a Psalm of Dr. Becker set to the melodies by the Kapell-meister Heinrich Schütz [shall be sung]. When it is too long, how-ever, it shall be divided in half or even in thirds and Psalm 119 divided [in this way] from time to time.
2. A German hymn.
3. Collect and a chapter from the New Testament (when [the chapter] is also too long, it shall be divided as well). In Lent, however, a section from the Passion shall be read.
4. German Creed.
5. Sermon.
6. Again a German hymn, but on Friday the Litany.
7. Collect and Benediction.

Third.

When an Apostle's Day falls [on a Wednesday or a Friday]
[fol. 22r]

1.	30 November	St. Andreas.
2.	21 December	Thomas.
3.	25 January	Conversion of Paul.
4.	24 February (in Leap Year, 25 February)	Matthew.
5.	1 May	Philip Jacobi.
6.	29 June	Peter Paul.
7.	25 July	Jacob.
8.	24 August	Bartholomew.
9.	21 September	Matthew, and
10.	28 October	Simon Judas.

If [an Apostle's] day falls on a Sunday, it shall be omitted that year.

If it falls on a Monday, Tuesday, or Wednesday, however, it shall be celebrated on Wednesday.

If it falls on Thursday, Friday, or Saturday, it shall be celebrated on Friday in the following order:

1. Introit: A Psalm of Dr. Cornelius Becker set to the melodies [fol. 22v] of the Kapellmeister Heinrich Schütz as the order specifies.
2. "Kyrie, Gott Vater in Ewigkeit."
3. "All Ehr und Lob soll Gottes sein."
4. Collect and customary Epistle.
5. A German hymn.
6. The Gospel.
7. A concerto.
8. German Creed.
9. The sermon.
10. A concerto.
11. A German hymn once again.
12. Collect and Benediction.

Fourth.

On whatever day it falls, 31 October [a day of] remembrance because on this day the holy Gospel [fol. 23r] was again brought to light by Luther, shall be observed and celebrated in the following manner:

If [31 October] falls on a Sunday, however, the court ensemble shall participate as is customary on other Sundays.

The Mass and the Credo.

1. Introit: "Ein feste Burg ist unser Gott."
2. "Kyrie, Gott Vater in Ewigkeit."
3. "Allein Gott in der Höh sei Ehr."
4. Collect, and a text rather than the Epistle which shall be selected by the senior court preacher.
5. "O Herre Gott, dein göttlich Wort."
6. A text instead of the Gospel, also selected by the senior court preacher.
7. "Nun lob meine Seele den Herrn."
8. "Wir glauben all an einen Gott."
9. Sermon.
10. "Erhalt uns Herr bei deinem Wort."

[fol. 23v]

11. Collect and Benediction.
12. "Ach bleib bei uns Herr Jesu Christ."

St. Martin's Day, in remembrance of Luther, shall be celebrated on 10 or 11 November exactly like on Apostle's Day.

This [holiday] shall be observed even when it falls on a Sunday.

14

Johann Georg II to the President and Advisors of the Privy Chamber of Dresden. Dresden, 27 March 1663

[SAD Loc. 10441. *Steuer-Sachen 1661–1664*, fol. 179]

[fol. 179r]
An Praesident und Räthe beÿ der Geheimen Cammer zu dresden
Dresden den 27. Martÿ 1663
     Johann George der Ander Churfürst etc.
Beste Räthe und lieben getreüe.
Wir haben vor diesen gnädigste verordnung gethan, daß Unserm alten
Capellmeister und lieben getreüen Heinrich Schüzen, die von Unsers
in Gott hochseelig ruhenden Herrn Vaters Gnd. ihme in das mittel der
Steüer assignirten Jährlichen zweÿhundert Gülden ferner gegen seine
quittung daselbst solten gefolget werden, damit er die unter handen
habenden Musicalischen sachen desto eher zum truck befördern könne.
Nun mögen ihme von etwa dreÿ Jahren hero dieselben zurücke
geblieben seÿn, umb deren abführung dann er in beÿgefügeten Suppli-
cato inständiges fleißes anhählt auch zu entrichtung der Currenten die
Merseburgische Steüergelder unterthänigst fürschläget.   Wann
wir dann nicht ungeneiget seÿn, ihme als einen alten ChurSächsischen
diener, und dar sich beÿ der [fol. 179v] Kirche mit seinem Musicalischen
fleiß gar wohl verdienet hat mit solcher Jährlichen beÿhülffe ferner
gnädigst versehen zulaßen Als ist hiermit Unser gnädigstes begehren ihr
wollet die verordnung thun, daß ihme hinfort gebethener maßen solche
besoldungs zulage der 200 f. von halben Jahren zu halben Jahren aus
den Merseburgischen Steüern gegen quittung gefolget, der bißhero
angelauffene Rest aber nach fürgegangener berechnung ihme von den
Steüerbuchhalter nach und nach vergnüget, und künftig unser Renth-
Cammer wieder zugerechnet werden solle. An deme etc. und etc. Geben
zu Dresden den 27. Martÿ Anno 1663.

14: Translation

Johann Georg II to the President and Advisors of the Privy Chamber of Dresden. Dresden, 27 March 1663

[SAD Loc. 10441. *Steuer-Sachen 1661–1664,* fol. 179]

[fol. 179r]
To the president and advisors of the privy chamber of Dresden.
Dresden, 27 March 1663.
    Johann Georg the Second, Elector
My dear advisors and beloved loyal servants!
    We have previously proclaimed with this most gracious command that our old Kapellmeister and beloved faithful [servant] Heinrich Schütz shall be granted against his receipt the further sum of the two hundred gulden from the taxes which was assigned him yearly by His Grace, our blessed late father, now at peace, with which he might expedite the printing of his musical works in progress.
    He shall now [be paid] this [amount] which has remained in arrears for approximately three years, the settlement whereof he urges in the appended petition of earnest diligence and humbly requests payment in Reichsgulden from the Merseburg tax revenues.
    Because we are not disinclined graciously to provide him further with such yearly assistance as an old servant of the Electorate of Saxony who has served very well in the church with his musical diligence, it is herewith our most gracious wish that you shall obey the command to grant him from this time forward the premium in the requested amount of 200 florins semiannually from the Merseburg taxes against receipt. The current accumulated balance, however, shall be paid out to him a little at a time by the revenue officer and henceforth again be credited to our chamber of finances. Sealed and administered in Dresden on 27 March 1663.

15

Schütz to Johann Georg II.
Dresden, 1 May 1666

[SAD Loc. 7287. *Einzelne Schriften. Kammersachen, 1592–1677*, fol. 171]

[fol. 171r. Not in Schütz's hand but bears his signature]
Capellmeister Schüze vom 1. Maÿ 1666.
Durchlauchtigster Hochgeborner Churfürst
Ew. Churf. Durchl. seind meine unterthenigste pflichtschuldigste und
gehorsame Dienste stets zuvor,

Gnädigster Herr

Ew. Churf. Durchl. ersehen aus der beÿlage sub [symbol of the sun for
Sunday] wie daß Dieselbe am 27. Martij Anno 1663. auf mein damahlig
unterthenigstes ansuchen an den gewesenen geheimen CammerPrae-
sidenten und Räthe befehl ergehen laßen beÿ dem SteuerBuchhalter die
verfügung zuthun, darmit derselbe wegen meiner restierenden bewilligten SteuerZulage von Reminiscere 1660. biß Trinitatis 1663. mit mir
abrechnung halten, den Rest vergnügen, und solchen dem RenthCammer wieder zurechnen solte, worfür ich mich nochmals unterthenigst
bedancken thue,
Ob ich nun wohl der hofnung gelebet, es würde erwehnter gnedigsten
Befehlich exequiret worden seÿn, Dieweil aber obgedachter Herr Praesident der von Haugwicz wegen seiner vielen reisen, und andern verrichtungen darzu nicht zubringen gewesen, biß er entlich seine bestallung genzlichen resigniret, mir aber an der sachen beförderung merck-
lich gelegen,
[fol. 171v] Alß gelanget an Ew. Churf. Durchl. mein unterthenigstes
bitten, Sie geruhen gnedigst mir anderweit befehl an den Steuer-
Buchhalter zuertheilen, darmit er berürte abrechnung förderlichst vor
die Hand nehmen, den befundenen Rest binnen Jahrsfrist auszahlen
und solchen der RenthCammer wieder zurechnen solle,

Wie nun solch mein suchen verhoffentlich der billigkeit gemeß, also bin umb Ew. Churf. Durchl. ich lebenslang zuverdienen schuldigst, Datum Dreßden den 1. Maÿ Anno 1666.

Ew. Churfl. Durchl.

[Schütz's hand]

Unterthänigster pflichtschuldigster
gehorsamer alter diener
Henrich Schütz Mpp
Capellmeister [flourish]

15: Translation

Schütz to Johann Georg II.
Dresden, 1 May 1666

[SAD Loc. 7287. *Einzelne Schriften. Kammersachen, 1592–1677,* fol. 171]

[fol. 171r. Not in Schütz's hand but bears his signature]
Kapellmeister Schütz on 1 May 1666
Most Serene Noble Elector,
My humblest, most dutiful and obedient service to Your Electoral Highness always and above all,

Most gracious Lord,
Your Electoral Highness will note from the enclosure under [the symbol of the sun for Sunday] how you, on March 27, 1663, [in response to] my most humble petition made at that time to the privy president and councillor, issued an order to the revenue officer to make arrangements that he should settle accounts with me regarding the remainder of the tax premium granted me from the second Sunday in Lent 1660 until the Sunday after Pentecost 1663, compensate me for the balance, and credit the chamber of finances again with the same, for which I am once again most humbly grateful.

I lived in the hope, indeed, that the aforementioned command would be graciously carried out, but meanwhile the aforementioned President von Haugwicz, due to his many trips and other duties, did not devote himself to it, until he finally resigned his post entirely. The furtherance of the matter is, however, of great importance to me.

[fol. 171v] I therefore address my most humble request to Your Electoral Highness that you graciously deign to command the revenue officer once more that he shall take action on the mentioned settlement of accounts immediately, pay the balance outstanding within one year's time, and credit the chamber of finances therewith.

As I hope that this my quest is in accordance with what is just, I am bound to serve Your Electoral Highness for life. Dated Dresden on 1 May 1666.

Your Electoral Highness's

[Schütz's hand]

> Most humble duty-bound
> obedient old servant
> Heinrich Schütz
> In his own hand
> Kapellmeister

16

Schütz to Johann Georg II.
Dresden, 3 May 1666

[SAD Loc. 7287. *Einzelne Schriften, Kammersachen 1492–1677*, fol. 219]

[fol. 219r. Not in Schütz's hand but bears his signature]
Wegen vorher aufgezeichneter, meiner bißhero zuruckgebliebenen
besoldung, kan ich nicht vorüber auf die begebenheit
untherthenigst erinnern zulaßen.
Daß Ihre Churfl. Durchl. albereit vor 3. Jahren, nemblich sub Dato den
27. Martij Anno 1663. an den damaligen Cammer Praesidenten Herrn
von Haugwicz seel. einen gnedigsten befehl haben ergehen laßen, daß
Er die verordnung thun, und wegen dieses Zettels den SteuerBuchhalter abrechnung mit mir pflegen, und den Rest so sich finden wurde,
mir gut thun und zahlen laßen solte, welches aber damals, von wohler-
melten Herrn von Haugwicz, wegen seiner absonderlichen vielen verrichtungen, so lange verschoben, biß er entlich solche bestallung resigniret, und also diese forderung biß dato noch unbezahlet blieben,
Ob nun Ihre Churfl. Durchl. sich annoch gnedigst belieben laßen wolle,
die einmahl mir bewilligte gnade durch einen anderweiten befehl an
den Herrn Buchhalter wiederumb zuverneüern, wird zu Deroselben
gnedigsten bereiffung und willen gehorsambst anheim gestellet.
[Schütz's hand]   Henrich Schütz Mpp
                                         Datum Dresden
                                         den 3 Maÿ
                                         Ao etc. 1666.

16: Translation

Schütz to Johann Georg II.
Dresden, 3 May 1666

[SAD Loc. 7287. *Einzelne Schriften, Kammersachen 1492–1677*, fol. 219]

[fol. 219r. Not in Schütz's hand but bears his signature]
Regarding the previously recorded [matter of my] pay, in arrears until now, I cannot but humbly bring [the matter] to mind that Your Electoral Highness three years ago, namely on 27 March 1663, issued a most gracious order to the chamber president at that time, the late Herr von Haugwicz, that he should issue a decree and, according to this note [from you], see to the revenue officer's settlement of accounts with me, and to compensate me and permit me to be paid the remainder which could be found. At that time, however, the aforementioned Herr von Haugwicz, because of his especially numerous trips, put [the matter] off so long until he finally resigned his post, and [therefore] this claim still remains unpaid at present.

If it may now please Your Electoral Highness once again to renew the favor once granted to me through another command to the revenue officer, [I] obediently present [the matter to you] for the same most gracious inspection and consent.

[Schütz's hand]   Heinrich Schütz
                                   Dated Dresden
                                   In his own hand
                                   3 May 1666

17

Schütz to an Unnamed Patron.
Undated

[SAD Loc. 8687. *Kantoreiordnung*, fol. 332]

[fol. 332r]
Hochegehrter Herr vnd Wolgeneigter förderer
1. Aldieweil mir die 200 fl. wormit Ich vorhin in Abschlag meiner
besolden in die Stewer verwiesen binn, Sauer genug gemacht, und mir
will fürgeworfen werden das derogleichen nicht eigentlich aus der
Steuer zu bezahlen sich gebürete, So habe ich mein petitum wegen des
Biers zu Naumburgk, auff meine Klare Steueranforderungen einrich-
ten wollen, damit derogleichen Vorwürffe ich hirnechst geubriget sein
möge, vnd versehe mich das derogestalt, solche sache desto ehe zu erhalten undt in der Steuer damit auch durch zu kommen sein werde,
vndt habe ich dieses hirbey nur noch zu erindern, das nach erlangeter
vnsers Gndsten Herrn gewunschten Resolution, der befehl nur in gnre
auf meine anforderungen in der Stewer, vnd nicht etwa in specie auf
das Capital, eingerichtet werden möge.
2. Im fall wegen des andern puncts mein hochgeehrter Herr (:betref-
fend nemblich das von mir gesuchte getreidicht:) vieleicht einer ab-
schlägigen andwort vermutens were, vnd denselbigen furzutragen bedencken haben möchte, So gebe Ich ihm dienstlich zu bewissen, ob er
deswegen mich nicht etwa dem Herrn Rentmeister zu recommendiren,
das auff ein jahr etwa von ihm und deren H. Cammer Räthen, mir in
hoc passu, gewilfahret werden möchte. Wiewol ich gleichwol auch vermeine vnser Gndste solche geringe sache, auff mein kurtzes leben mir
wol [*vieleicht* crossed out] zu bewilligen, nicht gros verweigern würde,
Ich aber dahin stellen v. Ihro Churfl. Durchl. gnade leben muss.
Bitte denselbigen Schlieslichen pp DEUM, Er wolle zu der von mir
solange zeit gesuchten freyheit mögliche grosgonstige förderung erweisen, Deum testor, das ich [*wegen* crossed out] pp in credulitatem

moderni novi mundi, qui nihil praeter extranea muliebria [*et* crossed out] puerilia et scurrilia, admiratur, alhier kein [strikeout] Zeichen thun können, oder wollen werde etc. Binn erbötig solche undt andere vorhin mir erwiesener gutthaten, v. meinetwegen gehabte bemühungen meinem Vermögen nach mit einen wircklichen danckzeichen in etwas zu recompensiren. Gott denselbigen zu allem gewunschten wolergehen hirmit [strikeout] treulichst entpfelende [closing flourish]

17: Translation

Schütz to an Unnamed Patron.
Undated

[SAD Loc. 8687. *Kantoreiordnung*, fol. 332]

[fol. 332r]
Most honored Lord and affectionate Patron,
1. Because the admonishment I received a little while ago [regarding] the 200 florin tax [premium] reduction in my income has annoyed me enough, and [because] I have been reproached that it is actually not appropriate to pay these [funds] from the [Merseburg] taxes, I have therefore applied my petition regarding the Naumburg beer directly to· my tax claim so that hereafter I might be relieved of these reproaches. And I am prepared in this manner to conclude this business as soon as possible and, in [the matter of] the tax, to make do with it. And in this regard I have only this to bring to mind: according to the resolution for which I asked and received from our most gracious lord, the mandate shall be applied only generally to my claim in the [matter of] the tax and not specifically to the capital.
2. Regarding the other point (concerning namely my grain apportionment), in case my most honored lord were perhaps inclined to refuse [the apportionment] and were to consider doing so, I wish kindly to request if he for this reason perhaps might not intercede on my behalf with my lord the chamberlain of the exchequer, in this case, so that in one year, he [the chamberlain] and the councillor of the exchequer shall grant [the grain apportionment] to me. Although it is my opinion that our gracious lord would not utterly refuse such a trivial matter [and shall] consent [to this] in my short lifetime, I shall, however, submit [this matter] to his decision and will have to live according to Your Electoral Highness's orders.
   In closing I ask him for God's sake that he show to the favor which I have sought for such a long time all possible favorable advancement. I

confess—God be my witness—that I can neither perform nor wish to perform a miracle here, confronted by the credulity of the modern new world, which admires nothing but what is foreign, effeminate, childish, and foolish. I am prepared in some respect to recompense this and other good deeds shown to me previously and efforts made in my behalf with a genuine show of thanks. May God commend you faithfully herewith for all desired well-being.

18

Dresden Instrument Chamber Catalog.
1681

[SAD Loc. 7207. *Verzeichnüs. Derer in das Churf. Sächß. Jüngste Gericht =
und Instrument = Cammer gehörigen Musicalischen = Sachen und Instrumenten, Welche sowohl die Italiäner, alß deüzshen der Capella Verwandten, biß
anhero zu Ihnen Exercitio und Gebrauch beÿ sich gehabt, und so viel vor iezo
von denen die voriezo allhier zugegen sind, wiederumb eingeantworttet worden,*
fols. 1–8]

[fol. 1r]
Durchlauchtigste Churfürst, Gnädigster Herr etc.
Ew: Churf: Durchl: ergangen gnädigsten befehliche vom $\frac{2}{12}$ Martij, zu
unterthänigst: undt gehorsambster folge, habe ich anbefohlener maßen,
die in das Jüngste = Gerichte und Instrument = Cammer gehörigen
Bücher und Musical: Instrumenta, so wohl von denen Italiänern und
Deüzschen, so viel sich deren voriezo allhier befunden, Insonderheit
aber von dem Geheimen Cämmerirer Gabriel Angelo de Battistini, ein-
gefordert, und die Sache so viel möglichen beschleuniget, Auch über
die jenigen, so wohl gedrückt alß geschriebne Musical: Sachen, und
Bücher, welche der Capellmeister Vincenzo Albrici undt gedachter Battistini (:so viel sie gestanden:) beÿ sich gehabt, mir nebenst einer von
Iedweden unterschriebener Specification, Sub Signo [symbols of the
sun, the planet Jupiter, and the moon] einantworrten lassen, und über
die Musicalischen Instrumenta, so mir von denen Andern der Capelle
zugethanen Personen (:welche solche [fol. 1v] im Gebrauch gehabt haben:) eingeliefert worden, ein richtiges verzeichnüß sub [the symbol for
the planet Mars] verfertiget, wie E: Churf: Durchl: auß beÿkommenden
Abschrifften, gnädigst werden zuersehen haben,   Alles aber immittelst wohl verwahret, in eine beÿ mir befindliche Stube und Cammer,
beÿgeleget, biß E: Churf: Durchl: ferner gnädigst befehlen werden (weil
die jenigen Orthe, allda diese dinge sonst hin gehören, noch versiegelt:)

wo sie sollen hingeschaffet werden, Wie denn zu E: Churf: Durchl: untherthänigsten Diensten, ich mich so gehorsambst willigst alß schuldigst befinde, und verbleibe:

E: Churf: Durchl:

Dreßden am   29. Martij   unterthänigst und
              8. Aprilis   gehorsambster
                                Christian Kittel.

[fol. 2r]

Abschrifft vom Original,

[Symbol of the sun]

Nachgesetzte Musical: Sachen, so ich endesbenanter, auß dem Churf: Sächß: Jüngsten = Gerichte und Instrument = Cammer biß anhero entlehnet und zu meinem Bedürffnüß bey mir gehabt, Alß:

I. Kirchen = Music

1. Psalm: Laudate Dominum omnes gentes.
    Von 4. Vocal = Stimmen, Mit Instrumenten, auch 6. Trompeten und Pauken,
    Des Durchlauchtigst = Höchstseeligsten Churfürstens zu Sachssen etc. Herzog Johann Georgen des Andern Composition,
2. Missa. Von 5. Vocal = Stimmen, mit Instrumenten und ohne Credo.
3. Dergleichen,
4. Ebendergleichen,
5. Missa. Von 5. Vocal = Stimmen, mit Instrum: und mitt einem Credo.
6. Missa und Credo von 5. Vocal = Stimmen, mitt Instrument: 6. Trompeten und Pauken,
7. Missa. sambt einem Credo von 5. Vocal = Stimmen, mit Instrum: 4. Trompeten und Pauken,
8. Dergleichen,
9. Magnificat. von 5. Vocal = Stimmen mit Instr: 4. Trompeten und Pauken,
10. Magnificat, von 5. Vocal = Stimmen, mit Instr: 2. Trompeten und Pauken,

[In the right margin, 2–10 above are bracketed with the following indication: Joseph Perandens Composition,]

[fol. 2v]

11. Magnificat alla breve. von 9. Vocal = Stimmen, und mitt Instrumenten,

12. Concert: Si diligitis me. von 3. Vocal = Stimmen, nehml: 2. Discänten und 1. Baß,

13. Concert: Veni Creator Spiritus. von 3. Vocal = Stimmen, nehml: Alt: Ten: und Baß, auch 2. Cornett: und 1. Fagott:

14. Concert: Repleti sunt omnes. Mitt 6en, alß Alt: Tenor, 2. Violin: undt 2. Cornetten,

15. Concert: Audite peccatores. Mitt 4en, Disc: und Baß und 2. Violinen,

16. Concert: Si Dominus mecum. mitt 6en, Disc: Alt: Ten: und Baß, 2. Violin: und 1. Fagot:

17. Concert: O! Altitudo. Mitt 5en, 2. Discänt: 1. Baß und 2. Violinen,

18. Concert: Abite dolores. Mitt 4en, 2. Disc: und 2. Violin:

19. Concert: Ad Coelestem Jerusalem. Mit 3en, 2. Discänten und 1. Alt:

20. Concert: Si vivo mi Jesu! Mitt 6en, Disc: Alt: und Baß, 2. Violin: auch 1. Fagot:

21. Concert: Languet Cor meum. Mitt 6en, Discant: Alt: und Ten: 2. Violin: und 1. Fag:

22. Concert: Dedit Abýssus. Mitt 4en, 2. Disc: und 2. Bässen,

23. Concert: O! ardor, o! flamma. Mitt 4en, Discant: und Baß, und 2. Violin:

[In the right margin, 11–23 above are bracketed with the following indication: Joseph Perandens Composition,]

[fol. 3r]

24. Concert: Fasciculis Mýrrhae. Von 5. Vocal = Stimmen, und mitt Instrumenten,

25. Concert: Laetentur Coeli. von 5. Vocal = Stimmen, und mit Instr: 2. Trompeten und Pauken,

26. Concert: Flavit auster. von 5. Vocal = Stimmen, mitt Instr: 4. Trompeten und Pauken,

[In the right margin, 24–26 above are bracketed with the following indication: Joseph Perand: Compos:]

27. VI. Psalmen = Bücher, alla breve, in Pappier gehefft, des D: Giov: Jacobi Gastoldi Composition.

28. Missa. ohne Credo. von 5. Vocal = Stimmen und mitt Instrumenten,

29. Missa ohne Credo. von 5. Vocal = Stimmen, mitt Instr: 2. Tromp: und Pauken,

30. Psalm: Beatus vir. von 4. Vocal = Stimmen, mitt Instrumenten, 2. Tromp: und Pauken,

31. Psalm: Laudate Dominum in sanctis ejus. Von 5. Vocal = Stimmen, mit Instr: 2 Trompeten und Pauken,

32. Concert: O! Jesu Brun aller Süßigkeit. Mitt 6en, alß Disc: und Bass, 3. Violin: und 1. Fagott:
33. Concert: Herr erbarme dich doch meiner, von 5. alß Disc: und Baß. und 3. Violin:
34. Concert: Moveantur cuncta sursum. Von 8tn, alß 2. Discänten, 2. Bäßen, 2. Violinen, und 2. Cornetten,

[In the right margin, 28–34 above are bracketed with the following indication: Meine Endesbenanten Composition,]

[fol. 3v]

35. Concert: Surrexit pastor bonus. Von 3en, alß 2. Discänt: 1. Alt:
36. Concert: Hodie beata virgo Maria. von 3en, nehml: Discant: Alt: und Baß,
37. Concert: Congratulamini michi omnes. Mitt 3en, alß Alt: Ten: und Baß,
38. Concert: Sancta et immaculata Virginitas. Mitt 4en, alß Disc: Alt: Ten: und Baß,
39. Motett: Factor factus est pro nobis. Von 6en Vocal = Stimmen, mit Instr:
40. Das Te Deum laudamus. von 5. Vocal = Stimmen, mitt Instr: 2. Trompeten und Pauken,
41. Die Litaneÿ deüzsch, von 5. Vocal = Stimmen, mitt Instrumenten,

[In the right margin, 35–41 above are bracketed with the following indication: Meine Endesbenanten Composition,]

II. Tafell = Music,

42. Madrigal von 5. Vocal = Stimmen, Mit Instr: auch 2. Trompet: und Pauken,
43. Madrigal, von 5. Voc: mitt Instr: undt 2. Trompeten,
44. Madrigal. von 5. Voc: mitt Instrum:
45. Dergleichen,
46. Madrigal. von 5. Vocal = Stimmen, mit Instr: und mitt 2. Trompeten,
47. Madrigal. von 5. Voc: mitt Instrum:
48. Ebendergleichen,
49. Madrigal mitt 2. Tenören,
50. Madrigal von 5. Voc: und mitt Instr: auch 2. Trompeten,

[In the right margin, 42–50 above are bracketed with the following indication: Joseph Perandens Composition,]

[fol. 4r]

51. Madrigal, von 5. Voc: und mit Instrument: auch 2. Trompeten,
52. Madrigal von 5. Voc: und mitt Instr:
53. Madrigal von 5. Voc: mitt Instr: und 2. Tromp:

54. Madrigal. Mitt 3. Voc: 2. Cant: und 1. Tenor,
55. Madrigal. Mitt 3. Vocal = Stimmen, alß Disc: Tenor und Baß,
56. Sÿnphonia, von 6en, alß 2. Trompeten und Pauken, 2. Violin: und 1. Fagott: woran die helffte des General = Baßes mangelt
57. Sÿnphonia. von 9en, nehml: 4. Trompeten, 4. Violin: und 1. Fagott:
58. Sÿnphonia. von 5en, alß 2. Trompeten, 2. Violin: und 1. Fagott:
[In the right margin, 51–58 above are bracketed with the following indication: Joseph Perandens Composition,]
59. Madrigal, von 3. Vocal = Stimmen, nehml: Disc: Alt: und Baß,
60. Madrigal, von 5. Voc: und mit Instr: auch 2. Trompeten,
61. Madrigal. von 5. Voc: und mitt Instr:
[In the right margin, 59–61 above are bracketed with the following indication: Meine Endesbenanten Composition,]
Händige ich hier benebenst wiederumb ein,
Signatum Dreßden, am 22. Martij Ao. etc.: 1681
               1. April:
Hierüber:
62. Introitus: Festo Trinitatis von 4. Vocal = Stimmen, und mitt Instr: Christoph Bernhards.

    Vincenzo Albrici,
    Mo: di Capella
[fol. 4v]
Abschrifft vom Original,
            [Symbol of the moon]
Nachgesezt = gedrückte Musical: Sachen, so mir endesbenanten, biß anhero auß der Churf: Sächß: Instrument = Cammer entlehnet und gereichet worden, Händige ich in Dieselbe wiederumb ein, Alß:
1. Primo libro de Madrigali. à. 5. Voci
    Di Oratio Brognonico Academico filarmonico
2. Terzo libro de Madrigali. à.5. Voci di Oratio
[In the right margin, 1–2 above are bracketed with the following indication: ohngehefft,]
3. Di luca Marenzio il Terzo libro de Madrigali à 5.
4. Di luca Marenzio. il 4to libr: à. 5.
5. Di luca Marenzio il 7. lib: de Madrig: à 5.
6. Madrigali di Domenico Obizzi. à 2.3.4 et 5. Voc: Sechß Bücher insgesambt
7. Madrigali di Paolo Giordano libro Primo.
    Sechß Bücher insgesambt,

8. Libro Secundo di Madrigali Concertati à. 2.3.4.5.6. et otto: parte, con Violini, di Giovanni Rovetta, Opera Sesta.
    Seÿnd insgesambt Sechß Bücher,
9. Libr: Secundo di Madrigali à. 5. Voci, di Steffano Bernardi. Opera Settima, Seÿnd insgesambt Sechß Bücher,
10. Di Claudio Monteverde, Madrigali, lib: 4.5.6. et 7. zusammen auch Sechß Bücher,
11. Canzoni di Antonio Mortaro, lib: 1. et 2. fünff Bücher zusammen,
[In the right margin, 3–11 above are bracketed with the following indication: Alles in Pappen und Pappier gehefft,]
Signatum Dreßden, am 27 Martij, Ao. etc.: 1681.
17
Gabriel Angelo de Battistini,
[fol. 5r]
[Symbol of the planet Mars]
Nun folgen die Musical: Instrumenta, welche die allhier in Dreßden anwesende Italiäner und Deüzschen, (:die abwesenden Italiäner und Deuzschen aber anlangende, weiß ich nicht, was ein oder Ander beÿ sich haben mag:) mir endesbenanten zu den Churf: Jüngsten = Gerichte, und Instrument = Cammer, eingeliefert habe, Alß:

1.

Vincenzo Albrici.
1. Clavicimbul. Mitt 2. Registern, und von Cipressenholcz, mitt einen Elffenbeinern Clav. biß in das Contra G. in einen schwarzen Futerale, Ist sonst ohne schaden, außgenommen daß der Resonanz = boden in etwas auffgerissen,

2.

Pietro Paolo Morelli,
1. Instrument, welches einfach bezogen und Eckicht daran das fördern Breth sambt dem Schlosse mangelt

3.

Johann Willhelm Forchheim,
1. Instrument, welches einfach bezogen und Eckicht von Cipreßen-Holcz, daran etwas abgebrochen, und vom Futerale der halbe Teckel über den Clavir weg,
[fol. 5v]
2. Viol: de Gamben   }   worbeÿ nur 1. Bogen, und mangeln 8.
1. Baß = Geÿge   }   Seÿten insgesambt daran,
5. Schallmeÿen, welche Er hatt zurichten laßen, nehml: 2. Disc: 2. Alt:

und 1. Tenor = Schallmeÿ, mit vergüldten Schlößern, Eßen, und 2. Balletten, mitt 2. Stifften, und 5. Röhren, welche 5. röhre in 1. Schächtelgen beÿsammen.

4.

Johann Füssell,
1. Instrument, welches einfach bezogen undt Eckicht, mitt einen lauten zuge, und mangelt das Schloß,

5.

Friedrich Westhoff,
1. Alte Tenor = Posaune. sambt dem Mund = Stücke
1. Alter Tertz = Fagott, Mitt einem abgebrochenen Schloße, ohne Eß und ohne Rohr,
worbeÿ unterthänigst erinnert wird, daß gedachter Westhoff noch eine neüe Posaune beÿ sich, welche er aber nicht eingeliefert, sondern vorgeben Sr: Churf: Dhl: etc. Höchstseel: gedächtnüs etc. hättens ihme gnädigst geschencket, wie deßen unterthänigstens Supplicat beÿliegende besaget, sub signo [symbol for the planet Mercury].
[fol. 6r. In Westhoff's hand]

Durchlauchtigster Churfürst
Gnädigster Herr

Eüer Churfl. Durchl. geruhen Gnädigst zu vernehmen, wie auff dero Gnädigsten Befehl, der geheimbte Cämmerier Christian Kittel die Instrumenta (so in die Churfl. Sächß. Instrument Cammer gehören und von Zeit zu Zeit ein und dem andern Musico zum Excercitio zu gebrauchen gegen gegebenen Schein darauß geliefern worden) wieder einfordern läßet, weil ich nun einen Alten fagot und eine alte Posaune beÿ mir gehabt habe ich solche zweÿ Stücke alsobald gehorsambster schuldigkeit nach außgeantworttet. Es haben aber Euer Churfl. Durchl. hochseeligster Herr Vatter als mein Gnädigst gewesener Churfürst und herr, schon vor 18 Jahren auß dero Instrument Cammer mir eine (damahls zwar Neüe nunmehr aber so lange Zeit gebrauchte und itzo auff 4 Thaler wehrt geschätzte) Trombone oder Posaune durch dero damahligen Capellmeister [fol. 6v] Joseph Peranden Gnädigst schencken laßen, solch mir damahls Gnädigstes geschencke, begehret nun der geheimbte Cämmerier Christian Kittel von mir auch eingeliefert zu haben. Habe dahero Eüer Churfl. Durchl. Gnädigsten willen hierdurch unterthänigst vernehmen wollen, damit dero Gnädigsten befehl ich in gehorsamster Schuldigkeit unverzüglich nachleben möge. Als der ich lebenszeit verbleibe

Eüer Churfl. Durchl.
Dreßden am 23 Martij Anno 1681
    Unterthänigste gehorsamster diener
    Friedrich Westhoff
[fol. 7v]
Dem Durchlauchtigsten Fürsten und Herren Herren Johann Georgen
dem Dritten, Hertzogen zu Sachsen, Jülich, Cleve und Berg, Des Heil.
Römischen Reichs Ertz = Marschallen und Churfürsten, Landgrafen in
thüringen, Marggrafen zu Meißen, auch Ober und Nieder Laußnitz,
Burggrafen zu Magdeburg, Gefürsteten Grafen zu Henneberg, Grafen
zu der Marck, Rauensberg und Berbig, Herren zum Rauenstein,
Meinem Gnädigsten Churfürsten und Herren.
[fol. 8r]

6.

George Taschenberg,
1. Quart = Posaune Sambt dem Mund = Stücke, in einem Futerale,
ingleichen
1. Tenor = Posaune, ohne Mundstücke, sonst ohne schaden,

7.

Paul Keÿser,
1. Clavicimbul, Mitt 4. Registern, mitt einem Elffenbeinern Clavire, bis
ins Contra G. welcher ohne Schloß, Item
1. Bücher-Puld, welches darzu gehöret,
1. Lÿera. sambt den Bogen, in einen verschloßenen Futerale, beÿ der
Lÿera mangeln 9. Seÿten,
1. Theorbe. Von EbenHolcze, mitt eingelegten Elffenbeine, und in
einen unverschloßenen Futerale, welche auch gar nicht bezogen,

18: Translation

Dresden Instrument Chamber Catalog.
1681

[SAD Loc. 7207. *Verzeichnüs. Derer in das Churf. Sächß. Jüngste Gericht = und Instrument = Cammer gehörigen Musicalischen = Sachen und Instrumenten, Welche sowohl die Italiäner, alß deüzschen der Capella Verwandten, biß anhero zu Ihnen Exercitio und Gebrauch beÿ sich gehabt, und so viel vor iezo von denen die vor iezo allhier zugegen sind, wiederumb eingeantworttet worden,* fols. 1–8]

[fol. 1r]
Most Illustrious Elector, most Gracious Lord,
To follow most humbly and dutifully Your Electoral Highness's most gracious command issued$_{12}^{2}$ March, I have ordered assembled as many of the books and musical instruments which belong in the instrument chamber [containing the painting of the] Last Judgment from as many [as possible] of the Italians and the Germans who were here up to now, but especially from the Privy Chamberlain Gabriel Angelo de Battistini, and expedited the matter as much as possible. I also made a proper list of those musical items and books, printed as well as handwritten, which the Kapellmeister Vincenzo Albrici and the aforementioned Battistini had in their possession (as many as they acknowledge), which were returned as written below with one or the other specification under the symbols [of the sun, the planet Jupiter, and the moon], and of the musical instruments handed over as well from the other persons associated with the court ensemble (who have been using [fol. 1v] them), under [the symbol for the planet Mars] has been completed, as Your Electoral Highness will graciously observe in the enclosed copy. Everything is put aside in safekeeping, however, in a room and chamber in my home, until Your Electoral Highness graciously gives further orders [regarding] where they are to be moved (because the places where these things ordinarily belong are sealed up). As one of Your Electoral High-

ness's most humble servants, I find myself as dutifully willing as [I am] indebted, and remain

Dresden   29 March   Your Electoral Highness's
            8 April [1681]   humble and obedient
                               Christian Kittel

[fol. 2r]
Copy from the original.

[Symbol of the sun]

I acknowledge that the following musical items were borrowed by me up until this time from the royal Saxon instrument chamber [containing the painting of] the Last Judgment and I have had them in my possession for my use, being:

I. Church Music

1. Psalm: *Laudate Dominum omnes gentes* in four vocal parts with instruments including six trumpets and timpani. Composition by the most serene late Elector of Saxony, Duke Johann Georg the Second.
2. Mass in five vocal parts with instruments and without Credo.
3. The same.
4. The same again.
5. Mass in five vocal parts with instruments and with a Credo.
6. Mass and Credo in five vocal parts with instruments of six trumpets and timpani.
7. Mass with a Credo in five vocal parts with instruments of four trumpets and timpani.
8. The same.
9. Magnificat in five vocal parts with instruments of four trumpets and timpani.
10. Magnificat in five vocal parts with instruments [including] two trumpets and timpani.

[In the right margin, 2–10 above are bracketed with the following indication: Compositions by Joseph Peranda.]

[fol. 2v]

11. Magnificat alla breve in nine vocal parts and with instruments.
12. Concerto: *Si diligitis me* in three vocal parts, namely two discant voices and bass.
13. Concerto: *Veni Creator Spiritus* in three vocal parts, namely alto, tenor, and bass, and two cornetti and one bassoon.
14. Concerto: *Repleti sunt omnes* in six parts, namely alto, tenor, two violins, and two cornetti.

15. Concerto: *Audite peccatores* in four parts, discant and bass and two violins.
16. Concerto: *Si Dominus mecum* in six parts, discant, alto, tenor, and bass, two violins and one bassoon.
17. Concerto: *O! Altitudo* in five parts, two discant voices, one bass, and two violins.
18. Concerto: *Abite dolores* in four parts, two discant voices and two violins.
19. Concerto: *Ad Coelestem Jerusalem* in three vocal parts, two discant voices and one alto.
20. Concerto: *Si vivo mi Jesu!* in six parts, discant, alto, and bass, two violins and one bassoon.
21. Concerto: *Languet Cor meum* in six parts, discant, alto, and tenor, two violins, and one bassoon.
22. Concerto: *Dedit Abÿssus* in four vocal parts, two discant voices, and two basses.
23. Concerto: *O! ardor, o! flamma* in four parts, discant and bass, and two violins.

[In the right margin, 11–23 above are bracketed with the following indication: Compositions by Joseph Peranda.]
[fol. 3r]

24. Concerto: *Fasciculis Mÿrrhae* in five vocal parts and with instruments.
25. Concerto: *Laetentur Coeli* in five vocal parts and instruments of two trumpets and timpani.
26. Concerto: *Flavit Auster*. In five vocal parts with instruments of four trumpets and timpani.

[In the right margin, 24–26 above are bracketed with the following indication: Compositions by Joseph Peranda.]

27. Six Psalm books, alla breve, bound in paper, compositions by D. Giov[anni] Giacomo Gastoldi.
28. Mass without Credo in five vocal parts and with instruments.
29. Mass without Credo in five vocal parts with instruments of two trumpets and timpani.
30. Psalm: *Beatus vir* in four vocal parts with instruments of two trumpets and timpani.
31. Psalm: *Laudate Dominum in sanctis ejus* in five vocal parts with instruments of two trumpets and timpani.
32. Concerto: *O! Jesu Brun aller Süßigkeit* with six parts, being discant and bass, three violins and one bassoon.
33. Concerto: *Herr erbarme dich doch meiner*, in five [parts], namely discant and bass and three violins.

34. Concerto: *Moveantur cuncta sursum* in eight parts, being two discant voices, two basses, two violins, and two cornetti.

[In the right margin, 28–34 above are bracketed with the following indication: I acknowledge that these are my compositions.]

[fol. 3v]

35. Concerto: *Surrexit pastor bonus* in three vocal parts, namely two discant voices and one alto.

36. Concerto: *Hodie beata virgo Maria* in three vocal parts, namely discant, alto, and bass.

37. Concerto: *Congratulamini michi omnes* with three vocal parts, namely alto, tenor, and bass.

38. Concerto: *Sancta et immaculata Virginitas* with four vocal parts, being discant, alto, tenor, and bass.

39. Motet: *Factor factus est pro nobis* in six vocal parts with instruments.

40. The *Te Deum laudamus* in five vocal parts with instruments of two trumpets and timpani.

41. The Litany in German in five vocal parts with instruments.

[In the right margin, 35–41 above are bracketed with the following indication: I acknowledge that these are my compositions.]

II. Tafelmusik

42. Madrigal in five vocal parts with instruments and two trumpets and timpani.

43. Madrigal in five vocal parts with instruments and two trumpets.

44. Madrigal in five vocal parts with instruments.

45. The same.

46. Madrigal in five vocal parts with instruments and with two trumpets.

47. Madrigal in five vocal parts with instruments.

48. The same again.

49. Madrigal with two tenors.

50. Madrigal in five vocal parts and with instruments and two trumpets.

[In the right margin, 42–50 above are bracketed with the following indication: Compositions by Joseph Peranda.]

[fol. 4r]

51. Madrigal in five vocal parts and with instruments including two trumpets.

52. Madrigal in five vocal parts and with instruments.

53. Madrigal in five vocal parts with instruments and two trumpets.

54. Madrigal in three vocal parts, two discant voices and one tenor.

55. Madrigal in three vocal parts, being discant, tenor, and bass.

56. Symphonia in six parts, being two trumpets and timpani, two violins, and one bassoon from which half of the continuo part is missing.
57. Symphonia in nine parts, being four trumpets, four violins, and one bassoon.
58. Symphonia in five parts, being two trumpets, two violins, and one bassoon.

[In the right margin, 51–58 above are bracketed with the following indication: Compositions by Joseph Peranda.]

59. Madrigal in three vocal parts, namely discant, alto, and bass.
60. Madrigal in five vocal parts and with instruments and two trumpets.
61. Madrigal in five vocal parts and with instruments.

[In the right margin, 59–61 above are bracketed with the following indication: I acknowledge that these are my compositions.]

I here return as well,
Signed Dresden 22 March 1681
                         1 April
Moreover:
62. Introit: Festo Trinitas in four vocal parts and with instruments by Christoph Bernhard.

Vincenzo Albrici
Maestro di Capella
[fol. 4v]
Copy from the original.
[Symbol of the moon]
I acknowledge that the following printed musical things were borrowed and procured by me up until this time from the royal Saxon instrument chamber which I return to same, being:

1. First Book of madrigals for five voices by Oratio Brognonico, Academico filarmonico.
2. Third book of madrigals for five voices by Oratio.

[In the right margin, 1–2 above are bracketed with the following indication: Unbound.]

3. Third book of madrigals for five voices by Luca Marenzio.
4. Fourth book of madrigals for five voices by Luca Marenzio.
5. Seventh book of madrigals for five voices by Luca Marenzio.
6. Madrigals by Domenico Obizzi for two, three, four, and five vocal parts. Six books altogether.
7. First book of madrigals by Paola Giordano. Six books altogether.

8. Second book of concerted madrigals for two, three, four, five, six, and eight parts, with violins, by Giovanni Rovetta, Opus Six. There are six books altogether.
9. Second book of madrigals for five voices by Steffano Bernardi [Stefan Bernard], Opus Seven. There are six books altogether.
10. Fourth, fifth, sixth and seventh books of madrigals by Claudio Monteverdi, six books altogether.
11. First and second books of canzonas by Antonio Mortaro, five books altogether.

[In the right margin, 3–11 above are bracketed with the following indication: Everything bound in cardboard and paper.]

signed Dresden, 27 March 1681

17

Gabriel Angelo de Battistini

[fol. 5r]

[Symbol of the planet Mars]

Now follow the musical instruments, which I acknowledge the Italians and Germans present here in Dresden (concerning the absent Italians and Germans, I do not know what either might have in their possession) have returned to the royal instrument chamber [containing the painting of] the Last Judgment, being:

1.

Vincenzo Albrici.
One harpsichord with two stops and of cypress wood in a black case with an ivory keyboard up to contra G. Except that the soundboard is somewhat cracked, it is otherwise undamaged.

2.

Pietro Paolo Morelli.
One harpsichord which is of simple decoration and edged. The front board along with the lock is missing.

3.

Johann Wilhelm Forchheim.
One harpsichord which is of simple decoration and edged of cypress wood, some of which is broken off, and the half lid over the keyboard is missing from the case.

[fol. 5v]

Two viole da gamba } with only one bow and from which
One bass viol   } eight strings altogether are missing.

Five shawms which he had repaired, namely two treble, two alto, and one tenor shawm with gilded keys, three S-shaped crooks, and two pirouettes with two staples, and five reeds which [are] together in one little box.

4.

Johann Füssell
One harpsichord which [is] simply decorated and edged, with one lute stop and missing the lock.

5.

Friedrich Westhoff,
One old tenor sackbut with the mouthpiece.
One old tierce bassoon with a broken-off key, without S-crook and without a reed.
Furthermore it should be remembered that the aforementioned Westhoff had another new trumpet in his possession which, however, he did not return but maintains His late Serene Highness of blessed memory graciously had given it to him as a gift, as his most humble petition purports, herein under the sign [symbol for the planet Mercury].
[fol. 6r. In Westhoff's hand]

Most Serene Elector
Most Gracious Lord

May it graciously please Your Serene Highness to learn how, on Your most gracious command, my lord the privy chamberlain, Christian Kittel, had the instruments recalled (which belong in the royal Saxon instrument chamber and which from time to time were provided to one musician or another to use for rehearsal upon presentation of a voucher). Because I then had in my possession an old bassoon and an old sackbut, I at once surrendered these two instruments with most obedient dutifulness. However, my Lord Your Serene Highness's late father, as my most gracious former elector and lord, through his Kapellmeister of that time, [fol. 6v] Joseph Peranda, graciously gave me eighteen years ago from your instrument chamber one trombone or sackbut (at the time quite new, but since then used for such a long time and now appraised at a value of four talers). My lord the privy chamberlain Christian Kittel now asks that I return as well this most gracious gift made to me at that time. I therefore wish humbly to know Your Serene Highness's most gracious will. I shall in most obedient dutifulness conform at once to your most gracious command.
Thus I remain for my lifetime,

Your Serene Highness's
Dresden, 23 March 1681
>Most humble, most obedient servant
>Friedrich Westhoff

[fol. 7v]

To the most serene Prince and Lord, Lord Johann Georg III, Duke of Saxony, Jülich, Kleve, and Berg; Erzmarschall and Elector of the Holy Roman Empire; Landgrave in Thuringia, Margrave of Meißen and Upper and Lower Laußitz, Burgrave of Magdeburg, princely Earl of Henneberg, Earl of Marburg, Ravensberg and Berbig, Lord of Ravenstein, my most gracious Elector and Lord.

[fol. 8r]

6.

Georg Taschenberg
One bass sackbut in a case together with the mouthpiece, likewise,
One tenor sackbut, without mouthpiece, otherwise undamaged.

7.

Paul Kaiser
One harpsichord with four stops with one ivory keyboard to contra G which is without a lock, *idem*
One music stand, which belongs to it.
One lira [da gamba] with the bow in a locked case. The lira [da gamba] is missing nine strings.
One theorbo of ebony with inlaid ivory in a nonlocking case which is not at all stringed.

19

Schütz to Sophie Elisabeth.
Brunswick, 22 October 1644

[PML Mary Flagler Cary Music Collection, fol. 27]

[fol. 27r]
Durchlauchtige Hochgeborne Princessinn,
Gnedige Fraw,
Das Ewre Fürstl. Gn. die bewuste Expedition bey der Hochfürstl. Fraw
Wittiben zu Schöningen, auff sich zu nemen, ihr in allen gnaden belieben laßen, Habe ich aus demjenigen, was Sie mir gleich itzo mit ihren
Lackeyen sagen lassen, mit unterthenigen großen danck, gnungsamb
vermercket. Worbey diese kleine erinnerung noch zu thun scheinet,
weil bewustes Positiff itzo in Hamburg und zwar in S. Peters Kirchen
nebenst der grossen Orgel empor, unter Jacobi Pretorii hand und inspection, öffentlich zu verkeuffen stehet, und dahero gewislich nicht
lange unverkaufft bleiben möchte, Das dahero hochgedachte Furstl.
Fraw Wittibe, sich balt zu resolviren in gnaden geruhen wolten [flour-
ish] Und da auch auff dem fall die Zahlung nicht also balt und
volkomlich miteinander gefallen könte, müßte hirinnen ich mich auch
accommodiren, wie wol mir gleich wol, auch mit der bahren Zahlung,
besser gedienet were [flourish] Werden in Summa Ihrer Hochfurstl.
Durchl. gemüth hierinnen gebürlich zu erforschen haben, dahinn ich
auch aller unterthenig und gehorsamb remittiren thue, sonder allen
meinen privat nutzen.

Weil gegenwertige Woche noch [strikeout] (:im fall es nur die [illeg-
ible word] unsicherheit zu lassen wirdt:) in meinen geschäfften nacher
Hildesheimb zu verreisen fürhabens binn, Ich auch vermutlich noch
eine zeitlang (wiewol wieder meinen willen und mit wenigen vortheil
war:) mich alhier in Braunschweig enthalten werde, Versehe ich mich
Ewer Furstl. Gn. in Gnaden geschehen lassen, und zufrieden sein werden, das meine hinüberkunfft bis auff die nachfolgende Woche, ich

verschieben thue, Da ich dann, im fall ich nur vernemen thue das es so dann deroselbigen auch gelegen sein wirdt, Ich mich gehorsamlich ohnausbleiblich stellen, und was zu verfertigung unserer unter handen habenden Musicalischen arbeit, dienlichen, bestes fleisses mit E. Furstl. Gn. unterreden und tractiren will. [fol. 27v] Dieselbige inzwischen Gottlicher beschirmung zu allem fürstlichen angenemen wolergehen hiemit treulichst empfelende und verbleibende

> E. Furstl. Gnaden
> so lange ich leben Werde
> unterthenigster trewer diener
> Henrich Schütz Mpp
> Braunschweig den 22 October 1644.

Die new uberschickten Arien haben wier von dem lackeyen wol bekommen, sehe daraus, das E. Furstl. Gn. aus [strikeout] meinen wenigen anleitungen sich mercklichen gebessert haben, wollen also verhoffen dieses Wercklein, nechst dem lobe Gott hatt, deroselbigen auch einen ewiges guetes gedechtnus gebehren, und erwerben werde.

[In a second hand]

Der durchleüchtiger Hogeboren Fürstin und Frawen Frawe Sophia Elisabeth Hertzogin zu Braunschweig und Lüneburg geborne Fürstin von Mechlenburg. Meiner gnädigen Fürstin vnd Frawen.

19: Translation

Schütz to Sophie Elisabeth.
Brunswick, 22 October 1644

[PML Mary Flagler Cary Music Collection, fol. 27]

[fol. 27r]
Serene Noble Princess,
Gracious Lady,
I am pleased to have just learned with humble great thanks what you have conveyed through your lackeys: that Your Royal Grace shall undertake the expedition in question to Her Royal Ladyship, the widow in Schöningen, at her most gracious pleasure. Regarding this, this small reminder seems appropriate because the positif in question which is now in Hamburg, and in fact in St. Peter's church in the gallery next to the great organ, is up for public sale under the supervision and direction of Jacob Praetorius and therefore will certainly not remain unsold for long, and therefore may it please the aforementioned Her Royal Ladyship, the widow, to come to a decision soon. And in case the payment could not be made both immediately and completely, I shall have to be as accommodating in this as best I can, though payment in cash would serve me better. Finally, if Her Royal Highness could make known her intention in this matter, I can most humbly and dutifully make a remittance without any personal profit.

Because during the current week I still intend to travel to Hildesheim on business (in case the [illegible word] uncertainty will permit this), and [because] I shall probably remain here in Brunswick still for some time (though contrary to my wishes and to little [financial] advantage), I expect that Your Royal Grace will graciously permit me and be content if I postpone my visit until the following week, for then, in the case that I learn that it shall be thus satisfactory, I shall present myself obediently without fail, and confer and discuss with Your Royal Grace immediately and most diligently the completion of our musical work which we have at hand. [fol. 27v] Meanwhile commending you faithfully herewith to divine protection for all suitable royal welfare, and remaining

Your Royal Grace's
Most humble faithful servant
as long as I shall live
Heinrich Schütz
In his own hand
Brunswick, 22 October 1644

We have safely received from the lackey the arias recently sent and see from them that Your Royal Grace has notably improved from my modest instruction and thus hope that this little work shall, apart from the praise of God, bring forth for Your Royal Grace an eternal good memorial.

[In a second hand]

To the serene noble Princess and Lady, Lady Sophie Elisabeth, Duchess of Brunswick and Lüneberg, born Princess of Mecklenburg. My gracious Princess and Lady.

20

Schütz to Sophie Elisabeth.
Brunswick, 17 March 1645

[NSAW 1 Alt 25 no. 294, fol. 4]

[fol. 4r]
Durchlauchtige Hochgeborne Fürstinn
Gnedige fraw
Indliegendes schreiben habe unter andern, zu meiner anhero kunfft,
Ich alhier in Braunschweig auch gefunden, woraus vnser Gnediger furst
und herr, nebenst E. F. Gn. zu dero gnedigsten beliebung, so weit sich
in gnaden selbst ersehen können, das derjenige Musicalische guete
Vogel, welchen bishero Ihrer beÿderseits furstl. Gnaden zu recommendiren ich würdig erachtet habe, an itzo disseits vorüber [*vnd* crossed
out] fliegen, undt dieser gegendt hernacher entgehen wirdt, weil nun
auch in diesem punct was zu thun seÿ ich nicht wissen kan, Als habe
dises E. F. unterthenig zu notificiren ich nicht unterlassen, vndt
daneben zu dero gnedigen beruffung anheimb stellen wollen, ob
vnseres Gnedgn herrn gutachten [strikeout] und meinung zu erforschen und mich wiederumb wissen zu lassen Sie die nothturfft befinden werden [flourish]
    E. F. Gn. hirmit gottlicher beschirmung zu allem furstl. wolergehen
hirmit trewlichst empfelende und verbleibende.
                E. F. Gn.
                allezeit unterthngr
                gehorsamer
                Henrich Schütz Mpp
                Braunschweig den
                17 Martii 1645
[fol. 4v]
Der Durchlauchtigen hochgebornen Furstin Vnd frawen, frawen Sophia Elisabeth, hertzoginn zu Braunschweig und Luneburgk [flourish]

Geborner Princessin zu Mecklenborg, meiner gnediger fürstinn und frawen [flourish]

20: Translation

Schütz to Sophie Elisabeth.
Brunswick, 17 March 1645

[NSAW 1 Alt 25 no. 294, fol. 4]

[fol. 4r]
Serene Noble Princess
Gracious Lady,
   Upon my arrival here in Brunswick, I found among others the enclosed writing from which our gracious prince and lord and Your Royal Grace, at your most gracious pleasure, can graciously learn that that musically good bird, whom up until now I considered worthy to be recommended to both of Your Royal Graces, has now on this side flown away and will afterwards leave this region. Because now I do not know what can be done in this regard, I cannot fail to notify Your Royal [Highness] of this humbly and in addition want to place [myself] at your gracious disposal to enquire into our gracious lord's judgment and opinion and to let me know in return how you decide [to correct] the need [for such a musician].
   Most faithfully commending Your Royal Grace herewith to divine protection for complete royal welfare herewith, and remaining
                              Your Royal Grace's
                              always humble obedient
                              Heinrich Schütz
                              In his own hand
                              Brunswick
                              17 March 1645

[fol. 4v]
To the serene noble Princess and Lady, Lady Sophie Elisabeth, Duchess of Brunswick and Lüneburg. Born Princess of Mecklenburg, my gracious Princess.

21

Schütz to the Wolfenbüttel Court.
Undated

[NSAW 1 Alt 25 no. 294, fol. 5]

[fol. 5r].
In noie dni
Punct
Derowegen Ich ümb etwas genauere nachrichtung unterthenig zu bitten habe.

1.

Wegen der Companey der instrumentisten
1. wie starck dieselbige sein solle
2. was instrument Sie gebrauchen sollen
3. woraus dann zu schliessen sein wirdt was Oberinstrumentist von nöthen thue

2.

Wegen der Companeÿ der Sänger
1. von wie viel personen
2. von den discantisten, knaben, falsetisten und Eunuchen
3. was fur sprache die Vocal Music sich gebrauchen soll [flourish]

3.

Vom gebrauch der Geistlichen Music
1. beÿ der Taffel
2. beÿ den predigten
3. beÿ einem Principal absonderlichen Musicalischen Gottesdienst in der Kirchen [flourish]

4.

Wegen der Weltlichen TaffelMusic

5.

Wegen der Weltlichen Academischen vndt Theatralischen Music.

6.

Von dem Ort zu Musiciren in der kirchen
1. dem Chor in der Schloskirchen
2. dem Chor in der Stadtkirchen.

7.

Von beyhanden schaffung allerhandt nothwendigen Instrumenten.
1. Einem Zimmer darzu [flourish] Woselbst auch das tegliche execi-
tiam geschehen kan
2. deroselben inspection und verandwortung [flourish]
[fol. 5v]
Schuzzen

21: Translation

Schütz to the Wolfenbüttel Court. Undated

[NSAW 1 Alt 25 no. 294, fol. 5]

[fol. 5r]
In the name of the Lord
Points
On which I have been humbly asked [to provide] somewhat more precise information.

1.

Regarding the company of instrumentalists
1. How strong it should be
2. What instruments they should use
3. From that will then be decided what principal instrumentalist is required

2.

Regarding the company of singers
1. Of how many persons
2. Of the discant voices, boys, falsettists, and eunuchs
3. What language the singers shall use.

3.

Of the use of sacred music
1. At table
2. With the sermon
3. At a principal special musical service in church.

4.

Regarding secular music at table

5.

Regarding secular, academic and theatrical music.

6.

Of the place to perform music in church
1. The gallery in the palace church
2. The gallery in the city church.

7.

Of the current procurement of all sorts of necessary instruments.
1. A room in which the daily rehearsals can also take place
2. The same for supervision of the instruments and the responsibility for them.
[fol. 5v]
Schütz

22

Schütz's Poem "Der Musen Glükwünschung."
1650

[HAB T 904 2° Helmst.; Gn 4° 766. Poem to Duke August. Printed in Martin Gosky, *Arbustum vel Arboretum Augustaeum, AEternitati ac domui Augustae Selenianae sacrum, Satum autem & educatum a MARTINO GOSKY, L. Silesio, Med. D. . . . EX OFFICINA DUCALI WOL-PHERBYTTANI. Typis Johan et Henr. Stern. Anno 150,* fols. 461–62]

[fol. 461v]

I.

Mit süssem Klang o schönst' Auror'
Wir Musen dich verehren/
Dein glentzend Kleid im gülden Cohr
Mit Lob wir hoch vermehren
Weil unser Leu
Wiedrumb jetzt neu
Dein Tages = Licht gesund noch kan anblicken.
[fol. 462r]
Darunter sich
Gantz sicherlich
Die Menschen und das Vieh im Land erquicken.

II.

Willkommen du gewünschter Tag
Wilkommen / weil darinnen
Sich kühnlich wol erfreuen mag
Der Chor der Schäfferinnen.
Gott Pan auch frey
Auff der Schalmey
Ein Waldliedlein den Satiren mag singen.

Die Najades
Die Driades
Gezieret und gekrentzet einher springen.

III.

Ihr Meer = Göttinnen eilt gepaart
Aus euren tieffen Quellen
Ihr Bäum und Blümlein mancher Art
Müst euch gesamt einstellen.
Der Welfen Held/
In dieser Welt
Mit Lob und Klang bis Himmelhoch erhebe.
Weil er im Schutz
Für Martis Trutz
Das Jugend = Volck und uns lest sicher leben.

IV.

Ihr Götter und Göttinnen auff
Die Welffenburg umringet
Augustus fodert euren Lauff
Lob / Ehr und Preiß ihm bringet/
Der Welfen = Stam
Hoch Lobesam
Gepflantzet in dem Edlen Nieder Sachsen
Mit Freud und Lust
Hertzog August
Sol weit ausbreiten sich / und hoch wachsen
Heinrich Schütz

22: Translation

Schütz's Poem "Felicitation of the Muses."
1650

[HAB T 904 2° Helmst.; Gn 4° 766. Poem to Duke August. Printed in Martin Gosky, *Arbustum vel Arboretum Augustaeum, AEternitati ac domui Augustae Selenianae sacrum, Satum autem & educatum a MARTINO GOSKY, L. Silesio, Med. D.... EX OFFICINA DUCALI WOLPHERBYTTANI. Typis Johan et Henr. Stern. Anno 150*, fols. 461–62]

[fol. 461v]

I.

With sweet sounds, o most beautiful Aurora
We Muses honor you
Your shining raiment in the golden choir
We multiply greatly with praise
Because our lion
Can now again
Behold in health your daylight anew.
[fol. 462r]
Under which
Most assuredly
Man and beast in this country quicken.

II.

Welcome, you awaited day,
Welcome, for there
The choir of shepherdesses
Shall rejoice boldly,
The God Pan shall play
A little forest song for the satyrs
On the shawm.

The naiads
The dryads
Leap about adorned and crowned with garlands.

III.

You sea goddesses, hasten in pairs
From your deep springs,
You trees and little flowers of many kinds
Must arrange yourselves together in many ways.
Raise the Guelf hero
In this world
To the heavens with praise and rejoicing.
Because he guards us from
The scorn of Mars,
He allows the young and us to live in safety.

IV.

You Gods and Goddesses
Surrounding the castle of the Guelfs
Augustus speeds your course,
Bring him praise, honor, and glory
The Guelf line
Highly laudably
Planted in noble Lower Saxony
With joy and delight
May Duke August
Spread far and grow tall.
Heinrich Schütz

23

Sophie Elisabeth to Schütz.
Wolfenbüttel, 22 June 1655

[NSAW 1 Alt 25 no. 294, fol. 8]

[fol.8r]
Sophia Elisabeth
Unsere gunst und gnädigen gruß zuvor Ehrbar kunsterfahrener wolgelahrter lieber besonder.
Wir haben auß eurem eingelangten schreiben von 12 dieseß mit mehren
Verstanden, was an unß ihr, wegen deß Falsetisten oder Mahlerß, und
deß Directoris reise, wie auch wegen deß Bassisten anhero gelangen
lassen, und der Discantisten halber in dem Postscripto angeführet. Wan
dan um deß hochgebornen Fursten Herrn Augusti, Hertzogen zu Br.
vnd Lunab. etc. unsers hertzvielgeliebten Herrn und Gemahls Ld, alle
die von euch gethane Vorschläge ihro gnadig mit gefallen lassen, Alß
werdet ihr dieselbe Vorgeschlagener massen werckstellig zu machen,
und daß vor nemlich [*erst* crossed out] ein guter Bassist, welcher, wan
er [*ein* crossed out] Instrumentalische darbeÿ ist, unß desto angenehmer
seÿn wird, heruber komme, dan weile uns noch keine antwort geword,
von dem [strikeout] bekandt bassist zu Caßel, wirdt dieser, wan gleich d
and kom solte umb abwechselung nicht undienlich sein, euch besteß
fleisseß angelegen halten, und sind wir dero ankunfft gewärtig, und
werden es an dero hierunter benötigten anordnung zu [strikeout] ihrer
reise nicht ermangeln lassen. Sofern auch dem Falsetist annoch beÿ
seiner meinung anhero zu kommen beruhet, so sind hochgedacht vnsers
fr. geliebten Herrn vnd Gemahles Ld, dessen ankunfft, ungeachtet er
dieselbe zimlich lang auffgeschoben, annoch in gnaden begehrend,
woltenß euch also andwortlich unverhalten, und verbleiben euch mit
gonstigen gn. willen wol beÿgethan.
Geben Wolffenb. am 22 Junii 1655
An Heinrich Schutzen

[fol. 8v]
**Sermae andwort an Heinrich Schutzen
d. 22 Junii 1655
CM**

23: Translation

Sophie Elisabeth to Schütz.
Wolfenbüttel, 22 June 1655

[NSAW 1 Alt 25 no. 294, fol. 8]

[fol. 8r]
Sophia Elisabeth
Our favor and gracious greeting first and foremost to our honorable, artistically experienced, learned, beloved, and special [servant].
   We have learned from your delivered letter of the twelfth of this [month], along with much [other information], what you have addressed to us here regarding the falsettist or artist, the director's trip, also the bass, and the matter of the discantists presented in the postscript. If then the nobly born prince, Lord August, Duke of Brunswick and Lüneburg, our most beloved lord and husband, His Dilection, is to consent graciously to all of your proposals, then you shall accomplish this in the manner proposed, and especially see that a good bass comes here who, if he also plays an instrument, would be even more suitable to us, because we, meanwhile, have still received no answer from the well-known bass in Kassel. The latter, even if the former should come, shall occupy your utmost diligence, for an exchange would not be inappropriate. We await your arrival and we shall spare nothing for the necessary arrangements for your trip. Inasmuch as this still depends upon the falsettist's intent to come, then our gracious beloved lord and husband His Dilection still graciously desires his arrival, regardless of the fact that he has put it off for some time. We wish you to show no restraint in your answer and remain faithfully yours with favorable gracious intent.
Given Wolfenbüttel 22 June 1655
To Heinrich Schütz
[fol. 8v]
Most serene answer to Heinrich Schütz
22 June 1655
CM

24

Johann Jacob Löwe von Eisenach's Contract as Kapellmeister.
Wolfenbüttel, 24 June 1655

[NSAW 3 Alt 461, fols. 12–13]

[fol. 12r]

Von Gottes gnaden, Wir Augustus, Hertzog zu Brunswÿg und Lüneburgk, etc. hiemit vor Unß und Unsere Erben, jegen manniglichen Uhrkunden und bekennen, daß wir den Erbarn und kunsterfahrnen Unsern lieben getrewen Hansen Jacoben Lowen von Eÿsenach für Unsern Directorem Chori Musici und Capelmeistern, ietzo in gnaden bestellet, auffe und angenommen haben. Thuen das auch, bestellen und nehmen ihn dafür auff= und an, hiemit und in Krafft dieses Briefes, derogestalt und also, daß Unß und gedachten Unsern Erben, er getrew und holt, auch gehorsamb und gewertig seÿn, Unser und deroselben bestes in allewege thuen und schaffen, schaden, arges und nachtheil aber nach höchstem seinem verstande, vernmögen und krafften abwenden und verhüten, bevorab aber <u>sich eußerst dahin bemühen, daß Er Unß eine außbündige Capellen und Music</u>, von sonders erfahrnen und kunstreichen Gesellen, welche Unß sowoll in Musica Vocali, alß auch Instrumentali woll anstehen, nebenst zweÿen gelernigen Capellknaben, die er den sonderlich darzu vor sich informiren soll [Sophie Elisabeth's hand from left margin] (:war zue wir Ihme Jährlich fur einen Jed Knab an Kostgeldt 52 Dreÿohrts Rtr und 18 ggl und [strikeout] für leinin geräth, schuh, strümpf, und waschgeldt und waß dem angehörig 20 Rtr und dann ein [*lincee Kleÿd* crossed out] lincee Kleÿd mantel und Hutt:) [first hand] [*den negsten auff Unser weitere ordinantz* crossed out] zuwege bringen, und beÿ die hand schaffen, und damit alle Son= und Festtage am ende und ohrten, woselbsten wir nach Unserer gelegenheit, Unsern fürstl. Hoffstadt und Residentz haben und anstellen werden, in der

Kirchen beÿ verrichtung des Gottesdienstes, wie auch zu Hoefe unter werenden Taffeln, ordinarie, wie auch Extraordinarie [fol. 12v] so offte es von nöthen, und von Unß erfordert wird, auffwarten, und dienstgewertig seÿn soll. Es soll aber er Hans Jacob Lowe vor allen dingen dahin sehen, daß er Ausbündige, und in der wißenschafft der kunst sonders erfahrne, und in Lehr, leben und wandel unärgerliche Musicos, so dem gesöff und anderer unartigkeit nicht zugethan seÿn, ausrichte, und mit denselben zu keines andern, wer der oder die auch seÿn, und nahmen haben mögen, es seÿn auch Officirer und Krieges Leute in Unserer Vestung Wulffenbüttel, oder sonsten andere ohne Unser sonderbahres Vorwißen und Special Concession derogestaldt auffwärtig seÿn, und in Summa eine solche Music anrichte, und zuwege bringe, damit er vor hohen Potentaten, und bevorab Unß, mit ruhm bestehen und passiren kan, wir auch dahero Ursach gewinnen mögen, nach befindung etwas mehr auff die Musicam zuwenden, So soll er auch vor sich selber, sich eines nüchtern, meßigen und unstraffbahren lebens befleißigen, sich Unserer Christl. Kirchen= Hoff= und andern nützbahren ordnungen gebrauchen, der erste mit in der Kirchen, und auff Unserm fürstl. Gemach, wan die Zeitt davon ist, und der letzte darauß und darvor wieder seÿn, seinen zuordenden Musicis mit gueten Exempeln vorgehen, und dieselbe zu aller Zucht und Ehrbahrkeit anweisen, auch da er Zeit wehrendes all [fol. 13r] solches seines Capelmeister dienstes in Unsern geheimen und angelegenen sachen etwas hören, sehen und erfahren möchte, so Unß und den Unserigen zu mercklichem praejuditz und nachtheil ausschlagen und gereichen wolte, davon niemand außer Unß, das geringste ppoliren und entdecken, sondern solches alles biß in seine Gruben, er seÿ auch Unser diener oder kein diener, verschwiegen beÿ sich behalten, und sich nach Unserer Ober Direction und Commando allein richten, und sonsten alles anders thuen und leisten, wie solches einem getrewen fleißigen und auffrichtigen dienern und Capellmeistern woll anstehet, eignet und gebühret, immaßen Unßer darüber gehörige pflicht und äÿyde abgeleistet, und seinen Reversbrief heraußer gegeben hat.

Darentgegen und zu ergetzlichkeit solches seines dienstes und mühewaltung, zusagen und versprechen wir ihme zu besoldung und kostgelde eines vor alles Jährliches und jedes Jahrs besondern, so lange er in diesem Unserm dienste verbleiben wirt, [second hand] drey hundt Taler, [first hand] halb auff weinachten, und halb auff Johannis Baptista tag auß Unserer fürstl. Zahl Cammer zureichen, und gegen Quietung abfolgen zulaßen, auch mit der wircklichen ausZahlung des ersten Termins auff negste [second hand] Weihenachten [first hand] einen anfang zumachen.

Wir behalten Unß aber beÿderseits bevor, da wir Ihn dergestalt vor Unsern Capellmeister und Directorem Chori Musici nicht lenger haben und behalten wolten, oder Unß er davor Zudienen weiters kein belieben tragen würde, daß alßdan [fol. 13v] ein theil dem andern ein viertel Jahr vorher eine bestendige losekündigung intimiren magk.

Wollen Ihn auch ungehörter sachen nicht beungnadigen, sondern auff etwa begebende fälle allemahl gnädig hören, und nach befindung ihn seiner Unschuld Fürstl. genießen laßen: Alles ohne gefehrde. Deßen zu Uhrkundt haben Wir diesen bestallungs brief mit eigenen handen unterschrieben, und Unserm Fürstl. Secrete besiegeln laßen: So geschehen in Unserer Residentz Wulffenbüttel, den 24. Junÿ. Anno. 1655. pw Serenmi etc. Bestallung dem newen Capellmeistern, Hansen Jacob Lowen von Eÿsenach gegeben d. 24. Junÿ Ao etc. 1655./.

Munditur nebst einem Revers

F: nro: 19

x–

24: Translation

Johann Jacob Löwe von Eisenach's Contract as Kapellmeister. Wolfenbüttel, 24 June 1655

[NSAW 3 Alt 461, fols. 12–13]

[fol. 12r]
By the grace of God we, Augustus, Duke of Brunswick and Lüneburg, herewith certify and acknowledge before us and our heirs one and all, that we now graciously appoint and employ the worthy and highly experienced artist, our beloved [servant] Johann Jacob Löwe von Eisenach as our director of choral music and Kapellmeister. That done, we also appoint, receive, and employ him herewith thus and in this manner by authority of this letter, that he shall be faithful and devoted as well as obedient and dutiful to us and our aforementioned heirs; always to do and perform our and our heirs' [wishes]; to avert and prevent injuries, offenses, and wrong, however, to the best of his understanding, ability, and power; but especially to strive to the utmost that he create an excellent *Kapelle* and ensemble of especially experienced and accomplished members, who serve well in the vocal as well as instrumental ensemble, along with two apprenticed choirboys whom he shall instruct specially [Sophie Elisabeth's hand from left margin] (he is due yearly for each boy's board 52 3/4 Reichstalers and 18 gold gulden and for linen apparel, shoes, stockings, and washing charges, and related items 20 Reichstalers and then a flaxen suit of clothes, coat, and hat) [first hand] and have in readiness; and shall have and commission them for all Sundays and feast days at the location and place in our royal court and residence according to our wishes; shall serve and be prepared to obey in church at the observance of the worship service as well as at the daily table at court, ordinarily as well as extraordinarily, [fol. 12v] as often as necessary and required by us. However he, Johann Jacob Löwe, shall

above all see that he conducts himself as an excellent musician and as one especially experienced in the knowledge of art and agreeable in his profession, life, and conduct, thus avoiding drunkenness and other indiscretions; and also to serve no other in this manner who is [either] the former or the latter and who wishes to have such privileges, namely, officers and soldiers in our fortress Wolfenbüttel, or any others without our particular prior knowledge and special permission; and in summary to prepare such an ensemble and create it so that it can withstand with glory and pass [scrutiny] before high potentates and especially us. If we also should find cause to devote something more to the ensemble according to circumstances, then he shall also above all devote himself to a sober, moderate, and irreproachable life, apply himself at our holy church, court, and other orders in effect, the first to be in the church and in our royal chamber at the proper time, and the last thereof and therefrom to set his associate musicians a good example, and to instruct them completely in discipline and respectability. And when in future should he, [fol. 13r] in his service as Kapellmeister, hear, see, and experience our private and important affairs, he shall then avert and deter obvious prejudice and injury from us and ours, of which no one but us shall have the slightest awareness and knowledge, but [take] all to his grave. He is either our servant or no servant at all; he shall maintain discretion and direct his attention to our supreme direction and command alone and otherwise do and carry out all else that is befitting, suitable, and becoming to a faithful, diligent, and true servant and Kapellmeister, on which he has sworn duty and oath to us, and which his letter of guarantee has specified.

In return and in compensation for his service and efforts, we pledge and promise him as salary and board once for all yearly and each year separately as long as he remains in our service [second hand] three-hundred talers, [first hand] half payable at Christmas and half on St. John's Day from our royal chamber of finances, and to give a receipt. The actual payment of the first term to begin at the next [second hand] Christmas.

[first hand] We mutually retain before us that if we no longer wish to have and retain him as our Kapellmeister and director of choral music or if he in return no longer sustains the inclination to serve in such a manner, then one shall [fol. 13v] give the other notice of a definite recision a quarter year in advance.

We shall not be ungracious to him in matters of impropriety, but in such circumstances which may occur, we shall always graciously hear him out and make our judgement as we think best. All without penalty. In witness thereof we have signed and sealed this letter of appointment in our own hand. Thus done in our capital Wolfenbüttel, 24 June 1655. Most serene appointment of the new Kapellmeister, Johann Jacob Löwe von Eisenach, done 24 June 1655.

Fair copy along with a guarantee

F: nro: 19

x—

25

Schütz to Sophie Elisabeth.
Dresden, 24 July 1655

[NSAW 1 Alt 25 no. 294, fols. 9–11]

[fol. 9r]
Durchlauchtige hochgeborne Fürstinn
Gnädige Fraw.
E. Furstl. Gnaden berichte ich hirmit in unterthngkeit was gestalt der
vermeinte Director Johann Jacob Löwe von Wien, nebenst denen beyden Discantisten am 19 Julii vor wenig tagen, mit etlichen alhier auff
der Elbe fortgefahrenen Schiffen, von hinnen bis nacher Magdeburgk
auch fortgereiset ist, worbey E. F. Gn. Ich auch nicht bergen kann, was
gestalt itzgemelten Director, ich entlich fast mit ernst [*auch* crossed out]
forttreiben müssen, welcher (:durch etliche ihm zu ohren gebrachte,
weis nicht durch wem, wiederwertige nachrichtung:) fur seinem abreisen, rükwendig war gemacht worden das er fast nicht fortgewolt, Nach
dem er sich aber numehr hatt behandeln lassen, vndt auf der Reise
albereit ist, So verhoffe ich, das (:wann es nicht albereit geschehen:) Er
sich nebenst denen knaben ehistes bey Ihrer Furstl. Hoffstadt glüklich
noch anlangen werde, vndt habe Ich dem Director Ein unterthngs
schreiben an E. F. Gn. hertzliebsten Herrn Gemahl mitgegeben, welches
Er zu seiner anhierokunft Ihrer Durchl. mit geburenden Reverentz zu
insinuiren wissen wirdt [flourish]
    Wie man solche leutlein Ihrer fürstl. hoffstadt änstandig und beliebet
sein werden, Stelle ich zwar dahinn, halte oder befinde Es aber an
meinem wenigen orte allerdings für Rahtsamb, (:ob man gleich solchen
director beharlich im dienste zu behalten nicht gesonnen were, oder Er
director in die lenge nicht verbleiben wolte:) Das man zum mindesten
1 Jahr bey der furstl. music ihn zu erhalten, man trachten solle, ümb
der rechten und gueten Manier halben, worzu er binnen solcher Zeit die
Musicanten verhoffentlich anführen u. gewehnen wirdt. Solte her-

nacher etwa einige Verenderung vorgehen, Stünde seine stelle (:ob
gleich nicht mit einem in der Music so wolgelerthen jedoch sonst:) mit
einem andern wol qualificirten kerl, der ein gueter Sänger daneben
were, allezeit zu besetzen, der die angefangene guete Manier der Music,
mit gueten compositionen, die man ihm zuschicken könte, Eben so wol
fortstellen könte, welches ich also, auf die begebenheit, nur gemeldet
haben will [flourish]

[fol. 9v] Dieser Johann Jacob Löwe (:massen ich auch an E. F. Gn. herrn
herrn Gemahl geschrieben habe:) ist ein auffrichtiger Ehrlicher mensch
an welchem Ich kein notabel laster, als lange Er sich bey mir angehalten
iemahls verspuret habe, alleine so ist er sonst frisches Östereichisches
humors v. sitten, will gerne alles nach seinem Embsigen sinn haben,
dahero ich mich auch besorgen mus das er die knaben vieleicht etwas
zu viel belästigen, undt Sie [*sich* crossed out] so dann über ihn klagen,
oder (:wie fur ihren abreisen sie sich etliche personen sollen haben
verlauten lassen:) wol gar wieder davon lauffen werden, solchen übel
nun fur zu kommen, were zwar mein wunsch E. F. Gn. (:wann es anders
sonder Unhöflikeit deroselbigen angemutet werden kann:) dieselbigen
zugleich etwas mit unter Ihre gnedige protection nemen vndt bis weilen
einen Zutritt vergönnen möchten, ümb ihr bewandnüs selbst anzubrin-
gen.

Sonst So hatt es wegen aufrichtung mehrgedachtes Directors Bestallung, Eben so gar gros Eilens nicht, Nur mus ich dieses hiebey noch 1
mahl unterthng erindern das Ich fur eine billikeit befinde das wegen
seiner aufgesandten schweren Reisekosten, auch Verzehrung der knaben auff der Reise hinab (:weil Sie für ihrem aufbruch undt fortzug
gentzlich unter meiner Verpflegung gewesen:) Ihme zu seiner an kunfft
eine ergetzung wiederfahren, vndt sonder masgebung, in die 50 thlr zu
einem gnädigen praesent so balt gegeben werden möge, Er ist zwar ein
Weit mehrers von Wien aus v. alhier looss worden, massen er anhero
noch von 30 in 40 thlr welche Er alhier erborget, noch schuldig zu
zahlen ist, vermeine aber Er auch mit so viel, Im fall Ihro durchl. nicht
Ein mehres aus eigenen bewegnüs thun wollen, sich anfänglich wol
vergnügen lassen werde, massen dann auch beÿ aufrichtung seiner Besoldung oder Verpflegung, Er sich verhoffentlich nichts minder zu
Einen billichen bequemen wirdt.

Vndt erwarte numehr mit Verlangen, Ihre ankunfft undt wie sie sich
zu ihren schuldigen unterthngn diensten anstellen und anlassen, zu
vernemen,   Wünschende, das wie alles von mir guth gemei- [fol.
11r] net worden ist, Es also auch ausschlagen undt [*wol* crossed out]
gerathen möge, Gott es auch in gnaden also wol gelingen lassen wolle,
dessen Göttlicher beschirmung zu allem gewunschten Wolergehen am

Seel v. leibe E. F. Gn. Ich auch hirmit trewlichst entpfolen haben will, verbleibende

E. Furstl. Gn.
Unterthngr schuldiger
diener allezeit
Henrich Schütz Mpp
Dresden am 24 Julii
Ao etc. 1655.

Ich binn auch von einem gueten freunde gebeten worden, Einen jungen menschen der ein Instrumentist ist v. Itzo mit dem Director zugleich auch fortgereiset, umb dienst sich in NiederSachsen zu bewerben, zu Recommendiren, Ob derselbe nun Ihrer Music anständig v. dabey von nöthen thun möchte, kan von Ihren albereit andern bestalten Musikanten v. dem zugleich mitkommende Director entschieden werden, v. werde ich meines theils es zu überflussigen leuten niemals rathen, will ihn aber in dessen so weit unterthng Recommendiret haben, das Er erstlich gehöret, v. wann bey der Music keine Stelle ledig ist, Er anderweit fort recommendieret werden möge [flourish]

[fol. 10r]

Postscriptum

Datum am 24 Julii 1655.

Demnach E. Fürstl. Gn. sich auch in gnade noch wol erindern wie Sie auff befehl dero hertzgeliebtesten herrn herrn Gemahl, mich hiebevor in bestallung genommen, undt über Ihre furstl. Music mir die Inspection von hause aus aufgetragen haben, deroselbigen ich mich auch bishero (:nicht alleine mit fleissiger fürsorge und bemühung, Sondern noch mit anschaffung dieser 2 discantisten und [*auch* crossed out] Verrpflegung deroselbigen, insonderheit mit fast köstbarer erziehung des meinigen von iugent auff:) verhoffentlich gar genugsamb angenommen habe, So kann ich numehr auch nicht unterlassen E. F. Gn. hochfleissig anzuliegen, Sie ihrer hohen discretion nach, vnd zu gelegener zeit, bey dero hochgedachten herrn herrn etc. Es dahin vermitteln helfen wollen, das ümb der mir angebotenen gnade versicherung willen, mir gleich wol auch eine kleine schrifftliche versicherung der bestallung zu handen gelangen möge, Eure furstl. Gn. Erindern sich das mir 100 goldgulden bewilliget worden sindt, mit welchen Ich auch annoch unterthanig vor lieb zu nemen erbotig binn, Auch hirüber noch geschehen lassen kann (:in erinderung der alten teutschen lehre, das mann grosser herrn zwar geniesen Sie aber auch bey Brohdte lassen soll:) das Es auf 100 thlr herunter noch moderiret werden möge, nur mit dieser angehengter bitte, das es also mit denen selbigen eingerichtet werden, das die helffte als 50 thlr Ostern vnd aber 50 thlr Michaelis, in

den zwey leibziger Messen des jahr über, mir zahlet undt kunfftig bevorstehenden Michaelis Markt der anfang mit denen Ersten 50 thlrn gemacht werden möchte. Zumahl ich dero Zeit, massen der Director meinen
Zustand berichten kann, wegen meiner jungsthinn in leibzigk verstorb-
enen letzten tochter vffgewandten begräbnuskosten, fast nottürfttig
binn.   Vnd wurde sich H. Steffann Daniel kauffmann zu Braunschweig, v. mein gueter freund, der alle leibziger Messen oder Markte
zu besuchen pfleget, auff gnädige anordnung Ihrer durchl. genugsamb
zu solcher auszahlung verstehen [flourish]   [strikeout] Getröste
mich dieses punctshalben, in Summa alleine E. F. Gn. gnädigen
beförderung der copist welcher mir zu Weissenfels E. F. Gn. psalmbuch-
lein hatt ausarbeiten, versichert sich auff kunfftigen leibziger markt
auch noch einer Recompens von 4 oder 5 Ducaten.
[fol. 10v]
Postscriptum
[fol. 11v]
Der Durchlauchtigen Hochgebornen Fürstinn vndt Frawen, Frawen Sophien Elisabeth, Hertzoginn zu Braunschweig und Lüneburg, Geborner
Hertzoginn zu Mecklenburgk, Fürstinn zu Wenden, Schwerin vndt
Ratgeburgk, auch gräffin zu Schwerin, der lande Rostock vndt Stargard
Frawen etc. Meiner gnädigen Fürstinn vnd Frawen [flourish]
[Sophie Elisabeth's hand]
Dß d Director ankom vndt vns nebenst d Knab noch zur Zeit wohl
anstendig, Dß er vorgestellet word vndt zwar wie ein Cappellmeister.
Dß man weg d Knab ein auge wolte mit auf sie hab, dß ihm den Director
50 Rtl. geliefert word. D Violiste weile die stelle alhir noch besetzt hatt
nicht unter kom. Dß sich seine bestallung hierbeÿ einstellet kön mit
verhofentlicher guter Satisfaction. D Copiist soll mit negstem dß seinige
auch bekom.

25: Translation

Schütz to Sophie Elisabeth.
Dresden, 24 July 1655

[NSAW 1 Alt 25 no. 294, fols. 9–11]

[fol. 9r]
Serene Noble Princess
Gracious Lady,
   I report to Your Royal Grace in humility herewith the manner in which the would-be director, Johann Jacob Löwe of Vienna, along with both discantists, departed a few days ago on July 19 on some ships which set out on the Elbe from here to Magdeburg. In so doing, I cannot conceal from Your Royal Grace the manner in which the newly announced director, whom I had to push forward rather seriously, who (because of disagreeable news that reached his ears, I do not know from whom) before his departure was made hesitant, so that he almost did not want to be off. After that, however, he then allowed himself to be convinced and has already set out. Thus I hope that (if it has not already happened) he shall yet arrive safely at your royal capital along with the boys very soon, and I have sent with the director a most humble writing to Your Royal Grace's most beloved husband which he [Löwe] shall present with proper reverence to Your Highness upon his arrival.
   How one is to be fair and just to such domestic servants of your royal capital, I am indeed uncertain. In my humble opinion, I consider or think it certainly advisable (if one were not disposed to continue to retain such a director in service or he would not want to continue as director for long) that one should strive to keep him with the royal ensemble at least one year for the sake of correct and good style, in which, it is to be hoped, during this period he shall train and instruct the musicians. If perhaps some changes should come to pass later on, replace him (although one so learned in music [will be difficult to find] however) with another well-qualified fellow who is also a good singer,

[one] who, so to speak, could carry on the newly established good musical style just as well with good compositions, which could be sent to him. This I just want to suggest, in any event.

[fol. 9v] This Johann Jacob Löwe (as I wrote to Your Royal Grace's husband) is a sincere honest person in whom I have observed no notable faults as long as he resided with me; but besides, he has bold Austrian disposition and manners [and] prefers to have everything according to his eager intentions. Therefore I fear that he works the boys perhaps a little too hard and they then complain about him, or (as they implied to a few people before their departure) run away from him altogether. To prevent such a misfortune, it would be my wish that Your Royal Grace (if it does not seem rude) might take them together somewhat under your gracious protection and occasionally permit them access to present their circumstances themselves.

Otherwise, regarding the establishment of the aforesaid director's appointment, there is certainly no great hurry, only I must herewith graciously mention one more time that I consider it fair that, due to his escalated heavy travel costs as well as the expenses for the boys on the trip down (because before their departure and embarkment they were entirely under my care) upon his arrival he be compensated, and (in my humble opinion) might be given 50 talers as a gracious gift immediately. He is in fact quite a distance from Vienna and got in trouble here because he in addition still owes about 30 to 40 talers which he borrowed here. However I think that, in case Your Highness does not want to provide anything more on your own initiative, he shall be satisfied at the start with this much, because then with the establishment of his salary and support, it is to be hoped he shall make the best of a [salary] which is small but fair.

And I now await with anticipation to be informed of their arrival and of how they take up and behave in their due humble services.

Wishing that all of my good intentions [fol. 11r] may thus develop and succeed, and also that they may be granted success by the grace of God into whose divine protection for all the prosperity of body and soul you desire I also faithfully wish herewith to commend Your Royal Grace, remaining,

> Your Royal Grace's
> humble indebted servant always
> Heinrich Schütz
> In his own hand
> Dresden 24 July 1655

I have also been asked by a good friend to recommend a young person who is an instrumentalist and who also just departed together with the director in order to seek employment in Lower Saxony. Whether he might now be suitable to perform with your ensemble and in so doing fill a need, can be decided by the other musicians already in your employ and the director traveling with him. And for my part, I never advise extra people, but nevertheless I want humbly to have recommended him this far, that he first might be listened to, and if no position in the ensemble is available, he may be further recommended.

[fol. 10r]

Postscript

Dated 24 July 1655

Whereas Your Royal Grace will graciously recall how you on the recommendation of your most beloved husband earlier appointed me and charged me with the inspection *in absentia* of your royal ensemble, which I hope that I have until now (not only with diligent care and effort but also with procuring these two discantists and providing for them, apart from the very expensive care of my own from childhood) undertaken quite sufficiently, I thus cannot now fail to entreat Your Royal Grace most diligently, according to your great discretion and at an opportune time, to help to negotiate with your aforementioned husband the assurance of the annuity offered me. A little written guarantee of my appointment might also at the same time reach my hand. Your Royal Grace will recall that 100 gold gulden were granted me which I am still humbly prepared to accept out of love. Also on this account I would even be content (remembering the old German proverb, that one shall not cause rich men to run short of bread) that [the agreement] may still be reduced to 100 talers but with the following request: that it may be so arranged that half (50 talers) be paid to me at Easter and again 50 talers [at] Michaelmas at the two Leipzig fairs during the year, and the first 50 talers might be paid at the upcoming Michaelmas fair. Especially since just now, as the director [Löwe] can report on my situation, I am very hard pressed due to the expensive burial costs for my last daughter who recently died in Leipzig.

And Herr Stephan Daniel, merchant of Brunswick and my good friend, who is in the habit of attending the Leipzig fair or market, would understand Your Highness's gracious instructions sufficiently for such a payment.

I wait patiently regarding this little point. In conclusion, only Your Royal Highness's dispatch [of funds] to the copyist who completed Your Royal Grace's little book of psalms for me in Weissenfels assures him of yet another recompense of four or five ducats at the next Leipzig fair.

[fol. 10v]

Postscript

[fol. 11v]
To the Serene Noble Princess and Lady, Lady Sophie Elisabeth, Duchess of Brunswick and Lüneburg, born Duchess of Mecklenburg, Princess of Wenden, Schwerin, and Radeburg, also Countess of Schwerin, the region of Rostock and Lady of Stargard. My gracious Princess and Lady.
[Sophie Elisabeth's hand]
[Inform Kapellmeister Schütz] that the director has arrived and is still at the present time quite acceptable; he has been introduced and indeed as a Kapellmeister.

That the choirboys will be looked after, that 50 Reichstalers shall be bestowed upon the director. The violinist, because the post here has been occupied for a time, found no employment. It is to be hoped that he [Schütz] could herewith be satisfactorily awarded his appointment. The copyist shall receive his [payment] at the next [fair].

26

Schütz's Contract as Kapellmeister *in absentia*. Wolfenbüttel, 23 August 1655

[NSAW 3 Alt 461, fols. 14–17]

[fol. 14r. Not in Schütz's hand]
Ich Heinrich Schütze, uhrkunde und bekenne Hiemit, das der durchlauchtiger, hochgebohrner Fürst undt Herr, Herr Augustus, Hertzog zue Braunschweig undt Lüneburgk etc. Mein gnädiger Fürst undt Herr, Mich für dero oberCapellmeistern von Hauß aus in gnaden bestellet undt angenommen hat, auch dero gnädige Bestallung darüber ertheilen laßen, Immaßen dieselbe wörtlich hernach folget:
Von Gottes gnaden Wir Augustus, Hertzog zu Braunschweig undt Lüneburgk etc. Vor uns undt unsere Erben jegen männiglichen uhrkunden undt bekennen, daß Wir den kunst sehr erfahrenen Unsern Lieben getrewen ietziger Zeit Churfürstl. Sächsischer Ld. zu dreßden bestalten Capellmeistern Heinrichen Schuetzen ebenfalß zu einem ober-Capellmeistern von Hauß aus in gnaden bestellet undt angenommen haben, thun das auch bestellen undt nehmen Ihnen darvor uff: und an, hiemit undt in Crafft dieses, deroge- [fol. 14v] stalt undt also, daß uns undt gedachten unsern Erben Er getrew undt holdt sein, unsere fürstl. Capellen alhier mit gueten düchtigen Musicanten die so woll in Vocali alß Instrumentali Musica woll abgerichtet sein, darneben auch undt insonderheit mit gueten Capellknaben undt Bassisten allemahl woll versehen, deßwegen stets mit unserm unterCapellmeistern welchen Wir an unserm fürstl. Hoffe alhie haben, der dan negst uns unter seiner oberDirection undt Commando mit sein soll, Wir auch denselben ohne sein Vorwißen nicht verendern wollen, Correspondiren, und wan Wir Zu Zeiten insonderbahren ins künfftig vorfallenheiten seiner praesentz undt gegenwarth benötiget sein würden, Er alßdan es beÿ vorhochermelter I. Churfürstl. [fol. 15r] Ld. zue Dresden dahin richten, und sich interimsweise Loß machen soll, daß uns er alhie uff eine geringe Zeit in

Musicalischen sachen undt deren oberDirection uffwerttig sein könne, gestaldt uns Er ein sonderbahres angelobnüs mit einen handtstreiche an aÿdes Statt ebenfalß daruff gethan, undt seinen Reversbrieff darüber heraußer gegeben hat;

Darentjegen undt zue ersetzlichkeit vor solche seine mühewaltung, zusagen undt versprechen Wir Ihme Jährlichs undt Jedes Jahrs besonderen so lange diese unsere Bestallung unuffgekündiget wehren wirdt Ein Hundert undt funfftzig Reichßthaler Ihme dieselbe in zweÿen unter schiedener Terminen, alß uff Michaëlis undt ostern, allemahl zue [fol. 15v] Leipzig uff Wechsel, durch unsern ietzigen unterthanen undt Kauffman in unserer Stadt Braunschweig Stephan Daniell, oder sonsten durch andere gelegenheit bahr gegen Quitung außZahlen zulaßen, undt mit den erst halbjährigen außZahlung, diesen itztbevorstehenden Michaelis tag dieses Jahrs an, mit Siebentzig undt fünff Reichßthalern ohnfehlbahr den anfang zumachen;

Wir behalten uns aber beyderseits bevor, da Wir mit dieser unserer Bestallung über kurtz oder Lang verenderung machen, undt Ihnen nicht lenger vor unsern oberCapellmeistern haben oder uns Er derogestalt darvor lenger zudienen kein beliebnüß tragen würde, [fol. 16r] daß alßdan ein theill dem andern ein viertheill Jahr vorher eine bestendige Lose intimiren laßen magk. Alles ohne gefehrde. Und deßen zue uhrkundt haben Wir diesen Bestallungs Brieff mit eigenen handen unterschrieben, undt unser fürstl. secret darunter uffs Spacium trücken laßen; So geschehen in unserer fürstl. Haubt undt Residentz vestunge Wulffenbüttell in den 8. tagen der heÿl. ostern Anno 1655./.

Verpflichte mich demnach hiermit undt in Krafft dieses, das Hochgedacht S. F. Gnad. Ich getrew undt holdt sein, S. F. G. undt dero Erben bestes befordern, schaden undt arges aber nach hochstem Vermögen [fol. 16v] kehren, wehren undt abwenden, bevorab aber inserirter fürstl. Bestallung in allen worten, Puncten und Clausuln schuldiger gebürr nachleben, und dan gegen was darin zue meiner behueff einverleibet, hinwieder gewertig sein soll und will; ohne gefehrde;

Uhrkündtlich habe Ich diesen Reversbrieff mit eigenen händen unterschrieben undt versiegelt; geschehen undt geben wie oben./. [Schütz's hand] In Dresden Am Vigilia S. Bartholomaei war der 23 Monats tag Augusti Ao etc. 1655.

[Seal]   Henrich Schütz
          Chürfl. Sächsischer
          Capellmeister Mpp
[fol. 17r. Third hand]
          Revers

Uber Mmj. Augusti etc. Bestallung von Heinrich Schutzen Churfurstl.
Sächsischen Capelmeistern zu Dresden
geben In den H. Ostern 1655.
F.i.
Vom Hoëf den 10t. 8bris ao 1655
Von Hofe kennen 3t. Maÿ:1660.

26: Translation

Schütz's Contract as Kapellmeister *in absentia*. Wolfenbüttel, 23 August 1655

[NSAW 3 Alt 461, fols. 14–17]

[fol. 14r]
I Heinrich Schütz herewith certify and acknowledge that the serene, noble prince and lord, my Lord August, Duke of Brunswick and Lüneburg, my gracious prince and lord, has graciously appointed and employed me as your senior Kapellmeister *in absentia,* and has bestowed your gracious appointment thereon, in the manner which follows verbatim hereafter:

By the grace of God we, August, Duke of Brunswick and Lüneburg, certify and acknowledge before us and our heirs one and all, that we have graciously appointed and employed the highly experienced artist our beloved Heinrich Schütz, currently appointed in Dresden as Kapellmeister as well to His Dilection, the elector of Saxony, as a senior Kapellmeister *in absentia.* That done, we also appoint, receive, and employ him herewith; and thus by authority of this [contract] [fol. 14v], that he shall be faithful and devoted to us and to our heirs mentioned above; to supply our royal ensemble here well at all times with good qualified musicians who are well trained not only as singers but as instrumentalists as well; moreover and particularly [to supply] good choirboys and basses in addition; regarding this to correspond regularly with our junior Kapellmeister [Johann Jacob Löwe] whom we have here at our royal court, who then next to us shall be under his supreme direction and command, and whom we shall not replace without his prior knowledge; and should we in times to come require his presence and attendance for special occasions, he shall at that time arrange it with aforementioned His Electoral [fol. 15r] Highness in Dresden and in the interim extricate himself for a short time so that he may attend to musical matters and their supreme direction. He shall likewise make to us a special vow to agree thereon in lieu of an oath and he has issued his letter of promise thereon.

Accordingly and as compensation for his efforts, we pledge and promise him yearly and every year separately, as long as this our appointment is not withdrawn, one hundred and fifty Reichstalers, this in two separate installments, namely on Michaelmas and Easter, always in [fol. 15v] Leipzig by promissory note through Stephan Daniel, currently our subject and merchant in our city Brunswick, or else through another arrangement, to be paid in cash against a receipt, and with the first semi-annual payment on this coming Michaelmas Day of this year to make the first payment without fail. We mutually agree, if we sooner or later make changes in this our appointment and would have you for our senior Kapellmeister no longer, or if he in return no longer sustains the inclination to serve in such a manner, [fol. 16r] then one shall give the other notice of a definite recision a quarter year in advance. All without penalty. And in witness thereof we have signed this letter of appointment in our own hand and stamped with our royal seal in the space below. Thus done in our royal capital and residence the fortress Wolfenbüttel in the eight days of Easter 1655.

I commit myself accordingly herewith and by authority thereof to be faithful and devoted to His aforementioned Royal Grace; to protect His Royal Grace and his heirs in the best manner possible; to divert, resist, and avert injuries and offenses, however, to the best of my ability; [fol. 16v] but above all to conform dutifully and properly to the official royal appointment in all words, points, and clauses; and then shall be in return ready and willing to attend to that contained therein. Without penalty.

As verification I have signed and sealed this letter of guarantee with my own hand. Done and delivered as above. [Schütz's hand] In Dresden on the Vigil of St. Bartholomew which was the twenty-third day of August 1655.

[Seal]   Heinrich Schütz
          Electoral Saxon Kapellmeister
          In his own hand

[fol. 17r. Third hand]

Guarantee

On His Majesty August's appointment of Heinrich Schütz, Electoral Saxon Kapellmeister in Dresden.
Done at Holy Easter 1655.
F.i.
From court, 10 October 1655. Designated at court, 3 May 1660.

27

Sophie Elisabeth to Schütz.
Wolfenbüttel, 10 November 1655

[NSAW 1 Alt 25 no. 294, fols. 6–7]

[fol. 6r]
Sophia Elisabeth
Vnsern gnädigen gruß zuvor etc.
Wir haben ab euren schreiben vom dato daß 30ten octobris iungsthin
unter andern ersehen, was an unß ihr wegen continuirung eurer bestallung gelangen laßen, auch wegen ubermachung der besoldungs gelder
unvorgreifflich vorschlagen, und daneben deß Capellmeisterß und
Theorbisten halber, mit anfuhren wollen.
Wir geben auch darauff in gnädiger antwort hinwieder zu
vernehmen, daß, so viel eure bestallung betrifft, unserß fry geliebten
Herrn und Gemahlß Ld, dieselbe zu continuiren, und die besoldungs
gelder dero behufes gebührend ubermachen zu lassen, in gnaden
entschlossen seyn. Aldieweil aber hochgedacht Seiner Ld eß commoder
und erträglicher fallen wird, sothane gelder durch ihren eigenen mann
zu erlegen, als vorgeschlagener massen uber machen zu lassen, alß werdet ihr verhoffendlich damit auch also einig seyn, undt könnet ihr im-
mittelß die sachen, so unserm Capellmeister zu uberschicken, demieni-
gen der euch die gelder außzahlet, nur einliefern, und bey demselben
die anstalt machen, solche sachen so lang an sich zu behalten, biß vnserß
herrn und Gemahls Ld verordnete ihme die gelder einliefern, und die
sachen en contr'eschange wieder von ihm abnehmen.
Der recommendirte Capellmeister ist [illegible word] hochgnd Seiner
Ld und unß nicht unanstendig, dafern er also fortfahret seind wir seines
Verhaltnuß halber mit demselben in gnaden zu frieden, vnd [fol. 6v]
zweiffeln nicht, unsere Music werde mittelß guten fleißeß und auffsicht
zu einem gutem stande endlich gebracht werden. Den Vorgeschlagenen
Theorbisten wollet ihr nur herüber schicken, Vorhero aber nach eurem

gutbefinden seineß unterhaltß halber mit ihme handeln, und uns davon ehests berichten. Wen derselbe die mahlerkunst beÿ seinem dienste treiben wil, soll ihm solcheß auch ungewehret seÿn.

Woltenß euch in Gnädiger andwort unverhalten dann wird ieder Zeit zu allen gn. geneigt seÿn.

Datum Wolffenb am 10 Novembr.

1655.

[fol. 7v]

Sermae Andwort an den Churf. Sachs. Capellmeister Heinrich Schutzen.

d. 10 9br

1655

J:H:H:

27: Translation

Sophie Elisabeth to Schütz.
Wolfenbüttel, 10 November 1655

[NSAW 1 Alt 25 nr. 294, fols. 6–7]

[fol. 6r]
Sophia Elisabeth
Our gracious greeting first and foremost etc.

We have learned from your last letter dated the 30th October, along with other [information], what you have addressed to us regarding the continuation of your appointment and regarding what you unpresumingly suggest about the remittance of your salary, and presented together with the matter of the Kapellmeister and the theorbo player.

In gracious response thereto, we give you to understand that, as far as your appointment is concerned, our lord and husband, His Dilection, is graciously resolved to continue the same and to remit the salary duly in your behalf. Since, however, it will be more convenient and tolerable to His aforementioned Dilection to remit such money through his own man than in the way you suggested, we hope that you will be in accordance with this [method of payment], and you can simply give the compositions to the person who delivers the money to you, and make arrangements with him to retain these compositions until such time as our lord and husband, His Dilection, orders him to hand over the money, and take the compositions from him again in a mutual exchange so that they can be handed over to our Kapellmeister.

The Kapellmeister whom you recommended [illegible word] is not unsuitable to His most gracious Dilection and us. If he continues in the same way [as he has started his service], we are graciously satisfied with his conduct and [fol. 6v] do not doubt that our ensemble shall ultimately be brought into good order through good diligence and supervision. You shall simply send here the theorbo player whom you have suggested, but beforehand negotiate with him his salary as you see fit and advise us thereof as soon as possible. Should he wish to pursue painting in his position, it also shall not be denied him.

We wish you to show no restraint in your gracious answer, then remaining faithfully yours in grace as always.

Dated Wolfenbüttel 10 November
                                   1655

[fol. 7v]

Most serene answer to the royal Saxon Kapellmeister Heinrich Schütz
10 November
1655
J:H:H:

28

Schütz to Sophie Elisabeth.
Dresden, 27 November 1655

[NSAW 1 Alt 25 no. 294, fols. 2–3]

[fol. 2r]
Durchlauchtige Hochgeborne Fürstinn
Gnädige Fraw,
Ewer Fürstl. Gnaden letzeres undt sub dato den 20 dieses Monats an
mich abgelassenes gnädge schreiben, habe ich heute 8 tage mit der
damahligen post wol entpfangen, vnd daraus gerne vernommen das
mein gethaner fürschlag, wegen das Falsetisten [*undt* crossed out] oder
mahlers in gnaden fur guth erkennet, undt beliebet worden ist, worauff
dann E. Furstl. Gn. Ich ferner nicht verhalten soll, wie Ich numehr
solche sache mit ihme in eine gewisheit versaget vnd dero gestalt abge-
handelt habe, das Er mir mit gegebenen handschlag zugesagt hatt, wo
nicht noch vor Weynachten, Doch zum lengsten auff den künfttges
newe Jahr In leibzigk befürstehenden markt, mit denen von dort
[strikeout] nacher Braunschweig zurücke reisenden kaufleuten sich mit
auf den Weg zu begeben, vndt an der hochfurstl. hoffstadt
Wolffenbüttell sich gehorsambst einzustellen.
Wegen seines tractaments, So habe ich ihm untersaget, das Mann
verhoffe, Er mit der jenigen Verpflegung welche ander wiederführe
auch sich vergnügen lassen würde, darwieder er nichts eingewendet als
nur dieses, das sein bitte were das alles Ihm nur In gelde angeschlagen
werden möchte Sintemahl er gerne im ubrigen nach seiner gelegenheit
sich kleiden v. sein leben anstellen wolte,   Wie hoch nun, ausser
des Capellmeisters, Eines andern besoldung bey ihnen anlauffen mochte ist mir vnwissend, vnd vermeine ich (:doch Sonder masgebung:) das
von anderthalb hundert thlrn, oder wochentlich 3 thlr bis auffs höchste
200 thlr mit ihme zu handeln vndt entlich zu schliessen sein werde
[flourish.] Vndt werden Sie verhoffentlich an Ihm, eine Ihrem hoch-

furstl. hoffe, gewislich wol anständige person zu verspüren haben, Als
welche bey allen furgehenden ferneren solenniteten, wol mit zugebrauchen sein wirdt, gibt einen zimlichen Poeten, und hatt darinnen
sonderliche guete inventionen, welche er selbst aufsetzet vndt hernacher in sein Tiorba absinget, welches sich dann bey Einer Furstl.
Taffell gar wol schicket, vndt zwischen der anderen Music, eine guete
abwechselung gibt [flourish] Derogestalt der ich auch nochmahls der
gewissen zuversicht binn, das mit annehmung und alimentirung dieser
person, auch nicht geirret sein solle [flourish] Gott verleyhe gluk dazu
[flourish]

Betreffende sonst den andern punct, wegen Zahlung der mir gndgst
bewilligten haus bestallung, ist Es niehmahls meine intention gewesen
Ihrer durchl. meinen auch gndsten herrn furzuschreiben, das Eben mit
dem Steffan Daniel, dieselbige erfolgen mochte, Sondern So ist es nur
mein vnvergreifflicher vorschlag darumb gewesen, aldieweill dieienige
person, welcher von Ihrer durchl. solche Zahlung aufgetragen gewesen
ist, sich niemahls, auch diese stunde noch, sich bey mir nicht angemeldet
hatt, mir auch von niemand geschrieben worden ist, bei weme Ich mich
wegen des entpfanges anzumelden, vndt meine sachen umb beforderung nacher wolffenbüttell zu recommendiren hette, welches wann
[fol. 2v] ichs nur noch erfahre [*werde* crossed out], meiner vnterthngstn
schuldikeit nach, Ich mich gehorsamblich vndt vergnüglich, dieses
puncts halben contentirt halten werde.   Sonst habe Ich auch des
von mir Recommendirten Capellmeisters bishero continuirter wolver-
halten erfreuentlich vernommenn, undt bleibe Ich ferner begierig zu
vernemen, das diese sache meiner gehabten gueten intention nach, zu
formirung einer (:zwar nicht allzuweitlauftigen:) doch kleinen vndt
zimlich volkommenen Capell undt Music entlich ausschlagen, [*möge*
crossed out] vndt Ihre furstl. hoffstadt, nechst dem lobe Gottes, dessen
auch Ehre in der Welt haben möge, Massen Ich dann von der (:will
hoffen nicht vergeblichen:) Einbildung binn, das gedachtes Ihr collegium Music sich albereit zu einem gueten Vorzugk fur andern Musiken,
an andern furstl. höffen anlasse, worvon Ich zwar an meinem orte [*nicht*
crossed out] mir kein sonderliches lob zuzuschreiben, als der ausser
meinen Raht Ich sonst bishero wenig dazu contribuiret, undt den
Capellmeister mit seinen eigenen erfindungen v. Compositionen habe
wollen handeln undt dieselbigen praesentiren lassen, Im übrigen aber
so erbotig als schuldig binn, nicht allein mit allem mir möglichen gueten
Raht, Sondern auch mit aller meiner v. anderer bey handen habenden
Musicalischen arbeit successive an die hand zugehen, vnd einzuschicken, wann nur vorher Ihre musick in etwas auf einen gewissen fuss

[strikeout] gestellet sein, v. ich wissen werde, wie ich gedachte meine sachen einzurichten haben werde,
    Befehle herauff E. F. Gn. dem starken schutz Gottes des allerhöchsten, Seine gottliche Maytt. anruffende, das deroselbigen, nebenst Ihren hochgeehrtesten herrn herrn Gemahl, Sie einen gueten ausgang des numehr abgelauffenen alten, vndt glükseeligen anfang und fortges des bevorstehenden lieben neuen jahrs, Ihnen in gnaden verleyen, vndt bey allem selbst gewunschten furstl. wolergehen Sie ferner noch viel lange jahr erhalten vndt festen [*möge* crossed out] wolle. Amen.
                        E. Furstl. Gnade
                        trew unterthnger alter
                        diener
                        Henrich Schütz Mpp
                        Dresden am
                        27 9brir
                        Ao etc. 1655.
[fol. 3r]
Ich habe E. F. Gn. unterthng umb verzeyhung meiner grobheit zu bitten, in dem ich nemblich dieselbige, in entstehung anderer gelegenheit vor dismahl mit der inlage an Ihren Capellmeister behelligen mus [flourish]
    Mit dem Tiorbisten v. Mahler, werde E. F. Gn. Ich anderweit mit einem meinem vnterthgen Schreiben [*auf* crossed out] wieder aufwarten, vndt wann Etwas vorher in dieser [strikeout] gegend zu verrichten noch forfallen möchte, binn deroselbigen gnädige ordinantz Ich vorher noch zuvernemen gewertig.
[fol. 3v]
Der Durchlauchtigen Hochgebornen Fürstinn und Frawen, Frawen Sophia Elisabeth Hertzoginn zu Braunschweig und Lüneburgk, Geborner Hertzoginn zu Mecklenburgk, Fürstinn zu Wenden, Schwerin, und Ratgeburgk, auch Gräffinn zu Schwerin, der Lande Rostock und Stargardt Frawen [flourish] Meiner gnädigen Fürstinn vndt Frawen [flourish].
[Sophie Elisabeth's hand]
Dem Falsisten, soll die 200 Rtlr einß fur all [strikeout] zur besoldung gewilliget werd. Nach d halb iärig geld die ihm versproch, erbiet sich S. Ld. mein H. H., dß für ihm gewiß werd soll, in leibzig. Wurde ihm also gleiche viel sein [strikeout] wen es ihm uber machte, wan es nur gewiß geliefert wurde.
[In third hand]
Heinrich Schütz den 27 9br 1655

28: Translation

Schütz to Sophie Elisabeth.
Dresden, 27 November 1655

[NSAW 1 Alt 25 no. 294, fols. 2–3]

[fol. 2r]

Serene Noble Princess

Gracious Lady,

Today I received safely with the eight-day-old mail Your Royal Highness's last gracious writing, sent to me on the twentieth of this month, and I was happy to learn that the suggestion I made regarding the falsettist or artist was graciously well received and is to your liking, whereupon I shall then not detain Your Royal Highness any longer as I have now discussed such matters with him definitely and have negotiated your position. He has given his word that, if not before Christmas then at the latest by the next approaching New Years fair in Leipzig, he shall set out with those merchants who are traveling from there back to Brunswick and present himself faithfully in the royal residence of Wolfenbüttel.

Regarding his pay, I have explained to him that one would hope he would be satisfied with such support as [any] other might receive. He has nothing against it but this: he requests that all shall be remitted only in cash since he prefers after all to clothe himself at his convenience and to manage his own life. As it is, I do not know how high you wish a salary other than that of the Kapellmeister to run, and I believe (indeed in my humble opinion) that from 150 talers, or three talers weekly, up to 200 talers at the most, will be negotiable and finally agreeable to him. And it is to be hoped that you shall recruit for your royal court this truly respectable person, as he may be put to good use, for example, at all ensuing solemnities, [for he] is a reasonably good poet who is capable of especially good inventions which he composes himself and afterwards sings to his theorbo which is then very well suited to a royal table and provides a good variety to other compositions. Thus I am once again quite confident that the employment and support of this person would not be an error. May God grant his blessing on it.

Otherwise, concerning the other point regarding payment of the salary agreement graciously granted to me, it was never my intention to dictate to Your Highness, nor to my most gracious lord that this same [payment] might be made through Stephan Daniel. However, it was only my suggestion, subject to correction, because that person who commissioned such payment from Your Highness has not up to the present hour ever reported to me nor has anyone written to me regarding to whom I report the receipt [of the money] and who is responsible for the conveyance of my compositions to Wolfenbüttel. When [fol. 2v] I am but informed [of your wishes], according to my humblest duty, I shall humbly and contentedly remain reasonably satisfied on this point.

Otherwise I am delighted to have learned of the prevailing good conduct of the Kapellmeister whom I recommended, and I remain eager to learn further that this matter of my good intention to assemble a small (indeed not too extensive) and reasonably complete *Kapelle* and ensemble has finally succeeded, and may your royal capital, second [only] to the praise of God, have glory in the world, because (I hope not in vain) I believe that your aforementioned collegium musicum already appears to surpass other ensembles at other royal courts, whereof I in my position indeed ascribe no particular praise to myself. Except for my advice, I otherwise contributed little to it up until now and [I] wished to have the Kapellmeister progress with his own inventions and compositions and to have these presented. In other respects, however, I am as willing as indebted not only to provide all of the good advice that I can, but also all of my and other available musical work successively and to present it, provided that beforehand your ensemble can stand on its own two feet and I understand how I am to have my aforementioned compositions delivered.

I wish Your Royal Grace the powerful protection of Almighty God, imploring His Divine Majesty graciously to grant you along with your highly respected husband a good departure from the present waning year and a very happy beginning and continuation of the approaching beloved New Year, and to preserve and fortify you in all of your wishes for royal prosperity for many long years yet to come.

> Your Royal Grace's
> loyal humble old servant
> Heinrich Schütz
> In his own hand
> Dresden

27 November 1655

[fol. 3r]

I humbly request Your Royal Highness to forgive my insolence, this being, namely, now that the opportunity has arisen, that I must trouble you about the money paid to your Kapellmeister [Schütz].

Regarding the theorbo player and artist, I will again attend Your Royal Grace with one of my humble writings at another time, and as it may still be possible to accomplish something in this area as before, I am still prepared as before to heed your gracious command.

[fol. 3v]

To the serene noble Princess and Lady, Lady Sophie Elisabeth, Duchess of Brunswick and Lüneburg, noble Duchess of Mecklenburg, Radeburg, also Countess of Schwerin, the region of Rostock and Stargardfrauen. My gracious Princess and Lady.

[Sophie Elisabeth's hand]

The 200 Reichstalers shall be granted to the falsettist as salary once and for all. Regarding the semiannual money promised him [Schütz], His Dilection, my lord, affirms that it will certainly be delivered to him in Leipzig. He is indifferent regarding who shall remit it to him, if it shall only be delivered definitely.

[In a third hand]

Heinrich Schütz

27 November 1655

29

Sophie Elisabeth to Schütz.
Wolfenbüttel, 2 January 1656

[NSAW 1 Alt 25 no. 294, fol. 12]

[fol. 12r. Sophie Elisabeth's hand]
Sophia Elisabeth.
Vnsere gunst und gnädigen willen zuvor Ehrbar wolgelahrter lieber besonder.
Wir haben ab eurem eingelieferten schreiben mit mehren ersehen, was an unß ihr wegen des bewusten Falsetisten uberkunfft und tractement unter andern gelangen lassen, auch wegen außzahlung dero euch ver-willigten Haußbestallung zugleich mit anfuhren wollen, und geben euch daruff in gnädiger andwort hin wieder zu vernehmen, daß so viel den Falsetisten betrifft, ihme zu seiner besoldung und unterhalt iährlich 200 thlr einß fur alles vermachet und ausgezahlet werden sollen.

Wegen eurem halb iährigen besoldung aber haben unserß freundlich geliebten Herrn und Gemahls Ld sich dahin erkläret, daß sie euch die-selbe in Leipzig unfeilbahr auszahlen zu lassen behufige anstalt machen wollen [flourish] Dannenhero wir dafur halten, daß euch eben wenig daran gelegen seÿn werden, durch wen endlich sothane gelder ubermachet und geliefert werden, wan nur die außzahlung richtig erfolget, deren gewisheit ihr euch dan wol versichert halten könnet, und wir verbleiben euch mit gunst und gn. w. stets beÿgethan.
Geben Wolffenb. am 2 Jan. Ao 1656.
An den Churfurstl. Sachsischen Capellmeister Heinrich Schützen
[fol. 12v]
Sermae Andwort an den Churfurstl. Sachsischen Capellmeister zu dreßden
d. 2 Jan. 1656
F.G.

29: Translation

Sophie Elisabeth to Schütz.
Wolfenbüttel, 2 January 1656

[NSAW 1 Alt 25 no. 294, fol. 12]

[fol. 12r. Sophie Elisabeth's hand]
Sophia Elisabeth
Our favor and gracious will first and foremost to our learned, beloved and special [servant].

We have learned from your delivered letter, among with much [other information], what you have addressed to us regarding the housing and pay among other [details] of the falsettist in question, and presented together with [the matter of] the payment of your retainer granted to you, and in return we inform you in gracious response thereto, as far as the falsettist is concerned, he shall be granted and paid yearly 200 talers for his salary and maintenance once and for all.

As for your semiannual salary, our benevolent lord and husband has declared that he will take proper measures to have it paid to you without fail in Leipzig. We are of the opinion that it will make little difference to you through whom such money will be finally remitted and delivered, if only the payment takes place correctly. And of this you can be well assured, and we remain faithfully yours in favor and grace as always.

Given Wolfenbüttel 2 January 1656.
To the electoral Saxon Kapellmeister Heinrich Schütz
[fol. 12v]
Most serene answer to the electoral Saxon Kapellmeister in Dresden
2 January 1656
F.G.

30

Schütz's Autograph Receipt.
Dresden, Michaelmas 1656

[NSAW 1 Alt 25 no. 294, fol. 14]

[fol. 14r]
Das an denen, von Ihrer Fürstl. durchl. Herrn Herrn Hertzogen
Augusto, Hertzogen zu Braunschweig und Lüneburgk, Meinem
gnädigsten Herrn [flourish] mir endesbemelten, verordneten,
hausbestallungs geldern, die unterm dato betagten 75 Thlr Ich bahr
bezahlt bekommen, vndt in entphang genommen habe, Bekenne ich
mit dieser meiner eigenen handt undt Quittung. Datum Dresden bey
werenden leibziger Michaëlis Mark Ao etc. 1656.
> [Seal]   Henrich Schütz
> Churfl. S.
> Capellmeister Mpp

[fol. 14v. Not in Schütz's hand]
Herr Heinrichen Schützen Churfurstl. Capellmeisters besoldungs quitung von Haus auß   auf
————75 T.
geben Im Michaelis Markte zu Leiptzig Ao etc.1656
uon hoëf allererst am 13 (17?) Julÿ etc. Ao etc. 1657

30: Translation

Schütz's Autograph Receipt.
Dresden, Michaelmas 1656

[NSAW 1 Alt 25 no. 294, fol. 14]

[fol. 14r]
The court appointment money, 75 talers due on this date, decreed by Your Serene Highness, my lord, the Duke August, Duke of Brunswick and Lüneburg, my most gracious lord, I have received in cash and accepted. This I undersign and acknowledge with my own hand and receipt. Dated Dresden during the Leipzig Michaelmas Fair 1656.

> [Seal]   Heinrich Schütz
> Electoral Saxon Kapellmeister
> In his own hand

[fol. 14v. Not in Schütz's hand]
Electoral Kapellmeister Herr Heinrich Schütz's receipt of wages for 75 talers given at the Michaelmas Fair in Leipzig 1656 from court first and foremost on 13 (17?) July 1657.

3

31

Schütz's Autograph Receipt.
Michaelmas 1658.

Statement of Schütz's Wages.
Wolfenbüttel, 1 May 1660

[NSAW 4 Alt 19 vorl. no. 5096, fols. 2–3]

[fol. 2r. Schütz's hand]
Das Ihrer hochfürstl. Durchl. und Herrens, Herrens Augustus
Hertzogens zu Braunschweig und Lüneburgk etc. Meines gndgstn
fürsten undt herrens ergangenen anordnung gemes, der vnterm dato,
betagte Termin derer mir gndgst bewilligten gnadengelder, nemblich
fünff und Siebenzigk Thlr, von herrn Henrich Günthern, Wolbe-
nambten handels man zu Wolffenbüttel, mir endesbemelten, wol erleget
und bahr zahlet worden sind, Bekenne ich mit dieser meiner Hand und
quittung. Actum am leibzieger Michaëlis Marckte darselbst Ao etc. 1658.

    [Seal]   Henrich Schütz
                 Churfl. S. Eltister Capellmeister Mpp

[fol. 2v. In another hand]
Fernere Chürfl. Cammer Abrechnung,
Mit dem OberCapellmeistern zu Dresden, H. Heinrichen Schützen, we-
gen seiner Bestallung von Haus aus [flourish]
Laut Letztgezogener Abrechnung, sub dato d 18t. Decembris, a. etc.
1657. seint Ihm auff Mich. selbigen Jahres, im Rest Verbleiben—75
Thlr

darzu

Gebühren Ihm weiters, Vermöge der Chrl: Bestallung:
Auff Ostern a. etc. 1658   75 Thlr
—Michaëlis, ejusdem anni   75 Thlr

—Ostern ⎫ a. etc. 1659	75 Thlr
—Michaëlis ⎭	75 Thlr
—Ostern a. etc. 1660	75 Thlr
Sa: Bis Jetztgel: Ostern:	450 Thlr

Daruff seint gezahlt

a. etc. 1658.

1. Auff der Neuen Jahrs Messen, in Leipzig, den Rest der Vorigen Abrechnung, als:	75 Thlr

a. etc. 658.

2. Im Oster Er zu Leipzig, p. Wechsel bis Ostern a. etc. 1658.	75 Thlr

1658

3. Auff der Michaëlsmesse, abere ins Mich. 1658 Betaget	75 Thlr
Sa: dieser Gezahlten Posten	225 Thlr

Abgezogen,

Wolten bis Ostern a. etc. 1660. im Rest Verbleiben:	225 Thlr

Wolfenb. 1t. Mayji, a. etc. 1660
Jobst Barthold Kranckenfeldt
[fol. 3. In another hand]

OberCapellmeister Schütze zu Dresden Quitiret über HalbJährige Besoldung	75 Thlr

Betagt und Zahlt auff Michaëlis a. etc. 1658.

/17

31: Translation

Schütz's Autograph Receipt.
Michaelmas 1658.
Statement of Schütz's Wages.
Wolfenbüttel, 1 May 1660

[NSAW 4 Alt 19 vorl. no. 5096, fols. 2–3]

[fol. 2r. Schütz's hand]
The appointment money alloted me, namely 75 talers due on this date, decreed according to the command of my most gracious prince and lord, Your Most Serene Highness and lord, my Lord August, the duke of Brunswick and Lüneburg, has been fully paid in cash by Herr Heinrich Günther, respected merchant of Wolfenbüttel. This I undersign and acknowledge with my own hand and receipt. Concluded during the Leipzig Michaelmas Fair 1658.

[Seal]　Heinrich Schütz
Electoral Saxon Oldest Kapellmeister
In his own hand

[fol. 2v. In another hand]
Further settlement of the royal account with senior Kapellmeister of Dresden, Herr Heinrich Schütz, in connection with his appointment *in absentia.*

As per the previous statement carried over on 18 December 1657, he is due on Michaelmas of the same year	75 talers
Moreover, according to the electoral appointment, he is further due	
On Easter 1658	75 talers
—Michaelmas of the same year	75 talers
—Easter ⎱ 1659	75 talers
—Michaelmas ⎰	75 talers
—Easter 1660	75 talers

Total up to Easter of this year   450 talers
On that is paid:

1658

1. At the New Years Fair in Leipzig, the balance of the
previous statement of   75 talers

1658

2. At Easter in Leipzig by promissory note until Easter
1658   75 talers

1658

3. At the Michaelmas Fair on Michaelmas however
[he is] due   75 talers

Total of these sums paid   225 talers
Deducted from this, the balance until Easter shall remain: 225 talers
Wolfenbüttel, 1 May 1660
Jobst Barthold Kranckenfeldt
[fol. 3. In another hand]
Senior Kapellmeister Schütz of Dresden. Receipt for half-year salary of
75 talers. Due and paid on Michaelmas 1658.

/17.

32

Johann Jacob Löwe von Eisenach to Schütz.
Wolfenbüttel, 5 May 1660

[NSAW 1 Alt 25 no. 294, fols. 19–20]

[fol. 19r]

Edler Vester Insonders Hochgeehrter Herr Vatter.
Demselben mein Vornehmen durch dieses Schreiben zu eröffnen hab
ich nicht vnterlaßen können, was gestalt ich in willens beÿ meinen Gndl:
fürstl: und Herrn auff ein Viertl Jahrlang nacher Wien zu den meinigen
zu reißen, umb gnädige erlaubnüs anzuhalten, auß ursach, weil Ich noch
viel wegen meines vätterlichen Erbtheils, vnd seiter meines abwesens
eingebrachten und noch außstehenden schulden mit Ihnen nothwendig
zu unterreden, wolle auch gerne meine frau Mutter und brudern dahin
vermögen, daß sie sich doch einmahl auß den Papstumb, und nacher
Dreßden, da wier ein hoches zu fordern, oder an ein andern guten
Evangelischen Orth begeben mögten: Wegen erhöblichen Ursachen
halber trag ich keinen Zweiffel, solches beÿ meinen Gndl: fürstl: und
Herrn zu erhalten, Insonderheit durch vorbitt des Herrn Vatters.
Negstem, weile Ihr fürstl. durchl. als ein Hachgelährter Herr so viel
auff die Bibliothec auch andern künsten wendet, so hab ich in willens,
so fern ich werde Gnädige erlaubnüs erlangen können, Meines H: Vattern Seel: Ersten frauen, der hachgelährten Elisabeta Johanna Wertonia
ManuScripta von Episteln und Carmen so sie in lateinischer vnd gri-
gischer Sprach (:am Keyser Rudolph, vnd andern Vornehmen Poten-
taten/auch hochgelahrten leuthen welche zu Ihrer Zeit gelebt:) geschrieben, inngleichen die ManuScripta vornehmer hachgelährten
leuthen Epistulen vnd Carmen so solche an sie haben lassen abgehen
mit Zu bringen, vnd in Ihr fürstl: durchl: Bibliotheck vnterthänigst zu
verehren: Es soll auch ein künstliches gemählt (:welches ein Original
von den hochberühmten künstliches Mahler Michael Raphuel ist,
welches mir in der Erbschafft heimgefallen, auff 200 Rthl. geschetzt,

Ihr fürstl: durchl: zu sehen mit anhero gebracht werden, vnd so fern es Ihr fürstl: durchl: alsdenn gnädigst mögte gefallen, wie es mir in der Erbschafft geschätzet, zu überlassen.

Schlüßlichen will Ich auff meine vnkosten von den besten musicalischen Sachen, So zu Wien von künstlichen berühmten Meistern auffgesetzt, abschreiben lassen, zum gebrauch unserer Capella. [fol. 19v] Zu dießem behuff bitte ich dem H: Vatter dienstfrl: d. Er mir möge behülfflichen seÿn, vnd beÿ Ihr fürstl: durchl: ein unterthänigste vorbitt einlegen, damit ich mein anderthalbjarige besoldung mögte fölig bekommen, welche vmb Jianni betaget, auff d. Ich alhie meine Stetsmannenden Creditores in etwas [strikeout] kunde befriedigen und mir auch gelt zur reiß in händen bliebe [strikeout]. Wormit dem H: Vatter in Schutz des allerhöchsten empfhelend, verbleibend deselben.

ieder Zeit dienstwill: und gehorsamer Sohn

Johann Jacob Löw von Eisenach Cpm.

Wolffenbüttl den 5. Maÿ 1660./.

[fol. 20r]

Dem Edlen Vesten vnd großachtbahren Kunst vnd Sinnreichen Herrn Heinrich Schützen, Churfürstl: Sachsischen wol verordneten Capel Meister. Meinen insonders HochgeEhrten Herrn Vattern.

32: Translation

Johann Jacob Löwe von Eisenach to Schütz.
Wolfenbüttel, 5 May 1660

[NSAW. 1 Alt 25 no. 294, fols. 19–20.]

[fol. 19r]
Noble, Worthy, Most Highly Esteemed Father,
   I could not refrain from making known to you through this writing my intention to request gracious permission from my most gracious prince and lord to travel to my family in Vienna for a quarter of a year for the reason that I still must discuss much with them regarding my patrimonial inheritance and debts, which are still outstanding and called in since my absence. I also wish very much to be able to move my mother and brother, for they wish one day to leave the papacy and to go Dresden where we have something waiting for us. Due to the importance of these matters, I do not doubt that I shall obtain such [permission] from my gracious prince and lord, especially through intercession of my father [Schütz].
   Next, because His Serene Highness as a learned man invests so much in the library and other arts, I therefore intend, if I am able to obtain gracious permission, to bring along for His Royal Highness's library and present most humbly the manuscripts of epistles and odes of my father's beloved first wife, the learned Elisabeth Johanna Wertonia, since she wrote in Latin and Greek (to the Emperor Rudolf [II] and other noble potentates and learned people who lived during her lifetime), similarly to let him have the manuscripts of epistles and odes which noble learned people sent to her. There is also an artistic painting (which is an original by the most famous gifted painter Michael Raphael) which was bequeathed to me in my inheritance, assessed at 200 Reichstalers, which His Serene Highness shall see when it is brought along here, and [I shall] relinquish it to His Serene Highness if it graciously pleases him [for the amount at which] it was assessed to me in my inheritance.

Finally I intend at my own expense to have copied in Vienna the best musical compositions by gifted famous masters for use in our ensemble. [fol. 19v] For this purpose I ask my father humbly if he might help me and present a most humble request to His Serene Highness that I shall receive my salary of one and one-half years in full which was due in January, from which I [could] somewhat satisfy my ever pressing creditors here and still leave money in my pocket for the trip. With which I commend my father to the protection of the Almighty, remaining

Your ever-faithful and dutiful son
Johann Jacob Löwe von Eisenach
Kapellmeister

Wolfenbüttel, 5 May 1660.
[fol. 20r]
To the noble, worthy, and highly respected gifted and brilliant Herr Heinrich Schütz, highly appointed electoral Saxon Kapellmeister. My most highly esteemed father.

33

Statement of Schütz's Wages. Wolfenbüttel, 5 June 1660

[NSAW 1 Alt 25 no. 294, fols. 16–17]

[fol. 16r]

Frl: Cammer Abrechnung mit dem Ober Capellmeistern H. Heinrich Schutzen zu dresden, wegen seiner Bestallung von Hauß auß [flourish] Laut Illmi [flourish] Bestallung, sub dato Ostern a. etc. 1655. gebühren demselben Jahrlichs pro salario—150 Thlr in zweÿen Terminen, halb außl. Michaelis und halb außl. Ostern zuerlegen, wolle thun Außl.

Michaelis a. etc. 1655. zum 1. Termin	75	
Ostern a. etc. 1656.	75	
Michaelis a. 1656.	75	Thllr
Ostern a. etc. 1657.	75	
Michaelis a. etc. 1657.	75	
Summa von 2 1/2 Jahren		375 Thllr

Daruß seint gezahlt

1.	d. 5t. 8bris. a. etc. 1655. per Wechsell am Christian König in Leipzig Wechsell Scheins	75	
2.	d. 1t. Maÿ a. etc. 1656 aber eins an denselben	75	
3.	Im Michaelis Margkt zu Leipzig a. etc. 1656. Laut H. Schutzens eigener Quittung	75	Thllr
4.	Im Leipziger Oster Markt a. etc. 1657 besage H. Schutzens eigener Quittung	75	

[5. *d. 1t. 7bris a. etc. 1657 per Wechsell an Heinrich Gunthern im Vollmacht Steffan Daniels zu Braunschweig 150* crossed out]

Summa [*450* crossed out]　　　　　　　　　　　　　300 Thlr

Damit also bis Michaelis a. etc. 1657. [strikeout]
Im Rest   75 Thlr
Bezogen Wollffenbuttel d. 18t. xbris. 1657.
                    Jobst Barthold Krankenfeldt
                    Vertatur
[fol. 16v]
Am 5t. Junÿ, a. etc. 1660. ist auff Sermi [flourish] gnädigsten Befehl diese Abrechnung continuiret, und seint dem Ober Capellmeister Schütz uff den Leipziger Messen weiters gezahlt, wie folget:

Im Januario, a. etc. 1658	75 Thlr
Ostern selbig Jahrs	75 Thlr
Michaëlis abereins	75 Thlr
Sa: dieses:	225 Thlr
Und Restiren Ihm uff Ostern a. etc. 1660. noch	225 Thlr

[fol. 17v]
Besoldungs Abrechnung mit dem Ober Capellmeistern H. Heinrich Schutzen in Dresden
d. 18t. Xbris a. etc. 1657

33: Translation

Statement of Schütz's Wages.
Wolfenbüttel, 5 June 1660.

[NSAW 1 Alt 25 no. 294, fols. 16–17]

[fol. 16r]

Settlement of the royal account with Senior Kapellmeister Herr Heinrich Schütz of Dresden in connection with his appointment *in absentia*. As per royal appointment, on Easter 1655 he is due 150 talers yearly as salary in two installments, half payable on Michaelmas and half payable on Easter, payable

Michaelmas 1655 for the first installment	75	
Easter 1656	75	
Michaelmas 1656	75	} talers
Easter 1657	75	
Michaelmas 1657	75	
Total for 2 1/2 years	375	talers

On that is paid

1. 5 October 1655 by promissory note by Christian König in Leipzig	75	
2. 1 May 1656 to him again	75	
3. At the Michaelmas Fair in Leipzig 1656 as per Herr Schütz's own receipt	75	} talers
4. At the Leipzig Easter Fair 1657 as per Herr Schütz's own receipt	75	
Total	300	talers
Thus the balance up to Michaelmas 1657 is	75	talers

Carried over Wolfenbüttel 18 December 1657

                 Jobst Barthold Krankenfeldt

                 See over

[fol. 16v]

On 5 June 1660 upon Your Serene Highness's most gracious command is this settlement of accounts continued and Senior Kapellmeister Schütz is further paid at the Leipzig fair as follows:

In January 1658	75 talers
Easter of the same year	75 talers
Michaelmas once again	75 talers
Total of these:	225 talers
And balance due him on Easter 1660 in addition	225 talers

[fol. 17r]

Settlement of wages with Senior Kapellmeister Heinrich Schütz in Dresden

18 December 1657

34

Statement of Schütz's Wages. Wolfenbüttel, 6 June 1660

[NSAW 1 Alt 25 no. 294, fol. 21]

[fol. 21r]
Fernere Besoldungs Abrechnung
Fürstl: Brunsw: Lünebr: ZahlCammer, Mit dem OberCapellMeister von
Hauß Aus, Heinrich Schütz zu dresd. [flourish]
Vermöge gezogener Abrechnung sub dato d. 28t. Decembr: a. etc. 1657.
seint demselben uff Michaëlis selbig Jahrs im Rest
geblieben   75 Thlr
Darzu gebüren Ihm ferner:
Uff Ostern a. etc. 1658   75 Thlr
—Michaëlis 1658   75 Thlr
—Ostern a. etc. 1659   75 Thlr
—Michaëlis selbigen Jahrs   75 Thlr
—Ostern a. etc. 1660   75 Thlr
Sa: dieses   450 Thlr
Daruff
Hat Er emphangen:
Im Januario a. etc. 1658. so Ihm durch Wechsel übermachet   75 Thlr
Ostern a. etc. 1658. abereins in Leipzig: 75 Thlr
Michaëlis selbigen Jahrs wiederumb: 75 Thlr
Sa: dieser dreÿen Posten   225 Thlr
Wolte Er also uff Ostern a. etc. 1660. annoch zu
fordern Leben   225 Thlr
Signatum Wolffenbüttel, d. 5ten Junÿ a. etc. 1660
                    J B Kranckenfeldt

[fol. 21v]

Besoldungs Abrechnug,

Für den Ober Capellmeistern von Haus aus, Heinrich Schützen zu dresd. [strikeout] zum Rest stechend auff:

225 Thlr [*und* crossed out] So nebst Reysegeldern

50 Thlr

bezahlt d. 6ten Junÿ, a. etc. 1660.

34: Translation

Statement of Schütz's Wages.
Wolfenbüttel, 6 June 1660

[NSAW 1 Alt 25 no. 294, fol. 21]

[fol. 21r]
Further settlement of wages of the senior Kapellmeister *in absentia,*
Heinrich Schütz of Dresden, from the royal chamber of finances of
Brunswick and Lüneburg.
According to the balance carried over on 28 December 1657, the balance
due him on Michaelmas of the same year is   75 talers

In addition he is further due:

On Easter 1658	75 talers
—Michaelmas 1658	75 talers
—Easter 1659	75 talers
—Michaelmas of the same year	75 talers
—Easter 1660	75 talers
Total of these:	450 talers

He has received from this:
In January 1658 thus remitted to him
   through promissory note   75 talers
Easter once again in Leipzig   75 talers
Michaelmas of the same year again   75 talers
Total of these three amounts   225 talers
In addition he shall be paid at Easter 1660 for cost of living 225 talers
Signed Wolfenbüttel, 5 June 1660
                    J[obst] B[artold] Kranckenfeldt
[fol. 21v]
Settlement of wages. Balance paid to the senior Kapellmeister *in absentia,*
Heinrich Schütz of Dresden, of 225 talers together with 50 talers travel
costs, paid 6 June 1660.

35

Schütz to Duke August.
Dresden, 10 April 1661

[HAB Cod. Guelf 376 Nov., fols. 320–21]

[fol. 320r]
Durchlauchtigster Hochgeborner Fürst,
Gnädigster Herr,
E. furstl. durchl. seind meine unterthänigste dienste Ungespartes fleisses iederzeit bereit, Demnach von E. fürstl. durchl. annoch continuirender gueter gesundheit, und dero anderweit fürstl. wolErgehen, Ich ohnlängst erfreuliche nachrichtung erhalten, So habe ich mich uff heutigen zehenden monatstag Aprilis, als des von E. fürstl. durchl. abermals erreichten vnd erlebten fröhlichen Geburtstags, nicht alleine höchlich in unterthänigkeit erfreuet, Sondern bin auch aus schuldigster Devotion veranlasset worden, unter andern dero trewen dienern auch für meine wenige person, zwar abwesend, mit gegenwertiger meiner schrifftlicher Congratulation unterthngst zu erscheinen, von hertzen wünschende, vndt Gott anruffende, das seine göttliche almacht, E. furstl. durchl. (:als dessen weltberümbter Name, an fürstl. Weisheit, löblicher Verständiger Regierung, höchst Repectirlichen alter, als ein helles licht unter andern fürnemen Potentaten, durch Tewtschland, und gantz Europa hervor leuchtet:) ferner noch viel lange jahr zulegen, zum Schutz der Evangelischen Kirchen, und Ruhm Ihres hochfürstl. hauses, auch dessen wolfahrt und aufnemen, in gnaden bey beständiger gesundheit und allem furstl. wolstande erhalten wolle.

Nechst diesem berichte E. furstl. durchl. unterthngst, das auff Ihrer Churfl. durchl. zu Sachsen, meines gndgsten Herrens befehl, ümb verfertigung und auslassung in druck, beÿkommendes Buchs halben, In den neundten Monat, Ich mich bishero alhier zu Dresden habe aufhalten müssen, worvon gegenwertige zwey Examplar, nebenst so vielen Bassis Continuis für die Organisten, E. fürstl. durchl. zu zu schicken, und solche meine zwar geringe arbeit auch anschawen zu lassen, Ich von meiner mir obliegenden schuldigkeit erindert worden binn, unterthngst bittende, dieselben in gnaden anzunemen, und dero gndsten beliebung nach, das Eine Exemplar davon, dero herzgeliebtesten furstl. frawen Gemahlin (:Einer, also wie in allen andern furstl. thugenden, also insonderheit in der löblichen Profession der Musick, unvergleichlich perfectionirten Princessin:) wiederfahren zu lasse.

Ferner So habe Ich auch der gueten Zuversicht, das Euerer fürstl. durchl. Collegium Musicum, annoch, allermassen Ich es letztmals, in meiner anwesenheit wolbestalt gefunden, und hinterlassen, in gueten zustande anzutreffen sey, vndt Euerer fürstl. durchl. beÿ dero hoffstadt, mit dessen unterthänigster aufwartung werden gndgst zufrieden sein können, Ich binn gebührend erbötig, So bald Ich wiederümb von hiedanen nacher Weissenfels, Wie Ich ehistes hoffe, zu meinen daselbst, sonder Ruhm, allerhand die fürnembsten Authoren in Vorraht beysammen habenden musicalischen sachen, gelangen werde, demselbigen alle fernere [fol. 320v] schuldige handreichung zu thun, und das jenige, was etwa bishero verseumet sein möchte, bestes fleisses wiederumb Einzubringen,

Wormit E. furstl. durchl. nebenst dero hertzgeliebteste angehörige sambt und sonders, Ich dem starken schutz des allerhöchsten trewlichst entpfele, Mich und denselbigen fürstl. Collegium Musicum zu dero beharrlichen gnaden und gewogenheit, hinfuro ferner unterthngst Recommendire, und hiermit bestes Vermogens Verbleibe,

E. furstl. durchl.

> Verbundener unterthngster
> gehorsambster diener
> Henrich Schütz Mpp
> Dresden Am 10den
> Monatstag Aprilis.
> Ao etc. 1661

[fol. 321v. Not in Schütz's hand]
Dem Durchlauchtigsten Hochgebornen Fürsten und HErrn, HErrn Augusto Herzogen zu Braunschweig undt Lüneburgk, Meinem Gnedigsten HErrn

35: Translation

Schütz to Duke August.
Dresden, 10 April 1661

[HAB Cod. Guelf 376 Nov., fols. 320–21]

[fol. 320r]
Most Serene Noble Prince,
Most Gracious Lord,
I am prepared at all times with most humble, [and] unsparing diligence to serve Your Royal Highness.

Because today, the tenth of April, I received delightful news of Your Royal Highness's abiding good health and your enduring royal prosperity, I not only rejoice greatly in humility at Your Royal Highness's happy birthday, which is here once more and which you have lived to see, but I have also been induced out of most indebted devotion, together with others of your faithful servants as well, from my insignificant person, though absent, to offer concurrently my most humble written congratulations. Wishing from my heart and appealing to God that His divine power shall mercifully preserve Your Royal Highness (as one whose world-famous name shines forth throughout Germany and all of Europe as a bright light among other noble rulers in royal wisdom, laudable and wise rule, and most venerable age) in lasting good health and royal well-being for many more long years to come for the protection of the Protestant church, the fame of your noble house, and its welfare and prosperity.

In addition I humbly report to Your Royal Highness that by command of His Serene Highness of Saxony [Johann Georg II], my most gracious lord, I had to remain more than eight months until now in Dresden in order to complete and publish the enclosed little books, of which I send two copies and just as many continuo parts for the organists to Your Royal Highness and to have my meager work inspected. I have been reminded of my incumbent responsibilities, asking humbly to take these up by your leave, and, according to your most gracious favor, to bestow a copy on your most beloved wife (a princess incomparably perfect in all other royal virtues, but especially in the noble profession of music).

Furthermore I also have the good faith that your royal collegium musicum is still to be found in good condition as I found it in every way during my last duly appointed visit, and that following my departure Your Royal Highness in your residence will be graciously satisfied by that most humble service. I am dutifully prepared, as soon as I leave here for Weissenfels, which I hope will be as soon as possible, where in my supply of musical things, I have together, without boasting, all sorts of musical compositions of the most distinguished composers with which to lend to [the collegium musicum] all further [fol. 320v] dutiful assistance and to bring again my best diligence to that which may have been somewhat neglected up until now.

With which I faithfully commend Your Royal Highness and your most beloved household to the powerful protection of the Almighty and furthermore humbly recommend myself and the royal collegium musicum to your steadfast grace and goodwill, and herewith remain to the best of my ability,
Your Royal Highness's

> Indebted most humble
> faithful servant
> Heinrich Schütz
> In his own hand
> Dresden 10 April 1661

[fol. 321v. Not in Schütz's hand]
To the Most Serene Noble Prince and Lord, Lord Augustus, Duke of Brunswick and Lüneburg, My most gracious Lord.

36

Schütz's Autograph Receipt.
Teplitz, 21 May 1663

[NSAW 1 Alt 25 no. 294, fol. 22]

[fol. 22r]
Das auff des durchlauchtigsten Furstens vndt Herrens, Herrns Augustus Hertzogens zu Braunschweig undt Lüneburgk etc. gndgste anordnung, mir Endesbemelten, von Herrn Steffen Daniclln fürnemen Handelsman zu Braunschweig, unterm dato dreyhundert Thlr vergnüget und bezahlet worden sindt, wirdt nebenst unterthägster dancksagung hirmit bekennet, undt darüber gebürlich quittiret, Urkunde dieser meiner handt. Signatum Töplitz in den warmen Bädern daselbst, Am 21 Maÿ Ao. etc. 1663.
                              Henrich Schütz Mpp
[fol. 22v. Not in Schütz's hand]
Des Ober Capellmeisters von Hauß aus Heinrich Schützen Besoldungs Quitung uff 300 Thlr
den 21t. May. a. etc. 1663,

36: Translation

Schütz's Autograph Receipt.
Teplitz, 21 May 1663

[NSAW 1 Alt 25 no. 294, fol. 22]

[fol. 22r]
The 300 talers that on the most gracious command of the most illustrious prince and lord, Lord August, Duke of Brunswick and Lüneburg, paid on this date by Herr Stephan Daniel, distinguished merchant of Brunswick, are herewith acknowledged with humble thanks, and thereupon properly settled. Deed of this my hand. Signed Teplitz in the warm baths, 21 May 1663.

Heinrich Schütz
In his own hand

[fol. 22v. Not in Schütz's hand]
Receipt of wages of 300 talers of the senior Kapellmeister *in absentia* Heinrich Schütz. 21 May 1663.

37

Statement of Schütz's Wages.
3 October 1663

[NSAW 1 Alt 25 no. 294, fol. 24]

[fol. 24r]
Vermöge letzt gezogener Abrechnung beÿ Fürstl. Braunschw. lüneburgl. Zahl undt dem Ober Capellmeister von Hauß aus Heinrich Schützen zu dreßden sub dato den 5. Juny 1660, biß ostern 1660 Seindt demselben im Rest geplieben—225 Thlr die Ihm dan auch damahls beÿ deßen anwesen, nebst 50 Thlr Reise geldern zahlet worden
Ferner wolte Ihm gehoren

Von Ostern biß Michaelis 1660	75
Von Michaelis 1660. biß ostern 1661	75
Von Ostern biß Michael: 1661	75
Von Michael: 1661 biß ostern 1662	75
Von ostern biß Michael: 1662	75
Von Michael: [*biß* crossed out] 1662 biß ostern 1663	75
Sa: dieses	450

Darauff demselben zahlt

den 30. September 1660. beÿ gehultener Michael: merckt in Leipzig	75
den 15. April 1661. in der ostern Meße	75
Sa: des Endpfangs	150

Von obigen Abgetzogen, wolte demselben biß ostern 1663.

ein nachstand bleiben	300

Extrahiret, den 3t. April: 1663.
[fol. 24v]
Besoldungs Abrechnung Für dem Ober Capellmeister von Haus aus Heinrich Schützen zu dreßden biß Ostern 1663, deßen Rest bis dahin belaufft sich uff 300 thlr
den 3 Octobris Ao etc. 1663.

37: Translation

Statement of Schütz's Wages.
3 October 1663

[NSAW 1 Alt 25 no. 294, fol. 24]

[fol. 24r]
According to previous drawn settlement of accounts of the Royal Chamber of Finances of Brunswick and Lüneburg and Senior Kapellmeister *in absentia* Heinrich Schütz of Dresden, the amount outstanding from Easter 1660 until 5 June 1660 is 225 talers which at that time was paid when he was here together with 50 talers travel money.
Furthermore he is due

From Easter to Michaelmas 1660	75 talers
From Michaelmas 1660 until Easter 1661	75 talers
From Easter until Michaelmas 1661	75 talers
From Michaelmas 1661 until Easter 1662	75 talers
From Easter until Michaelmas 1662	75 talers
From Michaelmas 1662 until Easter 1663	75 talers
Sum of these	450 talers
Therefrom has been paid	
30 September 1660 at the Michaelmas fair held in Leipzig	75 talers
15 April 1661 at the Easter Fair	75 talers
Total amount received	150 talers
Apart from the above, an amount shall remain outstanding until Easter 1663	300 talers

Extracted, 3 April 1663
[fol. 24v]
Settlement of accounts for the salary of senior Kapellmeister *in absentia* Heinrich Schütz of Dresden through Easter 1663, the remainder of which amounts to 300 talers
3 October 1663

38

Schütz to Duke August.
Leipzig, 10 January 1664

[HAB 376 NOVI, fols. 322–23]

[fol. 322r]
Durchlauchtigster Fürst, Gnädigster Herr,
In erwegung derer von E. Hochfürstl. Durchl. mir bishero wieder-
fahrnen vielen undt hohen fürstlichen Wolthaten, hab Ich mich billich
zu schämen, das mit einschickung deren gndgst begehrten, meiner in
druk ausgelassenen Musicalischen wercke, Ich bis dato so lange ver-
zogen, und seumig gewesen binn, welches meines verseumnüs und
verzugs aber Ich Eine gndste verzeÿhung zu bitten, undt dahero zu
hoffen habe, Aldieweil zu solchen meinen in druck gegebenen sachen,
Ich ehe nicht, als fur 3 Wochen, nach erfolgter meiner Wiederkehr von
Dresden nacher Weissenfels, habe gelangen, undt solche Exemplarien
zusammen bringen können,
   Werden aber numehr solche meine Wercke, so viel deroselben vor
dismal Ich aufbringen können, durch Steffan Danieln (:Einen bekanten
Braunschweigischen Kauffmann, welchem ich bey itzigen Mark alhier,
die selbigen, nebenst einem dazu gelegten Catalogo, persönlich selbst
zugestellet:) hirbey E. furstl. durchl. Herrn Hoffambtschreiber verhoffentlich richtig gelieffert werden, und derselbige so denn ferner, E.
furstl. durchl. gndgsten ordinantz noch damit zugebehren wissen,
   Und habe E. furstl. durchl. Ich bevorab unterthngsten grösten danck
zu sagen, das solcher meiner geringen arbeit, Sie gndgst gesonnen, die
Ehre und hohe gnade zu erweisen, undt deroselben auff dero furstl.
undt durch gantz Europa höchstberümbten Bibliotheck, noch Ein
räumlein gndgst zu gönnen, dahero Ich dann auch anlass bekommen
zu wünschen, das meine noch übrige in meinen handen mit der feder
abcopirte, noch rückständige [strikeout] (:meiner meinung nach:)
besser als die vorige elaborirte arbeit, Ich auf solche masse, Itzo zugleich

auch hette mit Einschicken können, welches auch wol erfolget, undt ich mit herausgebung deroselbigen in offentlichen druck fortgefahren were, wenn es mir an den verlag herzu nicht ermangelt hette, und meinem zwar gehabten vorsag nach, E. furstl. durchl. mir bishero gndgst abgefolgte hausbestallung oder gnadengelder, Ich dazu hette gebrauchen können, welche ich aber, wegen anderweit meines sparsamen Einkommens disseits, mehrentheils zu meiner nottürftigen Verpflegung und Rettung bishero hehrnennen und gebrauchen (:wo nicht mich sonst unterweilen kümmerlich behelffen und hinbringen:) müssen [flourish] [fol. 322v] In welcher meiner vnterthngsten Erinderung denn, wegen derer von E. hochfl. durchl. bishero von mir erhaltenen, So vielen hohen undt furstl. wohlthaten, deroselbigen undt dero gantzen hochfurstl. hause, Ich umb so viel desto mehr mich verbunden erkenne, hirmit mich auch zu aller mir möglichen unterthngsten vergeltung, bevorab auch zu anderweit continuirlicher handreichung dero furstl. löblicher hoffmusick, gehorsambst anerbieten thue, im fall Ich nur ferner hirtzu qualificiret erachtet werden möchte [flourish]

Wormit Ich schliesse, E. hochfstl. durchl. dem Starken schutz Gottes des allerhöchsten, zu dem abermahl wieder eingetretenen lieben newen jahre, zu beständiger gesundheit, undt noch In viel lange jahr verlängerung und fristung dero lebens, auch alle andern hochfurstl. und selbst gewünschten wolErgehen am Seel und leibe trewlichst empfelende, vnd verbleibende

E. hochfurstl. durchl.
Vnterthngste gehorsambste
und pflichtschuldiger diener
Henrich Schütz Mpp
Datum leibzigk
den 10. Januarii
Ao etc. 1664

[fol. 323. Not Schütz's hand] Dem Durchlauchtigsten, Hochgebohrnen fürsten undt Herren, Herrn Augusto, Hertzogen zu Braunschweig, vndt Lüneburgk, Meinem gnadigsten Fürsten und Herrn.

38: Translation

Schütz to Duke August.
Leipzig, 10 January 1664

[HAB 376 NOVI, fols. 322–23]

[fol. 322r]

Most Illustrious Prince, Most Gracious Lord,

In consideration of the many and great royal kindnesses which I have enjoyed up to now from Your Most Royal Highness, I should be ashamed that until now I have so long delayed and neglected presenting my published musical works which you graciously desired. I ask however your most gracious forgiveness for my neglect and delay, and I am hopeful in this regard, for I have not yet succeeded in gathering up my printed things as such since my return to Weissenfels from Dresden three weeks ago.

However, as many of my works as I could assemble for now will be hereby properly delivered, I hope, to Your Serene Highness's official court scribe by Stephan Daniel (a noted merchant of Brunswick to whom I personally delivered them along with an appended catalog at the current fair), and who furthermore knows Your Royal Highness's most gracious command and, in addition, your provinces.

And first I offer Your Royal Highness my most humble profound thanks that you are graciously disposed to show my modest work the honor and high favor graciously to grant it a little space in your royal library, famous throughout Europe. I therefore had occasion to wish that I could now have sent in such a manner as well my [works] still remaining in my hands [and] copied by pen with which I am still in delay and which (in my opinion) are better than the compositions completed earlier. This I could well have done and I could have proceeded with the publication of these works, if I had found a publisher, and in fact according to my original intention, I could have used for that purpose my retainer or salary granted me by Your Royal Highness. But due to my otherwise meager income here, I must for the most part count it up and use it for my necessary support and preservation (considering from time to time I barely manage to get by and eke out my existence). [fol. 322v] I most obediently offer with my most humble reminder, because of Your Royal Highness's many exalted and royal kindnesses which I have enjoyed up until now, and your entire honorable household to which I more than ever acknowledge my alliance, to make all possible most humble amends before further continuing to assist with your royal praiseworthy court ensemble, should I still be considered worthy.

With this I close, faithfully commending Your Royal Highness to the powerful protection of God the Almighty for the beginning of the beloved New Year coming around again and yet many long years for a lengthy and prolonged life and all the most royal prosperity you desire for body and soul, and remaining

> Your Serene Highness's
> humble obedient and dutybound servant
> Heinrich Schütz
> In his own hand
> 10 January 1664

[fol. 323. Not Schütz's hand]
To the Most Serene, Noble Prince and Lord, Lord August, Duke of Brunswick and Lüneburg, My most gracious Prince and Lord.

39

Catalog of Schütz's Published Works.
Undated

[HAB Cod. Guelf 54 Extrav., fols. 225–26]

[fol. 225r. Not in Schütz's hand]
Verzeichnüß meiner außgelaßenen Musicalischen Wercke, Zu mercken,
waß also gezeichnet * naher Wolffenbütel geschücket worden ist,

Opera Prima.*

*Madrigalia à 5. ao 1611, zu Venedig ged.

Opera Secunda.

Deutscher Psalmen Motetten und Concertten mit 8 und mehr stimmen
Erstertheil in folio ao 1619 zu dreßden gedruckt.

Opera Terza.

Historia Resurectionis Dominicae Teutsch zu dreßden gedruckt ao
1623.

Opera Quarta.

*Cantiones Sacrae Quatuor Vocum 1625 zu Freybergk gedruckt.

Opera Quinta.

Doctor Beckers. Psalmbüchlein ao 1628 zu Freybergk gedruckt

Opera Sexta.

*Symphoniarum Sacrarum Prima pars à. 3.4.5.6. 1629 Venedig ged.

Opera Septima.

Musicalische Exeqvien 1636 in Freybergk gedruckt.

*Opera Octava.

*Geistl. Concert Erstertheil mit 2.3.4.5. ao 1636 in Leipzig gedruckt
[fol. 225v]

Opera Nona.

*Anderertheil Geistl. Concert mit 1.2.3.4.5. ao 1639 in Dreßden
gedruckt.

Opera Decima.

*Symphoniarum Sacrarum Secunda Pars. à 3.4.5. 1647 in Dreßden
gedruckt

Opera Undecima.

*Musicalia ad Chorum Sacrum oder Geistliche ChorMusic à 5.6.7. 1648
in dreßden gedruckt

Opera Duodecima.

*Symphoniarum Sacrarum Tertia pars à 5.6.7.8. Dreßden gedruckt ao
1650.

Opera Decima Terza

*Zwölff Geistl. Gesänge mit 4 stimmen von H. Christoff Kitteln hoffOr-
gan: zu dreßden außgelaßen ao 1657.

Opera Decima Quarta.

Die übersehenen und Vermehrten Arien. über D. Beckers Psalmbuch
in folio Dresdae 1661.
[fol. 226r. In Schütz's hand]
Sind dahero die noch Ermangelnden opera die nachfolgenden

Opera Secunda

Die grossen psalmen v. Concert in folio, nach welchen auch mit fleis
getrachtet, undt dieselbigen hirnechst auch noch Eingeschickt werden
sollen.

Opera Terza, die historij
der Aufferstehung unsers Seelig machers Jesu Christi.

Worvon Einig Exemplar nicht mehr zu erlangen ist, vnd dieselbige auf
gndgsts begeren, abgeschrieben v. [strikeout] verbessert auch eingeschicket werden soll.

Opera Qvinta.

D. Beckers Gesangbuch in 8vo.
Weil dieses Werk zum andernmal ubersehen und verbessert in folio Ao.
etc. 61 wieder in Druk ausgelassen worden ist, als ist [strikeout] für
unnötig erachtet worden, solch buch einzuschicken.

Opera Decima Quarta.

Sindt Eben die itzo erwehnten aufs Newe Revidirten vnd vermehreten
Arien oder Melodeyen über D. Beckers psalmbuch In folio, welche,
dieweil sie in so geschwinder Eil Itzo nicht eingebunden [strikeout] v.
fertig werden können, gleichwol aber in der arbeit sind, förderlichst
noch eingeschicket werden sollen [flourish]
[fol. 226v. In Schütz's hand]
Catalogus, Derer von Capellmeister Schützen in druck ausgelassenen
Musicalischen Werke [flourish]

39: Translation

Catalog of Schütz's Published Works. Undated

[HAB Cod. Guelf 54 Extrav., fols. 225–26]

[fol. 225r. Not in Schütz's hand]
List of my published musical works.
Note that whatever is designated * has been sent to Wolfenbüttel.

Opus 1

*Madrigals for five voices. Published in Venice, 1611.

Opus 2

German Psalms, Motets and Concerti with eight and more voices, Part One. Published in folio in Dresden, 1619.

Opus 3

Story of the Resurrection of Our Lord. Published in German in Dresden, 1623.

Opus 4

*Cantiones Sacrae for four voices. Published in Freiberg, 1625.

Opus 5

Dr. Becker's Little Psalm Book. Published in Freiberg, 1628.

Opus 6

*Symphoniae sacrae, Part One, for three, four, five, and six voices. Published in Venice, 1629.

Opus 7

Musicalische Exequien. Published in Freiberg, 1636.

Opus 8

*Sacred Concerti, Part One, with two, three, four and five voices. Published in Dresden, 1639.
[fol. 225v]

Opus 9

*Sacred Concerti, Part Two, with one, two, three, four, and five voices. Published in Dresden, 1639.

Opus 10

*Symphoniae sacrae, Part Two, for three, four, and five voices. Published in Dresden, 1647.

Opus 11

*Musicalia ad Chorum Sacrum or Sacred Choral Music for five, six, and seven voices. Published in Dresden, 1648.

Opus 12

*Symphoniae sacrae, Part Three, for five, six, seven, and eight voices. Published in Dresden, 1650.

Opus 13

*Twelve Sacred Songs for four voices. Published by Herr Christoph Kittel, Court Organist, in Dresden, 1657.

Opus 14

The revised and augmented arias from Dr. Becker's Psalmbook. In folio, 1661.
[fol. 226r. In Schütz's hand]
Following are the works still missing:

Opus 2

The large psalms and concerti in folio, for which I have searched diligently, and which shall still be sent as well.

Opus 3, The Story of the Resurrection
of Our Holy Savior Jesus Christ.

A copy of this is no longer available and, according to your most gracious wish, it shall be copied by hand, improved, and sent.

Opus 5

Dr. Becker's Psalmbook in octavo.
Because this work has been examined, improved and republished another time in folio in 1661, it has been considered unnecessary to send such a book.

Opus 14

The newly revised and expanded arias or melodies on Dr. Becker's Psalmbook in folio, just mentioned, which, because they could not be now bound and completed in such great haste, but are nevertheless in preparation, are to be sent separately.
[fol. 226v. In Schütz's hand]
Catalog of Kapellmeister Schütz's published musical works.

40

Statement of Schütz's Wages.
28 April 1665

[NSAW 1 Alt 25 no. 294, fol. 23]

[fol. 23r]
Laut ans von Hauß aus bestelten oberCapellmeisters in Craften Heinrich Schutzen, in Fürstl. Cammer rechenden Besoldungs Quitung ist
derselbe biß Ostern 1660. richtig bezahlet
Gebühren Ihme also

Ostern	—	1661	—	150
		1662	—	150
		1663	—	150
		1664	—	150
Ostern	—	1665	—	150
		Sa.		750

Darauf seindt demselben zahlt,

den 30t. Septemb.	1660	—	75
15t. Aprilis	1661	—	75
21t. May	1663	—	300
	Sa.		450

Abgetzogen
Wolten demselben bis Ostern 1665. noch zu zahlen im Rest
verpleiben — — 300
Extrahiret den 28t. Aprilis ao etc. 1665
            HHinsamm
[fol. 23v]
Besoldungs Abrechnung [flourish]
Für dem Ober Capelmeister zu dresden Heinrich Schützen
[second hand] Resto 300 thlr
den 28t. Aprilis 1665

/14

40: Translation

Statement of Schütz's Wages.
28 April 1665

[NSAW 1 Alt 25 no. 294, fol. 23]

[fol. 23r]
As per receipt of wages from the royal chamber of finances, Heinrich
Schütz, empowered as appointed senior Kapellmeister *in absentia*, is paid
in full up to Easter 1660.
Thus he is due

Easter	—	1661	—	150 [talers]
		1662	—	150 [talers]
		1663	—	150 [talers]
		1664	—	150 [talers]
Easter	—	1665	—	150 [talers]
Total	—	—	—	750 [talers]

On that he has been paid

30 September	1660	—	75 [talers]
15 April	1661	—	75 [talers]
21 May	1663	—	300 [talers]
Total:	—	—	—	450 [talers]

Deducted from this,
The balance due him up to Easter 1665 shall remain outstanding
                                                              300 [talers]
Extracted 28 April 1665
                H. Hinsamm[en]
[fol. 23v]
Settlement of wages. For the Senior Kapellmeister of Dresden Heinrich
Schütz. Balance 300 Talers.
28 April 1665

/14

41

Schütz to Duke Moritz.
Dresden, 14 July 1663

[SAD Loc. 8592. *An Herzog Moritz zu Sachsen-Zeitz, 1663–1668*, fol. 9]

[fol. 9r]
Unterthänigst Memorial, betreffende die Anrichtung Ihrer hochfurstl.
durchl. herren Moritzens herzogens zu Sachsens Hoffmusick zu dero
Residentzstadt Zeitz.

1.

Wegen den beyden Merseburgischen Capellknaben, welche vermuhtlich
sich Itzo bey dem gewesenen Cantor zu Naumburgk werden aufhalten,
Das wir jüngsthin albereit fur 3 wochen, Ich deswegen an Ihrer durchl.
H. Rentmeister schrifftlich hette gelangen lassen, also auch an Itzo,
noch mein wolbereifftes unterthngstes bitten were, das solche 2 knaben
mir förderlichst anhero zugeschicket, undt die wenigen Reise kosten,
undt wochentlich 1 thlr zu eines ieglichen verpflegung das lehrgeld mit
eingeschlossen, nicht geschewet werden möchten, in erwegung das
gedachte knaben, unter denen churfurstl. auch denen anderen zweÿen
vorhin alhier vorhandenen Discantisten, binnen 2 Monaten alhier zu
besserer perfection, verhoffentlich gebracht werden solten, als darinden
wol in vieren kaum geschehen möchte [strikeout], vnd könten Sie
hirüber auch alle 4 alhier also beyeinander, fein zusammengewehnet,
mit gueten strecken versehen, undt hirnechst nebenst dem Altisten ingesambt mit Einen der von hinnen abgefordert undt hinabgeschafft
werden, vndt habe ich hirmit ferner auch dieses absehen, [*ümb* crossed
out] wenn Ich solche 4 discantisten alhier gegenwertig bey Einander
haben würde, ümb zuzusehen, ob Sie alle auch gleich tüchtig sein, undt
etwa einiger vertausch, mit andern alhier unterschiedlich vorhandenen,
zu versuchen undt zu erlangen sein wolte. Vndt demnach auff verseu-
mung solcher 4 discantisten, der gröste theil des untergangs Eines Colle-

gii Musici bestehet, als will die geburliche verpflegung undt instituirung
deroselbigen, fürnemblich auch am allerfleissigsten zu beobachten sein,
woran an meinem ort ich nichts zwar erwinden lassen will, aber dennoch
mühsamb genung fallen wirdt, der Discantstimme zu gewunschter perfection zu bringen.

2.

Wegen des von mir vorgeschlagenen newen Positifs beydes in der kirche
    am stadt der orgel, und auch zu hoffe zugebrauchen.
Das dasselbigen verfertigung, von Ihrer furstl. durchl. dem Orgelmacher gndgst undt Ernstlich anbefolen werden möge, Sintemal solch
wercklein bey aller undt iede Musick zum fundament mit gebraucht
müste werden, undt dahero der Orgelmacher, beÿ Itziger auffsetzung
der grossen Orgel, dasselbige zu gleich bey hehr mit machen solte, Den
auffsatz wegen des claviers, item der Register, undt beqvemung zum
forttragen in zweyen stücken, habe ich dem Capellmeister vorher zugeschickt, wornacher der Orgelmacher sich denn zu richten, aldieweil solcher Auffsatz mit gueter bereiffung undt berahtschlagung hiroben
derogestalt aufgezeichnet worden, und demnach mehrgedachter orgelmacher aus der Alten orgell, Ein stark pfeiffwerck aus der Brust (:wie
Sie es heissen:) zu sich genommen, vnd desselbige zu seinem guetem
vortheil, in Eine andere gemeine kirche wiederümb verhandeln kann,
als sehe Ich gar nicht, wie solch newe positiff, Er hoch werde schätzen
können, zumal auch in dasselbige nicht mehr als nur 4 Register (:uber
welche, auch zu Einer vollständigen Musick, mehr nicht von nöthen
sind:) hierein gebracht werden sollen [flourish]

Postscriptum wegen dieses andern puncts

Dieweil ich aber mit heutiger post nachrichtung erhalten, als ob der
orgelmacher das vorhin abgehandelte positif albereit fertig nacher Zeitz
mitgebracht haben solle, So mag es mit den newen Eine weile nach-
bleiben, und mit dem vom orgelmacher mitgebrachten man sich Eine
weile behelffen, welches sonder zweiffel dem orgelmacher auch lieber
sein wirdt, als das von mir angegebene newe anzugehen, welches ihm
wegen Etlicher grossen pfeiffen mehr Einzubringen mühsamb zwar
fallen, Aber weit besserer Effect der Music dienen würde, als sein un-
complet werk nicht thun kann [flourish]

[fol. 9v]

3.

Wegen etlichen newen nohtwendigen Instrumenten sind Itzo alhier in der arbeit

1. Eine Bassgeige zu denen violen di gamba undt sonst anderweit bey dem Taffelldienst vielfältig zugebrauchen kömbt nebenst dem Futral der preis auff—16 thlr

2. Der grosse violon, welcher mit gueter berahtschlagung, undt möglicher sparsamkeit, ausser den noch dazu nötigen kasten, zu dessen fortschaffung, von mir erhandelt undt bestellet worden umb—24 thlr
   Was das hirzu nötige futral, nebenst dem Schlösser beschläge nun zu steken kommen wird, gibt die erfahrung.

3. Eine chormässige spinetta, ist zu Meissen nun auch wieder bestellet, am stadt der vorigen, die von Einem andern hinweg genommen worden, dessen preis mir noch unwissend, vermeine aber dieselbige nebenst dem futral dazu, uber 12.13.14 thlr nicht anlauffen werde.

4.

Wegen anordnung noch etwas weiterer geldt mittell.

Berichte Ich auch, das am abgewichenen Ostermarck von dem herrn Rentmeister mir zu verpflegung der zweÿer Discantisten und des Altistens alhier zwar fünfftzig thaler übermacht worden sein, dieweil aber solche summa auff gedachte 3 Personen numehr bis auf ein geringes ubrige, gar aufgegangen ist, In dem ich nemblich dem Altistens von verwichenen Jubilate angehende, wöchentlich 2 thlr undt auff die beyden Capelknabe von Ostern angehendt mit derogleichen wöchentlichen 2 thlr auch richtig bezahle, vndt dahero zu dero weiterer verpflegung, wie auch zu bezahlung der bestellten Instrumenten (:dazu ich denen meistern auff ihr inständiges begeren, von meinen wenigen anmuht immittelst etwas auf der hand geben müssen:) nichts mehr vorhanden ist, So habe Ich dahero [*etwa* crossed out] noch umb anderweit gndgste handreichung und derogleichen newe anordnung unterthngst zu bitten, nebenst gewisser versicherung, das solcher gelder Ich anders nicht als mit aller möglichen sparsambkeit, an geburende örter, mich gebrauchen, darüber getrewste Rechnung halten, undt bey dem herrn Rendmeister dieselbige iedermahl Erbarlich abzulegen, in bereitschafft anzutreffen sein werde [flourish]

Datum Dresden den 14 Julii
Ao etc. 1663.

41: Translation

Schütz to Duke Moritz.
Dresden, 14 July 1663

[SAD Loc. 8592. *An Herzog Moritz zu Sachsen-Zeitz, 1663–1668*, fol. 9]

[fol. 9r]
Most humble memorandum concerning the establishment of the court ensemble of Your Most Serene Highness, my Lord Moritz, Duke of Saxony, in your capital Zeitz.

1.

Regarding the two choirboys from Merseburg, who presumably will now reside with the former cantor of Naumburg [Gottfried Kühnel].

I should have contacted Your Serene Highness's chamberlain of the exchequer in writing that we newly [arrived in Dresden] three weeks ago. Therefore at this time my carefully considered request would still be to send the two boys to me here as quickly as possible and not to be put off by the minimal travel costs and the one taler weekly for all provisions, including the costs for schooling. In considering the aforementioned boys and the two others who came here a short time ago, one would hope that they could be brought closer to perfection within two months here among the electoral [choirboys] as there in four [months], and moreover all four could thus, living together, be expected to make good progress, and thereafter they could be summoned back and conveyed together along with the alto by someone from there. And in this matter I have further anticipated, if I had these four discantists here with one another at the same time to see if they are all equally capable, I could perhaps interchange some with several others present here to try and match them. And since the greatest part of the ruin of a collegium musicum consists of the neglect of four such discantists, their appropriate nurturing and education must be especially and most carefully attended to, toward which I in my position indeed spare nothing.

But nevertheless it proves difficult enough to bring the discant voice to desired perfection.

2.

Regarding the new positif which I suggested for use both in church as well at court, instead of the organ.

Your Royal Highness should graciously and earnestly urge the organ builder to complete it [the positif] since such a small instrument must be used as the foundation in each and every musical composition, and therefore the organ builder, in the current renovation of the great organ, should build [the positif] at the same time. I sent the Kapellmeister in advance the instructions about the keyboard, likewise the stops and the ease in which it may be transported in two pieces. The organ builder should then be guided by this because such a treatise was written down in this manner with good counsel and advice. And furthermore the oft-mentioned organ builder can take the loud set of pipes from the *Brustwerk* (as one calls it) from the old organ and sell them for a good profit to another church parish, for I see no reason why he could value it as highly as such a new positif, particularly since [the latter] will not contain more than four registers (more than which are unnecessary for a complete ensemble).

Postscript regarding this other point

Because in the meantime, however, I have received news in today's mail that the organ builder, [with regard to] the positif just discussed, has brought one along to Zeitz which was already finished, we can hold off for a while on the new one and be content with the one the organ builder brought along. The organ builder will undoubtedly prefer this to starting the new one as I suggested, which would prove difficult for him because some additional large pipes would need to be installed. Yet it would serve the effect of the music far better, as his incomplete instrument cannot do.

[fol. 9v]

3.

Regarding some necessary new instruments presently under construction here.

1. A bass viol for the viol consort and [which] might otherwise be needed repeatedly for service at table. It should come close to the positif for the price of 16 talers.

2. The violone, which I took charge of and ordered on good advice and with all possible frugality, except for those cases still necessary to carry it, for 24 talers.

It remains to be seen how the case, also necessary, shall now be fitted with the lock clasp.

3. A spinet tuned at normal pitch has also been reordered in Meissen in place of the previous one which was removed by someone else. I still do not know the price of it but believe it to be comparable to that of the positif which should not exceed 12, 13, or 14 talers.

4.

Regarding the arrangement for still more financial matters.

I also report that at the last Easter market 50 talers were indeed remitted to me by the chamberlain of the exchequer for room and board of the two discantists and the alto here. In the meantime, however, of that sum for the aforementioned three persons, all but a tiny remainder is since all but gone. Out of it, specifically, I paid the two talers weekly for the alto beginning with the previous Jubilate, and also rightfully paid for the two choirboys the same two talers weekly beginning at Easter and saw to their further provision. Likewise nothing more is at hand to pay for those instruments ordered (toward which I had to supply something from my own limited resources at the urgent request of the builders). It is for that reason that I must still humbly ask in addition for most gracious assistance and similar new arrangements along with [my] certain assurance that I shall only use such money with the greatest possible frugality for appropriate expenditures, keep faithful records thereon, and always stand prepared to render this humbly to the chamberlain of the exchequer.

Dated Dresden 14 July 1663

42

Duke Moritz to Schütz.
Undated

[SAD Loc. 8592. *An Herzog Moritz zu Sachsen-Zeitz, 1663–1668*, fol. 8]

[fol. 8r]
Beantworttung
Auf des Churfürstl. Sächß. Capellmeisters Heinrich Schüzens sub 14.
Julÿ 1663. eingeschicktes unterthenigstes Memorial.

ad 1.

Wegen überschickung der zu Merseburg in der lehr gestandenen und
alhier befindtlichen beÿden Capellknaben naher Dreßden, achten Wir
für rathsamber daß selbige unter des hiesigebe Informatoris institution
gelaßen, alß daß mit solchen vor iezo erst einige enderung getroffen
werden möchte, Und wollen wir nicht unterlaßen, nach beschehener
Abforderung der anderen beÿden von dreßden unter Ihnen ein certa-
men anzustellen, und zu hören welche von diesen oder Jenen die besten
profectus erlanget.

ad.2.

Betreffende das albereit verfertigte Positif, [*h* crossed out] so hat es
darmit wegen [fol. 8v] unterlaßung des Neuen sein bawenden, biß Wir
sehen, wie unß der Orgellmacher mit dem grosen wercke zu rest fördert
da dann hernach zu [*sehen* crossed out] bedencken, ob mit Ihm kegen
wieder annehmung dieses auf ein anders [second hand, left margin]
nach seinem des Capelmeisters angeben [first hand] zu handeln seÿ.
[second hand, left margin] Inzwischen könte der Capelmeister den Orgel machen von der rechten orth des Clavirs undt der Pfeiffer nothdürf-
tig informiren.

[First hand] ad.3.

Soviel die in der Arbeit begriffenen und benannten unterschiedtliche Instrumenta anbelanget, seind Wir mit derer erhandtlung, iedoch aufs genaueste allerdings gnedigst zufrieden [second hand] und soll deren bezahlung beÿ der abholung oder lifferung geleistet werden.

ad.4.

Zu weiterer unterhaltung der eingangs erwehnten Discantisten und Altistens biß künfftig Mich: geliebts Gott, Solle durch Unsern Renthmeister ehistes noch 30. biß 40. Thlr übermachet werden [flourish]

42: Translation

Duke Moritz to Schütz.
Undated

[SAD Loc. 8592. *An Herzog Moritz zu Sachsen-Zeitz, 1663–1668*, fol. 8]

[fol. 8r]
Answer
To the electoral Saxon Kapellmeister Heinrich Schütz's memorandum sent on 14 July 1663.

Re: 1

Regarding sending to Dresden both choirboys apprenticed in Merseburg and living here, we consider it more advisable that they be left at the local educational institution than to make any changes for them at present. And after the other two return from Dresden we shall not fail to arrange an examination for them and to listen to see whether the former or the latter has attained the greatest perfection.

Re: 2

Concerning the positif which has already been completed, we have [fol. 8v] put off building the new [positif] until we see how the organ builder serves us in the completion of the great instrument. Afterwards, when after the Kapellmeister's report has been discussed, [we shall] consider whether to commission him to reundertake this [task] after the other. In the meantime the Kapellmeister could use the organ from the right side of the keyboard [of the great organ] and inform the pipemaker as needed.

Re: 3

As far as the various aforementioned instruments which are about to be made are concerned, we are nevertheless indeed graciously satisfied with the purchasing in every detail and payment shall be made upon pickup or delivery.

Re: 4

In order to support the aforementioned discantists and alto until this coming Michaelmas, another thirty or forty talers shall, God willing, be remitted as soon as possible through our chamberlain of the exchequer.

43

Schütz to Duke Moritz.
Dresden, Michaelmas 1663

[SAD Loc. 8592. *Schreiben an Herzog Moritz von Sachsen-Zeitz*, fol. 33]

[fol. 33r]
Durchlauchtigster Fürst, Gnädigster Herr,
Demnach mir auch zu ohren gekommen, als ob die newerbaueten zweÿ
Musicalischen Chore, In E. Fürstl. Durchl. Schloskirchen, nicht allerdings meiner meinung nach, recht gerahten sein sollen, Sondern das die
Musicanten, wegen der fördern Seulen dahinder verborgen, undt nicht
recht in das gesichte herausser werts zu stehen kommen, undt dahero
ich nicht anders vrtheilen kann, als das der Resonantz [*dahero* crossed
out] auch desto minder Recht herausser in die kirche fallen undt Einen
gebürenden effect geben werde,
Dahero Ich denn verursachet werde (:im fall wir anders solches Chor-
bawes Ehre haben, und dieselbigen recht gebrauchet wissen wollen:)
hirbeÿ unterthngst undt hochfleissig zu erindern, E. F. durchl. sich
gndgst belieben lassen wollen, mit dem H. Bawmeister bey zeiten noch
zu berahtschlagen, Auff was masse solche beyde chore mit Einer zierlichen zimmer undt Tischerarbeit, etwa noch Ein anderthalb Ele her-
auswertz (:So weit sichs etwa schicken möchte damit es keiner seulen
darunter bedürffe:) in die kirche gerükt heraus werden könten, Auff
welche weise denn, und anders nicht, solche chore, meiner meinung
nach Ihre perfection, vndt gebürendes lob erst erreichen würden,
welches Ich aber Entlich zu E. F. durchl. eigenen gndgste entscheidung,
auch noch vnterthngst anheimb gestellet haben will [flourish]
Anfänglich war mein vorschlag, solche beyde chor solten voran, an die
bey den kirchpfeiler Einander gegenüber, gesetzet werden [flourish]
Muste aber entlich des H. Baumeisters meinung stadt geben [flourish]
Undt stehe ich bey so thaner Itzigen bewandtnüs, bey mir an, auff
was masse der Orgelmacher die Itzige grosse Orgel, auf den Einen chor

recht aufsetzen, vndt dieselbige recht ins gesicht in die kirche fallen
werde. Will aber dennoch verhofen, das hirinnen auch gueter Raht
undt vorsichtigkeit gepflogen sein werde [flourish]
E. hochfurstl. durchl. verzeyhen mir gndgst, wenn Ich vieleicht aus
übriger   sorgfalt,   derogestalt   dieselbige   verunruhige,   verbleibe
deroselbigen

Vnterthngstr schuldigster trewer diener
allezeit
Henrich Schütz Mpp
Dresden am tage S. Michaelis
Ao etc. 1663.

Bey herausrückung obgedachter 2 chor könten dieselbigen, mit derogleichen zierlichen seulwerk, wie die O . . . nischen Musicalischen chore
über dem Altar, auch aus staffirret werden.

43: Translation

Schütz to Duke Moritz.
Dresden, Michaelmas 1663

[SAD Loc. 8592. *Schreiben an Herzog Moritz von Sachsen-Zeitz,* fol. 33]

[fol. 33r]

Most Serene Prince, Most Gracious Lord,

Because it has reached my ears that the two newly built choir lofts in Your Serene Highness's palace church have not, in my opinion, turned out well in every respect, but that the musicians are hidden and do not stand properly facing outwards because of the furthermost pillars inside, and therefore I can only conclude that the resonance will carry in the church and give the proper effect much less effectively.

For that reason, I am therefore induced (if we should have the honor of building such loft at all and wish to use it in the right manner) to suggest to Your Royal Highness most humbly and most diligently, at your most gracious pleasure, that you confer with the master builder in due time [to determine] to what extent both lofts with an ornate room and cabinet work could perhaps be moved out another one-and-one-half ells forward in the church (as far as seems fitting so that it does not need pillars underneath), for only in such a manner, and not otherwise, can such a praiseworthy loft be constructed perfectly, in my opinion. I shall, however, in the end submit to Your Royal Highness's own most gracious decision. Initially it was my suggestion that both such lofts should be set forward opposite one another next to the church pillars; however, I finally had to defer to the opinion of the master builder.

And I doubt in the present situation the extent to which the organ builder is correctly erecting the present great organ in the one loft so that it faces into the church correctly. It is to be hoped nevertheless, however, that good advice and prudence shall prevail.

I beg Your Serene Highness's most gracious pardon if I perhaps out of excessive conscientiousness stir up trouble in this way. I remain your

Most humble, most dutiful loyal servant always
Heinrich Schütz, in his own hand
Dresden, on St. Michael's Day [September 29]
1663

By moving the aforementioned two lofts out, they could even be provided with the same ornamental pillarwork as the [illegible word] choir lofts over the altar.

44

Schütz to the Superintendent in Zeitz.
Undated

[SAM Rep. A29d. Teil I, no. 19, fols. 22–23]

[fol. 22r]
An Ihro hochEhrwürden, den Herrn Superintendenten in Zeitz, wegen
mein Endesbemeltens dinstlich Memorial

1.

Das Ich nochmals Erbotig were, Ihrer hochfurstl. durchl. vorigen
gndgste begeren gemes, zu dero furstl. hoffmusick gebrauch, alle undt
iede meine zwar geringe musicalische arbeit, so da fur guht erkennet
werden möchte, gerne zu contribuiren, und nach und nach ein zu
schicken, Aber dieweil Ich bishero unterschiedene fast viel sachen eingeschicket hatte, worvon, mein diener nachrichtung geben könte, So
aber meistentheils vorhanden gekom [*sindt* crossed out] [flourish] und
Ich ubel damit zufrieden were, das dieselbigen nicht fur die furstl.
Capell, in gewisser verwahrung von iemandt gehalten würden, So were
ich hirdurch veranlasset worden mich zu erkühnen, undt von
deroselbigen hirmit zu vernemen, welche grobheit Sie mir grosg.
verzehen wolten, Ob Sie nemblich nicht gedächten solcher meiner arbeit, die Ich nach und nach einschicken würde, die sonderlicher Ehre
anzuthun, und dieselbigen anfänglich von mir anzunemen, vndt hirauf
iemandt Ihrer Musicorum, vnd insonderheit dem Concertmeister, wenn
Er sie wird haben wollen, in seine verwahrung zum gebrauch der furstl.
Capell, zu Recommendiren, worauf Ich denn auch wils Gott gesonnen
were, Ein gedoppelt in gewisse Classen abgetheilt Register uber
dasjenige was etwa albereit eingeschickt worden oder nach folgen
möchte, auch Einzuschicken, das Eine vor den H. Supintendenten, v.
des andere fur dem, welchem solche concert vntergeben würden werden, undt dieses nicht alleine umb erweisung meine vnterthngstn

schuldigkeit willen, Sondern auch damit solche sache (:da anders etwas würdiges sich darunter finden möchte:) bey der furstl. Capell beharlich und unverlohren verbleiben theten.

In was vnterschiedliche Classen solch Register ich Eintheilen werde und hirnechst iegliches Concert oder stück an seinen ort eingeschrieben werden könne, habe Ich meinen diener, Ein Notul Mitgegeben [flourish].

2.

Demnach Ihre furstl. durchl. auch gndgst gesonnen sind die Beckerschen psalmen mit meinen Melodeyen, In Ihre Schloskirchen (:massen zu Dresden Halle und merseburgk auch geschehen:) einführen undt unterweilen insonderheit in den wochenpredigten mitgebrauchen zu lassen, als habe Ich etliche Explr solcher Psalmen bey henden geschafft, undt beykommende 3 Explr von dem hiesichen Buchbinder Einbinden lassen, und zwar in meinung, das der beyde in gold eingebundene Explr, fur Ihre furstl. durchl. vndt dero fraw gemahlin in Ihr oratorium oder kirchstüblein, zu dero gebrauch solten bey geleget, und des dritte von den H. Supintendenten selbst in der kirche gebraucht werden, zu einer nachrichtung wenn einer oder der andere psalmen gesungen werden solte, undt dafern nun hochgedachte Ihre durchl. nochmals gesonnen sein möchte solche gesange ehistes vieleicht, zu introduciren, So were mein unterthngs bitten, das dem H. StadtCantori (:als von dessen SchulCantorey solche psalmen und nicht von der furstl. Music abgesungen werden müßen:) anbefohlen werden möchten, zu seiner gelegenheit, etwa sich einen weg hiruber zu mir zu machen, So wolte Ich ihm noch ander 4 Exemplar, nemblich zu den 4 discant Alt tenor und Bassstimmen, alhier mit zurücke geben, umb allezeit, Ihrer durchl. [fol. 22v] gndgstn beliebung, und des H. Supintendenten anordnung, in der SchlosKirchen damit einen anfang zu machen [flourish]

Dieweil es aber die erfahrung zu dresden [strikeout] Merseburg und Halle gegeben, das die zuhörer iedesmahl nach Explrien des [strikeout] blossen Texts solcher psalmen getrachtet haben, daraus Sie verstehen können was gesungen werden, und daneben entlich auch mitsingen können, So habe Ich [*alhier* crossed out] hirbeÿ deren auch 2 Explr, So in der [strikeout] lüneburgischen druckerey gedruckt, auch mit einschicken wollen, umb an zu sehen ob dieselbigen sich etwa zum gebrauch fur einen und dem andern zuhörer, Edell und vnedell zu hoffe, tüchtig befunden werden möchten, Solten denn mehr hernacher geschickt werden das Rohe Explr fur 3 gl. darumb Ich iedesmal Erlegen kann, vnd vermeine Ich, das wenn Es Ihrer furstl. durchl. beliebig sein würde, Sie unterschiedliche Explr [strikeout] komen, Einbinden lassen,

vndt das furstl. frawenzimmer, [strikeout] Cammerjuncker, v. andere
hoffbediente iegliche mit einem Explr, zum anfange damit verehren
könten, die ordnung aber, und zu welcher zeit solche psalmen Etwa
gebraucht werden solten, wurde billich bey Ihrer hochfurstl. durchl.
undt dero H. Oberhoffprediger stehen [flourish] Und binn Ich meines-
theils Einiger gndgstn nachrichtung deswegen gewertig [flourish]
[fol. 23r] Verzeichnüs in was Classen, das Register uber neue Musicalische arbeit, So ich gelibts Gott, hirnechst fur der furstl. hoff: Music
(:und zwar ohne einziges entgeld, ausser meiner hausbestallung:) einschicken werde, vertheilet undt gehalten werden soll:

1. Grosse Psalmen, Geistliche grosse Concert, Te Deum laudamus
   undt derogleichen volstimmigen sachen mit [strikeout] Vocal und
   Instrumental parteyen, zu allerzeit nach befindung zu gebrauchen
2. Kleine oder mit wenig stimmen Eingerichtete psalmen und Concerten, Jedes mal, auch deren etliche unterweilen eingangs bey
   Einer furstl. taffel zu gebrauchen
3. Auf die 3 haubtfest, weynachten Ostern vndt pfingsten Eingerichtete Concerten.
4. Auf die kleinen festage, als das newe jahr, heilige 3 Kong. Purifica-
   tions Ascensionis, Trinitatis [strikeout] und andre kleine festage eingerichtete Concerten [flourish]
5. Auff der Sontäglichen Evangelia
6. Weltlich undt Moralische gesange fur Eine furstl. Taffellmusic

Ingleichen binn Ich auch erbotig dem Herrn Cantori mit communi-
cirung etlicher gueten sachen fur seine Stadt Music, auf sein begeren
an die hand zu gehen [flourish]

Was aber Etwa an gedruckten Musicalischen sachen, auch etwa an
gantzen abcopirten opern, als an Geistlichen oder Biblischen [strikeout]
Historien oder andern geschafft werden möchte wird billig absonderlich zu bezahlen und zu recompensiren sein [flourish]

44: Translation

Schütz to the Superintendent in Zeitz. Undated

[SAM Rep. A29d. Teil I, no. 19, fols. 22–23]

[fol. 22r]
To my lord, the most honorable superintendent in Zeitz, regarding my humble memorandum given below,

1.

that I would be once again most willing to contribute, according to His Royal Highness's previous most gracious desire, each and every one of my truly meager musical works for use by your royal court ensemble so that they might be judged worthy, and to send them little by little. But in the meantime I had sent up to now quite a few miscellaneous compositions, which, according to information provided by my servant, for the most part, have been received, and I was most displeased that they were not placed in safe keeping by someone for the royal ensemble. Thus I was induced to take the liberty of ascertaining from him, for which insolence you must pardon me, that you namely did not give special honor to my aforementioned works, which I sent little by little, and [request that you] accept them from me initially and then recommend them to someone of your musicians, and particularly to the concert master [Clemens Thieme], if he should want them, to his safekeeping for use in the royal chapel. To this end I then am inclined to send, God willing, a double register divided into definite categories for those [works] that perhaps have already been sent or shall follow, and to send one to the superintendent and the other to him to whom such concerti shall be entrusted, and this not only as evidence of my most humble willingness to serve, but also [to assure] that these compositions (if indeed something worthy should be found among them) shall remain preserved and safe in the royal chapel.

I have sent along with my servant a memorandum regarding the various categories into which I shall divide such a register, and hereafter every concerto or piece could be written down in its place.

2.

Because His Royal Highness has also graciously decided to introduce the *Becker Psalter* with my melodies into your palace church (which has been done in Dresden, Halle, and Merseburg) and especially to have them occasionally used with the weekday services, I have produced some copies of these Psalms which I had on hand and had the accompanying three copies bound by the local bookbinder, and indeed with the intention that the two copies bound in gold should be put aside for His Royal Highness and his wife for use in your oratory or chapel and the third to be used in the church by the superintendent himself as a guide when one or the other Psalm should be sung. And should His aforementioned Highness perhaps decide again to introduce such songs immediately, my most humble request would be that the city cantor [Johann Longolius] shall be commanded (as such Psalms must be sung by his school choir and not by the royal ensemble) to make his way over to me at his convenience, because I want to give him here another four copies, namely for the four voices, discant, alto, tenor, and bass, to take back with him, so that [it will be possible], according to His Highness's [fol. 22v] most gracious pleasure and the superintendent's order, to begin to use them in the palace church at any time.

Given in the meantime the experiences in Dresden, Merseburg, and Halle, where the listeners each time wanted to have copies of just the texts of such Psalms from which they could understand what was being sung and furthermore could ultimately sing along, I have had two copies of these printed in the Lüneburg printing house and shall send them along in order to see if they shall be deemed sound for use by one and the other listener, noble or not. Should then more be sent thereafter, I can deposit three gulden on the rough copy each time, and I believe that if it were agreeable to His Royal Highness, [when] the various copies arrive, they should be bound, and each royal lady and lord of the court and other court servants could initially be presented with a copy. But [the decision regarding] the order and at approximately what times these Psalms should be used would stand deservedly with His Royal Highness and his senior court preacher, and I am for my part ready to provide a most gracious report on it.

[fol. 23r] List of categories into which the register of new musical works, which I for the love of God shall hereafter send for the royal court ensemble (and in fact without compensation except from my appointment), shall be divided and maintained.

1. Large Psalms, large sacred concerti, *Te Deum laudamus,* and similarly full-voiced compositions with vocal and instrumental parts to be used at any time at one's own discretion.
2. Small Psalms and concerti or those only intended for few voices, some of which can be occasionally used at the beginning of a royal banquet.
3. Concerti intended for the three principal celebrations Christmas, Easter, and Pentecost.
4. Concerti intended for the lesser holidays such as New Years, the Three Magi, Purification, Ascension Day, Trinity, and other lesser holidays.
5. For the Gospels every Sunday.
6. Secular and moralistic songs for royal Tafelmusik.

Likewise I am also willing to communicate with the cantor and supply him at his pleasure with good compositions for his municipal musicians.

However, whatever printed musical compositions or entire works copied out by hand are to composed, being sacred or biblical stories or others, shall be duly paid for and compensated separately.

45

Schütz to Philipp Hainhofer.
Augsburg, 23 April 1632

[SUBH Sup. ep. 48. fols. 457–58]

[fol. 457r]
Edler, Ehrenvester hochachtbar, grosgönstiger Herr Vndt hochgeehrter freundt, demselben seindt nebenst Wünschung von Gott aller Erprieslichen Wolfarth leibes vndt der Seelen Meine vermögende dienste bestes fleisses bevorn,
MEinem Grosg. Herrn gebe Ich hirbeÿ zuvernemen das albereit lenger als vor halber Jahres frist, H. Friedrich lebzeltern ümb vorschreibung etlicher musicalischen sachen [*sachen* crossed out] von Napoli ich angesprochen auch ein verzeichnüs hirüber zugestelt habe, vndt demnach ich die beÿsorge trage, auch von wolermelten H. lepzeltern so viel verstanden habe, das solche lista vntterwegens beÿ beraubung der bothen, auch von abhanden mag kommen sein, Als habe Ich nicht vntterlassen können anderweit die feder an Meinen Grosg. herrn noch einsten an zusetzen, dienstfreundlich bittende, Er mir die gunst wiederfahren, vndt, besag inliegender specification, etliche Musicalische gedrukte sachen durch die seinigen heraus verschreiben, den Costo auch beÿ zeiten mich avisiren lassen wolle, Soll h. lepzeltern die zahlung hirvor zugestelt, vndt sonst die mühwaltung, zu begebender occasion, mit dank beschuldet werden.   Vnsern zustandt alhier betreffendt wirdt mein grosg. herr von h. lebzeltern teglich berichtet, vnser gnedigster herr, so viel ich nachrichtung habe, bringet eine ausserlessene Armee auf zimlich viel 1000 Mann zu Ross vndt Fusse zusammen, welche der liebe Gott, sambt Seiner Churfl. durchl., erhalten beschirmen vndt zu fürhabender intention glük vndt Seegen verleÿhen wolle [flourish] Francesco Castelli discantgeiger welchen ich mitt aus Italia bracht ist albereit lenger als vor einem Jahr gestorben, vndt ist diese tage Sigr. Caspar Kittel mein ander Reise geferthe auch gefehrli-

chen an einem hitziger fieber krank gelegen, woraus ihn Gott doch errettet, vndt hiebeÿ meinen grosg. seinen fleissigen grus v. dienst vermelden lasset. Ich habe über die massen ohngerne gehöret was massen, mein Grosg. herr, hiebevorn, wegen eines intercipirten schreibens, mit den kaÿserlichen fast in ohngelegenheit gerathen were, Gott dem Almechtigen aber dem seÿ numehr lob Ehr Preis vndt dank, der meinem grosg. herrn vndt viel tausendt fromme Christen von Ihren gewissens, hab vndt gueter peinigern, wiederumb gnediglich erlöset vndt raum gemacht hatt [fol. 457v] In gestriger predigt Sontag Jubilate, Erwehnete vnser Ober hoffprediger h. D. Höe, was massen bishero die Evangelischen kirchen, wegen grosser vntterdrükung der Catholischen, auch viel trawrikeit erduldet, an itzo aber der h. Christus in oberteutschlandt v. namentlich auch zu Augspurg vieler 1000 Ja hunderttausend menschen herzen wiederumb zu erfrewen angefangen hette, vndt machte ferner ein schöne application [strikeout] heutiges zustandes auf das Evangelium. Das hiervon auch vor meine person ich voranlasset worden, meinem grosg. herrn vndt vnsern mitt Christen zu Augspurgk, wegen der wieder erlangeten gewissens freÿheit herzlichen zu congratuliren vndt das Jenige zu wünschen, was im beschlus des gestrigen Evangelii zu finden ist, das nemlich die frewde, wormit der h. Christ viel 1000 hertzen zu Augspurg zu erfrewen anfangen hatt, niemandt nimmermehr von Ihnen nemen könne [flourish] Amen. Mein grosg. herr wolle meinetwegen h. D. Nathan vndt alle die seinigen dienstfreundlichen salutiren, vndt mit beharrlichen gunst v. freundschafft mir vnverrukt zugethan verbleiben, denen Ich zu vermögenden diensten herwiederumb schuldig vndt allewilligst verbleiben, vndt göttlicher protection vns allerseits ein fleis hirmit empfelen thun. Signatum dresden den 23. Aprilis. Ao etc. 1632.

> MEines grosg. herrn
> allezeit trewdienstwilligster
> Henrich Schütz
> Chur. S. Capellmeister Mpp

[fol. 458r]

> Musiche da Napoli

Ascanio Majone Canzonette à 3.
Scipione Stella. 1.2.3.4. libro Madrigali à 5.
Scipione Dentice. 1.2.3.4.5. libro di Madrigali à 5.
Scipione l'Acorcia. 1.2.3. lib.º di Madrigali à 5.
Camillo Lombardi Canzonette à piu voci
Cico Lombardi Canzonette. 1.2.3.4 et 5. à 3 voci
Venosa à 6 voci ottavo libro.
D. Joan Maria Sabino. 1.2.3 et 4. libro di Motetti

D. Carlo pedata Canzonette à 3 voci. lib.º 1.2.ᵈᵒ etc.
Frottole del Padre Grillo à piu voci.
Francesco Grandesa Canzonete à 3 voci.
D. Alfonso Verde Motetti à piu voci
D. Alfonso Montesana Madrigali 1.2.3. à 5.
Canzonette di Giramo. il 3. 4.ᵗᵒ et 5.ᵗᵒ à 3.
Del Prencipe Venosa Lamentation. à 6.
Giovan macque opere die Chiesa à piu voci
      che si truovano.
Joan Maria Trabaci Motetti et altre robbe di chiesa.
Ancora [*li madrigali et* crossed out] le messe dell' istesso
L'Abbate Mattias Canzonetti à 3.
Teseo Canzonette et Motetti à piu voci etc.
     Priegasi che con consiglio di qualcun Musico si taccia scernire questi et altri Auttori buoni di più che si truoveranno nelle Librarie di Napoli [flourish]
[fol. 458v]
DEm Edlen Vesten vndt Grosachtbarn h. Philips Hainhöffer Fürstlichen Pommarischen Rahtt daselbsten, Meinem grosgönstigen herren vndt hochgeehrten freunde günstig zu handen.
Augspurgk.

45: Translation

Schütz to Philipp Hainhofer.
Augsburg, 23 April 1632

[SUBH Sup. ep. 48. fols. 457–58]

[fol. 457r]

Noble, most honorable, respected, most benevolent lord and highly esteemed friend, may the Lord's blessing for complete well-being of body and soul be with you, along with my most diligent service to the utmost.

I give my most benevolent lord herewith to know how already more than a half year ago, I requested Herr Friedrich Lebzelter to order some musical compositions from Naples and I submitted a list of them. I was to bear the responsibility thereafter, and I understood as much from the aforementioned Herr Lebzelter, for such a list could be stolen from the couriers on the way or might be lost. I could not forbear putting quill to paper to my most benevolent lord once again, asking submissively that he do me the kindness of ordering some printed musical compositions through his household according to the enclosed specification and to have me apprised of the cost in due time. Herr Lebzelter shall deliver payment for them and furthermore, when there will be an opportunity, will show his gratitude for your trouble.

Concerning our situation here, my most honorable lord will be informed by Herr Lebzelter daily. Our most gracious lord, as far as I know, is assembling a specially selected army of several thousand men on horseback and on foot whom the good Lord, along with His Serene Highness, shall maintain, protect, and grant luck and blessing on the purpose proposed. Francesco Castelli, treble violinist, whom I brought along from Italy, has been dead already more than a year, and in recent days Signore Caspar Kittel, my other traveling companion, lay ill with a dangerously high fever from which God saved him and herewith he offers my honorable lord his diligent greetings and service. Above all, my benevolent lord, I have reluctantly heard how earlier the imperial troops were nearly led into difficulty through an intercepted letter. God Almighty, however, to whom henceforth be praise, honor, glory, and thanks, again graciously delivered my benevolent lord and many thousand pious Christians, tormented by their consciences, goods, and chattel, and made room for them in heaven. [fol. 457v] In yesterday's sermon for Jubilate Sunday, our senior court preacher Dr. Höe mentioned how up until now the Prostestant church, because of great repression by the Catholics, suffered much sadness, but how now Christ had begun to gladden again the hearts of many thousand, indeed one hundred thousand, men in Northern Germany and specifically in Augsburg, and furthermore made a beautiful interpretation of the current situation based on the Gospels. I have been personally moved by this to congratulate my honorable lord and those with Christ in Augsburg from my heart regarding their newly acquired freedom and to wish them what is finally to be found at the conclusion of yesterday's Gospels, that is, namely, the joy with which the Lord Christ had begun to gladden many thousand hearts in Augsburg, which no one can ever take from them. Amen. My honorable lord might on my behalf greet Dr. Nathan and all his flock and with steadfast love and friendship to whom I remain firmly devoted and to whom I remain with everything in my power likewise obliged and ever-willing, and diligently commend us all to divine protection. Signed Dresden 23 April 1632.

> My honorable lord's
> always faithful and most willing
> Heinrich Schütz
> Electoral Saxon Kapellmeister
> In his own hand

[fol. 458r]

> Music from Naples

Ascanio Majone. Canzonettas for three voices.

Scipione Stella. First, second, third, and fourth books of madrigals for five voices.

Scipione Dentice. First, second, third, fourth, and fifth books of madrigals for five voices.

Scipione Lacorcia. First, second, and third books of madrigals for five voices.

Camillo Lambardi. Canzonettas for many voices.

Cico Lambardi. First, second, third, fourth, and fifth books of canzonettas for three voices.

[Gesualdo, Duke of] Venosa. Book 8 for six voices.

Giovanni Maria Sabino. First, second, third, and fourth books of motets.

Carlo Pedato. Canzonettas for three voices, books one and two etc.

Frottolas by Father [Giuseppe Veggiano dello] Grillo for several voices.
Francesco Grandesa. Canzonettas for three voices.
Alfonso Verde. Motets for more voices.
Alfonso Montesana [da Maida]. The first, second, and third books of
madrigals for five voices.
Canzonettas by Giramo. The third, fourth, and fifth books for three
voices.
Lamentation for six voices by [Gesualdo,] the prince of Venosa.
Jean de Macque. Sacred works for more voices if they exist.
Giovanni Maria Trabaci. Motets and other sacred works.
Also the masses by the same.
Abbate Matthias. Canzonettas for three voices.
Teseo. Canzonettas and motets for more voices, etc.

It is requested that he be commanded to find, with the advice of some
musician, these and other good composers as well that are found in the
bookshops of Naples.
[fol. 458v]
To the favorable hands of the noble and honorable Herr Philipp Hainhofer, royal Pomeranian Councilor there, my most benevolent lord and
highly esteemed friend.
Augsburg.

Notes

Preface

1. *Beiträge zur Geschichte der königlich sächsischen musikalischen Kapelle grossentheils aus archivarischen Quellen* (Dresden: C.F. Meser, 1849).

2. Rpt. ed., 2 vols. in 1 (Leipzig: Peters, 1971).

3. (Regensburg: G. Bosse, 1931). Rpt. ed. (Hildesheim: Olms, 1976).

4. *Jahrbücher für musikalische Wissenschaft* 1 (1863), pp. 147–286.

5. (Bückeburg and Leipzig: C.F.W. Siegel, 1922).

6. Allen Skei, *Heinrich Schütz: A Guide to Research* (New York and London: Garland Publishing, Inc., 1981), p. xxi.

7. 2nd ed. (Kassel: Bärenreiter, 1954). English translation by Carl F. Pfatteicher (St. Louis: Concordia, 1959).

8. Agatha Kobuch, "Neue Sagittariana im Staatsarchiv Dresden. Ermittlung unbekannter Quellen über den kursächsischen Hofkapellmeister Heinrich Schütz," *Jahrbuch für Regionalgeschichte* 15 (1988), pp. 118–24.

9. *Der Gottesdienst am kurfürstlichen Hofe zu Dresden* (Göttingen: Vandenhoeck & Ruprecht, 1961).

10. See bibliography.

Chapter 1

1. Schmidt, p. 29. For the exchange of letters between Johann Georg I and Duke Moritz of Kassel, see Werner Dane, "Briefwechsel zwischen dem landgräflich hessischen und dem kurfürstlich sächsischen Hof um Heinrich Schütz (1614–1619)," *Zeitschrift für Musikwissenschaft* 17 (1935), pp. 343–55.

2. This document no longer survives in SAD. For a description see Moritz Fürstenau, *Zur Geschichte der Musik und des Theaters am Hofe zu Dresden* (1861; rpt. Leipzig: Peters, 1971), vol. I, pp. 24–25. Also see Karl August Müller, *Kurfürst Johann Georg der Erste, seine Familie und sein Hof. . . .*, vol. 1 of *Forschungen auf dem Gebiet der neueren Geschichte* (Dresden and Leipzig: Fleischer, 1838), pp. 145–48.

3. Moritz Fürstenau, 1861 I, p. 10 and pp. 169–70.

4. SAD Loc. 8687. *Kantoreiordnung,* fol. 247. Reproduced in Fürstenau 1861 I, pp. 28–29 and 35–36; however, Fürstenau has omitted most of the names of the members of the elector's ensemble. This list also appears in Fürstenau, *Beiträge zur Geschichte der königlich sächsischen musikalischen Kapelle grossentheils aus archivarischen Quellen* (Dresden: C.F. Meser, 1849), pp. 69–70, with extraordinary inaccuracy.

5. SAD Loc. 33344. 1949. *Registratura über das 10te Bestallungs Buch,* 1646–51, no. 37.

6. Ibid., no. 66.

7. Ibid., no. 99.

8. Colin Timms, "Bontempi, Giovanni Andrea," *The New Grove,* vol. 3, p. 37.

9. Erich H. Müller, ed. *Heinrich Schütz: Gesammelte Briefe und Schriften* (Regensburg: G. Bosse, 1931. Rpt. ed. Hildesheim: Olms, 1976), no. 57. SAD Loc. 8687. *Kantoreiordnung,* fol. 289r. "Mit der dritten Companeÿ aber, nemblich der Vocalisten oder Sänger, wurde es etwas kostbarer undt schwerer hehrgehen, weil mann dieselbigen ausserlandes, vieleicht auch zum theil gar unter den Italianern würde suchen müssen. . . ."

10. Wolfram Steude, Ortrun Landmann, and Dieter Härtwig, "Dresden," *The New Grove,* vol. 5, p. 616.

11. Erich H. Müller, *GBS,* no. 66.

12. This document is reproduced in Wilhelm Schäfer, "Einige Beiträge zur Geschichte der kurfürstlichen musikalischen Capelle oder Cantorei unter den Kurfürsten Christian I. und II. und Johann Georg I." *Sachsenchronik für Vergangenheit und Gegenwart* 1 (1854), pp. 423–24.

13. See Joshua Rifkin, "Towards a New Image of Heinrich Schütz," *The Musical Times,* vol. 126, no. 1713 (November 1985), pp. 651–58, and no. 1714 (December 1985), pp. 716–20, for a clear summary of Hofkontz's plight and for excerpts from his letters.

14. Erich H. Müller, *GBS,* no. 27. Facsimile edition by Heinz Krause-Graumnitz, Heinrich Schütz, *Autobiographie (Memorial 1651)* (Leipzig: VEB Deutscher Verlag für Musik, 1972). Translated in Pierro Weiss, *Letters of Composers through Six Centuries* (Philadephia: Chilton Books, 1967), pp. 46–51.

15. Erich H. Müller, *GBS,* no. 86.

16. Ibid., no. 88.

17. Ibid., no. 92.

18. This list will be discussed later in this chapter.

19. Reproduced in Fürstenau, 1861 I, pp. 33–35.

20. Both letters in document 7 are previously unpublished.

21. SAD Loc. 33345. 1953. *Registratura über das 11te Bestallungs Buch,* 1652–56, fol. 232r.

22. SAD Loc. 7287. *Einzelne Schriften,* fol. 191.

23. SAD OHMA C. no. 8. *Begräbnis des Churfürstens zu Sachsen Herrn Johann Georgens des Ersten.* 1657.

24. Fürstenau, 1861 I, pp. 136 and 179–80.

25. Anton Weck, *Der Fürstl. Sächs. weitberuffenen Residentz- und Haupt-Vestung Dresden Beschreibung und Vorstellung* (Nuremberg: J. Hoffmann, 1680), p. 422.

26. See Ralph Giesey, *The Royal Funeral in Renaissance France* (Geneva: Librairie E. Droz, 1960), pp. 27–28.

27. "Die sämtlichen Churfürstl. Sächsischen Cammer = Herren und Cammer = Junckern." Weck, p. 423.

28. The funeral and processions are described by Weck, ibid., pp. 422–30. See also Moser/Pfatteicher, *Heinrich Schütz,* p. 211. For the procession order of the court ensemble members, see SAD OHMA C. no. 8, fols. 289v–290r.

29. *Begräbnis,* from the unnumbered printed pages bound in the front of the volume. "so die Lieder nicht zureichen/müssen andere gesungen/oder vorige wiederholet werden. . . ."

30. *Begräbnis,* fol. 169.

> Beÿ dem Memorial des Capellmeisters ist dieses zuerinnern: So die Hof Music müßen auch Frühe nach 6. Uhr in das Schloß Kirchen sämbtlich seÿn, und das Singen verrichten, daß Sie mit nach Freyberg gereiset, davon finde ich ganz keine nachrichtung, So sonsten, weil der Dreÿen Hof Pre. mit fleiß gedacht wird, nicht sollte mit stillschweigen übergangen seÿn, der Bassist aber uns mit dahin, und das Creuze trage, welches der Herr Hofmarschall, und wie es damit auf dem Wege soll gehalten worden, schon wird wißen anzuorden. [Margin] Sr Churfl. Durchl. gdtr erklärung Die sämbtl. Musici sollen mit in den Process bis in den Schmalen Gartten gehen, darnach kehren Sie zurücke.

31. Ibid., fols. 211v–212v.

> Die beyden Capellmeistere und die ihnen untergebenen haben beÿ dem Churfl. Leichbegängnüs zu verrichten.
> 1. Montags den 2. Februarÿ 1657. sollen sie ingesambt früh morgens bald nach 6. Uhr in der Schloß Kirche seÿn, und das singen vor: und nach der Predigt verrichten, Hernach gegen Mittags nach vor 11 Uhr sich in des Capellmeister Schüzens behausung versameln, alda nach dem albereit verfertigten Verzeichnüs in Ordnung stellen, und wenn die Schüler auferfahren über den neuen Marckt aufs Schloß gehen, hinter denen Herren Geistlichen bis uf den Schloßhof folgen, So balde nun der Process angehet, folget der Bassist denen 9. Marschallen, so den Process führen, und träget das Creucifix allezeit hier und zu Freÿberg im Process vor denen und darauf abermals die beÿden Capellmeister, sambt denen ihnen untergebenen Musicis, sowol verangehende Capellknaben, in guter Ordnung, in 2. und 2. in einem Gliede, biß in die Creuz Kirche, stille ohne singen in gebührenden Leide folgen, und daselbst an ihrer stelle unter wehrender Predigt beÿ der Sacristeÿ, auch hernach, biß der ganze Process aus der Kirchen verwarten, als dann aber mit stillem Leben ihren wege nach hause gehen.
> 2. Dienstages den Dritten Februarÿ sollen sie ingesambt frühe umb 6. Uhr sich in der Creuz Kirche beÿ der Schüler und Geistlichen wieder einstellen, aufwar-

ten, und als dann in angehenden Process wie voriges tages bis vor das Wilsdorfer Thor in den schmal Garten folgen, von dannen sie sambtlich mit denen Herren Geistlichen und andern wieder in die Stadt kehren und nur allein der Bassist mit nach Freÿberg reiset.

32. Ibid., fol. 291r.

Der Churf. Säcß. OberhofPredigers und Beicht Vaters, Herrn Dr. Jacob Wellers Anordnung. Was bey dem Herrn Capellmeister zu bestellen, daß er Verordnung thun solle.
a) Die sämbtl. Schloß Music puncto 6. frühe sich in der Schloß Kirche einfinde, den 2. Februarÿ
b) Gesetzte Lieder, wenn mit den Läuten aufgehöret, vor und nach der Predigt singen
c) Halbweg zwölf zu Mittag zur deduction in die Creuz Kirche sich hinwieder auf dem Schloß einstellen.
d) Den Tag drauf den 3. Februarÿ in der Creuz Kirchen vor 6. Uhr sich einfinden, und die Churfl. Leiche bis durch den Churfl. Garten begleiten, da Sie denn sich hinwieder nach Hause begeben können.

33. Ibid., fol. 312v.

Sollen den 2. Februarÿ Montags zu Mittags gegen 11. Uhr die 24. Trompeter, Keßellpaucker und die einigen, so die 2. KeßellPaucken tragen, in langen Trauer Mänteln im Churfl. Stalle erscheinen, derselbst auf andern der ihnen vorgeordneten Reitenden Cammerdiener, und des gefertigten Verzeichnüs sich in 2. Trouppen theilen, und ihnen nach bis vor das grüne Thor folgen. . . .

34. Ibid., fols. 213v–215r.

35. Weck, pp. 428–29.

36. Ralph Giesey, *The Royal Funeral in Renaissance France* (Geneva: Librairie E. Droz, 1960), preface.

37. See ibid. Also see Lou Taylor, *Mourning Dress: A Costume and Social History* (London: George Allen and Unwin, 1983), pp. 22–25.

38. *Begräbnis*, fols. 407r–408r.

39. Fürstenau, 1861 I, p. 136.

40. SAD OHMA B. no. 13/b, *Beylager Marggrafens zu Brandenburg, Herrn Christian Ernsts mit Churfürstens zu Sachßen Herrn Johann Georgens des andern Fräulein Tochter Fräul. Erdmuth Sophien*, fols. 750v–52r. See Fürstenau, 1861 I, pp. 136–37, and Becker-Glauch, "Peranda, Marco Gioseppe," *MGG*, vol. 10, col. 1033. The 1662 list is discussed later in this chapter and reproduced in its entirety in the appendix.

41. See Moser/Pfatteicher, *Heinrich Schütz*, p. 632.

42. *NSA* 31, pp. xii–xiii.

43. This document is mentioned by Moser/Pfatteicher, *Heinrich Schütz*, p. 211, but is previously unpublished.

44. One of Johann Georg II's compositions is cataloged as item number 1 in document 18.

45. Thomas J. Culley, *A Study of the Musicians Connected with the German College in Rome during the Seventeenth Century and of Their Activities in Northern Europe*, vol. 1 of *Jesuits and Music* (Rome: Jesuit Historical Institute, 1970), p. 216.

46. Ibid., p. 217.

47. Carl-Allan Moberg, "Vincenzo Albrici und das Kirchenkonzert. Ein Entwurf," *Natalicia musicologica Knud Jeppesen septuagenario collegis oblata*, eds. Bjørn Hjelmborg and Søren Sørensen (Oslo: Norsk Musikforlag, 1962), p. 202.

48. Carl-Allan Moberg, "Vincenzo Albrici (1631–1696): Eine biographische Skizze mit besonderer Berücksichtigung seiner schwedischen Zeit," *Festschrift Friedrich Blume zum 70. Geburtstag*, eds. Anna Amalie Abert and Wilhelm Pfannkuch (Kassel: Bärenreiter, 1963), p. 237. See Av Einar Sundström, "Notiser om drottning Kristinas italienska musiker," *Svensk Tidskrift för Musikforskning* 43 (1961), pp. 308–9, for a list of these musicians.

49. See later in this chapter for a discussion of the 1717 list, which is reproduced in its entirety in the appendix.

50. Fürstenau, 1861 I, p. 262.

51. Ibid., p. 160.

52. Moberg, "Vincenzo Albrici (1631–1696): Eine biographische Skizze," pp. 240–41.

53. Fürstenau, 1861 I, p. 143, and Moberg, "Vincenzo Albrici (1631–1696): Eine biographische Skizze," p. 240, note 40.

54. See appendix.

55. See J. A. Westrup, "Foreign Musicians in Stuart England," *Musical Quarterly* 27 (1941), pp. 70–98, and Margaret Mabbett, "Italian Musicians in Restoration England (1660–1690)," *Music and Letters* 67 (1986), pp. 237–43, for information on the Albricis' London activities.

56. SAD Loc. 8297. *Päße von reisende Personen*, 1634–93, fol. 61r.

57. Moberg, "Vincenzo Albrici (1636–1696): Eine biographische Skizze," p. 245.

58. Richard Engländer, "Zur Frage der *Dafne* (1671) von G. A. Bontempi und M. G. Peranda," *Acta Musicologica* 13 (1941), p. 74, note 27a.

59. SAD Loc. 8681 no. 6. 1662–67. See also Fürstenau, 1861 I, p. 11.

60. *Grundlage einer Ehren-Pforte* (1740), ed. Max Schneider (Graz: Akademische Druck-und Verlagsanstalt, 1969), p. 18.

61. Fürstenau, 1849, p. 73. The original list appears to be lost.

62. Wolfram Steude, "Peranda, Marco Gioseppe," *The New Grove*, vol. 14, p. 362.

63. Fürstenau, 1861 I, p. 15.

64. Ibid., pp. 11–12.

65. Ibid., p. 12.

66. Hans Schnoor, *Dresden: 400 Jahre Musikkultur. Zum Jubiläum der Staatskapelle und zur Geschichte der Dresdener Oper* (Dresden: Dresdener Verlagsgesellschaft [1948]), p. 63.

67. SAD OHMA O.IV. no. 21. *Hof-Journal* 1667. "Die Italiäner Dominico Melani und Bartolomeo Sorlisi haben in Ihren Neugebaueten Lust = Garten draussen in der Vorstadt ein Panquet angestellet, darzwischen eine Teütsche Comoedia oder vielmehr ein Festanspiel agiret worden."

68. Fürstenau, 1861 I, p. 13.

69. Ibid., p. 13.

70. Ibid., p. 14, note. See especially Martin Bernhard Lindau, *Geschichte der Haupt- und Residenzstadt Dresden*, 2 vols. (Dresden: Kuntz, 1859–63), pp. 144–47.

71. SAD Loc. 10293. *Reisen verschiedener Privat Personen.* 1522–1690, fols. 10–20. I am grateful to Matthias Herrmann of the Heinrich-Schütz-Archiv for showing me these letters.

72. SAD OHMA O.IV. no. 24. 1669.

73. Fürstenau, 1861 I, p. 14.

74. John Walter Hill, "Oratory Music in Florence, III: The Confraternities from 1655 to 1785," *Acta Musicologica* 58 (1986), pp. 139–40.

75. SAD Loc. 8682 no. 9. 1674–75.

76. Elvidio Surian, "Cherici, Sebastiano," *The New Grove*, vol. 4, p. 202.

77. Fürstenau, 1861 I, p. 147.

78. Sibylle Dahms, "Pallavicino, Carlo," *The New Grove*, vol. 14, pp. 141–42.

79. Fürstenau, 1849, p. 104.

80. Bernhard's contracts as alto (1649) and vice-Kapellmeister (1655) are previously unpublished.

81. This letter is published in its entirety in Ida Maria Lipsius, *Musikerbriefe aus fünf Jahrhunderten* (Leipzig: Breitkopf & Härtel, 1886), vol. 1, pp. 110–11. SAD Loc. 7287. *Einzelne Schriften. Kammersachen, insonderheit Besoldungsrückstände der Civil-Militär u. Hofdiener u. Bitten um deren Verabschiedung,* 1592–1677, fol. 204r.

Es werden sich Euere Churfl. Durchl. zweiffelsohne Gnädigst zu entsinnen wissen, wie das ich nunmehro im dritten Jahre Euere Churfl. Durchl. für einen Musicus und Altisten in dero HoffCapella und kammer Unterthänigst und fleißigst aufgewartet. In welcher Zeit ich denn mein vor diesem getriebenes Studium beÿ seiten gesetzen, umb das ich die Musica desto bässer excolieren, und Eurer Churfl. Durchl. contentieren möchte. Weilen aber ich vermercke das ietzige meine profession der Musica mir zu keiner mir anständigen beforderung behülfflich, ia auch nicht gnugsame mittel mich dabeÿ nur nothtürftiglich zu erhalten erwirket: Alß habe ich beÿ mir beschlossen, die profession der Musica hinfüro zu quittieren und hingegen durch wiederumb zur hand genomme Studia meinen aufenthalt und beförderung zu suchen. . . .

82. This letter is previously unpublished. SAD Loc. 7287. *Einzelne Schriften,* fol. 206r.

Wiewohlen ich auf vorgestern eingegebene meine Unterthänigste Supplication, von E. Churfl. Durchl., meine dimission zu erhalten gehoffet: so bin ich demnach dero Gnädigste resolution, biß auf des CapellMeisters ankunfft, in unterthänigkeit zu erwarten, wie schuldigst, also erbötig. Weilen aber des Capell-Meisters ankunfft sich noch etwas lange verziehen wird: und aber ich, annoch für gar zu starck hereinbrechender Kälte, gern eine reise nach Dantzig zu meinen Freunden thun wolte, umb mich mitt denselbigen wegen des Ortes, und der Mittel zu studieren, wie auch anderen angelegenheiten der noththurfft nach zu bereden. Alß gelanget an E. Churfl. Durchl. meine unterthänigste bitte, selbige wolle Gnädigst mich auf ein paar Monat beuhrlauben, umb selbigen reise zu vollbringen.

83.   This letter appears in Schäfer, "Geschichte der kurfürstlichen musikalischen Capelle," pp. 425–26, and Moritz Fürstenau, "Christoph Bernhard, kurfürstlich sächsischer Kapellmeister und Praeceptor der Prinzen Johann Georg IV. und Friedrich August I. von Sachsen," *Mitteilungen des königlichen sächsischen Altertumsverein* 16 (1866), p. 58. I am grateful to Joshua Rifkin for pointing out that Bernhard himself misdated this letter as 24 January 1651. See Joshua Rifkin and Colin Timms, "Heinrich Schütz," *The New Grove North European Baroque Masters* (New York: W. W. Norton, 1985), p. 51.

84.   1740 (Graz: Akademische Druck- und Verlagsanstalt, 1969), p. 18.

85.   See Bruno Grusnick, "Bernhard, Christoph," *MGG*, vol. 1, col. 1785.

86.   Fürstenau, 1861 I, p. 35, note *.

87.   Ibid., p. 149.

88.   Folkert Fiebig, *Christoph Bernhard und der stile moderno. Untersuchangen zu Leben und Werk* (Hamburg: Verlag der Musikalienhandlung Wagner, 1980), p. 40.

89.   Ibid., p. 49.

90.   Fürstenau, 1849, pp. 92–94. The original document seems to have been lost since that time. See also Eberhard Schmidt, *Der Gottesdienst am kurfürstlichen Hofe zu Dresden* (Göttingen: Vandenhoeck & Ruprecht, 1961), p. 166.

91.   See later in this chapter and chapter 4 for an analysis of this catalog.

92.   The Dresden court diaries are now in SLB and SAD. For characteristic diary entries, see chapter 4.

93.   See Eberhard Schmidt, *Der Gottesdienst,* p. 205.

94.   Ibid., pp. 166–67.

95.   One such rare occasion was recorded by a diarist on 23 December 1660, the fourth Sunday in Advent, when Bontempi and Albrici alternated conducting in the three worship services that day. SAD Loc. 10206. *Hof Diaria* 1650.

96.   Fürstenau, 1861 I, pp. 150–51.

97.   See Wolfram Steude, *NSA* 39, p. xiv.

98.   Fürstenau, 1861 I, p. 151. See also Fiebig, *Christoph Bernhard,* p. 51.

99.   Eberhard Schmidt, *Der Gottesdienst,* p. 200.

100.   Ibid., p. 169.

101. SAD Loc. 4384. *Churfürst Johann Georg des Ersten zu Sachsen, Absterben und Begräbnis. Ander Theil*, vol. 1.

102. Eberhard Schmidt, *Der Gottesdienst*, p. 169.

103. Ibid., p. 89, note 114.

104. This document is previously unpublished. Eberhard Schmidt proposes that while the order may have originated in conjunction with the consecration of the chapel, it seems more likely that it dates from 1667. See ibid., p. 89, note 114.

105. OHMA N. I. no. 6. *Ceremoniel bey Legung des Grundsteins zu Capelle in Moritzburg 1661 und bey Einweyung der Churfurstl. Hoff und Capelle . . .* fol. 13v. See Steude, foreword to *NSA* 39, p. xvi. See also chapter 3 concerning performance of this work at the consecration service in Zeitz in 1664.

106. Steude, *NSA* 39, p. xvii.

107. Wolfram Steude, "Die Markuspassion in der Leipziger Passionen-Handschrift des Johann Zacharias Grundig," *Deutsches Jahrbuch der Musikwissenschaft* 14 (1969), p. 103. The Matthew, Mark, Luke, and John Passions preserved in the manuscript copy of Johann Zacharias Grundig in the Musikbibliothek der Stadt Leipzig are available in facsimile edition by Wolfram Steude, Heinrich Schütz, Marco Gioseppe Peranda, *Passionsmusiken nach den Evangelisten Matthäus, Lukas, Johannes und Markus* (Leipzig: Zentralantiquariat der Deutschen Demokratischen Republik, 1981).

108. Steude, "Die Markuspassion," pp. 96–116.

109. Ibid.

110. Moser/Pfatteicher, *Heinrich Schütz*, p. 679.

111. Steude, *Passionsmusiken*, p. 8, no. 3. Schütz's *opus ultimum* is available as *NSA* 39 edited by Wolfram Steude, who rediscovered the work in SLB. See also Wolfram Steude, "Das wiedergefundene Opus ultimum von Heinrich Schütz. Bemerkungen zur Quelle und zum Werk," *Schütz-Jahrbuch* 4/5 (1982–83), pp. 9–18.

112. Hans Schnoor, *Dresden: 400 Jahre Musikkultur. Zum Jubiläum der Staatskapelle und zur Geschichte der Dresdener Oper* (Dresden: Dresdener Verlagsgesellschaft [1948]), p. 33.

113. See both Becker-Glauch, *Dresdener Hoffeste*, and Schnoor, *Dresden*, for a discussion of these sources and for reproductions.

114. Werner Braun, "Zur Gattungsproblematik des Singballetts," *Gattung und Werk in der Musikgeschichte Norddeutschlands und Skandinaviens*, vol. 26 of *Kieler Schriften zur Musikwissenschaft*, eds. Friedhelm Krummacher and Heinrich W. Schwab (Kassel: Bärenreiter, 1982), p. 45.

115. Becker-Glauch, *Dresdener Hoffeste*, p. 70.

116. Fürstenau, I 1861, pp. 96–134, 204–68.

117. Werner Breig, "Höfische Festmusik im Werk von Heinrich Schütz," *Höfische Festkultur in Braunschweig-Wolfenbüttel 1590–1666*, ed. Jörg Jochen Berns, vol. 10, no. 4 (1981) of *Daphnis. Zeitschrift für Mittlere Deutsche Literatur*, p. 714.

118. Ibid., p. 715.

119. Rifkin and Timms, "Heinrich Schütz," p. 47.

120. Richard Engländer, "Zur Frage der *Dafne* (1671), von G. A. Bontempi und M. G. Peranda," *Acta Musicologica* 13 (1941), p. 60.

121. Becker-Glauch, *Dresdener Hoffeste*, p. 74, and Richard Engländer, "Die erste italienische Oper in Dresden: Bontempis *Il Paride in Musica* (1662)," *Svensk Tidskrift för Musikforskning* 43 (1961), p. 125. Microfilm copy of the 1662 print in Gdansk, Biblioteka Polskiej Akademii Nauk, at the University of Illinois. See RISM entry for other locations.

122. Engländer suggests that the music was the result of collaboration of Moniglia and P. A. Ziani, who had come to Dresden as a guest from Vienna to conduct his own music that same year and had composed his own *Teseo* for a 1658 performance in Venice. See "Die erste italienische Oper," p. 132.

123. "Zur Frage der *Dafne*," p. 60.

124. A print of *Apollo und Daphne* is in the Sächsische Landesbibliothek in Dresden. The music to *Jupiter und Jo* is lost.

125. *Ein deutsches Opernballett des 17. Jahrhunderts, ein Beitrag zur Frühgeschichte der deutschen Oper* (Leipzig: Frommhold & Wendler, 1931), a study based on a manuscript version of the work in SLB as Ms. SLB B44a.

126. This document is previously unpublished.

127. SAD Loc. 7287. *Einzelne Schriften, Kammersachen*, 1592–1677, fol. 216v. See also Erich H. Müller, *GBS*, p. 317. "Inhalts des, vor diesen ergangenen gnedigsten befehlichs, seind nachfolgende quittungen so u des Capellmeisters, Herrn Heinrich Schüzens besoldungs zulage, eingerichtet, beÿ der Churf. Sächß. RenthCammer künftig in Zurechnung hinwiederumb anzunehmen, alß...."

128. Erich H. Müller, *GBS*, nos. 112 and 113.

129. Ibid., no. 114.

130. See Moser/Pfatteicher, *Heinrich Schütz*, p. 212, note 118.

131. SAD OHMA O. IV. no. 29. *Hof-Journal*. 1672. "Nachmittag um 4. Uhr hat der alte Churfl. Capellmeister Heinrich Schüze, durch ein Seel. ende, sein in Dreßd. geendigete, seines alters 87 Jahr 4. Wochen 19 3/4 Stund. Ist gebohren den 8. Octobr 3/4 auf 9. uhr des abends Ao 1585."

132. Translated by Robin Leaver and Martin Franzmann, "The Funeral Sermon for Heinrich Schütz," *Bach*, vol. 5/2 (1974), pp. 26–28. Facsimile edition ed. by Dietrich Berke, Martin Geier, *Kurtze Beschreibung Des (Tit.) Herrn Heinrich Schützens/Chur Fürstl. Sächs. ältern Capellmeisters/geführten müheseeligen Lebens-Lauff* (Kassel, Basel: Bärenreiter, 1972).

133. Johann Mattheson, *Grundlage einer Ehren-Pforte* (1740), ed. Max Schneider (Graz: Akademische Druck- und Verlangsanstalt, 1969), p. 323. See also Moser/Pfatteicher, *Heinrich Schütz*, p. 223, and Fürstenau, 1861 I, p. 238. "Mein Sohn, er hat mir einen grossen Gefallen erwiesen durch Ubersendung der verlangten Motete. Ich weiß keine Note darin zu verbessern."

134. Fürstenau, 1861 I, pp. 254–56. The complete list appears in the appendix.

135. This list is reproduced in the appendix.

136. Compare with Becker-Glauch's table, *Dresdener Hoffeste,* pp. 18–19. Because her information is compiled from Fürstenau, the table is inaccurate.

137. Steude, "Das wiedergefundene Opus ultimum," p. 16. See pp. 17–18 for a list of Schütz's late works.

138. "new gemacht."

139. Steude, "Das wiedergefundene Opus ultimum," p. 17, no. 36.

140. Rifkin, "Towards a New Image," p. 720.

141. Eva Linfield, "A New Look at the Sources of Schütz's *Christmas History,*" *Schütz-Jahrbuch* 4/5 (1982/83), p. 19.

142. George Buelow, *A Schütz Reader: Documents of Performance Practice, Journal of the American Choral Foundation, Inc.* 27, no. 4 (October 1985), p. 8. I am grateful to Werner Breig for calling this point to my attention.

143. *Vespers at St. Marks: Music of Alessandro Grandi, Giovanni Rovetta and Francesco Cavalli,* 2 vols. (Ann Arbor: UMI, 1981).

144. Ibid., pp. 98–99.

145. SAD Loc. 8687. *Kantoreiordnung,* fol. 53. Schütz's list is reproduced in Erich H. Müller, *GBS,* no. 21.

146. Translated in Heinrich Schütz, *Musikalische Exequien,* vol. 8 of the *Stuttgarter Schütz-Ausgabe* (Neuhausen-Stuttgart: Hänssler-Verlag, 1973), p. xxxi. For the letter in its entirety, see Hans Rudolf Jung, "Ein neuaufgefundenes Gutachten von Heinrich Schütz aus dem Jahre 1617," *Archiv für Musikwissenschaft* 18 (1961), pp. 241–47, and Jung's commentary on the document in "Ein unbekanntes Gutachten von Heinrich Schütz über die Neuordnung der Hof-, Schul- und Stadtmusik in Gera," *Beiträge zur Musikwissenschaft* 4 (1962), pp. 17–36.

147. *NSA* 38, p. xxix.

148. Moser/Pfatteicher, *Heinrich Schütz,* p. 580.

149. Buelow, *A Schütz Reader,* pp. 29–30.

150. *NSA* 39, pp. xiv–xv. For a facsimile reproduction of this inscription, see *NSA* 28, p. xxi.

151. Weck, pp. 201–2.

152. *NSA* 39, p. xv.

153. The part is shown in facsimile in *NSA* 32, p. xx.

154. Gerhard Kirchner, *Der Generalbass bei Heinrich Schütz* (Kassel: Bärenreiter, 1960), p. 29.

155. Ibid., p. 18.

156. Buelow, *A Schütz Reader,* p. 9.

157. See J. Michele Edwards, "Schütz's *violone,*" forthcoming in the symposium proceedings for the 1985 International Heinrich Schütz Conference and Festival. I am grateful to the author for sharing her manuscript.

158. Buelow, *A Schütz Reader*, p. 21.

159. Kirchner, *Generalbass*, p. 29.

160. Ibid., p. 23.

161. Michael Praetorius, *Syntagma musicum III* (1619), facsimile edition by Wilibald Gurlitt (Kassel, Basel: Bärenreiter, 1958), p. 168.

162. Kirchner, *Generalbass*, p. 26.

163. *NSA* 3, p. 4.

164. See Kirchner, *Generalbass*, pp. 23–27. Other works by Schütz calling for lutes are SWV 47, 467, 474, 477, and 500.

Chapter 2

1. Heinrich Sievers, *Hannoversche Musikgeschichte. Dokumente, Kritiken und Meinungen* (Tutzing: Hans Schneider, 1979), p. 38, and Sievers, *Die Musik in Hannover* (Hanover: Sponholtz, 1961), p. 43, and Moser/Pfatteicher, *Heinrich Schultz*, pp. 83–85.

2. Sievers, *Die Musik in Hannover*, pp. 42–43.

3. Sievers, *Hannoversche Musikgeschichte*, p. 49.

4. Ibid., pp. 44 and 52.

5. Ibid., pp. 52–53.

6. Jost Harro Schmidt, "Heinrich Schützens Beziehungen zu Celle: ein Beitrag zur Schütz Biographie," *Archiv für Musikwissenschaft* 23 (1966), pp. 274–76.

7. Heinrich Sievers, "Die Orgel der ehemaligen Schloßkapelle zu Wolfenbüttel. Beitrag zur Geschichte der Kirchenmusik in Wolfenbüttel," *Jahrbuch des Braunschweigischen Geschichtsvereins*, series 2, vol. 5 (1933), p. 101.

8. Martin Ruhnke, "Wolfenbüttel," *MGG*, vol. 14, col. 803.

9. Sievers, *Die Musik in Hannover*, p. 26.

10. For a history of this church, see Gustav Spies, "Geschichte der Hauptkirche B.M.V. in Wolfenbüttel," vol. 7 of *Quellen und Forschungen zur Braunschweigischen Geschichte* (Wolfenbüttel: Julius Zwisslers Verlag, 1914).

11. Hans Joachim Kunst, "Die Marienkirche in Wolfenbüttel eine Siegkirche?" *Höfische Festkultur in Braunschweig-Wolfenbüttel 1590–1666*, ed. Jörg Jochen Berns, vol. 10, no. 4 (1981) of *Daphnis. Zeitschrift für Mittlere Deutsche Literatur*.

12. The view to the west is also reproduced in Werner Braun, *Die Musik des 17. Jahrhunderts* (Wiesbaden: Akademische Verlagsgesellschaft Athenaion, 1981), vol. 4 of *Neues Handbuch der Musikwissenschaft*, ed. Carl Dahlhaus, p. 190.

13. See Friedrich Chrysander, "Geschichte der Braunschweig-Wolfenbüttelschen Capelle und Oper vom 16. bis zum 18. Jahrhunderts," *Jahrbücher für musikalische Wissenschaft* 1 (1863), pp. 153–55.

14. Ruhnke, "Wolfenbüttel," col. 803.

15. Wilibald Gurlitt, "Der kursächsische Hoforgelmacher Gottfried Fritzsche," *Festschrift Arnold Schering zum 60. Geburtstage* (Berlin: A. Glas, 1937), p. 110.

16. Ibid., p. 116.

17. Uwe Pape, *Die Orgeln der Stadt Wolfenbüttel* (Berlin: Verlag U. Pape, 1973), pp. 4–7 and 10–11.

18. Ibid., p. 9.

19. Ibid., pp. 51–52.

20. Ruhnke, "Wolfenbüttel," col. 807.

21. Martin Bircher, "Der Gelehrte als Herrscher. Der Hof von Wolfenbüttel," vol. 1 of *Europäische Hofkultur im 16. und 17. Jahrhundert. Kongreß des Wolfenbüttler Arbeitskreises für Renaissanceforschung und des Internationalen Arbeitskreises für Barockliteratur* (Hamburg: Dr. Ernst Hauswedell & Co., 1981), p. 110.

22. Walter Haacke, "Gambenspiel am Hofe August der Jüngere zu Wolfenbüttel," *Zeitschrift für Musik* 111 (1950), p. 585.

23. Ruhnke, "Wolfenbüttel," col. 804; Haacke, "Gambenspiel," p. 585; Siegfried Fornaçon, "Sophie Elisabeth," *MGG*, vol. 12, col. 919.

24. Sievers, *250 Jahre Braunschweigisches Staatstheater (1690–1940)* (Brunswick: Verlag E. Appelhans, 1941), pp. 28–30. Hans-Gert Roloff, however, in "Absolutismus und Hoftheater. Das Freudenspiel der Herzogin Sophie Elisabeth zu Braunschweig-Wolfenbüttel," *Höfische Festkultur*, p. 739, states that Sophie Elisabeth's presence in Kassel has never been proven.

25. The painting is reproduced in Haacke, "Gambenspiel," and Braun, *Die Musik des 17. Jahrhunderts*, p. 268.

26. Jörg Jochen Berns, "Trionfo-Theater am Hof von Braunschweig-Wolfenbüttel," *Höfische Festkultur*, p. 684.

27. NSAW 100 N 250, fols. unnumbered. "das er allemahl zu Sont: und Feyertagen, oder wan es sonsten beÿ Trawung oder Hochzeiten die Notturfft erfodert daß Gottesdienstes vleißig abwarten, und sich nach gelegenheit, so wohl im Choral alß anmuhtigen und der Zeit bequemen Figural stucken unverdroßen hören laßen. . . ."

28. NSAW 100 N 250, fols. unnumbered.

29. NSAW 1 Alt 25 no. 293, fol. 2. Chrysander, "Geschichte," p. 155.

30. NSAW 1 Alt 25 no. 293, fol. 2. Partially reproduced in Chrysander, "Geschichte," pp. 156–57.

31. NSAW 1 Alt 25 no. 293, fol. 3r. "zumahle auch solches allwege beÿ den voriegen Fürst, vndt Herrn Hochseel. angedenckens also gehalten worden, vndt daß Kostgeldt beÿ Ietziegen schwierigen Zeitten ohne dieß geringe ist." Chrysander, "Geschichte," refers to this letter on p. 157.

32. NSAW 1 Alt 25 no. 293, fol. 3v. "Persöhnlich nacher Hamburgk vndt Lübeck Vorfügen vndt ohne allen Zweifell gutte Wolgeübte Instrumentalisten bekommen, die Vocalisten aber Weill daran ein grosser vnterschied vndt leicht nicht also qualifi-

ciret daß sie beÿdes Woll praesentiren können, zufinden. . . ." Chrysander, "Geschichte," refers to this letter on p. 157.

33. Not 12 January 1638 as given erroneously by Chrysander, "Geschichte," p. 157. NSAW 3 Alt 461, fol. 3r.

> daß er uns behueff des Gottesdienstes In der Kirchen, wie auch zu aufwartung vor unserer f. Taffel in unserm Gemache Gott dem allerhochsten zu sonderm Lob und ehren, und dann uns und den unsern zur recreation eine Ausbündige gute Capellen anrichten vnd dero behuef außerlesenen Außbündige Musicos welche sich nicht allein vf allerhandt Musicalische Instrumenta verstehen und dieselbe zur Lieblichkeit zugebrauchen wißen, in vnsren namen hin vnd wieder sich bewerben. . . .

This passage appears in Chrysander, "Geschichte," p. 157.

34. NSAW 3 Alt 461, fol. 3r.

> Als Einem Altisten welcher zugleich ein Instrumentalis Musica 120 thlr deßgleichen einem Tenorist so zugleich vff dem Pandor auch ein Instrumentalis—120 thlr Einen Bassisten der nebenst des Bass auch Instrumentaliter den Bassum gebrauchen vnd des Choralistenstelle mit vertretten vnd die Knaben in literis informieren könne: die Gr. Geigen zugleich mit woll streich od. sonst— 100 thlr Einen guten Violonist so vieleicht ein guten Lautenist daneb.—140 thlr Einen Cornet vnd Violisten—120 thlr Dulcian vnd Fagottist—120 thlr. . . .

Körner's list appears in Chrysander, "Geschichte," p. 156, as discussed earlier in this chapter.

35. NSAW 3 Alt 461, fols. 6–8. Not 24 January 1638, as in Chrysander, "Geschichte," p. 157.

36. Fair copy for Colerus's contract, NSAW 1 Alt 25 no. 296, fols. 2–4, dated 2 May 1663. All three contracts are previously unpublished. See later in this chapter and chapter 4 for more on Löwe.

37. In England and Ireland these musician-watchmen were known as the town "waits." In Germany the *Türmer* were members of the *Stadtpfeifer*. See Don L. Smithers, *The Music and History of the Baroque Trumpet before 1721* (London: J. M. Dent & Sons Ltd., 1973), pp. 116–31.

38. NSAW 3 Alt 503, fol. 12r.

> auf unserm Schloße, vndt dehme darauf erbauten thurme, nebenst 4. düchtigen, vndt in der Music erfahrnen gesellen. . . . zuweile auch, auf erfoderenten nachfall, vnserer Music: aufm Schloße oder sonsten in der HoffCapellen, mit seinen musicalischen Instrumenten, nebenst seinen gesellen, beÿwohnen. . . . Deßgleichen auch d. spielen beÿ hochzeiten, Kindtauffen vndt andern Convivÿs. . . . so wohl in Wolfenbüttel, alß auch in den gantzen ambt Wolfenbüttel, aufm lande mit musicalischen vndt andern Instrumenten vor sich vndt mit seinen gesellen allein. . . . Er soll aber allemahl wan er sich zu derogleichen hochzeiten vndt gastungen gebrauchen leßt, zum wenigsten einen gesellen aufm Schloßthurm laßen. . . .

This document is previously unpublished.

39. Ronald Gobiet, ed., *Der Briefwechsel zwischen Philipp Hainhofer und Herzog August der Jüngere von Braunschweig-Lüneburg* (Munich: Bavarian National Museum, 1984), p. 666.

40. Ibid., pp. 670 and 689–90.

41. NSAW 1 Alt 25 no. 293, fol. 11r.

42. NSAW 1 Alt 25 no. 293, fol. 13r.

43. NSAW 1 Alt 22 no. 225. Scheidt's letter appears in Chrysander, "Geschichte," p. 158. The madrigals are lost while the sinfonias were published in 1644 dedicated to Duke August of Saxe-Halle, where Scheidt was Kapellmeister. See Kerala Johnson Snyder, "Scheidt, Samuel," *The New Grove*, vol. 16, p. 605.

44. NSAW 1 Alt 25 no. 303, fol. 1r. "waß maßen mir von gutter handt auß Braunschweig berichtet, daß Ihr fürstl. Gnade zu Wolfenbüttel ohnlengst ihren Capellmeister, und dero andere Musicanten abgeancket, wobeÿ uff künftigen Sommer (:geliebts Gott:) etliche sehr gutte leute wieder zu bestellen. . . ."

45. NSAW 1 Alt 25 no. 293, fol. 8r.

46. NSAW 17 III Alt 87, fol. 33v.

47. Ruhnke, "Wolfenbüttel," cols. 803–4.

48. Friedrich Thöne, *Wolfenbüttel. Geist und Glanz einer alten Residenz* (Munich: Bruckmann, 1963), p. 97.

49. Ibid., p. 99.

50. Ibid., p. 98.

51. Ibid., p. 100.

52. I am grateful to Joshua Rifkin for information regarding the whereabouts of this letter, which is in the Pierpont Morgan Library in New York. The letter was discovered by Moser and it appears in its entirety in Moser/Pfatteicher, *Heinrich Schütz*, pp. 156–57.

53. Jörg Jochen Berns, "'Theatralische neue Vorstellung von der Maria Magdalena.' Ein Zeugnis für die Zusammenarbeit von Justus Georg Schottelius und Heinrich Schütz," *Schütz-Jahrbuch* 2 (1980), p. 120.

54. Ibid.

55. Erich H. Müller, *GBS*, no. 54.

56. Ibid., no. 57.

57. Martin Geier, *Kurtze Beschreibung Des (Tit.) Herrn Heinrich Schützens . . . Lebens-Lauff*. Facsimile edition by Dietrich Berke (Kassel: Bärenreiter, 1972), fol. 2v. See also chapter 1.

58. Sievers, *Die Musik in Hannover*, p. 43, and Rifkin and Timms, "Heinrich Schütz," pp. 32–33.

59. Chrysander, "Geschichte," p. 159.

60. Hans Haase, "Nachtrag zu einer Schütz-Ausstellung," *Sagittarius* 4 (1973), p. 88, note 6.

61. Chrysander, "Geschichte," p. 160.

62. Erich H. Müller, *GBS*, no. 55.

63. NSAW 17 III Alt 87, fol. 34r.

64. NSAW 3 Alt 461, fol. 19r. "d. Music mit d. Stimme od. vf and. musicalisch Instrten, Orgel Positiv vnd derogleich vndthenig willig vffwarten. . . ."

65. NSAW 3 Alt 461, fol. 21.

66. NSAW 3 Alt 461, fol. 22r. "Benedictus Höfern in unsrer Fl. Capellen fur einen Musicanten und Hofforganisten nun an die 3. Jahr trewlich vnd fleissig aufgewartet. . . ."

67. NSAW 1 Alt 25 no. 299, fol. 5.

68. NSAW 1 Alt 25 no. 299, fol. 2r.

69. NSAW 3 Alt 461, fol. 19r.

70. NSAW 3 Alt 448, fol. 2r. "Ich werde es auch nicht lang mehr aushalten können, wo sonst ich nicht gar zum betler werden. . . ."

71. NSAW 3 Alt 448, fols. 212–13.

72. NSAW 1 Alt 25 no. 299, fols. 28v and 35r.

73. Teubener's appointment is dated 24 June 1646, NSAW 3 Alt 461, fol. 29.

74. NSAW 17 III Alt 95, fols. 14, 27v–28r, 34v–38r. This list is previously unpublished.

75. NSAW 3 Alt 461, fol. 32.

76. NSAW 4 Alt 19 vorl. no. 4864, fol. 1.

77. This treaty between the emperor and the Guelf dukes promised the return of Wolfenbüttel, which had been in the hands of the emperor since 1627. See Joseph Leighton, "Die literarische Tätigkeit der Herzogin Sophie Elisabeth von Braunschweig-Lüneburg," *Europäische Hofkultur*, p. 484.

78. Several of the engravings are reproduced in Heinrich Sievers, *250 Jahre*, pp. 31–35. See also Berns, "Trionfo-Theater am Hof von Braunschweig-Wolfenbüttel," *Höfische Festkultur*, pp. 689–90.

79. Joseph Leighton, "Deutschsprachige Geburtstagsdichtungen für Herzog August d.J. von Braunschweig-Lüneburg," *Höfische Festkultur*, p. 764.

80. Two prints exist in HAB. See Wolfgang Schmieder and Gisela Hartwieg, *Musik. Alte Drucke bis etwa 1750*. Vols. 12 and 13 of *Kataloge der Herzog-August-Bibliothek Wolfenbüttel* (Frankfurt am Main: Vittorio Klostermann, 1967), vol. 1, pp. 316–17.

81. Hans-Gert Roloff, "Absolutismus und Hoftheater. Das Freudenspiel der Herzogin Sophie Elisabeth zu Braunschweig-Wolfenbüttel," *Höfische Festkultur*, p. 736.

82. Hans-Gert Roloff, "Die höfischen Maskeraden der Sophie Elisabeth, Herzogin zu Braunschweig-Lüneburg," *Europäische Hofkultur*, pp. 489–96.

83. The music of this Singspiel is lost.

84. Roloff, "Die höfischen Maskeraden der Sophie Elisabeth," *Europäische Hofkultur*, pp. 490–91.

85. James Haar, "Astral Music in Seventeenth-Century Nuremberg: The 'Tugend-sterne' of Harsdörffer and Staden," *Musica Disciplina* 16 (1962), p. 175. See also Robert Eitner, "Das älteste bekannte deutsche Singspiel Seelewig," *Monatshefte für Musikgeschichte* 13 (1881), pp. 55–147, for a modern edition.

86. Harsdörffer was a member of the Fruit-Bearing Society as well as the German-Minded Society (*Deutschgesinnte Genossenschaft*) and was cofounder with Johann Klaj of the Society of the Pegnitz Shepherds or the Pegnitz Flower-Order (*Pegnitzer Hirtengesellschaft* or *Pegnisischer Blumenorden*) in 1644. The Pegnitz Flower-Order was based in Nuremberg and included among its members Schottelius and Anton Ulrich, Duke August's son. See Karl F. Otto, *Die Sprachgesellschaften des 17. Jahrhunderts* (Stuttgart: J. B. Metzlersche Verlagsbuchhandlung, 1972), p. 46.

87. Frederick Lehmeyer, *The Singspiele of Anton Ulrich von Braunschweig* (Ph.D. diss., Berkeley, 1971), p. 102.

88. Ibid., p. 117.

89. NSAW 3 Alt 448, fol. 217.

90. Ingrid Brainard, "Der Höfische Tanz. Darstellende Kunst und Höfische Repräsentation," *Europäische Hofkultur*, p. 381.

91. Werner Breig, "Höfische Festmusik im Werk von Heinrich Schütz," *Höfische Festkultur*, pp. 711–33.

92. This letter appears in Chrysander, "Geschichte," p. 161.

93. NSAW 3 Alt 461, fol. 34.

     alle fest: und Sonntage beÿ verrichtungs deß Gottesdienstes, wie auch sonsten beÿ: und vor unserer furstl. Taffeln in anwesenheit frembder Herrschafften, oder deren Abgesandten und sonsten unter andern seinen Cameraden auffwarten und sich mit allerhand Musicalischen Instrumenten, wie dieselbe nehmen haben mügen, und Er darauff gelernet, auch Vocal Musica, allermahl auff unser erfordern praesentiren. . . .

     Wilcke's contract is previously unpublished. He is named by Chrysander, "Geschichte," p. 182.

94. Erich H. Müller, *GBS*, no. 94. Sophie Elisabeth's penned sketch is previously unpublished.

95. Ibid., no. 96.

96. This contract is previously unpublished.

97. This letter is previously unpublished.

98. Erich H. Müller, *GBS*, no. 97.

99. This letter is previously unpublished.

100. NSAW 3 Alt 461, fol. 37.

101. Erich H. Müller, *GBS*, no. 66.

102. Ibid., no. 99.

103. Documents 16, 17, 19, and 20, which are all pages from Duke August's account books, are previously unpublished.

104. NSAW 1 Alt 25 no. 294, fol. 18.

105. Moser/Pfatteicher, *Heinrich Schütz*, p. 206.

106. Rifkin and Timms, "Heinrich Schütz," p. 60. The letter is reproduced in Ferdinand Saffe, "Wolfenbüttler Komponisten des 17. Jahrhunderts," *Mitteilungen des Universitätsbundes Göttingen* 2,2 (1921), pp. 74–75.

107. I am grateful to Joshua Rifkin for this information.

108. Erich H. Müller, *GBS*, no. 106.

109. NSAW 17 III Alt 99, fol. 32v.

110. NSAW 17 III Alt 99, fol. 53v.

111. Earliest available contract dated 26 April 1660, NSAW 3 Alt 461, fol. 41.

112. NSAW 17 III Alt 99, fols. 32r–33v, 76v.

113. Saffe, "Wolfenbüttler Komponisten des 17. Jahrhunderts," p. 81.

114. Chrysander, "Geschichte," p. 182.

115. NSAW 1 Alt 25 no. 295, fol. 5. Also in Chrysander, "Geschichte," p. 182.

116. Hans Haase, *Heinrich Schütz (1585–1672) in seinen Beziehungen zum Wolfenbüttler Hof*. Exhibition catalog of the Herzog-August-Bibliothek, no. 8 (Peine: Druckhaus A. Schlaeger, 1972), p. 13.

117. I am grateful to Joshua Rifkin for this information and to Jennie Rathbun of the Houghton Reading Room for a description of the volume.

118. Erich H. Müller, *GBS*, no. 110.

119. Horst Walter, "Ein unbekanntes Schütz-Autograph in Wolfenbüttel," *Musicae scientiae collectanea: Festschrift Karl Gustav Fellerer*, ed. Heinrich Hüschen (Cologne: Arno Volk, 1973), pp. 621–22.

120. Haase, "Nachtrag," p. 93.

121. Ibid., p. 95. See also Schmieder and Hartwieg, *Kataloge*, vol. 1, pp. 301–6.

122. Appointment dated 25 July 1659, NSAW 3 Alt 461, fol. 43. Listed as choirboy in 1645, NSAW 17 Alt 94, fol. 16v.

123. Appointment dated 3 May 1665, NSAW 3 Alt 461, fol. 58.

124. Appointment dated 9 May 1665, NSAW 3 Alt 461, fol. 53.

125. Appointment dated 26 January 1663, NSAW 3 Alt 461, fol. 49.

126. NSAW 17 III Alt 100, fols. 42r–43v, 67.

127. *SGA* I, p. xxviii.

128. Eva Linfield, "A New Look at the Sources of Schütz's *Christmas History*," *Schütz-Jahrbuch* 4/5 (1982/83), pp. 19–20.

Chapter 3

1. Erich H. Müller, *GBS*, no. 108.

2. SAD Loc. 8563. *Correspondenz Johann Georg II mit Wilhelm Hz. v. Sachsen-Weimar.* 1655–60, fols. 801–2.

3. Ibid., fols. 803–4.

4. SAW Abteilung A. VII. 2b, fol. 83r.

5. For Schütz's other known visits to Weimar, see Adolf Aber, *Die Pflege der Musik unter den Wettinern und wettinischen Ernstinern* (Bückeburg, Leipzig: Siegel, 1921).

6. Karl August Müller, *Kurfürst Johann Georg der Erste*, p. 234.

7. "Neues zum Thema 'Heinrich Schütz und Weimar,'" *Schütz-Jahrbuch* 9 (1987), pp. 105–15. See pp. 110–11 for a description of the ceremony.

8. SAW Abteilung A. VII. 2b, fol. 135r. "Sonnabt den 29 Julÿ, ist der Kapell. Schütz von Weissenfelß anhero kommen."

9. Ibid., fol. 136r.

10. I wish to thank Wolfram Steude for suggesting the connection between Schütz's presence in Weimar and Duke Moritz.

11. See chapter 2 for more on Löwe in Wolfenbüttel.

12. SAD Loc. 33344. 1949. *Registratura über das 10te Bestallungs Buch*, no. 76. Thieme's appointment in Dresden is dated 1 June 1650.

13. Published in Arno Werner, *Städtische und fürstliche Musikpflege in Zeitz bis zum Anfang des 19. Jahrhunderts* (Bückeburg and Leipzig: C. F. W. Siegel, 1922), p. 64. The documents cited by Werner are found in SAM A29 d, nos. 18 and 19. These materials were unfortunately not available at the time of this study.

14. Ludwig Sulz's appointment is found in SAD Loc. 33345. 1953. *Registratura . . .* 1652–56, fol. 410, dated 20 December 1655. See also chapter 1.

15. This letter appears in Werner, *Städtische und fürstliche Musikpflege*, pp. 63–64.

16. Erich H. Müller, *GBS*, no. 109.

17. Ibid., no. 115.

18. For more on this register and Tafelmusik, see chapter 4.

19. SAD Loc. 8682. no. 10. *Hof Diaria* 1676, fol. 88r.

Als ich die beÿ Unserer wahren Religion Augspurgischer Confession übliche Kirchen gesänge an D. Cornelÿ Beckers Psalmen und andern geistreichen Liedern, wie solche auch in meiner Hoff Capella alhier pflegen gesungen zu werden, mit ihren Melodeÿen unter Discant und Basso sambt denen gewöhnlichen Kirchen gebehten wieder aufpflugen, und in diesem deütlichen truck und forma herauß geben laßen, habe ich E. Lbd. ein paar exemplaria darvon wohlmeinende zusenden wollen.

20. Werner, *Städtische und fürstliche Musikpflege*, p. 71.

21. For a condensed version of the consecration service, see ibid., pp. 73–74.

22. Ibid., p. 73.

23. Moser/Pfatteicher, *Heinrich Schütz*, p. 218.

24. Rifkin and Timms, "Heinrich Schütz," p. 65.

25. Wolfram Steude, foreword to Heinrich Schütz, *Der Schwanengesang*, NSA 39 (Kassel: Bärenreiter, 1984), pp. xvi–xvii.

26. Werner, *Städtische und fürstliche Musikpflege*, p. 74.

27. SAM A29d, no. 19, fols. 5–7. This document is mentioned by Werner but is unpublished.

28. *Fürstl. S. Capellordnung zur Moritzburg an der Elster*. For the complete statute, see Werner, *Städtische und fürstliche Musikpflege*, pp. 67–71.

29. See chapter 1 for more on the Dresden order.

30. Moser defines *musicaliter* or *figuraliter* as concepts signifying polyphonic performance and *choraliter* as simpler music. "The distinction is made between *choral* Sundays and *figural* Sundays, that is, Sundays on which there was simple music and Sundays on which there was polyphonic music" (Moser/Pfatteicher, *Heinrich Schütz*, p. 216). Eberhard Schmidt, *Der Gottesdienst*, p. 206, suggests that *choraliter* could mean a plainer style of polyphony, or even unaccompanied, or that the church music would be performed by the choir in which the choir could perform polyphonically and with instruments.

31. Löwe states in a letter dated 28 November 1664 to Privy Chamberlain Johann Heinrich Menio that at most courts the Kapellmeister directs the vocal Tafelmusik and the concertmaster the instrumental Tafelmusik. See Werner, *Städtische und fürstliche Musikpflege*, p. 76.

32. Werner, ibid., p. 83.

33. Ibid., pp. 66 and 74–78. Werner describes the quarrel between Löwe and Thieme in detail.

Chapter 4

1. See Moritz Fürstenau, "Churfürstliche Sechsische Cantoreiordnung (1555)," *Monatshefte für Musikgeschichte* 9 (1877), pp. 235–46.

2. This order is published in Arthur Kern, *Deutsche Hofordnungen des 16. und 17. Jahrhunderts*, 2 vols. (Berlin: Weidmannsche Buchhandlung, 1905), pp. 66–79.

3. Eberhard Schmidt, *Der Gottesdienst*, p. 32.

4. Ibid., pp. 162–63.

5. See chapter 1.

6. Document 13. Another undated order in SAD OHMA N. I. no. 8, *Ordnung wie es an hohen Fest- und Sonntägen auch in der Wochen in der Residentz Dreßden gehalten werden solle,* contains similar but less specific information.

7. Eberhard Schmidt, *Der Gottesdienst,* p. 165.

8. Ibid., p. 164.

9. Ibid., p. 165.

10. Ibid., p. 164.

11. Ibid., p. 165, note 35. See Praetorius, *Syntagma musicum III,* p. 135.

12. Eberhard Schmidt, *Der Gottesdienst,* p. 165.

13. Ibid., p. 152.

14. Ibid., pp. 165–66.

15. See chapter 1.

16. Eberhard Schmidt, *Der Gottesdienst,* pp. 168–75.

17. Ibid., p. 171. "domit S. Churf. Gn. Ihre Music bey den frembden Ehre und rhum habenn mögenn."

18. Loss's entire letter appears in Wilhelm Schäfer, "Heinrich Schütz," *Sachsenchronik* 1 (1854), p. 501. This passage is translated in Moser/Pfatteicher, *Heinrich Schütz,* p. 89.

19. Translated in Rifkin, "Towards a New Image," p. 656.

20. Eberhard Schmidt, *Der Gottesdienst,* p. 169.

21. SAD Loc. 8687. *Kantoreiordnung,* fol. 271v.

> Wiewohl nun, Gnädigster Churfürst und Herr, dem Capellmeister Schützen sehr wohl anstünde vnd rühmlich wehre, wann er als das membrum Principale und Haubt der Capellen, beÿ seiner anvertrawten Capelle standhaft verbleibe, Sie mit Musicalischen Sachen versorgte, mit rath und that deroselben veranderlich beÿwohnte, vnd also verrichtete quod sui oset officÿ [flourish] So ist doch E. Churf. Durchl. vnd fast iedermänniglich bekant das Er, wie sonstem einem Hirten gebührhet, viel iahr hero seiner Schäffe wenig geachtet, sondern sie verlaßen, von Ein provintz in die andern gereÿset, E. Churf. Durchl. Capelle hat mögen versorget werden oder verlaßen stehen [flourish] Hergegen werden E. Churf. Durchl. in Gnädigstem Andencken tragen, das nicht allein die 3. iahr über, also Herr Schütze sich in Dennemarck, zu Braunschweig vnd Weißenfelß aufgehalten, Ich dero Churf. Capella mit auserstem fleiße nach bestem Vermögen bestellet, beÿ fürstlichen kindtauffen, adelichen beÿlagern vnd andern Taffelaufwartungen das meine gethat, sondern habe auch . . . die itzigen 4. Jahr hero so wohl die fest- Sonn- vnd fÿertage mit gehörigem Musiciren, als die wochenpredigten vnd tägliche bethstunden mit ordentlichem Singen bestellen, und also [fol. 272r] dem Capellmeister Schützen zugleich Seine bestallung vnd brod verdienen müßen.

A partial translation appears in Moser/Pfatteicher, *Heinrich Schütz*, p. 181. This letter has never been published in its entirety. See chapter 1 for the outcome of Hofkontz's petition.

22. See chapter 1 regarding Schütz's theatrical compositions.

23. Rifkin, "Towards a New Image," p. 656.

24. Eberhard Schmidt, *Der Gottesdienst*, p. 174

25. This contract appears in Schäfer, "Geschichte der Kurfürstlichen musikalische Capelle," pp. 423–24.

26. Eberhard Schmidt, *Der Gottesdienst*, p. 172.

27. Ibid.

28. Ibid., p. 177.

29. Ibid., pp. 178–79.

30. Friedrich Chrysander, "Geschichte," p. 156. "Ein Calcant, dazue man einen discipulum nehmen kann, so zur Orgel und sonsten zum Absetzen und Schreiben dienlich, in allen als Kleidung und Kostgelde...."

31. Fürstenau, 1861 I, p. 169.

32. Hainhofer's descriptions of his visits to Dresden are published nearly in their entirety by Oscar Doering in *Des Augsburger Patriciers Philipp Hainhofer Reisen nach Innsbruck und Dresden* (Vienna: Carl Graesser & Co., 1901) based on HAB Cod. Guelf 11.22.Aug.20, fols. 299–527. "mit darein gemahltem Jüngsten gericht, aus welcher man in die hofkirchen zue der grossen orgel gehen kan, vnd müssen in diser kammer die trommeter vnd kesselbaugger an hohen festen in die instrumental musicam musicieren, vnd echones machen ..." (p. 210). See also pp. 231–35 for Hainhofer's description of the instruments kept in the chamber in 1629 and document 18 for an inventory of music and instruments missing from the collection in 1681.

33. Wolfram Steude, Ortrun Landmann, and Dieter Härtwig, "Dresden," *The New Grove Dictionary of Music and Musicians*, ed. Stanley Sadie (London: Macmillan, 1980), vol. 5, p. 616.

34. Don Smithers, *The Music and History of the Baroque Trumpet before 1721* (London: J.M. Dent & Sons Ltd., 1973), p. 113.

35. Ibid., p. 114.

36. Ibid.

37. SAD Loc. 10568, fol. 193r.

38. See appendix.

39. Werner Braun, *Die Music des 17. Jahrhunderts* (Wiesbaden: Akademische Verlagsgesellschaft Athenaion, 1981), p. 50.

40. For a fine discussion, see Erich Reimer, "Tafelmusik," *Handwörterbuch der musikalischen Terminologie*, ed. Hans Heinrich Eggebrecht (Wiesbaden: Franz Steiner, 1972).

41. Fürstenau, "Churfürstliche Sechsische Cantoreiordnung," p. 236. "In der Capellen vnd für vnnsere Taffel. . . ."

42. SAD Loc. 33344. 1949. *Registratura über das 10te Bestallungsbuch,* 1646–51. no. 99.

    wegen der auffwarttung in vnser HofCapell, vor der Taffel vnd sonsten, ge-schaffet, verordnet vnd befohlen wird. . . . Daneben soll er über alle vnsere blasende, beröhrte, geigende vnd andere instrumenta, wie auch über das in vnserm Schlosse dazu eingereümte zimmer, die vffsicht vnd verwaltung haben, vnd fleissiger achtung darauf geben, daß deren keines beschädiget noch verloren werde, Wiedriges falles aber den schaden od. verlust zu erstatten schuldig sein, Die Jenigen Instrumenta, deren man in der Kirche, bey der Taffel, oder an-deren vorfallenden aufwarttungen bedürfftig, stets fertig halten, vnd an den ort, wo sie gebraucht werden sollen, durch den Calcanten oder die knaben bringen lassen. . . .

43. Erich H. Müller, *GBS,* no. 93.

44. I am grateful to Wolfram Steude for calling Hainhofer's observations on Tafelmu-sik to my attention.

45. HAB Cod. Guelf 11.22.Aug.20. Published in Doering, *Des Augsburger Patriciers,* p. 217. Also partially in Moser/Pfatteicher, *Heinrich Schütz,* p. 138.

    [fol. 443v] Hinder iedem bild ist es hool, vnd dergestalt gerichtet, das man aine sondere music darhinder halten kan. Wann man in disem obern saal speiset, so stellet man die musicanten auch in vndern saal, schleusset zu, so gehet die re-sonanz durch die lufftröhrer lieblich hinauf.

    Oben hero vnder der deckin ist es auch zu verborgner music gerichtet, so, das man von 32 orthen verborgne music, iede absonderlich, hören kan.

46. HAB Cod. Guelf 11.22.Aug.20. [fol. 480] "nemlich zu vil gäste gar zu gros getümmel vnd geschraÿ machen; Es ist aber beÿ dieser Churfrl mahlzeit alles gar still, gravitetisch, vnd respectierlich zugangen, vnd niemand, als der churfürst an der Tafel vnd wer Ihme geantwurtet hat, laut geredet." This passage is not pub-lished by Doering.

47. See also Moser/Pfatteicher, *Heinrich Schütz,* p. 139.

48. HAB Cod. Guelf 11.22.Aug.20. [fol. 453v] "Darnach aine hüpsche collation aufge-setzt, musicam vocalem vor dem Zimmer [fol. 454r] draussen, ein Zimmer musicam instrumentalem (als ainem instrumentisten vnd lautenisten, der sonsten der Churfürstin aufwartet vnd mit ainander alternierten) gehabt. . . ." This passage is also not published by Doering.

49. SAD OHMA N.I. no. 8. *Ordnung wie es an hohen Fest- und Residenz Dresden, gehalten sollte,* 1657–1721.

    haben die sämbtl. Trompeter Er Churfl Dhl das Neue Jahr geblasen und solches folgender gestalt verrichtet: Entlich haben Sie sich auf den Riesen Saal beÿ die Fenster nachmittags gestellet, und als Er Churf. Durchl. zur Tafel gangen sobald Er Churfl. der Herr Ober Hofmarschall in den Riesen Saal getreten, geblasen, Nun Last uns Gott den Herren, welches sie solange continuiret biß Er Churfl. Dhl. und alle deroselben hohe officirer und bediente in das Tafel Gemach, Hernach als Ihr Durchl. die Churfürstin und das Churf. Fräulein zur Tafel kamm ebenfalls obgeseztes Lied und biß Selbige in das Tafel Gemach geblasen, Als aber die Königl. Ungar und erzhogl. Osterreichl. freÿherren Abgesandten zur Tafel geführet worden nur eine Intrade geblasen, Wie aber die Chur: und Fürstl. Herrschafft zur Tafel, haben sich die Trompeter auf einseit der Riesen Stube in das vorgemach beÿm Mitlern Gange vorfüget, und da selbst geblasen Joseph lieber Joseph mein, Darauf die Trommel schläger und Pfeiffer in dem Gange zwischen der Riesen Stube und Riesen Saale ihre schuldigkeit auch abgeleget, und sich also diese, geendet,

50. SAD OHMA O.IV. no. 5. *Hof-Journal* 1641–50. "haben Ihre Churfl. Durchl. dero das mit Gott 66sten erhabten Geburtstag celebriret, auch ist deroselben beÿ gehaltener Tafel, von Ihr Chur Prinzl. Durchl. Herzogk Johann Georgen, Abents umb 9 Uhr, durch die Musicanten ein singend Ballet praesentiret,"

51. SAD OHMA O.IV. no. 27. *Hof-Journal* 1671. "umb 5. Uhr zur Tafel geschlagen und geblasen . . . darbeÿ auffm Theatro die Comoedia vom Orlando Furioso agiret wurde, und die Berg-Sänger, das Türchische Paückgen und Schallmeÿ-Pfeiffer unter wehrender Tafel auffwarteten,"

52. SAD OHMA O.IV. no. 16. *Hof-Journal,* 1665–66.

     die meisten Dames und Cavalliers fingen eine Branslee zu tantzen an, Worzu die von dem König auß Franckreich, dem Königl. Prinzen zugeschickte 8. Violens aufwarteten, nach dem Bransle, tantzete man Couranden, und worden damit ein Paar Stunden pashiret. . . . Nach der Tafel continuirete man das tantzen mit courantes, Bransles, und Teütschen Tänzen; zwischen solchen ward Confect und Wein herumb getragen, und endigte sich dieser Ball mit einem Engelländischen Tantze.

53. SAD Loc. 8682. no. 13. *Hof Diaria,* 1679–80, fol. 286r. "Die französischen Violisten, der Cammer Cymbalist, Churf. und Tragoner. Schallmey Pfeiffer, bergsänger, Wallachischen bockpfeiffer und die Stadt Pfeiffer."

54. Fürstenau, 1861 I, pp. 200–201.

55. Ibid., pp. 201–2.

56. SAD OHMA O.IV. no. 23. *Hof-Journal* 1668. "Die Italiänische und Teütsche Musicanten haben beÿ der Tafel mit Ihrer Music auffgewartet."

57. SAD OHMA O.IV. no. 24. *Hof-Journal* 1669. "Dabeÿ wartete der Capell-meister Vincenzo [Albrici] mit der sammtlichen Churfürstl. Musica auff."

58. SAD Loc. 8682. no. 9. *Hof Diaria,* 1674–75. "Abends aber im tafel gemmach tafel, bey welcher der Cammermusicant, balthasar Seydanck mit der Viola da gamba aufwartet."

59. SAD Loc. 8682. no. 12. *Hof Diaria,* 1678. "Bey der Tafel ließen sich zwey frembde Brandenburgl. Musici einer auf der Laute und der andere auf der Viol di Gamba hören. . . ."

60. LAG n. Rep. Gera/K, Kap 59, 1 no. 1, fol. 82v. Published by Hans Rudolf Jung, "Ein neuaufgefundenes Gutachten von Heinrich Schütz aus dem Jahre 1617," *Archiv für Musikwissenschaft* 18 (1961), p. 245.

Anlangende die beiden Tischknaben, die da sollen gehalten werden, gnediger Herr, achte ich meinem Guthachten nach, das E. Gn. hierauf das ganze Fundament Ihrer Music bauen können . . . mußen dießelben Knaben—ihr seind wenig oder viel—vom Cantore im Singen und von E. Gn. Hofinstrumentisten auf Geigen necessario alle, auf andern Instrumenten aber, alß Zincken, Posaunen, nach Lust und Beliebung der Knaben abgerichtet werden. . . .

61. SAD Loc. 8687. *Kantoreiordnung,* fol. 210r.

Dieses ist, Gnedigster Churfürst, meinem wenigen gutachten nach dasjenige undt füglichste Mittel wodurch E. Churf. Durchl. Ihre HoffCapell nicht alleine in etwas erhalten, eine kleine Music bey dero Churfl. Taffel erlangen, Sondern auch zu begebenden, helffe Gott baldt bessern zeiten (:mit annemung ein bahr gueter Italianischen oder andern Instrumenten, undt so viel gueter Sänger:) das Collegium Musicum iederzeit, nach deroselben gnedigsten Wolgefallen gar balt completiren undt ergentzen können. . . .

62. SAD Collection Schmidt, Amt Dresden, vol. 10. *Hof Sachen,* no. 2841, fol. 3. This autograph letter is still unpublished. Facsimile of fol. 1 in Becker-Glauch, *Dresdener Hoffeste,* frontispiece. "Ob Ihr Churfl. durchl. kan geschehen lassen das diese woche etwa, wann sonst kein aufwarten ist, Ich sembtliche knaben gros v. klein etwa einmal beÿ der taffel aufwarten lasse. . . ."

63. SAD OHMA O.IV. no. 23. *Hof-Journal,* 1668. "Speisten Eure Chur-Prinzl. Durchl. Abends beÿ Dero Prinzessin. . . . Eure Durchl. haben die Capellknaben holen lassen, welchen beÿ der Tafel, den Neuen Eheverlobten zu Ehren, sich haben hören lassen. Wurd darauff biß in die Nacht getanzet."

64. Praetorius, *Syntagma musicum III,* pp. 129–30.

Also vnd dergestalt kan man es mit anordnung einer guten Music vor grosse Herrn Taffel oder bey andern frölichen Conventibus auch halten/daß/wenn man zween oder mehr Knaben/oder auch andere Alt: Tenor: vnnd Bass: Vocal-Stimmen (so von mir Voces Concertatae genennet werden) zu ein Clavicymbel, Regal oder dergleichen Fundament Instrument hat singen lassen/also bald mit Lauten/ Bandorn, Geigen/Zincken/Posaunen vnd dergleichen/etwas anders ohne Vocal-Stimmen/allein mit Instrumenten zu Musiciren anfange; Darauff dan wiederumb mit Vocal-Stimmen/vnd also eins vmbs ander mit Instrumenten vnd Stimmen vmbwechsele. Ebenermassen/daß man nach eim Concert oder sonsten einer prechtigen Mutet, bald ein lustig Canzon, Galliard, Courant oder dergleichen mit eitel Instrumenten herfür bringe. Welches dann auch ein Organist oder Lautenist vor sich alleine in acht nemen kan/daß wenn er in Conviviis, eine Mutet oder Madrigal sein langsam vnd Gravitätisch gespielet/also bald darauff ein frölich Alemande, Intrada, Bransle oder Galliard anfange; hernacher wiederumb etwa eine andere Mutet, Madrigal, Pavan oder kunstreiche Fugam vor sich neme.

65. Erich H. Müller, *GBS,* no. 28.

66. Eberhard Schmidt, *Der Gottesdienst,* p. 205. See also F.A. Drechsel, "Alte Dresdener Instrumentinventare," *Zeitschrift für Musikwissenschaft* 10 (1927–28), pp. 495–99, for a discussion of the instruments listed in this catalog.

67. See the appendix for the 1680 list and chapter 1 for more on Battistini.

68. Gesualdo di Venosa, *Collected Works*, vol. 10, ed. Glenn Watkins, p. ix. See pp. 37–47 for a facsimile of the surviving Quinto partbook.

69. *NSA* 37, p. x. "An/Vorhergedachten/Hoch-Fürstl. Altenburgischen Verlobungs-Tage/Unterthänigst gesetzte/ und vor Churfürstl./Taffel in darzu kommende Music/abgesungene/Ode."

70. Ibid., p. x. "Folgende/von/Herrn Heinrich Schützen/Chur-/Fürstl. Sächs. hochverdienten Capell-/meister/Gesetzte Melodey/Kömmet zu der Hoch-Fürstl. Altenburgischen/Verlobungs-Ode./Am 125.Blat." Modern edition available in *NSA* 37, p. 3.

Chapter 5

1. Erich H. Müller, *GBS,* pp. 380–81.

2. Ibid., no. 91.

3. NSAW 1 Alt 25 no. 295, fol. 7.

4. 150 gulden, or florins, are equal to 100 Reichstalers.

5. NSAW 1 Alt 25 no. 296, fols. 2–4.

6. Chrysander, "Geschichte," p. 158.

7. NSAW 17 III Alt 87, fols. 33v and 46v.

8. See Erich H. Müller, *GBS,* appendix, no. 7.

9. Ibid., no. 6.

10. Fürstenau, 1849, pp. 92–93.

11. Erich H. Müller, *GBS,* no. 49.

12. *Syntagma musicum III,* p. 125.

Bibliography

Aber, Adolf. *Die Pflege der Musik unter den Wettinern und wettinischen Ernstinern.* Bückeburg, Leipzig: Siegel, 1921.

Becker-Glauch, Irmgard. *Die Bedeutung der Musik für die Dresdener Hoffeste bis in die Zeit Augusts des Starken.* Kassel: Bärenreiter, 1951.

———. "Dresden." *Die Musik in Geschichte und Gegenwart.* Ed. Friedrich Blume. Kassel: Bärenreiter, 1949–. Vol. 3 (1954), cols. 757–94.

———. "Peranda, Marco Gioseppe." *Die Musik in Geschichte und Gegenwart.* Ed. Friedrich Blume. Kassel: Bärenreiter, 1949–. Vol. 10 (1962), cols. 1033–35.

Béhar, Pierre. "Anton Ulrichs Ballette und Singspiele. Zum Problem ihrer Form und ihrer Bedeutung in der Geschichte der deutschen Barockdramatic." *Höfische Festkultur in Braunschweig-Wolfenbüttel 1590–1666.* Ed. Jörg Jochen Berns. Vol. 10, no. 4 (1981) of *Daphnis. Zeitschrift für Mittlere Deutsche Literatur*, pp. 775–92.

Berns, Jörg Jochen. "'Theatralische neue Vorstellung von der Maria Magdalena.' Ein Zeugnis für die Zusammenarbeit von Justus Georg Schottelius und Heinrich Schütz." *Schütz-Jahrbuch* 2 (1980), pp. 120–29.

———. "Trionfo-Theater am Hof von Braunschweig-Wolfenbüttel." *Höfische Festkultur in Braunschweig-Wolfenbüttel 1590–1666.* Ed. Jörg Jochen Berns. Vol. 10, no. 4 (1981) of *Daphnis. Zeitschrift für Mittlere Deutsche Literatur*, pp. 663–710.

Bircher, Martin. "Der Gelehrte als Herrscher. Der Hof von Wolfenbüttel." Vol. 1 of *Europäische Hofkultur im 16. und 17. Jahrhundert. Kongreß des Wolfenbüttler Arbeitskreises für Renaissanceforschung und des Internationalen Arbeitskreises für Barockliteratur.* Ed. August Buck et al. 3 vols. Hamburg: Dr. Ernst Hauswedell & Co., 1981, pp. 105–27.

Bittinger, Werner. *Schütz-Werke-Verzeichnis. Kleine Ausgabe.* Kassel: Bärenreiter, 1960. Supplement by Werner Breig. "Schützfunde und -zuschreibungen seit 1960— Auf dem Wege zur Grossen Ausgabe des Schütz-Werke-Verzeichnis." *Schütz-Jahrbuch* 1 (1979), pp. 63–92.

Bittrich, Gerhard. *Ein deutsches Opernballett des 17. Jahrhunderts, ein Beitrag zur Frühgeschichte der deutschen Oper.* Leipzig: Frommhold & Wendler, 1931.

Brainard, Ingrid. "Der Höfische Tanz. Darstellende Kunst und Höfische Repräsentation." Vol. 2 of *Europäische Hofkultur im 16. und 17. Jahrhundert. Kongreß des Wolfenbüttler Arbeitskreises für Renaissanceforschung und des Internationalen Arbeitskreises für Barockliteratur.* Ed. August Buck et al. 3 vols. Hamburg: Dr. Ernst Hauswedell & Co., 1981, pp. 379–94.

Braun, Werner. *Die Musik des 17. Jahrhunderts.* Vol. 4 of *Neues Handbuch der Musikwissenschaft.* Ed. Carl Dahlhaus. Wiesbaden: Akademische Verlagsgesellschaft Athenaion, 1981.

———. "Zur Gattungsproblematik des Singballetts." *Gattung und Werk in der Musikge-schichte Norddeutschlands und Skandinaviens.* Vol. 26 of *Kieler Schriften zur Musikwissenschaft.* Eds. Friedhelm Krummacher and Heinrich W. Schwab. Kassel: Bärenreiter, 1982, pp. 41–50.

Breig, Werner. "Höfische Festmusik im Werk von Heinrich Schütz." *Höfische Festkultur in Braunschweig-Wolfenbüttel 1590–1666.* Ed. Jörg Jochen Berns. Vol. 10, no. 4 (1981) of *Daphnis. Zeitschrift für Mittlere Deutsche Literatur,* pp. 711–33.

———. "Schütz-Aspekte im Vorfeld des Jubiläumsjahres 1985." *Musica* 38 (1984), no. 6, pp. 527–31.

Brodde, Otto. *Heinrich Schütz. Weg und Werk.* Kassel: Bärenreiter, 1972.

Buelow, George. *A Schütz Reader. Documents of Performance Practice. Journal of the American Choral Foundation, Inc.* 27, no. 4 (October 1985).

Chrysander, Friedrich. "Geschichte der Braunschweig-Wolfenbüttelschen Capelle und Oper vom 16. bis zum 18. Jahrhunderts." *Jahrbücher für musikalische Wissenschaft* 1 (1863), pp. 147–286.

Culley, Thomas J. *A Study of the Musicians Connected with the German College in Rome during the Seventeenth Century and of Their Activities in Northern Europe.* Vol. 1 of *Jesuits and Music.* Rome: Jesuit Historical Institute, 1970.

Dahms, Sibylle. "Pallavicino, Carlo." *The New Grove Dictionary of Music and Musicians.* Ed. Stanley Sadie. London: Macmillan, 1980. Vol. 14, pp. 141–42.

Dane, Werner. "Briefwechsel zwischen dem landgräflich hessischen und dem kurfürstlich sächsischen Hof um Heinrich Schütz (1614–19)." *Zeitschrift für Musikwissenschaft* 17 (1935), pp. 343–55.

Doering, Oscar. *Des Augsburger Patriciers Philipp Hainhofer Reisen nach Innsbruck und Dresden.* Vienna: Carl Graessner & Co., 1901.

Drechsel, F.A. "Alte Dresdener Instrumentinventare." *Zeitschrift für Musikwissenschaft* 10 (1927–28), pp. 495–99.

Edwards, J. Michele. "Schütz's *violone.*" Unpublished manuscript.

Eitner, Robert. "Das älteste bekannte deutsche Singspiel Seelewig." *Monatshefte für Musikgeschichte* 13 (1881), pp. 55–147.

———. *Biographisch-Bibliographisches Quellen-Lexicon der Musiker und Musikgelehrten der christlichen Zeitrechnung bis zur Mitte des neunzehnten Jahrhunderts.* New York: Musurgia [1947].

Engländer, Richard. "Die erste italienische Oper in Dresden: Bontempis *Il Paride in Musica* (1662)." *Svensk Tidskrift för Musikforskning* 43 (1961), pp. 119–34.

———. "Zur Frage der *Dafne* (1671) von G.A. Bontempi und M.G. Peranda." *Acta Musicologica* 13 (1941), pp. 59–77.

Fiebig, Folkert. *Christoph Bernhard und der stile moderno. Untersuchungen zu Leben und Werk.* Hamburg: Verlag der Musikalienhandlung Wagner, 1980.

Fornaçon, Siegfried. "Sophie Elisabeth." *Die Musik in Geschichte und Gegenwart.* Ed. Friedrich Blume. Kassel: Bärenreiter, 1949–. Vol. 12 (1965), cols. 920–21.

Fürstenau, Moritz. *Beiträge zur Geschichte der königlich sächsischen musikalischen Kapelle grossentheils aus archivarischen Quellen.* Dresden: C.F. Meser, 1849.

———. "Christoph Bernhard, kurfürstlich sächsischer Kapellmeister und Praeceptor der Prinzen Johann Georg IV. und Friedrich August I. von Sachsen." *Mitteilungen des königlichen sächsischen Altertumsvereins* 16 (1866), pp. 56–68.

———. "Churfürstliche Sechsische Cantoreiordnung." *Monatshefte für Musikgeschichte* 9 (1877), pp. 235–46.

———. "Fürstlicher Gottesdienst im 17. Jahrhundert." *Monatshefte für Musikgeschichte* 3 (1871), pp. 58–61.

———. *Zur Geschichte der Musik und des Theaters am Hofe zu Dresden.* 1861. Reprint (2 vols. in 1). Leipzig: Peters, 1971.

Geier, Martin. *Kurtze Beschreibung Des (Tit.) Herrn Heinrich Schützens/Chur Fürstl. Sächs. ältern Capellmeisters/geführten müheseeligen Lebens-Lauff.* Facsimile edition by Dietrich Berke. Kassel: Bärenreiter, 1972.

Giesey, Ralph. *The Royal Funeral in Renaissance France.* Geneva: Librairie E. Droz, 1960.

Gobiet, Ronald, ed. *Der Briefwechsel zwischen Philipp Hainhofer und Herzog August der Jüngere von Braunschweig-Lüneburg.* Munich: Bavarian National Museum, 1984.

Grusnick, Bruno. "Bernhard, Christoph." *Die Musik in Geschichte und Gegenwart.* Ed. Friedrich Blume. Kassel: Bärenreiter, 1949–. Vol. 1 (1949–51), cols. 1785–89.

Gurlitt, Wilibald. "Der kursächsische Hoforgelmacher Gottfried Fritzsche." *Festschrift Arnold Schering zum 60. Geburtstage.* Berlin: A. Glas, 1937, pp. 106–24.

Haacke, Walter. "Gambenspiel am Hofe August der Jüngere zu Wolfenbüttel." *Zeitschrift für Musik* 111 (1950), pp. 583–86.

Haar, James. "Astral Music in Seventeenth-Century Nuremberg: The 'Tugendsterne' of Harsdörffer and Staden." *Musica Disciplina* 16 (1962), pp. 175–89.

Haase, Hans. "Besondere Erwerbung auf dem Gebiet der Musik." *Sammler Fürst Gelehrter Herzog August zu Braunschweig und Lüneburg 1579–1666.* Exhibition catalog of the Herzog-August-Bibliothek, no. 27. Brunswick: Druck- und Verlagshaus Limbach, 1979, pp. 335–40.

———. *Heinrich Schütz (1585–1672) in seinen Beziehungen zum Wolfenbütteler Hof.* Exhibition catalog of the Herzog-August-Bibliothek, no. 8. Peine: Druckhaus A. Schlaeger, 1972.

———. "Music am Hofe." *Sammler Fürst Gelehrter Herzog August zu Braunschweig und Lüneburg 1579–1666.* Exhibition catalog of the Herzog-August-Bibliothek, no. 27. Brunswick: Druck- und Verlagshaus Limbach, 1979, pp. 265–78.

———. "Nachtrag zu einer Schütz-Ausstellung." *Sagittarius* 4 (1973), pp. 85–97.

Hill, John Walter. "Oratory Music in Florence, III: The Confraternities from 1655 to 1785." *Acta Musicologica* 58 (1986), pp. 129–79.

Jung, Hans Rudolf. "Ein neuaufgefundenes Gutachten von Heinrich Schütz aus dem Jahre 1617." *Archiv für Musikwissenschaft* 18 (1961), pp. 241–47.

———. "Ein unbekanntes Gutachten von Heinrich Schütz über die Neuordnung der Hof-, Schul- und Stadtmusik in Gera." *Beiträge zur Musikwissenschaft* 4 (1962), pp. 17–36.

———. "Neues zum Thema 'Heinrich Schütz und Weimar.'" *Schütz-Jahrbuch* 9 (1987), pp. 105–16.

———. "Zwei unbekannte Briefe von Heinrich Schütz aus den Jahren 1653/54." *Beiträge zur Musikwissenschaft* 14 (1972), pp. 231–36.

Keller, Peter. "New Light on the Tugendsterne of Harsdörffer and Staden." *Musica Disciplina* 25 (1971), pp. 223–27.

Kern, Arthur. *Deutsche Hofordnungen des 16. und 17. Jahrhunderts.* 2 vols. Berlin: Weidmannsche Buchhandlung, 1905.

Kirchner, Gerhard. *Der Generalbass bei Heinrich Schütz.* Kassel: Bärenreiter, 1960.

Kobuch, Agatha. "Neue Sagittariana im Staatsarchiv Dresden. Ermittlung unbekannter Quellen über den kursächsischen Hofkapellmeister Heinrich Schütz." *Jahrbuch für Regionalgeschichte* 13 (1986), pp. 79–124.

———. "Neue Sagittariana im Staatsarchiv Dresden. Ermittlung unbekannter Quellen über den kursächsischen Hofkapellmeister Heinrich Schütz." *Jahrbuch für Regionalgeschichte* 15 (1988), pp. 118–24.

———. "Quellen über Heinrich Schütz in Staatsarchiv Dresden. Ein Uberblick anläßlich der 300. Wiederkehr seines Todestages." *Archivmitteilungen* 23 (1973), pp. 16–19.

Kraft, Günther. "Zeitz." *Die Musik in Geschichte und Gegenwart.* Ed. Friedrich Blume. Kassel: Bärenreiter, 1949–. Vol. 14 (1968), cols. 1188–92.

Kunst, Hans Joachim. "Die Marienkirche in Wolfenbüttel eine Siegkirche?" *Höfische Festkultur in Braunschweig-Wolfenbüttel 1590–1666.* Ed. Jörg Jochen Berns. Vol. 10, no. 4 (1981) of *Daphnis. Zeitschrift für Mittlere Deutsche Literatur,* pp. 643–62.

Kunze, Stefan. "Höfische Musik im 16. und 17. Jahrhundert." Vol. 1 of *Europäische Hofkultur im 16. und 17. Jahrhundert. Kongreß des Wolfenbüttler Arbeitskreises für Renaissanceforschung und des Internationalen Arbeitskreises für Barockliteratur.* Ed. August Buck et al. 3 vols. Hamburg: Dr. Ernst Hauswedell & Co., 1981, pp. 69–80.

Leaver, Robin A. and Franzmann, Martin. "The Funeral Sermon for Heinrich Schütz." *Bach* 4/4 (1973), pp. 3–16; 5/1 (1974), pp. 9–22; 5/2 (1974), pp. 22–35; and 5/3 (1974), pp. 13–20.

Lehmeyer, Frederick. *The Singspiele of Anton Ulrich von Braunschweig.* Ph.D. diss., Univ. of California at Berkeley, 1971.

Leighton, Joseph. "Deutschsprachige Geburtstagsdichtungen für Herzog August d.J. von Braunschweig-Lüneburg." *Höfische Festkultur in Braunschweig-Wolfenbüttel 1590–1666.* Ed. Jörg Jochen Berns. Vol. 10, no. 4 (1981) of *Daphnis. Zeitschrift für Mittlere Deutsche Literatur,* pp. 755–67.

────── . "Die literarische Tätigkeit der Herzogin Sophie Elisabeth von Braunschweig-Lüneburg." Vol. 3 of *Europäische Hofkultur im 16. und 17. Jahrhundert. Kongreß des Wolfenbüttler Arbeitskreises für Renaissanceforschung und des Internationalen Arbeitskreises für Barockliteratur.* Ed. August Buck et al. 3 vols. Hamburg: Dr. Ernst Hauswedell & Co., 1981, pp. 483–88.

────── . "Die Wolfenbütteler Aufführung von Harsdörffers und Stadens Seelewig im Jahre 1654." *Wolfenbüttler Beiträge* 3 (1978), pp. 115–28.

Lindau, Martin Bernhard. *Geschichte der Haupt- und Residenzstadt Dresden.* 2 vols. Dresden: Kuntz, 1859–63.

Linfield, Eva. "A New Look at the Sources of Schütz's *Christmas History.*" *Schütz-Jahrbuch* 4/5 (1982/82), pp. 19–36.

Lipsius, Ida Maria (pseud. La Mara). *Musikerbriefe aus fünf Jahrhunderten.* Leipzig: Breitkopf & Härtel, 1886.

Mabbett, Margaret. "Italian Musicians in Restoration England (1660–90)." *Music and Letters* 67 (1986), pp. 237–43.

Mattheson, Johann. *Grundlage einer Ehren-Pforte* (1740). Ed. Max Schneider. Graz: Akademische Druck- und Verlagsanstalt, 1969.

Moberg, Carl-Allan. "Vincenzo Albrici (1631–1696): Eine biographische Skizze mit besonderer Berücksichtigung seiner schwedischen Zeit." *Festschrift Friedrich Blume zum 70. Geburtstag.* Eds. Anna Amalie Abert and Wilhelm Pfannkuch. Kassel: Bärenreiter, 1963, pp. 235–46.

────── . "Vincenzo Albrici und das Kirchenkonzert. Ein Entwurf." *Natalicia musicologica Knud Jeppesen septuagenario collegis oblata.* Eds. Bjørn Hjelmborg and Søren Sørensen. Oslo: Norsk Musikforlag, 1962, pp. 199–216.

Moore, James. *Vespers at St. Mark's: Music of Alessandro Grandi, Giovanni Rovetta and Francesco Cavalli.* 2 vols. Ann Arbor: UMI, 1981.

Moser, Hans Joachim. *Heinrich Schütz: sein Leben und Werk.* Kassel: Bärenreiter, 1936. Rev. ed. 1954. English trans. by Carl F. Pfatteicher, *Heinrich Schütz: His Life and Works.* St. Louis: Concordia Publishing House, 1959.

Müller, Erich H., ed. *Heinrich Schütz: Gesammelte Briefe und Schriften.* Regensburg: G. Bosse, 1931. Rpt. ed. Hildesheim: Olms, 1976.

Müller, Karl August. *Kurfürst Johann Georg der Erste, seine Familie und sein Hof, nach hand- schriftlichen Quellen des Sächsischen Haupt-Staats-Archivs.* Vol. 1 of *Forschungen auf dem Gebiet der neueren Geschichte.* Dresden and Leipzig: Fleischer, 1838.

Otto, Karl F. *Die Sprachgesellschaften des 17. Jahrhunderts.* Stuttgart: J.B. Metzlersche Ver- lagsbuchhandlung, 1972.

Pape, Uwe. *Die Orgeln der Stadt Wolfenbüttel.* Berlin: Verlag U. Pape, 1973.

Praetorius, Michael. *Syntagma musicum III* (1619). Facsimile ed. by Wilibald Gurlitt. Kassel and Basel: Bärenreiter, 1958.

Reimer, Erich. "Tafelmusik." *Handwörterbuch der musikalischen Terminologie.* Ed. Hans Heinrich Eggebrecht. Wiesbaden: Franz Steiner, 1972.

Rifkin, Joshua. "Towards a New Image of Henrich Schütz." *The Musical Times* 126, no. 1713 (November 1985), pp. 651–58, and 126, no. 1714 (December 1985), pp. 716–20.

Rifkin, Joshua, and Timms, Colin. "Schütz, Heinrich." *The New Grove North European Baroque Masters.* New York: W.W. Norton & Co., 1985, pp. 1–150.

Roloff, Hans-Gert. "Absolutismus und Hoftheater. Das Freudenspiel der Herzogin Sophie Elisabeth zu Braunschweig-Wolfenbüttel." *Höfische Festkultur in Braunschweig-Wolfen- büttel 1590–1666.* Ed. Jörg Jochen Berns. Vol. 10, no. 4 (1981) of *Daphnis. Zeitschrift für Mittlere Deutsche Literatur,* pp. 735–53.

――――. "Die höfischen Maskeraden der Sophie Elisabeth, Herzogin zu Braunschweig- Lüneburg." Vol. 3 of *Europäische Hofkultur im 16. und 17. Jahrhundert. Kongreß des Wolfenbüttler Arbeitskreises für Renaissanceforschung und des Internationalen Arbeitskreises für Barockliteratur.* Ed. August Buck et al. 3 vols. Hamburg: Dr. Ernst Hauswedell & Co., 1981, pp. 489–96.

Roloff, Hans-Gert, ed. *Sophie Elisabeth, Herzogin zu Braunschweig und Lüneburg, Dichtungen, Spiele.* Vol. 6 of *Arbeiten zum Mittleren Deutschen Literatur und Sprache.* Frankfurt a.M., Bern: Cirencester, 1980.

Rose, Gloria. "Albrici, Bartolomeo." *The New Grove Dictionary of Music and Musicians.* Ed. Stanley Sadie. London: Macmillan, 1980. Vol. 1, p. 226.

――――. "Albrici, Vincenzo." *The New Grove Dictionary of Music and Musicians.* Ed. Stanley Sadie. London: Macmillan, 1980. Vol. 1, pp. 226–27.

Ruhnke, Martin. "Wolfenbüttel." *Die Musik in Geschichte und Gegenwart.* Ed. Friedrich Blume. Kassel: Bärenreiter, 1949–. Vol. 14 (1969), cols. 801–9.

――――. "Zur Hochzeit: die Psalmen Davids. Ein Brief von Heinrich Schütz an die Stadt Braunschweig." *Beiträge zur Musikgeschichte Nordeuropas. Kurt Gudewill zum 65. Geburtstag.* Ed. Uwe Haensel. Wolfenbüttel: Möseler, 1978.

Saffe, Ferdinand. "Wolfenbüttler Komponisten des 17. Jahrhunderts." *Mitteilungen des Universitätsbundes Göttingen* 2,2 (1921), pp. 69–93.

Schäfer, Wilhelm. "Einige Beiträge zur Geschichte der kurfürstlichen musikalischen Capelle oder Cantorei unter den Kurfürsten August, Christian I. und II. und Johann Georg I." *Sachsenchronik für Vergangenheit und Gegenwart* 1 (1854), pp. 404–51.

――――. "Heinrich Schütz." *Sachsenchronik für Vergangenheit und Gegenwart* I (1854), pp. 500–587.

Schmidt, Gustav Friedrich. *Neue Beiträge zur Geschichte der Musik und des Theaters am Her- zoglichen Hofe zu Braunschweig-Wolfenbüttel.* Munich: Verlag Wilhelm Berntheisel, 1929.

Schmidt, Eberhard. *Der Gottesdienst am kurfürstlichen Hofe zu Dresden.* Vol. 12 of *Veröffentlichungen der Evangelischen Gesellschaft für Liturgieforschung.* Göttingen: Vanden- hoeck & Ruprecht, 1961.

Schmidt, Jost Harro. "Heinrich Schützens beziehungen zu Celle: ein Beitrag zur Schütz Biographie." *Archiv für Musikwissenschaft* 23 (1966), pp. 274–76.

Schmieder, Wolfgang and Hartwieg, Gisela. *Musik. Alte Drucke bis etwa 1750*. Vols. 12 and 13 of *Kataloge der Herzog-August-Bibliothek Wolfenbüttel*. Frankfurt am Main: Vittorio Klostermann, 1967.

Schnoor, Hans. *Dresden: 400 Jahre Musikkultur. Zum Jubiläum der Staatskapelle und zur Geschichte der Dresdener Oper*. Dresden: Dresdener Verlagsgesellschaft [1948].

Schütz, Heinrich. *Autobiographie (Memorial 1651)*. Facsimile ed. by Heinz Krause-Graumnitz. Leipzig: VEB Deutscher Verlag für Musik, 1972.

————. *Sämmtliche Werke*. Ed. Philipp Spitta et al. Leipzig: Breitkopf & Härtel, 1885–1927.

————. *Neue Ausgabe sämtlicher Werke*. Ed. Werner Bittinger, Werner Breig, Wolfram Steude et al. Kassel: Bärenreiter, 1955–.

————. *Sämtliche Werke*. Ed. Günter Graulich. Stuttgart: Hänssler-Verlag, 1971–.

Sievers, Heinrich. "Braunschweig." *Die Musik in Geschichte und Gegenwart*. Ed. Friedrich Blume. Kassel: Bärenreiter, 1949–. Vol. 2 (1952), cols. 227–41.

————. *Hannoversche Musikgeschichte. Dokumente, Kritiken und Meinungen*. Tutzing: Hans Schneider, 1979.

————. *Die Musik in Hannover. Die musikalischen Strömmungen in Niedersachsen vom Mittelalter bis zur Gegenwart und besonderer Berücksichtigung der Musikgeschichte der Landeshauptstadt Hannover*. Hannover: Sponholtz, 1961.

————. "Die Orgel der ehemaligen Schloßkapelle zu Wolfenbüttel. Beitrag zur Geschichte der Kirchenmusik in Wolfenbüttel." *Jahrbuch des Braunschweigischen Geschichtsvereins*, series 2, vol. 5 (1933), pp. 101–6.

————. *250 Jahre Braunschweigisches Staatstheater (1690–1940)*. Brunswick: Verlag E. Appelhans, 1941.

Skei, Allen B. *Heinrich Schütz: A Guide to Research*. New York: Garland Publishing, Inc., 1981.

Smithers, Don. *The Music and History of the Baroque Trumpet before 1721*. London: J.M. Dent & Sons, Ltd., 1973.

Snyder, Kerala Johnson. "Bernhard, Christoph." *The New Grove Dictionary of Music and Musicians*. Ed. Stanley Sadie. London: Macmillan, 1980. Vol. 2, pp. 624–27.

————. "Scheidt, Samuel." *The New Grove Dictionary of Music and Musicians*. Ed. Stanley Sadie. London: Macmillan, 1980. Vol. 16, pp. 604–11.

Spies, Gustav. "Geschichte der Hauptkirche B.M.V. in Wolfenbüttel." Volume 7 of *Quellen und Forschungen zur Braunschweigischen Geschichte*. Wolfenbüttel: Julius Zwißlers Verlag, 1914.

Steude, Wolfram. "Bemerkungen zur Erforschung und Darstellung der Musikgeschichte Dresdens zwischen der Stadtgründung um 1200 und dem ausgehenden 17. Jahrhundert." *Sächsische Heimatblätter*. Dresden 28, no. 6 (1982) pp. 259–64.

————. Foreword to Heinrich Shütz, Marco Gioseppe Peranda, *Passionsmusiken nach den Evangelisten Matthäus, Lukas, Johannes und Markus*. Facsimile ed. Leipzig: Zentralantiquariat der DDR, 1981.

————. Foreword to Heinrich Schütz, *Der Schwanengesang*. NSA 39. Kassel: Bärenreiter, 1984.

————. "Die Markuspassion in der Leipziger Passionen-Handschrift des Johann Zacharias Grundig." *Deutsches Jahrbuch der Musikwissenschaft* 14 (1969), pp. 96–116.

————. "Neue Schütz-Ermittlungen." *Deutsches Jahrbuch der Musikwissenschaft* 12 (1967), pp. 40–74.

————. "Peranda, Marco Gioseppe." *The New Grove Dictionary of Music and Musicians*. Ed. Stanley Sadie. London: Macmillan, 1980. Vol. 14, pp. 362–63.

————. "Das wiedergefundene Opus ultimum von Heinrich Schütz. Bemerkungen zur Quelle und zum Werk." *Schütz-Jahrbuch* 4/5 (1982/83), pp. 9–18.

Steude, Wolfram; Landmann, Ortrun; and Härtwig, Dieter. "Dresden." *The New Grove Dictionary of Music and Musicians*. Ed. Stanley Sadie. London: Macmillan, 1980. Vol. 5, pp. 612–27.

Sundström, Av Einar. "Notiser om drottning Kristinas italienska musiker." *Svensk Tidskrift för Musikforskning* 43 (1961), pp. 297–309.

Surian, Elvidio. "Cherici, Sebastiano." *The New Grove Dictionary of Music and Musicians*. Ed. Stanley Sadie. London: Macmillan, 1980. Vol. 4, p. 202.

Taylor, Lou. *Mourning Dress: A Costume and Social History*. London: George Allen and Unwin, 1983.

Thöne, Friedrich. *Wolfenbüttel. Geist und Glanz einer alten Reisdenz*. Munich: Bruckmann, 1963.

Timms, Colin. "Bontempi, Giovanna Andrea." *The New Grove Dictionary of Music and Musicians*. Ed. Stanley Sadie. London: Macmillan, 1980. Vol. 3, pp. 37–38.

Walter, Horst. "Ein unbekanntes Schütz-Autograph in Wolfenbüttel." *Musicae scientiae collectanea: Festschrift Karl Gustav Fellerer*. Ed. Heinrich Hüschen. Cologne: Arno Volk, 1973, pp. 621–25.

———. "Löwe von Eisenach." *The New Grove Dictionary of Music and Musicians*. Ed. Stanley Sadie. London: Macmillan, 1980. Vol. 11, pp. 289–90.

Walther, Johann Gottfried. *Musikalisches Lexicon* (1732). Facsimile ed. by Richard Schaal. Kassel: Bärenreiter, 1953.

Weck, Anton. *Der Fürstl. Sächs. weitberuffenen Residentz- und Haupt-Vestung Dresden Beschreibung und Vorstellung*. Nuremberg: J. Hoffmann, 1680.

Weiss, Pierro. *Letters of Composers through Six Centuries*. Philadelphia: Chilton Books, 1967.

Werner, Arno. *Städtische und fürstliche Musikpflege in Zeitz bis zum Anfang des 19. Jahrhunderts*. Bückeburg and Leipzig: C.F.W. Siegel, 1922.

Westrup, J.A. "Foreign Musicians in Stuart England." *Musical Quarterly* 27 (1941), pp. 70–89.

Young, Percy, "Brunswick." *The New Grove Dictionary of Music and Musicians*. Ed. Stanley Sadie. London: Macmillan, 1980. Vol. 3, pp. 391–92.

Zanetti, Emilia. "Bontempi, Giovanni Andrea." *Die Musik in Geschichte und Gegenwart*. Ed. Friedrich Blume. Kassel: Bärenreiter, 1949–. Vol. 2 (1952), cols. 127–32.

Index

The name of each court musician is followed by his instrument(s), voice part, or post, if known, and the court(s) where he was active. Page references within the documents pertain to the English translation only.